D1626631

Revenge

Revenge

Maureen O'Brien

Little, Brown and Company

A *Little, Brown* Book

First published in Great Britain by Little, Brown
and Company in 2001

All characters in this publication are fictitious and any resemblance to real persons, living or dead, is purely coincidental.

A CIP catalogue record for this book
is available from the British Library.

ISBN 0 316 85575 8

Printed and bound in Great Britain by
Omnia Books Ltd, Glasgow

Little, Brown and Company (UK)
Brettenham House
Lancaster Place
London WC2E 7EN

www.littlebrown.co.uk

This book is for Fred
and, as always,
for Michael.

ACKNOWLEDGEMENTS

My special thanks to Mark Davies (without whom there would be no book) and to Linda Razell, homeopath, and Stephen O'Brien, medical herbalist. The Metropolitan Police at Kentish Town HQ were, as always, very good to me, especially Inspector John Whittaker and Dave Nixon, as was Eric Gordon, Editor of the *Camden New Journal*, and Nick Fagge. I received generous help from the Hong Kong Police Bureau, the Hong Kong Customs and Excise Bureau, and from Senior Superintendent Albert NG Kam Wing of the Narcotics Bureau who gave me hours of his time and knew instinctively the kind of information a writer of fiction needs. To René Tan for his kindness and hospitality. To Derik Tan not just for putting me right on Chinese names but for the initial inspiration to write about Hong Kong. And to Hilary Hale my editor for her faith and for her constant injunction not to fret.

Revenge is a kind of wild justice, which the more man's nature runs to, the more ought law to weed it out.

—Francis Bacon

1

The head thumped against stone, was lifted and thumped, lifted and thumped. Each impact sizzled through her fingertips, sent shock waves juddering up her arms. One final lift and drop, and the thing was done. Finished. Jude swayed, muscles trembling, panting.

Lee came down the garden in a series of short flights, using one leg and a crutch. He halted, gazing around. 'It's transformed. It's a different place.' He sat on the low wall surrounding the pond. 'It's very beautiful.'

Leaning heavily on the mallet handle Jude tried to see it as he did. Yes, you could now see the bones of the design. Maybe at last it was beginning to look good.

'You've created a paradise, Jude. Please, smile.'

'Later, okay?' She smiled.

'Now come and have some tea.'

'Did you say tea?' Jude let the mallet fall and stood up straight.

Lee laughed.

Jude watched him, his laugh, his lovely teeth, his short black hair, his caramel-coloured skin. He looked so cool. Her clothes were stuck to her flesh, working all day in this heat. 'You're not offering a shower as well, are you, by any chance?'

'Thank you. I would love to take a shower with you.'

Jude grinned.

They walked back through the garden towards the house.

The water was heaven, not too warm, not too cool, needling into her knotted shoulders, sliding over her upturned face. Jude drank the fine white cup of honey-coloured scented tea, letting the water run and bounce, letting all the tension and effort loose, letting it all go.

Lee's hand came round the curtain and took the empty cup. Then he came round the curtain naked. He held on to the edge of the tiles to steady himself. He'd had this operation on his knee, an old injury, 'Got it playing cops and robbers,' he'd told Jude, 'years ago when I was a kid. Couldn't afford the operation till now.' The knee was taking a long time to mend, the scar a lumpy white worm wriggling round the smooth curve of his thigh.

Jude said, 'The swelling's gone down.'

Lee looked affronted. 'Down?'

Jude laughed. 'Does it hurt?'

'No actually. And nor does my knee.'

The water splashed over him turning his fine black hair to a shiny helmet. Jude moved her body closer to his, pressed hard against him, only the sheets of water snaking down between them. She soaped his neck, his back, down the long hollow of his spine between the sinewy muscles to his narrow waist, and followed the curve of his hip bone. She disentangled her tongue from his and backed a little to soap his flat stomach whose nerves visibly quivered at her touch. The silkiness of the lather, the silkiness of his skin.

Lee took the soap from her and she watched him caress it between his hands. He massaged the lather over her shoulders, her breasts. His soapy hand slid down between her thighs, the water flowed over her and round her. She felt that divine weakness, no longer the strength to stand.

She gave a little moan. Lee moaned also and his soapy fingers moved inside her. Jude slid from conscious thought into acute concentrated sensation, her muscles biting round his fingers, again and again.

Lee said, 'You make such wonderful noise.'

'I never did before.'

'No?'

'No, always very quiet before.'

'I make you scream and shout. Only me?'

'Yes.'

Lee laughed, hugged her close to him, 'Jude, I'm ten feet tall! I'm so proud of myself!'

She opened her eyes and looked into his face. He smoothed her wet hair away from her brow, placing delicate kisses on her eyebrows, her eyelids, cheeks, chin, mouth. The water flowed between them, rinsing the soap from her flesh and his. He dried her with a big white towel. She dried him, kneeling to dry his feet, then moving upwards, gently dabbing him, first with the towel then with the tip of her tongue, till he shouted feebly, 'Stop.'

'Come on then.' Jude put a strong arm round his waist. He put an arm round her neck. She found it endearing of him to be an inch or two shorter than her and slighter, leaner. Entwined they limped into his bedroom, the small sucking noises of damp flesh touching and parting, touching and parting as they went.

Slatted blinds sliced up the afternoon sun. Lee slid between the sheets like a fish. He lay on his back and held the upper sheet open for her. Jude stretched herself full length on top of him. He groaned. 'Wait till my knee is better. Then I'll show you what I'm capable of.'

'You're capable of quite enough, my boy.' Jude lowered her mouth to his mouth and her hand to his cock. Her fingers played along the tensile shaft to its silky mushroom tip.

Lee moaned low. And moaned again and again. He reached to the bedside table. 'Ah, Jude, the prophylactic nuisances of post-Aids life . . .'

'I almost love you,' Jude said, 'when you say things like that.'

* * *

Sometime after five Jude got up and took another shower, cooler, shorter, practical, cleaning up to go home, hating to wash off the smell of him, like straw, like a hay field in summer. She groaned and wondered why this swoony ecstasy and love did not always go together. She and Lee, this perfection, this Garden of Eden stuff before the fall. How come this didn't add up to love?

She pulled on her jeans and T-shirt and, carrying her creased old gardening boots, tiptoed into the bedroom to look at him. His face was turned towards the window, almost smiling in sleep. She stroked his silky black hair.

He didn't stir, in that fathoms-deep sleep he fell into after sex. She touched her mouth, then his, with two fingertips, lingering there, his soft vulnerable mouth. Her hand hovered over his eyelids like a blessing. 'See you next week,' she whispered. He made a small noise, half hearing her in sleep. She crept out of the room, and quietly let herself out of the flat.

They had papayas in Paradise Food. She picked out two, sunshine yellow, just ripe, next stage rotten, and a lime to squeeze on them. Good for breakfast tomorrow. Dan liked them, especially on mornings when she wasn't working and they had plenty of time.

Strange, walking down the aisles of the narrow shop among the spices and sauces and pulses and breads, people chattering round her, feeling the sense of Lee all over her, inside her, this swooning ecstasy of the flesh. And nobody knew. Saying Hi to Charlie and yes it was good gardening weather and how had his holiday in Cyprus been.

She bought a bunch of his amazing rocket with big pungent leaves, some Cyprus potatoes with that fine red soil on them, organic onions, and a couple of tandoori naans. She'd knock out something Indian, not too complicated, comforting and fast. Dan loved her Indian things. Dan loved her. She loved him. This was the continuum of her life. She was grateful, content. She wished he loved her in the way she loved him. But that had never been and would now never be and she had found a way to live. She was okay. She was fulfilled. As much as any woman ever could be.

'You look happy,' Charlie said.

She smiled, her whole self in the smile. 'I am.'

This was nearly the truth.

2

The explosion blew the window out. Inside, flames blasted from floor to ceiling, filling the room.

Gregor from number thirteen called 999. The engines from Kentish Town fire station were there within seven minutes. Seven minutes is quick but fire is quicker. Fire is quicker than breath, quicker than thought. And quicker than flesh. The ambulance arrived just after the fire engines and the rescue teams went to work. But the body they carried out was not recognisable.

The fire brigade informed the Area Major Incident Pool. A senior detective officer was despatched from Colindale. The scene was frozen, the scene was sealed. Detective Inspector John Bright of Kentish Town CID happened to be on the second shift so he also was despatched to the scene. The duty officer, setting up the incident van, informed him that the senior fire officer suspected the fire might not be an accident. John Bright, not allowed into the cordoned-off scene till the FIT team from Scotland Yard had finished with it, despatched DC Llewellyn to accompany the burned man in the ambulance to the hospital and to stay with him in the hospital until further notice. 'Have we got his clothes bagged up?'

'He was naked, guv.'

'Naked?'

'He was in bed.'

'Was he?' Bright looked at his watch. Six thirty in the evening. 'Got the bedding bagged up?'

'What was left of it, guv.'

'Jesus. Who treble-nined?'

'Little old foreign bloke from number thirteen. Greg or something, they call him.'

The lab sergeant, as duty officer, designated a narrow path into and out of the house. But it would be a while before the scene was declared safe for anyone but the rescue teams. Kicking his heels was not John Bright's favourite occupation. He picked Gregor out of the crowd round the cordon. He was easy to spot. He was the one telling everyone how it happened. Bright removed him.

'I wass joss walkin' downa street. They tell you, I'm ina streeta lot. I got nothina do, I like talka my neighbour, ya know? So I'm walkin' by, gonna do my bitta shoppin' over Prince a Wales Road, an' wha! whoom! Diss flame come roarin' outa dere! Lika big essplossion, ya know? Look! I gota glass stickin' in me. Da ambolence lady fix me up okay.' Bits of sticking plaster dotted his face. He leaned closer and whispered, 'She give me somink fora shock.'

'Brave man, Gregor. Good work phoning so fast.'

'I'm a citizen, issn't it? Iss my duty, yah?'

'You know the guy that lives there? In number nine? Guy that got burned.'

'Oh yah! I speak him often, juss up an' down, ya know? How are you, Greg? And so. Juss chattin' ina street, I never been inside dere. He a nice guy. Chinese.'

'He's Chinese?'

'We both foreigner. I from Poland. He from Hong Kong.'

'What's the guy's name, you know, Gregor?'

'Lee.'

'Lee? That it?'

'All I know, sir.'

'How long's he lived here?'

'Ina street? Ohh. Maybe two year? Three maybe? I been here fifty year, same house. I come here aftera war, ya know?'

'Fifty years!' And never learned the language, Bright thought.

'Amazing,' he said. 'Anyone live with him – the victim – this Lee?'

'Liddle Chinese girl. Lovely girl.'

'She his wife or what?'

'I think. I donno.'

'What's her name?'

Gregor shrugged. 'She don' speaka me. Lossa fights, Lee an' her. Policemen came two three times.'

'That right?' Bright punched a number on his mobile. 'When was the last time, Gregor?'

Gregor shrugged again. 'She been gone four five month now, since the baby came.'

'Baby, hn?'

'She tooka baby wiss her and—'

Bright batted out the name and address. 'Check the records. We were called out at least twice to a domestic, last incident at least – six months ago?' Gregor nodded, shrugging. 'Try six months,' Bright said. 'What does this Lee do for a living?'

Gregor shook his head. 'I don' know, sir.'

'How old is he?'

'Young man. Nice-lookin'.' Gregor and Bright exchanged a look. The thing they'd brought out of the house hardly looked human. 'Thirty maybe?' Gregor's eyes went as sad as a dog's. 'Nice boy. Always had a word for me.'

Bright jumped in fast before grief took over. 'They got him out pretty quick, thanks to you. They can do amazing things these days. Take it easy, okay? Now listen. You see anyone go in, come out, hanging around? Any time today?'

'The gardener.'

'Gardener? Know his name?'

'Her. Big girl. Oh, nice girl. She been makina nice garden for Lee.'

'That right?'

'Come three four days ina week, work all day.'

'She was here today? You sure?'

'Sure. Seen her iss morning 9 a.m! Hi, Gregor, nice day, ya know?'

'See her leave?'

'Sure! Haff pass five, quar'to six. Sure!'

'Which? Half five or quarter to six?'

Gregor scratched his face, hit a sticking plaster and winced. 'Er . . . I donno, sir.'

'Where were you?'

'Up dere, my gate.'

'Doing what?'

'Havina smoke. My wife don' like I smoke ina house. Yah! Havina smoke before I go my bitta shoppin'. Ha' pass five, sir.'

'Sure?'

'Sure! She wave to me. Garden girl.'

'She waved, so that proves it was half-past five?'

'No, sir. I go shop quar'to six.'

'A-ha. Did she speak to you?'

'No. Juss wave. She wen' down atta way.' He gestured toward Kentish Town Road. 'Nice girl.'

'And you don't know her name?'

'Sure. Lee tell me. Jule. Somink like 'at.'

'Jewel? Julie?'

'Mm . . . well . . . maybe.'

'A-ha. And she's been working there how long?'

'Five six week maybe?'

'Five six weeks. You never saw her round here before that?'

Gregor shook his head.

'Sure?'

'See her once, you don' forget, okay?'

'Okay. She the only person you saw? Come in or go out? Today?'

Gregor thought. He nodded. Then he shook his head. 'I din' see no one else.'

'The Chinese girlfriend, wife, whatever, you know where she lives now?'

Gregor shook his head. 'She come four five times witha baby in buggy. Lass time I see her? One week maybe?'

'Anyone else visit the last few days? Anyone stand out?'

Gregor tried hard. At last he said, 'Fat guy come sometimes.'

'Fat guy?'

'Yeah. Fat guy. Look old but he ain't. They go drinkin', fat guy an' Lee.'

'Go drinking where?'

'I see 'em ina Prinsa Wales nown-again.'

'But you didn't see him here today?'

'No, sir.'

'Good man, Gregor.'

'Welcome, sir.'

'You think of anything, mate, remember anything, you get in touch, okay? John Bright. Here's my card.' He tucked his little police issue card into Gregor's top pocket. Gregor plodded off back to the patient crowd.

Bright got on the mobile again, this time to the lab sergeant inside the flat. From here you could see into the front room where the ghostly socos of the FIT team glided about, white figures against the blackened walls.

'Yes?'

'John Bright.'

'Hi, John. We'll be a while yet. Mind you, in this black bog there's not a lot we can do. Have to come back when it's dried out a bit.'

'How's it looking so far?'

'Off the record there's not much chance it could have started by accident.'

'A-ha? Why's that?'

'Too fast. And the explosion blew the window out.'

'You saying a bomb of some sort?'

'More like the bed was doused in petrol or something. Off the record like I said. Okay?'

'When can I get in there?'

'We can't do a lot more in this mess. We'll leave you the scene in about an hour? You going to be in charge?'

'Just what I'm going to find out. Let you know.'

Bright bounced on the balls of his feet. He jingled the change in his pockets. He looked for a cigarette in the pocket of his scuffed old leather bomber jacket. That was weird – he hadn't smoked in years. Must be the smell of wet smoke, the whole street drenched in it. He went back to Gregor. He said, 'Anyone else live in that house?'

'Dere's a flat upstair. You know. People comin' an' goin'. No one stay too long.'

'No one moved in lately? Into the upper flat?'

Gregor shrugged, blinked. The shock absorber the ambulance woman had given him was wearing off. 'Don' think so, sir. I donno. Haven't seen no one three four week.'

'Okay, mate, you think of anything, okay? – let me know. No rush.'

But there was a rush, there was always a rush. These were the moments that mattered. You didn't get somewhere in the first forty-eight hours, the scent got cold. He wanted in there now. This nice house. Not the smartest in the street, he guessed, even before the fire, but it still had its curlicued iron balcony along the first-floor windows and its decorative plaster mouldings. It was certainly not the smartest now, with its ground-floor front burnt out, and black tongues licking up the wall to the first-floor windows.

Bright's phone rang. He moved out of earshot of the crowd. 'Bright.'

'It's Helen, John.'

'A-ha?'

'Owner of flat is Lee Han. British citizen brought up in Hong Kong. Married six years to Chloe Liu. Both came here six years ago. Lee Han living at present address two years. We were called to three violent incidents. In each case it was him who called – Lee Han. Twice she'd attacked him with a weapon.'

'What weapon?'

'Kitchen knife. But the last time she accused him of hitting her. He admitted slapping her to stop her hysterics.'

'When was that?'

'Five weeks ago.'

'Five weeks? That right?'

'Everything got calmed down on the spot. No charges brought. The couple's well known to uniform branch.'

'And the landlord of the house?'

'Big company. Embrey Estates. Address in the City. They'd all gone home, I couldn't speak to anyone.'

'First thing tomorrow check their records. Looks like the last tenant left the upstairs flat about three weeks ago.'

'So it's empty?'

'A-ha. I want to know who lived there last, who's been shown round the place last few weeks. You know.'

'Yes, I know.' She was waiting.

He lowered his voice. 'Helen, I've gotta call off tonight.'

She sounded cool. 'That'll make a change.'

'Sarcasm. Doesn't suit you.'

She ignored that. 'Will this be your case?'

'I'm trying.'

'You are.' She touched it lightly. 'Very.' Her voice got official; someone had come into the CID room, he could tell. 'So that's the information so far. Okay, guv?'

'Sorry, Helen.'

'That's all right, sir. Any time.'

She was on his conscience. But as usual she'd have to wait. More urgent things on his mind. He climbed into the incident van to see the AMIP man.

He managed not to groan out loud. He knew the guy. They'd been at Hampstead together ten years ago. Roger Gould. Oxford graduate, one of the new breed, destined for high office. He'd shot up the ladder like a rocket into orbit. 'How'ya, Rog?'

'John! Good to see you! Thought you'd have made DCI by now.'

'Yeah, well, we can't all be high-flyers like you, Rog. You're doing good with AMIP, last I heard.'

'Can't complain, John, can't complain.' He always had said everything twice. And that was one of his more charming qualities.

Bright asked him dead offhand, 'You taking this case on?'

'What do you think, John? Think it's serious enough for us?'

Bright shrugged. His slight squint that came and went now came and stayed, fixed on a point the big DCI couldn't identify. 'Well, you know, Rog, we're hellish busy. This is Kentish Town, remember? The new East End.'

'I thought the Addams Family had retired to sunny Spain.'

'The new boys are worse, believe me.'

'Yes, yes. Sorry about your last case, John. Your only witness killed. Must have been a big disappointment. Big disappointment. You might have got promotion out of that.' He sounded real sad.

'Brennan on the loose again is worse than disappointing, Rog, it's a disaster.'

'But you're not connecting Brennan with this little conflagration, surely?'

'Nah. Different MO. The bad boys round here just shoot – bang, bang you're dead – don't go to the trouble of lighting bonfires under their victims. Not that efficient, right, fire? Not that predictable. Not nice and safe like shooting point blank in the back of the head. Element of chance. Your big bad boys don't like that.'

'No, no . . .' Roger looked thoughtful.

'Look, Uniform have been called out a few times on a domestic here—'

'A bit violent perhaps for your average domestic, John?'

'Violent girl, the wife. Moved out a few months ago with her kid. They're Chinese apparently.'

'Chinese? That's interesting. Don't you have some of the Snakehead Syndicate living round here too?'

'Organised Crime Squad got them banged up, Rog, coupla years ago. Total of forty-five years between the four of them. And it's a bit far-fetched, innit?'

'No connection then, you think?'

'This poor burned geezer's from Hong Kong, Rog, That's what they tell me. Snakeheads are mainland China, right?'

'Mmm, but the Triads are Hong Kong . . .' Big Rog from AMIP wasn't happy, something worrying him. 'Snakeheads are big rivals of the Triads, John. Big rivals. You know that.'

'I'm not ruling anything out, Rog, but our intelligence says the victim's clean.'

'Even the clean ones can get blown away.'

'A-ha, keep reminding me.'

'And the er – wife? Any form?'

'Chloe she's called. No form here. Only come to our attention attacking the victim.'

'I'll get on to a mate in the Interpol Office at the Yard. They'll contact Hong Kong Police Bureau, check her out. It's the middle of the night HK time but there'll be a duty officer, start the ball rolling.'

'Rog, before you do that – there's a gardener. A woman.'

'A woman gardener? Is that so . . . ?' Roger got very interested.

'Left the scene around five thirty, maybe ten minutes before the fire.'

'Not the one on the telly by any chance, is she?'

'Been here all day, working. Plenty of opportunity. Probably the means. Might even turn out to have motive. Never know.'

'Who saw her?'

'Old Polish guy.'

'Reliable witness?'

'Seems compos mentis. Doesn't seem to have an axe to grind.'

'Who is this gardener girl? Do we know?'

'No, but we will as soon as I can get in there. I hope. Meanwhile we're tracing the wife.'

'I see. I see . . .' Gould was rubbing his chin, thumb one side, fingers the other, very sage.

'And the upper flat's been empty three weeks, far as we know. I need to get up there and have a look.'

'Not yet I'm afraid, John. Not yet. Patience, patience, catchee monkey.'

The lab sergeant came out. He nodded to Bright but addressed Roger Gould. 'You the AMIP officer?'

'Yes. DCI Roger Gould. Yes.'

'Are you taking the case?'

Gould turned to Bright. 'What do you think, John?'

Bright shrugged. Mustn't look too keen – Big Rog was counter-suggestible. 'Like I said, we're overworked, what's new? Seems like a local affair but, as you say, could be wider implications . . .' He scratched a hand through his hair so it stood up in short spikes. 'It's up to you, Rog.'

'You may be right. You may be right. Maybe it would be better, handled locally. Let me check police records in Hong Kong and we'll make a decision on the basis of that.'

'Whatever you say, Rog.'

Bright's mobile rang again. It was Llewellyn. 'Guv? I'm at the hospital burns unit. The victim has not yet regained consciousness.'

'They expect him to live?'

'Seventy-five per cent burns, guv.'

'Jesus.'

'But they got him in intensive care. They're working on it.'

'Any drugs or alcohol in his system?'

'No.'

'Okay, Taff. Stick around the hospital till I get you replaced. Keep me up to date.'

Roger Gould looked inquiring.

Bright said, 'Well, it's not a murder, Rog. Not yet.'

'Hmm . . .' Gould turned away. 'Well, you know, I think perhaps it might be best handled locally. For now. For now. So . . . if you think you have the capability . . . ? We'd keep a watching brief, of course, be of any help we could.'

Bright's expression became concentratedly blank.

'Okay by you, John?'

Hands bunched in his jacket pockets, Bright shrugged in a resigned kind of way. 'A-ha, yeah. Okay by me.'

The lab officer addressed Bright, deadpan. 'We can give you a path in and out, guv. The front room – that's the bedroom – is frozen. Sealed pending further investigation. Fire was more or less confined to there. But they've finished with the rest of the flat for now. All yours.'

The socos were filing out. The light getting dusky. The street lamps came on, lighting the scene like a stage set. The audience still hung around, agog, waiting for the next act to begin. Bright said, 'Coming in, Rog?'

'Don't think so, John, no. I'll let you get on. Just keep me informed.' Big Rog stood at the gate, arms folded, with an almost wistful look, gazing in down the blackened corridor of the flat. 'Let me know what happens with the female gardener.'

3

'Dan?' Her voice echoed round the hall. You can always tell when a house is empty. He wasn't back yet. She was glad. She'd be content for an hour, drinking a scotch, listening to *The Archers* and then the arts programme on Radio 4 while she put the meal together. She took off her boots and threw them into the cloakroom, then ran upstairs to slip into something comfortable, a long cotton frock, deep blue, loose and cool. She brushed her hair and looked at her face. She bit her lip. Could you tell? By looking at her? Smelling her? Couldn't you tell? She sniffed her wrist but could only smell Imperial Leather soap.

Her freckles were packed closer now after weeks in the sun. She didn't mind. As a girl she'd hated them but now she knew that they added to her *je ne sais quoi*, bringing out the dizzy child-like blue of her eyes, and the thick spring of her dark red hair. She knew she looked great – healthy, sizzling with energy, shining and gleaming, she'd never looked so good. And maybe she never would again. Thirty-four was perfect, but sadly would not last for ever. She had always thought she'd get to her perfect age and stay there. But no. It didn't work like that. Time did not stop. Oh, well. She was enjoying it while it lasted, because it sure as hell wouldn't come again.

She hummed while she chopped the potatoes and measured out her spices. Some tune, she couldn't think where she'd heard it before or what it was. She opened the french windows. A train went by and the house shook. She loved this house but one day those trains might drive her to violence. Especially the heavy ones during the night, carrying the nuclear waste, their heavy metallic groaning, the shrieking, the vibration. She and Dan didn't wake these days. The timetable data was entered in their brains, enabling them to sleep. The brain shut out habitual useless information. Brains were good at that. She had discovered they could do it with anything.

She added water to her pan of peas and potatoes and stirred. The juice thickened and turned the colour of cinnamon, then boiled. She turned the heat down to simmer. Then she took her scotch outside, rattling the ice, swallowing the first mouthful, flinty and cold on the tongue, numbing the roof of the mouth. Oh that was good. She wandered down the garden. The clump of delphiniums in the corner needed tying up. She stretched. She'd do it tomorrow.

She ducked under the apple tree. Lots of little apples, swelling, rosying up. She loved this tree in all its seasons, surviving the filth and pollution of the railway, the London emissions of lead and sulphur and CO_2, the accelerating destruction of the planet. It was her symbol of hope. The little apples reddening.

She sat on the bench with her back to the house. At least you couldn't see the railway from the garden. The walls were six feet high, and the trains ran in a cutting thirty feet below. You could see cars however. All along the top of the right-hand wall cars of all kinds appeared to float in air. *Car Repairs*, the notice said on the street. She liked this surreal view of old Beetles, MGs, Citroëns, reclining in their eternal rest, higgledy-piggledy, along the top of her garden wall. Her climbing roses wound in among them, decorating them, tying up the battered metal shapes. She wished she could paint. Gardening was her painting, the nearest she could get.

George appeared from his hiding place under the New Zealand flax, a large stripy plant with strap-like leaves. George was himself large and stripy, with a battered air, somehow suited to this garden, and a cheerful disposition. He strolled towards her with his rolling sailor's walk, big white feet on the end of bandy legs, making that growling purr that was almost a chirrup. He stretched, dipping his back, then drew his feet together and raised his body in a steep arc. He shuddered all over with the pleasure of stretching, then came on towards her.

'Hello, my George.' She bent, hanging an arm down for him. He stood on his hind legs and rubbed his face hard against her knuckles, both sides, then rolled over on his back while she rubbed his stomach.

Dan came out while they were absorbed in this daily love-in, George on his back and Jude on her knees, both making chirruping noises of passionate affection. Dan stood watching the intimacy between her and the cat. Suddenly George smelt Dan, turned his head to see him, then jumped away. Love-in over. Jude turned and jumped too. 'Christ, Dan, you gave me a fright.'

'Didn't you hear me come in?'

'It's all right, George, it's Dan, not the Kentish Town axe murderer.' But George sat with his back to them on the edge of the terrace. He lifted his left back leg straight up and began methodically to clean his claws, scraping hard at each one with his teeth. Jude got to her feet, falling over the long blue dress. 'Have you been in long?'

'Long enough to have a shower and change.'

'Oh yes, you do look rather suave, now you mention it.' She reached both her arms round his waist and looked up into his face.

He was big, Dan. Six foot two and big with it. His head a large round cherub's with light brown curls. No fat on him, nothing spare, but a look of softness, something in him never quite emerging from childhood. This air of boyishness the thing that Jude had loved first and loved still. Jude squeezed him tight.

But there was nothing pliable in Dan. The softness was a mirage. Nothing ever truly softened in him, nothing melted. He retained his physical integrity, whatever you did to him. She sighed, smiling up at him. 'Why do I love you?' she said.

'Fuck knows.'

She laughed and kicked over her drink. The ice cubes and golden liquid spilled on the old red bricks. Drat. Another embrace over. 'Clumsy cow,' she said.

'I'll get you another one.' Dan went back into the dim light of the kitchen. He lifted the lid of the pan. 'Mmm, Indian.'

Jude, picking up the glass, throwing the ice in the pond, looking at the apple tree and the evening sky and George almost invisible now back in his hiding place, suddenly felt like weeping and didn't quite know why. Everything all at once felt terrible, the euphoria of the afternoon gone, replaced with a sweep of despair. Dan brought her new drink.

'Cheers,' she said. They clinked glasses.

Dan saw her sadness. He bent his head and touched her forehead with his. 'Cheers,' he said solemnly. They drank but Jude for some reason could not smile.

'What's up?'

'Oh, I don't know. I'm hungry maybe. Low blood sugar, that's all.'

'So let's eat.'

Once during dinner Jude got a sudden memory of herself and Lee in the shower, a shock shooting up inside her from groin to throat. Dan was looking at her. He was speaking and she hadn't heard. For a moment she was about to say, Dan, Lee is my lover, or: how would she put it? Lee and I – what? Do it, after the gardening; make love? have sex? make heavenly play, flesh with flesh, hand and eye and tongue, and cock and fleshly orifice, and all my nerve ends are tingling, and my blood is fizzing round my veins and I float around in a kind of dream even when I'm heaving rocks about and deep-digging a vegetable bed. And yet I'm not in love. And yet that's not quite true. I'm as in love as it's possible to be when we're doing it, the silken game. But I don't want to be doing *this* with Lee – sitting on either side of our old kitchen table, eating a curry, then lounging like book-ends on the old velvet sofa watching the telly, reading, talking idly of this and that, for ever and ever and ever, in this dear old house which fits us like a warm coat.

She didn't say any of this. She didn't say a word. What would Dan do if she spoke? Apart from suffer, that is. Walk out? Throw her out? Speak? Be silent? She didn't know. And she was not in the least tempted to find out. She feared that her dalliance with Lee would strike at the core of his being. And that to let him know would, like coring an apple, remove the middle of him, clean, in one piece, leaving him empty, hollowed out.

He looked at her now, and stopped speaking. He said, 'You're looking well, you know.'

'Comes of having an outdoor job.'

'Arr,' he said. "'tis workin' on the la-and.'

'I was miles away. I haven't heard a word you said.'

'I know.'

'What have I missed?'

'Nothing. Just work.'

'*Just* work?'

He took a mouthful of beer and did not respond to this. 'Where were you?'

'What mean?'

'Miles away, you said.'

'Oh. In Lee's garden.' This was not strictly true; she had been in Lee's shower.

'What were you *doing* in Lee's garden?' He spoke lightly.

'I was – I don't know now. Just sort of – looking about.' Her neck felt hot. She hoped she wasn't blushing.

Dan nodded slowly. 'How's it coming along?'

'How's what coming along?'

'The garden, what else?'

'Oh. Lee says I've created a paradise.'

'Does he?' Dan didn't take his eyes off hers. 'He's happy then.'

'You could say that, yes.'

'You'll be sorry when it's finished.' Again his tone was light.

'Oh, I don't know.' She had lived in the present, the last five weeks. 'I haven't thought about it.' This at least was true.

'No?'

'No.' She didn't want to think about it. 'Well,' she said. 'It's always nice to start something new.'

'I never suspected you of fickleness, Jude.' He did not smile when he said this.

Did she detect—? No, her guilt heard accusation in everything he said. But she looked away from him. 'Well, you know, I always tend my gardens afterwards. I never leave them in the lurch.'

'You'll be going back there then? When it's finished?' A hint of anxiety? Grimness? Again, no; just her guilty imagination.

'I suppose so. Once a month, once a week. Whatever.'

'Whatever?' Now Dan was not looking at her.

'Whatever's necessary. Whatever he can afford.'

'Mmm . . .'

Silence. Just the quickened rhythm of her heart. Guilt was new to her, deception unnatural.

Dan stretched and got up from the table. 'That was good.'

While he piled the dishes in the sink, she dropped on to the sofa and punched the remote control. The old telly crackled into life. People having secret affairs always deluded themselves. Friends of hers, saying *I'm sure he/she knows. He/she just doesn't want to talk about it*. She did not want to fall into such self-delusion. There was no way Dan could know. And no way she would enlighten him.

Dan squeezed up next to her and put his arm around her. It was okay, then; only guilt making her imagine things. She turned her radiant face to him and snuggled against his shoulder.

4

The heat was still coming off the walls. But it looked more like a flood than a fire. Like it had rained black rain for forty days and forty nights. Bright stood in the cordoned-off doorway. Everything in the room was drenched, charred, black. The firemen had hacked jagged gaps, checking the fire had not got into wall cavities, ceiling joists, under the floor, to start up again and race through the house. The mattress, where flames had ripped through the cover, a lumpy grey stew of wet wadding. The floor a swamp, the carpet rippled in hillocks and squelching hollows where lumps of wet plaster floated, disintegrating into mud. That cold dank burnt smell. Walls, floor, ceiling, furniture, black, black and wet. And the smell of fire and water was the smell of despair. Like the two elements were never meant to mix.

He left the bedroom doorway, followed black wet footsteps down the pale wood floor of the passage and opened a door on his left. Neat little bathroom under the stairs. Blinding white tiles. Clean but for the black smears, some the fire, some the socos' fingerprinting mess. A white kimono hung on the door. He put his nose to it. A scent. Couldn't place it. Like fresh-sawed pine. Nice. Door at the end to the kitchen. This Lee Han liked white all right. Dazzling. Clean. But for the dusting of black snowflakes. Made the holocaust in the bedroom more of an outrage.

From the kitchen you took a sideways step into the living-room. Long windows on to a terrace. A pale wood floor like the corridor. A low white sofa. Not so white any more. Flecked with smears of black. A coffee table with a glass top. He started work – wandering round the room, getting the feel of it.

Hi-fi stuff, not quite state of the art but good. A tower of CDs. Eclectic selection of music, from the Japanese bamboo flute through jazz to pop Bright had never heard of and Mozart, Bach. He moved to the desk – smooth pale wood, smart but not expensive, Ikea rather than Conran. A small Toshiba laptop. Nice design but again a few years old. This guy is doing okay but not rolling in it, or if he is he spends his money on other things.

Bright opened a desk drawer. Neat files, some labelled *Letters/work, Letters/friends*, some with the names of newspapers, magazines. He riffled through, looking for an address, a number. A plain letter-heading on a sheet of A5 said *Jude Craig Gardens. Design and Maintenance* with an address just the other side of Kentish Town Road, ten minutes from here, five minutes from police HQ. He got Cato on the mobile. 'This lady gardener. Left the place ten, fifteen minutes before it erupted. The victim will probably be a corpse by morning. Looks like one now. But play it cool, nothing heavy, feel your way. We'll have to bring her in, swab her for petrol traces, whatever. But don't set off any alarm bells. Had enough of those round here to last awhile.'

'I'll take Helen with me, guv?'

'You do that, Cat, and tell Atkins to get his ass round here pronto.'

The other drawer was also full of neat files, labelled with topics: *Environment. Race. Homeless.* Under them another file. The guy was a meticulous labeller. So when Bright saw this unlabelled file he got one of his feelings, a little lurch of the stomach, little pinpricks over his skin. He went very quiet, he purposely slowed down. He lifted out the file. He put it on the top of the desk and opened it.

The first page was headed *Gangland Execution.* Then came some sheets of computer print-out, single-spaced. And behind them pages of newsprint, the same words, but with photos. Bright recognised the cuttings. He'd hardly forget. They were from the local freebie newspaper and they related to his own aborted case. The top article was headlined *Gangland Shooting in Kentish Town.* The date a year ago. There were six follow-up articles in the file. All close to the knuckle. The by-line on each of the articles was Lee Han.

In the old days Bright would have known this guy, talked to him, told him just what he wanted him to know, no more, no less. Nowadays the journos were briefed by the appointed duty officer every Tuesday, fed the party line. It was all PR now. So the reporters went nosing about on their own, they had to. They found out too much, they disclosed too much. To the villains as well as the punters. Lee Han had taken the bland PR information and made two and two add up to more than four. But he wasn't far out.

Robert Mahoud was killed yesterday in a junkyard in Kentish Town. Mahoud witnessed the drug-war murder in broad daylight of 30-year-old Harry Flaherty six months ago outside a betting shop in Gospel Oak. At the time of the junkyard killing, Mick Brennan, also of Kentish Town, was in prison awaiting trial for the murder of Flaherty. Mahoud, the only witness against Brennan, had given a very full statement to the police.

The police applied to the CPS for permission to use Mahoud's statement at the trial. The CPS have turned down the application. A witness has to be able to stand up in court, be identified and cross-examined on his testimony. A dead witness is no witness.

The Brennan trial was scheduled for next week. Now Brennan has been released. Detective Inspector John Bright, heading the inquiry, when asked by our reporter why Mahoud did not have 24-hour protection, spoke feelingly about the undermanning of the Metropolitan police.

Though Brennan was in prison at the time of the Mahoud murder, the same gun was used to murder Flaherty and Mahoud. The gun, the only real clue to connect the two killings, has never been found.

Bright bagged up the file. He sat there thinking, playing a

light rhythm upon it with the fingers of his right hand. This Lee Han was a clever bloke. Maybe he had been a little bit too clever for his own good? It was an angle he had to bear in mind.

His eyes were resting on the spines of some big books in the alcove. He got up to examine them. They were art books, mainly photographs – Magnum, Bill Brandt, Salgado, Suau. He came to a big black ring binder with no title on the spine. He got the feeling again. The buzz.

He took out the ring binder, slow and careful. Opened it. Clear plastic wallets, each containing two ten by eight prints back to back. This was Han's personal photo album. He sat down on the sofa, laid the album on the table and began to turn the pages.

Good prints, these. No colour snaps. All black and white. All portraits. At the beginning they're mostly of a Chinese woman, sophisticated, rich-looking. Thirties? Forty? Maybe older. Hard to say. Then comes a young girl, also Chinese.

She's a little cracker, short black hair, straight fringe over the straight eyebrows. There's one of her with the older woman, face to face in profile. Then the Little Cracker takes over from the other woman; she's in every picture, against this background or that. One of them, in a night-club or bar, she's turning to look over her shoulder, lights all around her, the barman out of focus behind looking at her. A great picture, like a still from a movie. Bright turned the page and stopped a minute. He scratched a hand through his hair. 'Shit,' he said.

She's naked. Page after page. Here in this flat he'd guess. Some on this very sofa. He shifted, a bit uneasy. But they're great black and white prints, and if you made the effort and stood back a bit from the subject, you could see they were great nudes. Full of atmosphere. Good lighting, all that, not just—

'Christ, guv, I thought you were here to work.'

Bright jumped. He hadn't heard Atkins come in. 'Fuck, Tommy, don't do that, right? I'm approaching heart-attack age.'

'Jeez, guv.' Atkins' chin was glued to Bright's shoulder, he could feel the heat of his breath. 'She'd give you one.'

'A-ha. And a heart attack as well.'

'Who is she?'

'Victim's wife?'

'Lucky geezer.'

'You didn't see him taken out of here.'

'Doesn't look the wife type to me,' Atkins leered.

'She didn't think so either.'

'What? Split?'

'A-ha. Ex-wife now.'

'His luck ran out then.'

'Maybe.'

'Where is she now?'

'What I want to know.' Reluctant, Bright turned the page.

And there she stood in her wedding gear. With a young Chinese bloke. And this bloke, if you could use the word beauty for a man, he had it in spades. But he didn't look conceited with it. He looked a bit solemn. A bit sad. But she looked just the way a bride is meant to look. Radiant. She barely came up to his shoulder. And her wedding dress barely came down to her crotch. Atkins whistled.

Bright said, 'What's the building?'

'You're looking at the building?'

'Come on, Tommy.'

'It's Camden Town Hall. That back bit, so-called garden. The weddings all have their pictures done there.'

'The Japanese garden.'

Atkins smirked. 'That figures.'

'Hong Kong is not Japan, Tommy.'

'Well, it's all the mysterious bloody East, innit, guv?'

Bright stood up. 'Get this album bagged up, I'll take it with me.'

'I bet you will.'

Bright couldn't stand Atkins. But he was one of the team. You had to keep them cheerful. He gave the DC what passed for a smile. Nothing in his face changed except for maybe the muscles round his eyes or the concentration of his now-you-see-it-now-you-don't squint. 'And that file of newspaper articles.' He was looking through a plastic box of floppy disks. He came to one that wasn't labelled. He said, 'Bag these up. And the computer. We need someone who can hack into it. Maggie's the best. Get her on to it. We need Han's address list. And anything else we can find in this machine.'

'Right, guv.'

Bright wanted to go out in the garden. He liked gardens. Got it from his ma. But he'd better go up to look at the first-floor flat. 'Tommy? Finish bagging this lot up, then follow me upstairs, okay?' He let himself out of Han's front door into the small lobby.

The FIT team had left him a narrow path up the side of the stairs. The smell got colder as he went up. On the landing the firemen had broken the door in, used a hatchet and splintered the lock. Then they'd doused the place to be on the safe side. Sopping wet carpet. Windows blackened, runnels of black water still dripping from the sill, sinking into the general ooze. No furniture.

He opened a door: a bleak little shower room; not like the one in the flat below. Next to it a sad little kitchen, blackened grease on the cheap cooker, tile-pattern lino on the floor. No wonder the place wasn't let. Sure, it wasn't helped by the layer of wet soot, but even so, whoever was managing this place, they weren't earning their keep.

Sticking to the designated path he squelched into a small back room. Hardly any damage back here. Just like below, the fire had been confined to the front. A phone. He lifted it, listened. Dead. Nothing else except a slipping-down pile of magazines on the floor under the back window. He flipped a few pages and sighed. Atkins came in. 'Bag 'em up, Tommy.'

'Oah, whoah, just my cuppa tea, guv.'

'Bit on the soft side for you, innit? Strictly top shelf stuff.'

'What? Get a loada this!' Atkins held a mag open at a centre page spread. 'That's strictly under the counter, that is, guv. You'd need to know where to get it.'

'Get it anywhere on the Internet these days. It's called progress.'

'You're a bloody puritan, guv.'

'A-ha. What do you think? Left behind by the last tenant or what?'

Atkins, preoccupied, didn't reply.

'Or maybe a bloke sitting up here, meant to be keeping watch on the comings and goings below, using these to keep himself amused, till he hits the right moment? The perpetrator or just the lookout man? And that's the other question – what makes it the right moment? What's right about today, quarter to six or thereabouts on this particular Monday evening? Why not at night when the victim would be sleeping anyway?' Bright stood at the window, bouncing on the balls of his feet. 'Then again, maybe the timing isn't significant. Maybe this flat up here's got nothing to do with it either.' He didn't like the smell up here. He didn't think he'd have liked it even before the fire. He wanted air. He went to the window. Stood there looking out. 'Nice garden,' he said.

'Mmm.' Atkins barely gave it a glance, absorbed in his congenial task. Horticulture couldn't compete.

'Looks like the gardener was the last to see him alive. Cato should be talking to her now.'

Atkins looked up at last. 'Her?' he said. 'If she's anything like that one on the telly Cato has all the luck.'

5

Jude was white, the suntan of the summer sucked from her skin by shock. Her freckles the only colour in her face. 'Dan? This is . . .' She gazed at the two people, not knowing how to introduce them. Stupid, at this moment, to be wondering what was the form, but she couldn't recall the names they had given her. The man was a natty-looking fellow with a beard, wearing a blazer and immaculate grey trousers with a crease. The girl a pretty blonde, early twenties.

'Yes?' Dan zapped off the sound and got up from the sofa.

The man said, 'Mr Craig? Sorry to disturb you. I'm Niki Cato and this is Helen Goldie. We're from Kentish Town CID.'

Jude watched Dan too go white. He seemed almost to stagger before he came forward to shake hands with the man. Shake hands? Somehow this seemed an extraordinary thing to do. Indeed the police people did look taken aback. But they politely allowed their hands to be shaken.

Dan pushed a hand through his hair. 'What's happened? Is it my old office? I don't use it any more, it's up for rent. I know the burglar alarm goes off at odd times. People have complained before—'

'Actually, sir, it's Mrs Craig that we need to talk to.'

'It's about one of my clients, Dan.' Jude spoke almost without voice. 'The place where I was working today? Lee? He's been—'

'Mr Lee Han was badly injured earlier this evening, sir.'

'Badly injured? How? Look, if he's had an accident in the garden because of some negligence on Jude's part—'

'No, Dan. He was . . .' Jude put her hand up to her face and covered her mouth. Tears filled up her eyes and spilled down over her hand. She hunted in her pocket and found a tissue. She covered her eyes with the tissue. She wiped her nose, her mouth.

The girl, Goldie, put a hand on Jude's arm and sat her down at the kitchen table. She said to Dan, 'Could you get her a glass of water, Mr Craig?'

Dan came to life.

Cato, watching Jude, said, 'It was a fire in actual fact, sir.'

'A fire?' Dan gave the water to Jude, who could not manage to drink.

'They think – they think . . .' Jude couldn't go on.

'We're not sure, but there's some doubt about whether it was an accident.'

'How do you mean?'

'It looks like someone threw petrol over him and set him alight.'

'He was in bed at the time.'

Jude let out a cry, a shout, of anger, of helpless sorrow.

'Someone tried to kill him?' Dan's voice was weak.

'Well, it's too early to say for certain. We just want to ask your wife a few questions.'

'Why Jude?'

'We found her name among his papers.'

'And someone of your description was seen leaving his place, Mrs Craig, about half five this evening? So we wondered if you might be able to shed any light . . . ?' Cato's smooth manner suited his blazer and natty grey trousers, but not his innocent Geordie accent.

Dan said, 'Jude's been working there for a few weeks, redesigning the guy's garden for him.'

'Yes, sir, we know that.'

'So you did leave about half five?' the blonde girl said.

'Yes.'

'Was he – all right – when you left, Mrs Craig?'

'Yes. He— As far as I know. Yes.'

'Was he in bed when you left?'

'Well . . .' She must not lie. 'He was in his bedroom.' She must tell strictly the truth. 'He didn't answer when I said I was going.' That was true. She didn't need to say she had left a kiss with her fingertips on his eyelids and his beautiful mouth. 'I let myself out.' She was lying by omission. *And I don't know how much they'll be able to find out. They're bound to find traces of me in the bedroom, aren't they? In the bed? But no, the bed must have been burned. Does that remove traces—? I'm thinking like a criminal.* She felt that her skull was no longer big enough to contain the thoughts she had to hide. From Dan even more than from the police. The breezy Geordie policeman was looking at her, expecting a response. She wanted to ask how extensive was the fire, how much she needed to fear. *If I ask that they'll think I'm asking out of guilt. And they'll be right. And how can I be thinking like this when Lee—?*

Dan said, 'I think Jude's in shock.'

Jude said, 'Is it possible to see Lee?'

Natty Cato said, 'Not just yet, I'm afraid. He's in intensive care. It's touch and go whether he'll survive.'

Goldie said, with less callous cheerfulness, 'But I'm sure if you ring the hospital, they'll give you news.'

She stared at them and they stared at her, almost vacantly. Cato took a meerschaum pipe out of his pocket. No one could take their eyes off this object. He said, 'Mr Han's Chinese, isn't he?'

'He's from Hong Kong.' Jude sounded bewildered.

'Are you suggesting this could be a racist attack?' Dan said.

'Not that you could tell what race he is now,' Cato said, 'apparently.'

Dan said, 'What?'

The young woman answered. 'Seventy-five per cent full thickness burns.'

'Can you survive that?' Dan said.

'We don't know yet, sir.'

'I thought seventy-five per cent burns meant certain death.'

Jude's features on her white face blurred with shock and grief, like the shadows on the face of the moon. 'I'm sorry—' She went out to the garden, holding on to things, the table, chair backs, the window frame. She sat on the outside bench. The police followed Dan out. Dan stood near her but didn't touch her. George, despite his fear of strangers, sprang on to her lap and butted her chin with his head. She put her arms round him, her face in his fur. She had to stop them seeing – all of them – she had to be just the gardener and Lee just a client. She had to get herself under control. *His face. His beautiful face.* 'He had an operation on his knee a few months ago,' she said. 'He wouldn't be agile enough to—'

Dan handed her the water and she drank some. She said, 'I'm sorry. But he's – he was – very beautiful. Lee.' *His face. His hands.* 'I'm sorry. I can't believe it's racist. I can't believe someone would do that.'

'You can't think of any reason . . . ?'

Jude knew things were bad between him and his ex-wife Chloe. She knew Chloe was furiously jealous and had behaved with violence towards Lee. Many times. But not this? Surely not this? And anyway, it wasn't Jude's place to suggest a person to blame. 'No,' she said.

'Did you talk at all, while you were there today?'

'Yes. He came out to the garden at teatime. He said—' she swallowed – 'he was pleased with – what I'd done.'

'That's all?'

Jude nodded. She couldn't risk her voice again. She couldn't risk another compromise with the truth. Not in front of Dan.

'Okay.' The policewoman smiled at her.

'Did you see anyone hanging round? In the garden? In the street?'

'No.'

'Not when you were leaving?'

'No. Only Gregor. A neighbour. But he's always there.'

'He's the one who called 999,' Goldie said. 'He might have saved Mr Han's life.'

'Look, Mrs Craig, would it be all right with you if we asked you to come round to the station with us?'

'What for? She hasn't done anything. For Christ's sake!'

'Take it easy, sir. It's just routine.'

'It's just it's a good idea to take swabs as close to the incident as we can—'

'Swabs!'

'Your wife's hands. If you've handled petrol or anything. You know. There'd be traces—'

'But she's driven her van for Christ's sake. There's a hundred ways she could have—'

'We're not accusing your wife of anything, sir.'

'We just thought you might like to get things cleared up now instead of—'

'Instead of what? Waiting till the poor guy's dead?'

'It's okay, Dan. It's really okay.'

'I'm phoning our solicitor. You're not going to the police station without protection.'

'Dan, I don't mind.' She looked at the policeman. 'But I've had a shower. I've cooked. I've washed my hands lots of times since I—'

'They can still find traces.'

'If there's any to be found.'

'Very sophisticated processes they've got now, Mrs Craig.'

'If not, you're eliminated. That's the idea.'

'For your own good, kind of thing.'

She took George's head in her hands and looked in his eyes. She rubbed his forehead with her nose. 'I've got to go, my George. But I'll be back soon.' George stepped from her lap to the table and jumped from there to the top of the wall where he crouched with his shoulders up, glaring. Jude stood.

'Thanks, Mrs Craig.'

'I'm coming with you.' Dan ran ahead of them up the stairs and fetched her jacket from the cloakroom. He draped it round her, squeezing her shoulders in a reassuring way before opening the front door.

'Nice house, this,' Cato said. 'Pity about the council flats right opposite.'

His breezy manner, now he was on the doorstep, seemed an affront, but Jude supposed policemen were used to terrible events and, like doctors and nurses, couldn't afford to get involved.

She followed them down the steps to the waiting car. Behind her Dan shut the door on their house.

6

Bright stepped out on to the terrace. The geometric pattern of stone and brick surrounded a square formal pond. Green blades of rushes and iris leaves shot up out of the water, around a verdigris bronze sculpture, also of blade-like leaves. A trickle of water bubbled over the curving leaves of the sculpture and ran down, back into the pond, making a rippling, tinkling, clean little song.

Beyond the pond a brick path curved between a small tree and a screen of bamboo. Bright followed the path and found a small courtyard paved with stone, with a bench and a small shed, in the shelter of the end wall which was well over ten foot high. A rambling rose with flowers like apple blossom clambered all over the wall. Its scent battled with the stench of doused fire even this far from the house.

The shed, crouched at the foot of the wall, was not your average garden shed. It was small, square, stained a dark blue-grey. Very smart, hand-built, he'd guess. It seemed to have a flat roof. From the roof of the shed to the top of the wall maybe five feet.

The big trees on the other side of the wall were thick with summer leaf. Behind the trees the long neck of a crane sketched its silhouette on the sunset sky.

Bright pulled open the shed door. The smell of new wood. A slatted potting bench and shelves above, clips on the wall to hang the tools on. A long window at one end letting in cool greenish light. This was a dream of a shed. But then it was still newly built, barely used, everything in its place, not the usual dusty jumble of rusting implements and garden twine. He noted a five-litre plastic drum, opened it and sniffed: paraffin, nearly full. He also noted a clean twelve-inch square next to it on the floor, outlined in chalk by the socos. He went out again into the heat and round behind the shed.

It stood two feet away from the wall, on brick paving. Very neat. Recessed into the back of the shed, part of its design, a ladder of wood slats led conveniently up to the roof. Bright climbed the rungs. Got the forensic print stuff all over him.

The top of the shed was flat, as he'd imagined, with wood decking in the same smart slate-grey and a balustrade of narrow horizontal wood slats. He crept under the overhanging branches of sycamore and looked down at the garden. You could lie up here as long as you liked, as long as you needed. See and not be seen. Even someone working in the garden just below wouldn't be aware.

He felt like a kid again, up in the tree house, the bamboo fronds, the rippling water, a little bird pippling away close by. From this haven of peace, looking up at the windows of the house, how could you believe that someone had set fire to the place, deliberately set fire to a man?

He lay there, on his front, and looked down the gardens either side. Not a soul. Three, four gardens in both directions. Nobody. Not even a kid playing on a climbing frame. No face at a window, not to the right, not to the left. Natch. They were all out in the street now, gawping at the rescue circus, no one keeping a lookout, no one checking back here, not from the upper floors of Han's house and not from the houses either side.

How had it been earlier in the day? A sleepy hot Monday afternoon? Maybe a sun worshipper covered in sun block, flat out, eyes shut, or a gardener bent double, eyes down. But everyone else would be at work.

The side walls of the gardens were four feet high topped with a few feet of trellis. You'd be daft to come that way. No. You come over this end wall. You wait your moment, hidden in the leaves, then drop on to the roof of this shed, hole up here and wait till the coast's clear.

How do you know when the coast's clear? Someone inside the house gives you a sign, that's how. Either from Han's flat or the vacant flat upstairs. Then you climb down the convenient built-in ladder at the back here. You keep low. Make a low run. Into the flat through the open french windows, down the passage in there, see the bloke's in bed asleep, douse the bed in petrol, light your fuse, and leave. How? Not over the side walls – too dangerous, too likely to be seen. You'd have to go up over the back wall here. Trees to hide you. But you'd snag yourself to buggery on the rose thorns. Wouldn't be quite as easy as getting in.

The petrol was in the shed? The perpetrator was in cahoots with the gardener? That would figure. But then the gardener wouldn't need an associate; she had the total opportunity to carry this out alone. She was in the garden all day. She was legit. She had no need to climb over walls, lie low on the shed roof. She had plenty of time to set the fire up. She would have known for sure Lee Han was in bed. Sleeping. She could take her time. And then she didn't even try to hide. Leaving at her normal time, she strolled out, waved to Greg and sauntered off, leaving her employer behind, about to become barbecued meat. That was cool.

She was the obvious suspect, no question about that. Somehow he couldn't square it with the person who'd created this garden. But you never know. People are wilder than fable, weirder than witchery. People can turn on a sixpence—

'Who are you?' The voice came from just behind him.

'Christ! People keep trying to give me a heart attack today.' He flashed his ID at the head looking over the wall. A guy from the FIT team. 'John Bright. Kentish Town CID.'

'You in charge?'

'You got it.' Bright examined the wall above the shed. Ivy had recently been cleared, you could trace the stitching of branches on the brick. Thorny roses looped and whorled. 'This how they got in?'

'Well, there's a few broken branches over this side, shredded leaves. Signs of someone climbing the ivy. But couldn't say when. Nothing conclusive.'

'No conveniently snagged bits of clothing like you get on the telly?'

'Not yet.'

'That's a surprise.'

'Yup.'

'Find anything interesting over here in the garden?'

'Too dry for footprints.'

'What about inside the shed?'

'Drum of paraffin, bit of rope. All fingerprinted. Be in the report.'

'And something a foot square that was on the floor and isn't now.'

'Oh, yes.'

'Recently removed.'

'Yup.'

'By you?'

'No, we just did a floor scraping, might be traces of what was there.'

'When will you know?'

'It'll be in the report.'

'That it?'

'Yup.'

The head disappeared.

Bright pulled himself up on to the top of the wall and peered through the clotted summer leaves. The place was a building site.

Bright remembered now. They'd knocked down this nice Victorian school to put up a cluster of mean little houses with mean little windows, crammed together, for working-class folk. The architect that designed them wouldn't live in one for love nor money.

Some of the ivy branches on that side of the wall were pulled out from the mortar, some of its leaves were crushed.

He could see a few Uniforms over there hunting through the undergrowth with sticks, watching where they walked. Immediately below him on a ladder, the soco he'd spoken to scrutinised the vertical surface of the wall. 'Anything?' Bright said.

Without looking up the soco said, 'You're fucking up our crime scene.'

'You've already done the top of the wall.'

'How do you know?'

'I just saw you up here.'

'What if you hadn't?'

Bright sighed. 'Find anything up here?' No reply. 'No fibres, nothing?'

The pause was so long he was on the point of pulling rank. Then the soco muttered, 'It'll be in the report.'

'It'll be in the report,' Bright said. 'Thanks. I'll remember this moment with gratitude.' He dropped to the shed roof and skimmed down its integral ladder. Time to go back indoors, get stuck into the freaking paperwork.

He settled himself on the sofa. He groaned through the headings: lines of inquiry he intended to pursue; how he intended to proceed with the case. By following my nose, assholes. This was the bullshit they strangled you with. How the fuck did he know how he was going to proceed with the case? How did he know how the case was going to proceed with him?

Roger Gould stuck his head round the door. This was the reason, this big sandstone face with its sheen of self-satisfaction, this overbearing presence looming over him, this was why he was feeling wrong-footed, hampered, constricted, constrained.

'Oh good, good, filling in the forms. Not your favourite occupation, John, if I remember right.'

Bright groaned. 'You remember right.'

'You'll never rise higher, you know, always kicking against the pricks.'

'Any particular prick you got in mind, Rog?'

The Great Chieftain came and looked over his shoulder. 'And what lines of inquiry do we intend to pursue? Are we clear?'

'Don't know about you, Rog, but I'm managing to figure out a few main strands. I'm gonna sit here and write them all down on the nice clean forms and when I've finished you can read them. How about that?'

'At least you've got a prime suspect.'

'A-ha? Who's that?'

'Well, the gardener. Your sergeant called, by the way. They've got her round at the station now. They've swabbed her for petrol traces. All under control.'

7

She's amazing. Chestnut hair. Curly, out of order type hair. Not long but thick and springy. She's big. But she's not fat. She's strong. Imagine her striding along mountain tops. Imagine her in the sack. Closer, she's no beauty. Freckles and these bright blue eyes, kind of face wouldn't look wrong on a street kid. You look at her and you can't help but imagine her stark bollock naked, that's the thing. She'd take care of a bloke all right. And enjoy it, my God. All this went through his head in one sharp jolt while he went into the room and shut the door behind him and strolled round to the head of the table where he could see her better.

This was the nice interview room. The room for the innocent. You might or might not get this room again. After this interview, if you gave the wrong impression, the next time you'd get the room without the window, space for just two people either side the table and mean cruel bars of fluorescent light.

When he came in she looked at him not like a prisoner but like a hospital visitor, waiting. Her eyes grappled his, close wrestling. She said, 'Is there any news?'

'What of, Mrs Craig?'

'Of Lee.'

'Just the same, I'm afraid.'

The eyes pulled away from his. She swallowed and nodded. She didn't say a word.

Bright said, 'One of my officers is with him all the time. We'll be the first to hear if anything – if there's any change. You're in the right place.' Just testing. She glanced his way again. Got his irony. In spite of the hole she was in. They usually didn't. She wasn't thick, then. He stayed standing. He liked to be free to go walkabout. He said, 'Can we get you anything? Cuppa tea?'

She shook her head: no.

'Don't blame you. Police issue. Can't recommend it. So you're his gardener, you been working there five weeks and you left his place today fifteen minutes before the fire broke out.'

She watched him talking, like a kid, expectant, waiting for the bit that might mean something to her. He paused. She went on watching. Then she realised something was expected of her. 'Yes,' she said.

'Okay. You know him before he hired you to do his garden?'

'No.'

'So how come he picked on you?'

'Another client. It's always like that. Word of mouth. I don't advertise.'

'Why's that?'

'I can't afford it. And word of mouth is better.'

'So who was this person recommended you to Mr Han?'

'A client in Lady Margaret Road. Kate Creech.'

Bright went still. Cato went still. Helen went still. The gardener girl looked at them, wondering why.

Cato's little smirk moved the corners of his mouth. 'Kate Creech the actress?' he said.

'Yes.' People did get funny about actresses. It seemed policemen were no exception. 'I did her garden over a year ago. I just maintain it now. Three or four times a year.'

'And Kate – Creech – knows Mr Han?' Bright's squint concentrated somewhere middle distance.

'Yes. He photographed her for the local freebie when she was appearing at the New End theatre a few months ago. He told her he needed someone to design his garden. So . . .'

It hurt her to talk about him, you could see.

Bright wanted Cato and Helen out of here but he couldn't think of a reason that wouldn't look mad. Kate and this Chinese bloke that looked like an advert for Levi's? Your past life running past your eyes, thick like treacle. Never mind that now. 'So you first met him- when? Early July?'

'End of June, yes. He showed me the garden. It was just concrete paths and weeds. Nothing worth keeping except that rose on the end wall. I did a design and a price and he accepted it.'

'What you charge him?'

'About two thousand.'

'Is that a lot?'

'No. I came down on the original estimate because . . .' She half smiled. Sadness made it a grimace. 'I don't know why really. He couldn't afford any more. And I needed the job.' But she looked like it was more than that.

He wasn't going to push it. Yet. 'So you started the garden when?'

'About a week later. Beginning of July. Initially I worked for a week, every day. That was the clearance work. I had to hire a skip and shift a lot of debris. But since then I've just done a couple of days a week.'

'So today was just a normal day?'

She gave him another look. No, she was far from thick. She didn't smile. Wasn't capable any more. She sighed. 'Just a normal day.' Her body shrank round itself, an empty frock on a washing line. She said, 'I could do with a glass of water if you could run to that.'

'I think we could run to a glass of water. Cato?' Some reason, he minded Cato's presence more than Helen's. Cato went with bad grace. 'Okay.'

Bright walked round the table, closer to her. He sat on the

table, one foot on the ground, one leg swinging. Close to, she smelled of Imperial Leather soap, he knew, his ma always used it. 'You arrived what time this morning?'

'Half nineish.'

'That normal?'

'Yes.'

'You have a van, what?'

'I have a van. But—'

He looked at Helen.'Has it been searched?'

The gardener's head came up. 'Searched?'

'Don't mind, do you, Mrs – er – Craig?'

'I – I don't know. Why would you . . . ?'

'Well, far as we know, you were the last to see him before he got nearly burned to death. Best we know what's in your van. Just to eliminate it, right?'

'Don't you—? I mean – don't you need a warrant or something? I—'

'Well, strictly we do, but if you just give us the go-ahead it saves us all a lot of trouble. I mean, if you got nothing lurking in there that looks like criminal intent . . .'

'But I—' She didn't want to say anything can look like criminal intent if you want to make it look that way. She didn't say she'd heard of coppers planting evidence either. She was too polite, too well brought up, not like the usual yobbos they had in here. And she didn't want to refuse in case that went down bad for her – lack of co-operation with the police, all that. She floundered, then said, 'Will I be able to be there while you . . . ?'

This was quite a clever question to come out of all that floundering. 'Oh, I think so.' He turned to Helen. 'Can't see anything against that, can you?' He didn't give Helen time to reply. 'Where is the van?' he said.

'Outside my house.'

'Your husband there, is he?'

'No. Well, I don't think so. He came with me. Here. He's waiting for me.'

'You got the keys on you?'

She fumbled in a big cotton bag. Brought out this big bunch of keys.

'Christ,' he said. 'What are all those?'

She sorted through them. 'These are my house and the van and Dan's car. The others are my clients'.'

'They trust you then.'

She looked upset. 'Yes.' Like no one had ever not trusted her before and the experience was new and frightening.

She was guilty. He felt it then, coming off her in waves. She was ashamed and guilty but he wasn't sure what of. Yet. He'd get to that shortly.

Cato came in with a plastic bottle of water and a paper cup, poured a cup of water and handed it to Jude Craig with a courtly gesture. Put the bottle down on the table in front of her. Stood back against the wall and folded his arms: *I am above this butler stuff; Helen should be sent on menial errands, not me. She's of lower rank and, more to the point, she's female.*

Bright waited for the performance to finish. 'Okay, we'll go round there later and have a look at the van. You can be there. Your husband can be there. No hanky-panky. See?' He raised his hands in a conjuror's gesture: look, nothing up my sleeve. 'So this van was parked outside Mr Han's flat all day today?'

'No. I walked round to Lee's today. My tools were there already. I didn't need the van. I walked. Erm, I'll need to get my tools, by the way.'

'We'll go round there together, Mrs Craig.'

Again her eyes acknowledged the menace. She nodded but didn't speak.

'So the van was outside your own house all day.'

'Yes. As far as I know.'

'Your husband ever use it?'

She looked at him. The blue eyes got this dead look. Tired. She shook her head. 'Not as a rule. He uses his car.'

'And where was he today?'

'Working at home when I left this morning. He was going to see a client in the afternoon, I think.'

'Was he at home when you got back this evening?'

Something happened to her when you mentioned the husband, like life was draining out of her. She shook her head: 'Not when I first got in, no.'

'So what time did he get back?' He asked this, squeezing his nasal corncrake South London voice into an insinuating purr, an intimate sensuous threat.

She glanced his way, she couldn't help it, and very fast away again. She looked at her hands in her lap, black nails, bruises, scratches, a workman's hands. If you weren't a hardboiled copper these hands might make you weep. 'I'm not sure what time I got back myself. I did some shopping in Kentish Town Road—'

'Where?'

'Paradise Food – you know? – Kentish Town Road, next to the Oxfam Shop—'

'I know Paradise Food . . . Take you five, seven minutes to get there from his place.'

'I was there five minutes or so—'

'Call it ten. It's now getting on for quarter to six. The fire was just breaking out. A-ha?'

'Then I got back—'

'Ten minutes? Five to six?'

'—changed out of my work gear—'

'Ten past six?'

'—put some food on to cook—'

Yes, she would cook. 'How long that take you?'

'The food? Half an hour, maybe more?'

'Okay, we're talking ten to, five to, seven?'

'Yes. Dan must have got home about – I don't know – about a quarter past, I suppose? You'll have to ask him. I don't wear a watch. They get damaged in my work.' She swallowed. She'd run out of breath, and words, to obfuscate the fact that she didn't know, and they didn't know, where her husband had been when Lee Han was being burned to a crisp in his bed.

'Where had he been?'

'Who?'

'Your husband.'

'To see a client, I think.'

'This client, a-ha. Where is that?'

Again the waves of guilt coming off her. 'He did say, but I was miles away. I'm sorry. I think this client – I think it's the one that – I think he said the house he's designing for him is in Essex. I'm not sure. I'm sorry.'

'Don't apologise to me. Most wives don't hear a word their husbands say.'

She gave a wan smile. She was tired. She was tired deep inside. And sad. And sadness wasn't natural to her. It was new to her. Made her uncomfortable like a garment that didn't fit. She shifted round inside it, trying to find a way to wear it and carry on like things were normal. He was getting to her, he could feel it, he was getting there. Round and round the garden like a teddy bear, one step, two step . . .

He said, 'What time did you stop working in Mr Han's garden?' This was it. This was the question. He'd got there. 'A-ha, you don't wear a watch but roughly, give me a rough guess – just before you left? An hour before you left? Half an hour? What?' She was gazing at the opaque glass of the window, facing away from them, from all of them. He gave her time: 'Go on, just a rough guess.'

She didn't reply. Some kids shouted outside, insults flew, then high laughter, the sound of running feet. Someone tried to start a car, the engine coughed then died. At the third go it started. The car drove away. Nobody said anything.

Cato shut the window. 'Teatime, wasn't it, Mrs Craig?'

'She told us she saw him, sir.'

'He came out to the garden, that's what you said, wasn't it?'

'Is that right, Mrs Craig?' Bright's voice still this insinuating nasal purr, like a cat's tail wrapping itself round your leg.

She turned to Bright. 'Yes. He came out to see what I'd done. The garden's nearly finished you see, the main structure—'

'I saw. It's nice.'

'He offered me a cup of tea.'

'So what time was that? Roughly. Take your time.'

'Half four maybe?'

'You'd be ready for it by then.'

She didn't respond to the double meaning.

'So you had a cup of tea at teatime. In the garden?'

'I – No. Well, on the terrace, yes.'

Her first lie, he could see it clear as day. Because he could see it he knew she wasn't used to lying, it didn't come easy to her, she didn't know how to prevent that particular shrinking of the skin round the mouth, like sucking on a lemon, that slight defocusing of the eyes.

'Did Mr Han have a cup of tea with you?'

'Yes.'

'On the terrace?'

No hesitation. 'Yes.'

'What did you talk about?'

'Oh, erm, just – the garden.'

'Had he paid you yet, by the way?'

'No.'

Her eyes filled with tears. Not for her possibly lost couple of thou either, Bright guessed.

'Was that a bone of contention?'

'How?'

'You said you were nearly finished. Like shouldn't he have paid you by now?'

'No. He was to pay me next week. That was the deal.'

'Not a problem then.'

'No.'

'Will it be a problem now?'

'How?'

'You won't get paid. Maybe.'

The blue eyes swam under water. She said in a tired flat tone that stopped just short of insult, 'No, that won't be a problem.'

'A-ha. So go on.'

'Go on?'

'So you had a cuppa tea on the terrace. You and Mr Han. How did long did that take?'

'Erm . . .'

'Just a rough idea. See, it's quite a long time, isn't it, between half four and half five when you left? Just like to get an idea what you were up to.'

'I had to finish off in the garden. Put the tools away.'

'In the shed, right? What time did you do that?'

'Erm . . .'

'Like – before you had the tea – and the chat – on the terrace? Or after?'

'Oh, after. Just before I left.'

'Notice anything funny?'

'Like what?'

'Like anything had been disturbed. Anything missing.'

'Like what?'

Nobody replied. They all watched her, waiting.

'No, I didn't. I just put the tools away and left. Why?'

Quietly he said, 'Have you ever handled that drum of paraffin in the shed?'

She said, 'I should think I've handled everything in that shed at some time.'

'There was a clean place on the floor, a foot square? Next to the drum of paraffin.'

'The petrol!' she said. 'Is that what they used?'

'You knew there was petrol in the shed? How long had it been there?'

'Always. I mean it was in the old shed. I took down the old one, so everything had to be moved. Then I built this one, and put everything back.'

'So when did you last see the petrol there?'

She put both roughened hands over her eyes, kept them there, breathed deeply into them. Then she took them away and shook her head. 'I can't remember. I just didn't notice. I'm so sorry. I'm so sorry.'

'It's a nice little shed. Unusual. Nice little hidey-hole on the top of it. All overhung by next door's tree. You could lie up there for hours and not be seen.'

'Lee was intending to do that when his knee mended. Lie up there and read. It's peaceful there.' She was close to breaking, remembering him and the peaceful garden. The garden of remembrance it might turn out to be.

Bright said, 'Someone could have been up there all the time you were doing the garden. Waiting. Watching you. Waiting for you to go.'

She turned her whole body to stare at him. She was imagining. Wondering. She said, 'How would they get up there without me knowing?'

'Over the wall at the back?'

'That wall is very high.'

'There's trees on the other side. To give you a leg up.'

'How would they get over it without me hearing?'

'You were making noise. The building site makes noise.'

'But that close – I'd have seen them surely.'

'Not if you were working hard. Someone could wait on top of that wall. Plenty of tree cover. Stay up in the leaves. Bide their time. Wait for the moment. Then jump down and make themselves cosy on top of the shed. And just wait.'

She pushed the creepy feeling out of the way to give this idea some rational thought. You could see her doing that. She shook her head at last. She said, 'It's possible. But I don't think it's likely.'

'Why?'

'I think I'd have known. I'd have felt there was someone there. I'd have felt it.'

'You go indoors for lunch?'

'I don't stop for lunch. Not really. I eat on the hoof. I sat down for a few minutes. By the pond. Ate a sandwich.'

Cato leered. 'Didn't your friend Lee bring you tea?'

Bright wanted to throttle Cato. She was motoring now, speaking free, out of danger, innocent. This was when they incriminated themselves, walked into traps. Natty little Sherlock never knew when to leave well alone.

'No,' she said. 'He brought me fizzy water as a matter of fact, and went back to work.'

'Where did he go?'

'I suppose to his desk in his living-room. That's where he works normally. I don't know.'

'See, what I'm trying to establish, Mrs Craig—' Bright became open, confiding, the squint almost imperceptible – 'was the garden empty at any time during the day or were you out there all the time? See what I mean? If you'd gone indoors at some time, that could be the time that someone climbed in over that wall and hung out on the shed roof. See?'

'Yes, I see.'

'What did you do about – er – toilet arrangements? Go in the house?'

'It's weird but when I'm working I don't need to wee. I think it's because you sweat so much—' She stopped a split second, reminded of something, brought up short, made a swift U-turn away from it. 'Anyway, I didn't go in at lunchtime. Or at all till I finished work.'

Bright said, 'We found a red curly hair in Mr Han's bathroom. Same length as yours.'

She waited and she didn't look at anyone. She moved her head to one side then the other like her neck was in a collar that was too tight.

'In the shower,' he said.

She had to cough to get her throat clear. She said with a candid look, at Bright only, 'I had a shower before I left.'

'A-ha?'

'Lee said I could.'

'He brought you a cuppa tea, you had a chat, and then he let you use his shower.'

'Yes.'

'Why didn't you tell us this before?'

She looked at Cato. 'I thought you might – jump to conclusions.'

'I see. Was this the first time you – used his shower?'

'No. It was— From the— I nearly always did.'

'Kind of him. Wasn't it?'

'Yes.'

'So you had a shower and then put your work clothes back on again. And then put the tools away.'

She knew how it sounded. Her eyes were not frightened exactly, more supplicating. 'Yes.' She breathed out through her nose like a little pony. 'Look, I'm so sorry. I've remembered. We didn't drink the tea on the terrace. I took mine into the shower and drank it there.'

'And where was Mr Han all this time?' Bright left a pause

but she didn't fill it. 'Was he back indoors by now?'

'Yes, he – he came in when I did.'

'And how was he feeling?'

'Feeling?'

'Mrs Craig, he was in bed. At five thirty in the afternoon. Was he feeling ill? Tired? I mean, was he normally in bed at five thirty of an afternoon? Was he all right?'

They all watched her. She said, 'He'd had an operation on his knee recently. It's been taking a long time to heal. He still uses a crutch. It's tiring for him, I think.'

'So he was just resting then, that it?'

She looked at his bland expression, his squint at its most impenetrable. She didn't reply.

'This is quite a long shower? Take you from half four to what – twenty past five? You see, Mrs Craig, if there was something going on between you and Mr Han and you'd had some kind of – well, if there was jealousy involved or – blackmail maybe—'

'Blackmail?' She was shocked.

'He could've threatened to tell your husband.'

'Lee? Oh, this is ridiculous.' She rose from her chair then remembered where she was and sat again. 'Lee is a nice man. He cares about big issues – crime and the environment and the homeless and – he's a civilised person. It's ridiculous what you're saying. He's kind and good.' She got out a tissue and rubbed her eyes but she went on talking; she'd got strength from his accusation. 'You must meet people who do dreadful things all the time, threaten each other, injure each other, try to kill each other. But Lee's not like that. Any more than I am. Even if – well, you've implied all kinds of things, but – even if some of that were true, people like him and me, we don't resort to . . .' She lifted her shoulders and let out a sigh, not of exasperation, but like her lungs were constricted so she couldn't breathe. She shook her head many times but had run out of words.

Bright said, 'You're right, we see all sorts. A lot of it, other people wouldn't be able to stomach. But we get to know that human beings are capable of all kinds of stuff you'd never suspect. In a corner, anyone will fight to keep what they got. Even nice people like you and Mr Han . . .' He waited. They all waited.

She didn't answer. She didn't look at anyone. She looked at her hands. She unclasped them and placed them flat on her knees, she straightened the fingers, lifting them, stretching them, studying the short nails, the scratches and bruises. She took a breath. She looked up at Bright. She said, 'Is my husband still here?'

This brought them all up short. 'Er . . .'

'Because if you're going to keep me here any longer, you should tell him to go home. And I'd like him to ring our solicitor please as well. You won't stop us doing that, will you?' No aggression. Just the pleading eyes again. Not like they meant to plead; she couldn't help the look they had.

Bright gazed at her for a while. He said, 'No idea who could have done this to Lee Han, then? You really can't help us at all?'

'He writes about criminals . . .' She shrugged.

'A fat man used to visit him. Ever see a fat man there?'

She shrugged again, and shook her head: no.

'Ever see anyone in the upstairs flat?'

'There was a man with red hair. But he left a few weeks ago. I never spoke to him. He waved from his back window once, in the first week or two when I was making the pond. Since then the estate agents have brought a couple of people to see the place. Well, I assume it was that – I just got a glimpse. People at the window. Do you think—?'

'What about today?'

'No, I didn't see anyone up there today.'

'What about Mr Han's wife? History of violence there. Did you know that?'

Her back straightened. 'I don't know anything about . . . It's not my business.'

Bright nodded. He'd never get a word out of her that might incriminate anyone else. It was weird to meet a nice person in here, specially at his level. The Uniforms met ordinary decent citizens from time to time. But CID were the sewage workers, they worked the stink and the creatures that had their living in it. They themselves had their living in it. A hair found in the shower wasn't enough to arrest her on, even if they thought she was guilty. And he wasn't going to push her on the sex thing. It would keep. You need something to use in an emergency. That might be it. Lee Han might be above blackmail, and so might Jude Craig. But he wasn't. He couldn't afford to be. 'Okay,' he said. 'Well, at least we've established about half an hour when you weren't in the garden and maybe someone else could have got in over the wall.'

They looked at him, all three. He went to the door and opened it. 'Thanks for your help.'

Bewildered, she stood up. She came slowly to the door, wary, like it might be a trick. He nearly let her go without a word. But close to her in the doorway he said, 'We will need to speak to you again. Don't go away anywhere without letting us know?'

She nodded. 'I won't.'

'Tell your husband sorry we kept him waiting.'

She didn't look round as she walked away.

8

He stood up and hugged her. They clung together a moment. Oh the relief to find him waiting there, the heaven of being clasped in his arms again and protected by him. Then she saw his eyes. He wasn't looking at her.

The policeman, the dangerous one in the scruffy leather jacket, stood in the inner doorway watching them. He said to Dan, 'Mind if I ask you where you were this afternoon, Mr Craig? Your wife thought you went to see a client but she's not sure.'

'No, I didn't, Jude. I just went out for a walk. I often do that when I run out of inspiration, don't I? Go walkabout.'

'Where did you go?'

'Oh God, just over to Parliament Hill Fields. By way of Gospel Oak.'

'Gospel Oak. What route?

'Well now . . . I went past here actually, then down along Spring Place, into Grafton Road and—'

'So you'd have passed quite close to Mr Han's flat then.'

'Well, I suppose so, but I'm actually not quite sure exactly where it is. Willes Road, is it, Jude?'

She smiled. 'Close.'

The policeman was watching. But she felt fine. She'd have known if Dan was lying. He wasn't. 'Can we go now?' she said.

The policeman looked amused though he didn't smile. Just these metallic points of light that snapped on and off in his little brown eyes. 'Sure, you can go now,' he said. 'Thanks for your help.'

His voice set her teeth on edge. Dan looked like he might say something else. But he didn't. He just opened the door for her and they were out, into dear old Kentish Town Road, littered pavements, deafening traffic, amiable winos, all the ordinary people going about their ordinary business, not knowing how a moment could change your life from a jogging along okay sort of affair to a minefield where one wrong step could blow it sky high. Where someone you loved was lying sick unto death and you must not breathe a syllable of how you felt to the other person you loved.

'What did they ask you?' Dan said. 'What did they want to know?'

She couldn't tell Dan the half of it. 'They think someone got over the wall and waited till I finished work. Waited till I left. Or maybe someone was hiding, waiting, in the upstairs flat.'

'They don't suspect you then?'

'They – they found a red curly longish hair in the—' *not the shower, don't say shower* – 'in Lee's bathroom.'

'Well of course they did. You must have used the bathroom while you were there. Christ!'

She nodded, the breath all gone lumpy and wet in the back of her mouth, choking her so she couldn't speak.

'They didn't threaten you, did they, Jude?'

Oh, she wanted to howl like a banshee. *Yes, yes, yes! They're threatening everything. They're threatening me. They're threatening us. Especially us.* She wanted to tell him everything, to prepare him, pre-warn him, pre-arm him. She wanted him to hear it from her first, not the police, not that frightening detective inspector with the small brown glittery eyes that he used like a sharp instrument, scalpel, or gouging tool. He was relentless. He was driven. He was screwed tight like a spring and he would choose his moment and catch you in his coils. She knew he would get it out of her about her and Lee. She knew this quite surely. But he would wait till he needed it. He was fair the way an animal is fair. Like George, who never used his claws on her until he absolutely had to; they both knew the claws were there, like they both knew his feline teeth could bite clean through a finger, but he only ever bit her gently. That's what John Bright did, he was biting her gently, letting her know, the teeth were waiting, to close round her secret and bite. And Dan was waiting now for an answer from her. And if she said one word of their insinuations his questions would unravel. If she mentioned the shower, she could not go back. Dan would ask and ask and ask and all would be known and all would be a devastation and a ruin.

They stood at the window of Dan's workroom and watched through the slats of the venetian blind, while two men in papery white spacesuits climbed all over her van, searching it inside and out. The policeman in the blazer and sharp-crease trousers stood around smoking his Sherlock Holmes pipe. A small crowd had spilled out of the flats opposite and the kids arsed about, getting smart with the policeman who ignored them. Jude and Dan felt shivery with shame.

At last the forensic people finished. They got back in their van and drove off. The poseur policeman waved to her and Dan, giving them the thumbs up in his jaunty way.

Dan's hand gripped hers so hard it hurt. 'What on earth did they think they were looking for?'

'They asked me about a drum of petrol missing from the shed.'

'Oh yes, you'd set fire to your employer and leave the remains of the petrol in your van for the police to find. What do they want to charge you with – idiocy?'

'They have got to eliminate me, I suppose.'

'But why,' Dan said, 'would you want to kill him?'

This question was the dangerous one. She shook her head,

letting the movement take her gaze with it, scattered, unfocused. 'That's it, that's just it, why would I?'

'I mean,' Dan said. 'You like him so much. Don't you?' His voice was quiet, serious.

Every question seemed loaded, sinister. 'Well, yes—'

'And after all—' Dan looked down and into her eyes, stilling them – 'he hasn't paid you yet.'

When she gazed at him, frozen in the headlights of his regard, he smiled.

And after a long hesitation she smiled palely back.

He led the way downstairs and put the kettle on. He had dropped the questions, decided to cheer her up. She was relieved and paradoxically disappointed. She knew she must tell Dan about her and Lee before she was forced to tell the police. They must not know before Dan. They must not be able to use it against him.

Use it against him? This idea brought her up sharp. *Dan could be guilty. Dan had a motive.* But only if he knew about her and Lee. She shut her eyes and groaned.

'Sit down. Come on.'

She opened her eyes. And there stood the real Dan, the Dan she knew, the Dan who looked after her, cared for her, in sickness and in health, for richer for poorer, all the days of his life. Handing her a mug of tea, the symbol of all that.

'Tea's good for shock. And I'll give you some arnica.'

'You don't believe in homeopathic remedies.'

'I know I don't. But the bloody things do work.'

Now she did smile. 'You even know that arnica's the right one—'

'—for shock and bruising. Just shows you—' he smiled at her as he went to the cupboard – 'I know more than you think.'

Every time she thought she had a safe piece of road to follow, the conversation took a bend. *I know more than you think?* Her head felt full of rolling rocks, heavy, full of difficult movement, weighted this side then that. All she could do was shut her eyes and drink the tea. And wait. And hope. And let the problem approach so close it would meet her head on. As Dan was approaching her now with the little glass bottle of homeopathic remedies.

If her mouth had been able to form the words at this moment she would have told Dan her secret. But she sat there while he shook two little pills into the lid of the bottle and all she said was, 'No, you first, I have to wait a while – after the tea.'

'Me?' he said. 'Why me?'

'It's been a shock for you as well. Hasn't it?'

He looked at her a moment, his head on one side. Waiting for her to elaborate? Considering his reply? But she said nothing else. And whatever else he might have said, he decided against it.

'I suppose it has,' he said slowly. And she watched him toss his head back and the pills into his mouth and they said nothing more.

He sat her on the sofa and covered her legs with the green tartan rug. When George came in he jumped on her lap, kissed her face three or four times, turned round and round, kissed her once more, and settled, curled like the shell of a snail. Dan gave her the arnica, and settled close to her on the sofa too. It would appear a normal night in the basement of the Craig household, to anyone looking in.

9

'Interpol have contacted the Hong Kong Police Bureau, asked them to do background checks on the victim and his wife. Which they did. Neither of them has a police record, no known criminal connections, no Triad business.'

'A-ha.'

'I broke the news to Mr Han's mother.'

'How'd she take it?'

Roger Gould made a slight hesitation. 'Well, she was shocked, of course.'

'She coming over to see him?'

'No.'

'No?'

'No. She runs a large firm. She can't spare the time.'

'No love lost there then.'

'Well, I suppose that's how it looks but—'

'A-ha, that's how it looks, Rog.'

'I think I'll set further checks in motion. Just in case there's something they've missed. Leave that end to me.'

Bright shut down his phone and scratched his head. Atkins came in and sat at the far end of the table. He put his feet on the next chair and leaned back against the wall. Bright felt, as he often did, like punching his face in.

The CID room was surprisingly quiet considering Camden's colossal crime count, an air of calm routine, even tedium. It was a big room, four huge tables, one for each team. And running the length of the room, facing the tables, the crime desk, where five uniformed officers manned the computer terminals and the phones.

Bright stood up. All the team, except Atkins, sat to attention. 'Right,' he said. 'Four main lines of inquiry. Number one, the gardener. Interviewed her and swabbed her for petrol traces. Awaiting results from the lab. Two, the ex-wife. History of violence against the victim, and she couldn't be traced last night. Taff's interviewing her now. Three is, the victim and her both come from Hong Kong—'

'Well, look no further, it's the Triads, guv.'

'What about the Snakeheads? Some of them only live over the road.'

'Snakeheads?' Helen laughed.

'Straight out of crime fiction, right?' Cato went into his kindly mentor act. 'But it's for real. Deadly enemies of the Triads.'

'The Snakehead case was all over, well before Lee Han came to the area,' Bright said. 'However . . . the AMIP DCI—' subdued groans round the table – 'A-ha, ain't we lucky? Area Major Incident Pool is keeping a watching brief – DCI Roger Gould is checking out the Hong Kong end. Victim's ma still lives there.' Bright handed out some pictures of Lee Han.

'Fuckinell, man, he a model for Calvin Klein or what?'

'Not any more, that's for sure.'

A young Uniform came into the CID room and handed Bright a folder. Bright looked through it. 'Right, I got the scene report.' He lifted out some pictures – graphic close-ups of Lee Han's burned face, hands, torso. He looked through them without expression then launched them down the table. 'A few ambulance shots,' he said. They were passed round, studied with clinical attention.

Someone said, 'Shame the poor bastard lived.'

Even Atkins sounded subdued. 'Any leads, guv?'

'Fingerprints, at least ten sets. None of them on our records.'

'So he doesn't associate with known felons.'

'One of the few round here who doesn't, then.'

'You got a jaundiced view of life, mate.'

'Tell me something new.'

'Pity you can't tell if they're male or female,' Helen said.

'What?'

'The fingerprints.'

Bright nodded. 'Good point.'

'Yeah, might tell us what he was doing in bed in the afternoon.'

Bright handed round a plastic bag. 'A hair. Found in the shower. Reddish. Curly.'

'Pubic?'

'Apparently not.'

'Shame.'

'That's the gardener,' Helen said. 'Jude Craig.'

'A-ha.'

'For definite, guv?'

'For definite.'

'*Mrs* Jude Craig.' Cato showed his little eye teeth in a canine grin.

'In the shower!'

Helen bristled. 'It's possible to take a shower in a place without screwing the owner.'

'Come off it, Goldilocks. She's got motive, she's got opportunity, and she's seen leaving the flat quarter of an hour before!'

'And what is her motive exactly?'

'I don't know. He was two-timing her and she found out? He was blackmailing her – threatening to tell her old man what she got up to in the afternoons?'

Helen said, 'What about the husband, guv? Has he accounted for his time? Do we know where he was before he came home yesterday?'

'Out walking, he says.'

Cato brightened up. 'That's a great alibi!'

'He admits he went in that direction but says he didn't know exactly where the flat was.'

'It was him, guv.'

'Think so, ha?'

'If she was two-timing me,' Cato said, 'I might burn the bloke to death.'

Bright let the laughter roll around. Helen was watching him. He didn't join in. 'Don't rule it out, don't rule anything out, goes without saying. But I've got a feeling we might be frying bigger fish here.' He let a little silence hang, to get their attention. 'Our fourth line of inquiry, right? . . . Lee Han is a crime reporter for the local freebie.'

Puzzled looks. 'Yeah?' Cato said. 'So?'

'He's shit hot on Mick Brennan.'

The guys round the team table murmured.

'He's been looking into our shooting in the junkyard.' Bright passed round the print-outs of Han's articles. 'I been studying these this morning and I'm telling you, he's no slouch.' He gestured at the crime desk behind him. 'Maggie's hacking into his files to see if there's anything else in there on the Brennan killings.'

Maggie said without looking up, 'I'm in. But there's an awful lot of stuff. And logic's not his strong point. I haven't even found his address list yet.'

'You'll get there. Right. Atkins, you take the landlord. It's a property company in the City. Embrey's, something like that.'

Cato took his meerschaum out of his mouth. 'Embers? That's a joke.'

'Bernard, you take the estate agents. Everyone who's had keys or been taken to the flat, and the last tenants. Just for a start.'

'Right, guv.' Bernard was their token black DC. He got the

same kind of treatment as Helen, but not so overt: he was bigger, he rolled with the punches. He was more used to taking the shit. He'd been taking it all his life.

'Listen. One other thing we got is the fat man. There's a fat man, looks older than he is. He's a regular visitor to the victim's place. They drink together in the Prince of Wales. So I suggest, Atkins, that after – and not till after – your visit to the City folk, you pay a visit to the Prince of Wales tavern. And remember, an officer does not drink on duty unless not to do so would impede the course of his inquiry.'

'Thanks, guv. You buying?'

'In fact, don't anyone forget the fat man. Wherever you go, keep an eye out. Anyone answering that description we want to speak to him.'

At that moment his mobile rang.

10

Coming over the canal bridge, swans gliding amidst the litter, Bright had a few clichéd thoughts about the mire of city life and beauty shining through the filth and corruption, when a swan bore down on a moorhen and dive-bombed it out of the water. An unprovoked attack on a puny adversary. So much for purity and beauty in the mire. A Royal Mail van tried to cut him up just then on the Sainsbury's roundabout. He pulled himself together, put the mail van in its place – behind him – and looked up the address Llewellyn had given him. He parked in a residents-only place and then walked.

Palton Mews was a little yard off Portobello Road. Scruffy but bright. Brave red and yellow window boxes balanced on the crumbling sills.

Llewellyn was waiting for him. 'She lives upstairs, guv. Number 4A. Her name's Chloe.'

'So, what she say exactly when you told her?'

'She said, "A fire? Oh."'

'*A fire, oh?* You tell her her ex-husband's in intensive care with seventy-five per cent burns and she says *a fire oh*?'

Llewellyn shrugged. 'People get a shock, it takes them different ways.'

'Well, that's different all right. *A fire oh*. Like she expected it to be something else?'

'I wouldn't necessarily want to read that into it.'

'Christ, Taff. You got a bad attack of political correctness. I'd get it seen to if I was you.'

A piece of driftwood was tied to the railings with string, on it the number 4A roughly done in white paint and an arrow pointing up. The frail-looking iron staircase creaked and shifted as they climbed.

'She say anything else?'

'She said, is he alive? I said yes, but he's in intensive care.'

'And she said?'

'Nothing. I told her which hospital and she said thanks.'

'That's it?'

'That's it.'

'Where was she last night?'

'Staying round a friend's.'

'Call the friend?'

'Yes. Friend confirms she was there.'

'Whole time span?'

'Yes.' Taff looked glum. 'All night, matter of fact.'

'Oh. A bloke.'

'A bloke, ay. Black bloke. Round the corner.'

'He for real?'

'Far as I can tell.'

The bright green paint was lifting off the door. The lock had been broken sometime and not well fixed. A child cried inside.

She looked like she'd been crying too, the black stuff round her eyes and her bright red lipstick all smudged. But you couldn't tell – maybe she just hadn't washed since she'd got up. She wore black, a frock as short as her wedding dress in the picture. Bright showed her his ID. 'You've already met DC Lewellyn.'

Her eyes moved to Taff and back again. 'Lee?' she said. She had a slight accent, so slight it was hardly there, more a hesitation than an actual sound, with just a slight cockney edge. 'Has he died?'

'No. But there's no plans yet for him to get out of intensive care.'

No way of knowing if she was relieved or not. She let them in with a shrug. The child was still crying. She picked him up, a small creature in Gap dungarees. He stopped crying to watch their faces, watch the words coming out of their mouths, staring in that disconcerting way kids do before they learn to put on the face that's expected of them. He sat in the crook of her right arm supported by her angled hip. There was no spare flesh on either of them, mother or child.

The place was a mess. Kid's clothes strewn about, half-eaten kid's messes, a wet rusk. A couple of disposable nappies, used. A baby smell: urine, thin sour vomit, talcum powder.

Unlike Lee's place, this was a riot of colour, red and gold and magenta silk, a sofa covered in imitation leopard with an imitation leopard rug. Mirrors with jewelly glass decorations. Posters of – Bright supposed – film stars or singers too young and trendy for him to recognise. It looked like a whore's place. He'd seen plenty. Couldn't tell if it was her taste or temporary. 'Lived here long?' he said.

'Since Lee and I split up.'

'How long's that?'

'Six months and three days.'

'A-ha.'

'It's not my taste if that's what you're thinking.'

'A-ha?'

'You think I'm a whore or something?'

'It's whore's decor all right.'

'I know that. You think I wouldn't know that?'

'What do you do for a living?'

'I look after Lee's kid. I baby sit.' She said these words clearly, separately. *Baby. Sit.* Even taking her accent into account it sounded odd.

'He's your kid too, right?'

'And mine, yes.' She spoke wearily on a sigh. She sat, the child held carelessly on her hip, and crossed her long, long, thin, thin legs.

Llewellyn couldn't take his eyes off these legs.

Bright said, 'Take a look round, Taff.'

Taff, mesmerised, did not respond.

'You don't mind if DC Llewellyn has a look round, do you, Chloe?'

'Have you got a warrant?'

'No, but we can get one and—'

'Who cares anyway.' She shrugged. 'It's okay. I've got nothing to hide.'

'Thanks. Go on then, Taff.'

The DC came round like from an anaesthetic. 'Yeah. Er – yeah. Okay, guv.' He moved like one of those guys in the fairy tales, the prince who's had a spell put on him by the beautiful witch and can never ever after find his way out of the forest. Not till the nice woodcutter's daughter comes along and gives him a kiss. And leads him out by the nose.

The girl watched Llewellyn gather his wits and leave the room. She seemed to be considering something but her eyes were opaque. Bright wondered if maybe another oriental might have a clue what she was thinking. He supposed he was being racist. He couldn't help that. Her mouth gave nothing away either. Only the skin on the inside of her arms gave away what she was.

'Expensive habit,' he said. 'And I'm not talking just money either.' The kid didn't look sick, though he was maybe thinner than you'd expect, with a sad, wise expression and sallow skin. Not that Bright knew anything about babies. 'Was he born a junkie?' he said.

For a second those eyes almost revealed something. But then they blanked out again. He reckoned the answer was yes. But she wasn't answering. She looked at him a long time. She sighed. She said, 'I thought you came to tell me about Lee.'

'To ask you about Lee.'

'What about him?'

'Who might have set fire to him.'

'Not me anyway.'

'How do we know that?'

'He pays me an allowance. Without that I've got nothing.'

'If Lee dies, who gets his property?'

'I do. The baby does.'

'A lot?'

'No. He's not rich.'

'Just a living?'

'Not much of one.'

'You deserve it?'

'I didn't want to have a baby; he did. When the kid was born Lee took no more notice of me, only of the kid. I didn't like that. So I moved out. With his precious kid. Because everyone knows a child must be with his mother.' She gave Bright a defiant stare. 'Anyway Lee can't look after him. He has to work.'

'To keep you and his kid.'

'That's right, yes! And if he's all burned up he can't work any more so then what happens to us? You think I'm stupid? You think I'm going to burn up my meal ticket?'

'You have been known to do things in anger without thinking too much about the consequences.'

'I don't think you burn someone in anger. You have to think about that ahead of time.'

'Do you?'

She minutely raised her eyes, gave him an *is that the best you can do?* look and disdained to reply.

Llewellyn returned. He stood in the doorway staring again in a dumbfounded way. Bright glanced at him. Taff dragged his gaze from the girl to Bright. 'Some photos in the bedroom. Her and Lee and some other people.'

'There were a lot of photos of you at Lee's place. He take them?'

'He's a photographer.'

'That right?' he said. Dumb cop. She was getting under his skin. She was annoying him. Not that she'd know. She was a girl who liked to think she was clever. Cleverer than blokes especially. He'd play as dumb as she liked. Let her think on.

'That's how he came to be a journalist,' she explained with extreme patience to the moron cops. 'He sold pictures of local things to that stupid local newspaper. Then he started to find out things, just local stuff going down, nothing big, so he started doing a few words for them. He sometimes does stuff for the *Big Issue* too. He has this thing for the underdog. He was always like that. As a kid he had a whole menagerie. Always taking in strays.' Her tone expressed contempt for such a pitiable weakness.

'You knew him when he was a kid?'

'We grew up together. In Hong Kong.'

'Mind showing me your pictures, Chloe?' Very 'umble, very Uriah Heep.

She led the way. The kid leaned his chin on her shoulder and stared like Bright might hold the answer to the big questions of the universe. Poor kid. No one was going to give him the answer to anything.

A whore's bedroom. Black feather boa over the brass bed rail. Black patent shoes with four-inch stiletto heels. Flesh-coloured satin sheets. A red scarf over the lamp. 'You share this place,' Bright suddenly said.

She stood still. The baby turned his head inquiring. He felt the change in her. She looked into the baby's eyes. For a second Bright saw something more than indifference there. Well, maybe he did. He couldn't be sure. That was the trouble, he couldn't be sure of anything with her.

She gave a long sigh. 'She lives somewhere else now. She brings her – clients here sometimes. She pays half the rent. How do you think I could afford to live here otherwise?'

'How d'you meet her?'

Chloe shrugged. 'I don't know. A club or pub or somewhere? We got talking. She offered me this place.'

'Can you give me her name and address?'

'I only know her name's Shelley. Don't know her address.' The blank gaze defied them.

Bright kept his temper. 'You must have her phone number.'

'No. She phones me. Then we go out until she's finished.'

'You always go out?'

Opaque her expression might be, but contempt she could do so it socked you between the eyes. 'You think I'd let my kid witness that stuff?'

'Junkies will do a lot of things—'

'I am not a junkie. My use is strictly recreational. I have my habit under control. I do not buy. I do not need to buy.'

'That means you're getting enough. Where from?'

She gave what passed for a laugh, a little puff of audible breath through her nose. 'That would really be clever, to tell you lot.'

Taff looked in pain. He said, 'You should go into detox. There's a place now would let you keep the kid.'

'Oh yes, the Priory. And who pays? You?' Then she smiled at him. She said, 'You're too nice for a cop.'

Bright couldn't stand the sight of Taff's stricken face. He looked at the photos spread on the slippery bed. They were all of Chloe. All in black and white. All by Lee Han, he'd say at a glance. Three of her with the baby. Classy, not your average Technicolor fatso kid beaming for the nice man with the camera; these were lovely mother and child jobs. With a kind of sexy – no – sensual – life to them, shadows and shafts of light. Ah, one small picture, different, a faded Polaroid: Lee and Chloe on either side of that woman again, the one in her – what – late thirties? Forty? He held it out to her. 'There were pictures of this woman at Lee's.'

She turned from Taff to the photo. Her eyelids drooped slowly over her eyes in a gesture of loathing. Or was it loathing? How would he know? 'His mother,' she said.

'In Hong Kong?'

'That's right.'

He waited. If you stay quiet long enough people fill the silence. Even people who are good at sitting out a silence. Even Chloe.

'She hates me.'

'Why's that, Chloe?'

'I married Lee.'

'When was this?'

'Six years ago.'

'And that's why you left Hong Kong – because of his mother, right?'

'In Hong Kong I would see her all the time. Lee would see her all the time. Believe me, life is too short.'

'Where'd you live when you first came here?'

'All over. With friends. Then we got a room in Ladbroke Grove. Then a friend told us about the flat in Kentish Town—'

'What friend?'

'I don't know. Friend of Lee's.'

'You sure you don't know?'

The flat dead eyes gazed their flat dead gaze. Chloe didn't waste words. What she had said she had said.

'You lived there two years, right?'

She shrugged, meaning give or take a month or so.

'You like it there?'

'I don't like it anywhere.'

'A-ha. Well, looking like you do, with your small but private income, with your steady supply of what you need, living in a mews in Notting Hill, that's pretty tough. No wonder you're unhappy.'

'What do *you* know?'

'With a nice little kid who was born a junkie like his mum but he's okay now?'

The eyelids came down half mast over her eyes. She said, 'You're asking me all kinds of things and insinuating stuff and I don't like that, okay? So you have something to ask me, you ask me and I'll answer and then you go. Okay?'

'Fair enough. Where were you yesterday afternoon?'

'I went out in the street, down the market, bought some milk, tins for the kid, bread, stuff like that.'

'How usual is that?'

'It's usual. I'd go crazy in here all day, so I put him in his chair-thing and we go down the market. Every day.'

And she'd score down there. Paying with whatever she had. Not always money. Yeah, and ask down the market and all the guys, they'd nod, yeah, man, she down here every day, yeah sure she down here Monday, yeah! Never give the scum a crumb, and who could blame them, waste of time asking, but they'd go through the motions for the record, for all the forms in triplicate. He wouldn't send Bernard down the market, no way, his one black DC, they'd give Bernard the worst time, take the piss – they didn't like traitors and they'd never see a black copper as anything but that – gone over to the enemy – and who could blame them? He'd send Helen. She had the best chance. And a good nose for a lie.

'And you didn't get on the 31 bus and take a trip down Camden way to burn your ex's face off, after you'd bought the milk?'

She sighed, a little bit rattled, not much. 'Have you ever tried waiting for a 31 bus?'

'I hear you had rows with Lee. Big rows. We were called out twice, three times. Because you got violent.'

'Sure. Before I moved out. But now? What's to row about?'

'People can generally find something. Custody of the kids. Money. Who gets the telly.'

She gestured with contempt at a smart TV with built-in video in the corner. 'I got it.'

'You attacked him many times. Once with a knife. Once you nearly scratched his eyes out.'

'More than once.' She stood up. Bright found himself tensed, ready to restrain her, ready to defend himself. She walked past him to the cot where she put the child down. The child played with a small plastic dog with a nodding head. The dog was green.

She said, bending over the kid, 'I'm glad they spoiled his face actually. Now the girls won't run after him the way they used to. It serves him right. He'll be okay. Lee is always okay. Is his mother coming over to see him? She better not come near me.'

She said all this in her neat little voice like she was reciting her shopping list. Only when she said *his mother* did they hear that slight shake in the sound. Bright was beginning to recognise what passed for passion in there. He'd like to stay awhile, find out what had filled her up with hate, and other substances. If he'd been alone he'd have stayed, let the whole thing expand a little. He didn't fancy her – she left him cold – but he liked her, the way a lepidopterist might like a rare specimen, might like pinning it to a board and noting its particulars with precision, with pleasure.

Instead he said, 'Thanks for your help. We'll be on our way. Taff?'

Taff looked woken from his hundred-year spell.

She didn't turn round as they went to the door. But just as Taff opened it she said, 'Don't you know who did it, then?'

Bright said, 'You didn't answer my question.'

'What question was that?'

'Did you go to Lee's flat yesterday?'

'No. I haven't been there for a week. Chico hasn't been well.'

'Chico?'

'The kid.'

'You call him Chico?' Llewellyn was aghast.

'They call you Taff, don't they?'

Bright rarely showed amusement in a grin – she'd made a rare achievement. He turned in the doorway. He said, 'You talk to Lee on the phone yesterday?'

'Yes.'

'What time?'

'In the morning.'

'What about?'

'He hadn't sent the cheque on time. As usual. He said that gardener girl was there.' She paused and breathed in, controlling something. 'She's a big thing. Bigger than him. She has red hair and awful freckles. She's very strong. I saw her once carrying paving slabs and banging them with a big hammer made of wood.' Her voice held fastidious horror. 'He'd never have a girl bigger than him. He never liked big girls. I don't give a shit about her.'

'And you're sure? You didn't go to Kentish Town yesterday? You didn't go to see Lee?'

She shrugged.

'So you couldn't have seen anyone go in or out?'

She didn't bother to shrug: just stared.

'So long, Chloe.'

She'd already turned away. She lay down on the leopard couch in one movement, a sideways roll without bending at the knees. He realised she was fit. Wearing a pair of new trainers that he guessed to be the ultimate in street cred, on the end of those amazing legs.

The child sat in his cot, watching from behind the bars as the policemen went out of the door.

11

She was stranded on a desert shore and Dan in his little boat got farther and smaller and if he got much farther and much smaller she wouldn't be able to see him at all and she'd never get him back. For the first time in fourteen years she felt alone.

Last night she'd lain awake, stiff as a plank so's not to wake him. Should she tell him about her and Lee, get it out in the open? It might be bad, but could it be worse than this? Yes, it was the only way: tell him and take the consequences.

Then she plunged into a sleep in which she was chased, hounded, caught, trapped. And she woke in the dark, and knew she wouldn't tell him. Not yet anyway. And knew she was just putting off the hour and piling up nightmares to come. She picked up the little alarm clock. Four thirty.

Then she became aware she couldn't hear Dan breathing. She turned on her side. He wasn't there. George, curled at the end of the bed, stirred as she got up, rolled on his side while she stroked his face, but then covered his eyes with a paw, determined not to wake.

She crept down the stairs in her kimono and knocked on his door. Even her knock sounded wrong, diffident. 'Dan?' And her voice: shy, like a stranger. There was no reply. She had to nerve herself to open the door.

First she felt relief, just to see him there, at his big table all littered with plans and drawings. He sat tousle-haired, vacant-eyed, not working. His face looked soft, like putty, as faces roused from sleep do look in the middle of the night. 'Dan?'

He didn't even shift his eyes to look at her. She slipped into the room and stole up close to him. The plans of the Tower House, his present project, were open on the table. She put her hand to the back of his neck. He switched off his working lamp and the room turned ten shades of grey in the leaden pre-dawn light.

He turned and pressed his face between her breasts. She held him tight in her arms but they didn't speak. Not then, and not back in bed where he turned his back to her and she wrapped her warmth round him and he slept before she did and was gone again from her side when she woke, very late, to another perfect summer day.

When she came down he had already prepared breakfast. Cut open the limes and papayas she'd bought yesterday on the way home from Lee's. Yesterday? It seemed a year ago, all the uneasy joy, the physical well-being. She couldn't eat.

'They're good,' Dan said. 'Just right.'

She said, 'I'll just ring the hospital.'

He said, 'I already did.'

She turned to him.

'No change. Still critical. Still in intensive care.'

He was on his way upstairs. She couldn't see his face.

She squeezed the lime juice into the golden flesh of the papaya and ate feeling like Judas.

The phone rang. Dan picked it up. She heard the low drone of his voice and later, when the call ended, the echoing ping of the kitchen extension. After she'd washed up she went up to his workroom and knocked. The Tower House design was on the drawing board. He ran his hand over it like he was stroking a beloved animal, the way she stroked George.

'Who was on the phone?'

'My present master.'

'What about?'

'Second thoughts.'

'Yours or his?'

'I told you yesterday we were having some disagreements.'

'Yes . . . ?'

'Your mind was on other things.'

'Oh. Yes.'

Dan put his hand to his face a moment. Over his mouth. He gave a small – she didn't know what to call it – almost a shiver. And she suddenly knew Dan couldn't hack it on his own, not his work, and not his life either. So maybe this collapse she sensed in him was not caused just by her. Maybe her guilt had prevented her seeing his real trouble? 'Dan?' In a surge of sympathy she touched his back. He started away from her touch, like her hand was a flaming torch burning between his shoulder blades— She shut her eyes. Flames, fire, that's all she could see since yesterday. Anyway, who was she kidding? She was the one who had hurt Dan. *He was my man And I done him wrong.* 'You love this job,' she said.

'I did, yes.'

'Can't you just change it a little bit, convince him you've changed it a lot? Just wait and see? It might all calm down, blow over.'

He turned and looked at her. Right into her eyes. But not as though he saw her. She felt herself disappearing into his long regard. 'Calm down,' he said. 'Blow over . . .' He gave a sort of laugh and shook his head. 'No.'

'He's the client. You have a contract.'

'Absolutely, Jude. With characteristic clarity you have hit the nail on its head. I have a contract.'

'You were glad of this job when it came in.'

'And if it goes there may never be another? Again, you have hit it in one.'

'Can't you compromise?'

'Compromise? Me? This is Dan Craig you're talking to. The Great Dan Craig. What did that review say – *the future beckons, rosy with promise*?' He laughed. 'How long ago was that?'

'You might be able to use the design somewhere else?'

'It won't work somewhere else. It's meant for here. This particular flat landscape. This particular watery light, off the estuary, off the River Blackwater. It's meant for here.' His voice wandered into despair.

She wished she hadn't knocked. Hadn't come in. Hadn't spoken. She was mixed up in this, in his implacable attitude, in his despair. She knew it. And this was not just her conscience biting; it was the truth. She said suddenly, 'Do you miss Martin badly, Dan?'

He turned on her, his face stretched over the bones with the emotion he didn't want to let out. 'I don't like working alone. You know that.'

'Yes but—'

'Yes but nothing. I'm forty. I'm not going to get into another partnership now. Martin was a hack but he was good at the office work, keeping the clients sweet. I can't do that. I'm probably going to lose this job. The thing is falling apart.'

'Don't decide now, Dan, in the heat of the moment. Not while all this terrible—' She didn't want to mention Lee, the police, the fire. But he hadn't heard her, she realised. He wasn't aware of her. She felt yesterday hit her like a punch in the stomach, a sick heave of panic. She had to go. This was his problem. She had to leave him with it. She had problems of her own.

Downstairs, she phoned the hospital. A sibilant male voice said, 'Mr Han is still in intensive care. Still critical. The surgeon is with him now deciding whether they can operate or not.'

'Operate?'

'Skin grafts. But he's got to be well enough, you see.'

'I see. Thank you.'

'You're welcome, madam.'

She made camomile tea. She stretched on the sofa under the tartan rug. George came in from the sun but refused to sit on her. He crouched in the shade of the doorway chattering his teeth at the birds, imagining.

This was her morning for her own garden. She should be out there working. But she felt as though someone had taken the great mallet she had been using on Lee's York stone flags and repeatedly cudgelled her head with it. To get her mind off Lee she tried to think about Dan. That was as bad. She shifted her mind to her garden. A blue colour scheme for the end bed; hibiscus, delphinium, *Tweedia cerulea*, clematis, and in the fragile blue haze of her imagination she fell asleep.

She woke because the kitchen phone extension pinged. She felt groggy, drugged. She heard Dan's door open. He came downstairs.

'You talked to him?' she said.

'I've pulled out.'

'No?'

'Yes.'

'You didn't try to persuade him?'

'No point.'

'There's always a point—'

'Not about this.' He stood looking out at the garden. George on the windowsill watched him. Dan put a hand out and rubbed George's head. 'It's the tower,' he said at last.

'What about the tower?'

'He's decided he doesn't want it.'

'Doesn't want it? Your tower?'

'That's right.'

'But why?'

'Thinks it'll cut out light.'

'Will it?'

'Of course not.'

'And you couldn't convince him—?'

'I'd have to put the staircase somewhere else!'

'And you can't do that?'

'The tower is the centre of the design. The glass in the top, drawing down light, the staircase moving up to the light, the floors opening off, you've seen the drawing, everything on this organic curve like the inside of a conch shell. How can he—? How can he—?' His eyes were full of tears. 'You walk into the house and you walk into light. But he can't see that.'

'Why can't he see it? I can see it.'

'You're a human being. He's a – he's a – Oh Christ—' He sat on the arm of the sofa next to her. Harsh noises came out of him, not quite sobbing, more gasping, tangible clods of anger and hurt, all his anger and hurt going into this.

Instead of into me, Jude thought. And wondered at her propensity for taking blame. And for deserving it. She held his hand till the storm subsided. 'You're not going to try to rethink then?'

'Why should I? Why? He is wrong! Wrong! Wrong!'

'Yes, but . . .' But what? *But you're not lying burned near to death in an intensive care unit; you have health and strength and talent and therefore hope; and despair is a sin?* What was his tower compared to Lee's predicament?

'And it's not just the tower,' he said. 'There's – other things.'

'What things?'

'His whole attitude. Like he owns me.'

'But it's his house, Dan. I know I've said it before but he is the client. He gave you the commission.'

He left her side, got up from the sofa, strode out to the garden and picked up the fallen rake. Leaves had already started to fall. He raked the grass in furious dragging movements, leaving scratches like finger-scratches on skin, lumps of soil and grass flying, clogging the tines of the rake. He hated her to find fault with him. Why had she been so stupid? Woken from sleep she had only half her wits about her. That's what she was – a half-wit. And now she'd hurt him. He knew he should have compromised, but that was Dan. He could not compromise. He never had. And she admired him for his steadfastness, his principles. She followed him out.

She said, 'I'm sorry, Dan.'

He said, 'No one buys me.'

'No.'

'No one owns me.'

'No.'

'So he can fuck off and buy himself a tame hack who'll build him the shit he wants, build him a fucking seaside bungalow out of breeze-block with dinky little imitation Dutch gables and PVC double glazing.'

'Yes—'

'Because I don't do that. I don't sell out.'

'I know that—'

'So why did you say—?'

'I didn't mean it! I'm sorry!'

'You of all people!'

'Me—?'

'Blaming me!'

'No! I wasn't! I don't. I don't.'

'So apologise!

'I do, I do. I apologise. I do.'

He stopped dragging at the grass, leaned on the rake, breathing hard.

'Anything,' she said, 'if you'll only leave me a little bit of grass in the lawn.'

It was touch and go. He looked at her for some time frowning.

But then he breathed a laugh through his nose. He threw her the rake. 'Fucking well do it yourself then.'

'I'm resting after my ordeal.'

But this time he didn't laugh. 'Sorry. I'm out of work again. You're keeping me again. You're right to blame me.'

'Oh Dan, leave it out. For fuck's sake. I can't spend my whole life saying we keep *each other*, what's yours is mine, for better for worse. It's insulting to think I even think about such things. You know I don't. What the fuck does it matter who keeps who?' In the face of his bleak expression she went to him and put her arms around him. He made no response. She said, 'What would I do without you? I wouldn't want to live.'

He looked at her face, all over her face, in bits, like he was taking it apart and putting it back together. He placed a hand on either side of her face. He had large expressive hands. His fingers framed the sides of her face. He pulled his hands forward, still holding the edges of her face. He gazed with wide eyes into hers. Slowly his face approached hers till she could no longer focus and his eyes became a blur, till the edges of his face touched his hands also and shut out the light. Their two faces so close but not touching, and blind, unable to see in the tunnel of his hands, Jude and Dan stood breathing the same darkness in the bright hot afternoon sun.

12

There were two bells. One of them had a notice over it saying *Bell.* Bright tried that one with no result. A blonde woman sat at a desk in the window, visible through the vertical slats of the blind. She refrained from seeing him. He tried the bell that was not designated *bell.* That had no effect either. He rapped on the window. The blonde at last looked up. With a disdainful movement of her eyes she indicated that the door was not locked. Pity they couldn't run to a notice saying *push.*

Feeling a right pillock he flashed her his ID. This did not impress the blonde. She was bored, unsmiling. And older close up than the general image she was aiming at, short leather skirt, tight scoop-neck top. 'Who d'you want?'

'I want the boss, love.'

'You mean the editor?'

'If he's the boss.'

She unwound her legs and lounged over to a partition door. She opened it and leaned in, treating Bright to a full view of the back of her thighs. She returned. 'Mr Priest'll just be a few minutes.' She subsided on to her chair and tapped at her keyboard, ignoring him.

Another blonde came through the pass door, the image of the first blonde but young enough to be her daughter. This one's hair gleamed, her skin glowed pale.

The receptionist bounded to her feet. 'Alice, have you got a minute? I want to show you something.' Alice smiled obligingly. The receptionist opened a carrier bag and unfolded a turquoise suede skirt with a four-inch fringe. 'What do you think? Could I wear this?'

A serious discussion followed, Alice offering advice, Receptionist smiling, simpering, till Alice extricated herself and went on through to the editor's office, when Receptionist relapsed into her state of suspended animation. The young are meant to model themselves on the more mature? In this case it was the other way round. Bright felt sad watching. Perhaps he was getting old himself?

Then a light flashed on Receptionist's phone display. She said, 'Mr Priest says go through.'

'Go through where, love?'

She waved a limp hand at the pass door. It had a code pad but was opened as he reached it by Alice who gave him a sweet pure smile, led the way, first up some stairs then down some stairs, and indicated a flimsy door.

The editor worked in a cubicle made of plywood and glass, papers piled on shelves, desk, windowsill, in constant threat of slippage. 'Yeah? Sorry to keep you. Bloody phone never stops. This business, you can't tell people phone back; you might miss something. Who'd you say you were?'

Bright introduced himself. Again.

'Oh yeah, God, poor old Lee, eh? Such a good-looking guy as well, God. Terrible.' Priest had a rich Midlands accent, not poshed up by London. Strangely for a journalist, he talked more than he listened. Maybe he was nervous? Reflections off his thick pebble specs made it hard to check out his eyes. 'Who could have done that to him?' he said.

'That's what we'd all like to know.'

'How is he? I keep meaning to go in but you can see what it's like here, I hardly have time to go home let alone hospital visiting. It's our press day tomorrow. All hell breaks loose here. I might make it on Thursday though. That's our quiet time.

While you're all reading the paper we start thinking about next week's.'

'He's not allowed visitors. Still in intensive care.'

'Oh poor swine.'

'He might not survive.'

Priest at last looked up and paid attention. 'What?'

'A-ha. It could get to be a murder case any day now.'

'Jee-sus.' When he sat still Bright could see his eyes. They got that glassy, intent, blind look that means a lot of activity is going on behind.

'So what can you tell me, Mr Priest?'

'About what?'

'Articles he was working on, people he was interviewing—'

'Well, you know, I don't know the detail of what the reporters are getting up to, they do their own stuff. But he was still working on this gangland thing, couldn't let go of it, it seemed to have a grip on him, bit obsessed if you ask me, couldn't move on. He knew everything, stuff we couldn't print. Actually come to think of it, he was interviewing one of you lot last I heard.'

Bright went still a moment. 'A copper? Who would that be?'

'As I said, I wouldn't know . . .' Priest shunted vaguely through the shifting drifts of paper.

'Would anyone else here know?'

'Might have been the bloke in charge of the gangland case, you know? Witness that got shot in the junkyard.'

If Bright had been driving a car he'd be doing an emergency stop. His mind reeled, fast rewind, then fast forward.

The sense of hiatus brought Priest's restless movement to a halt. He stared at Bright. He said, 'Oh shit. That's you, right?'

Bright said, 'I promise you Lee Han never spoke to me.'

Priest lifted a pile of computer print-out. 'Ah, there it is.' He leaned over and with long strong fingers lifted a battered old red tin ashtray with the message Coca-Cola fading away to bare metal. 'I need a fag.' He opened the door and Bright followed him downstairs. He waved a hand at the room on the left – 'Sales. All those people selling advertising space' – and turned right into a big basement room, a worktop running all round it, four or five people at computer terminals. 'This is where the paper's assembled. Mayhem Wednesday nights.'

He led the way out to a large square garden the width of two houses, a strip of concrete flags next to the building and a big square of flat grass confined by a grimy brick wall. 'The smokers' club meets out here. Democratic decision. Not my doing. You need special outdoor clothing these days to be a smoker. Is it worth it, you ask yourself.' He lit a Camel-light from a crumpled pack and sat down on one of the white plastic chairs. He sucked hard on the cigarette and exhaled with a satisfied sound. 'Aah, that's better.'

Bright didn't sit.

Priest said in a quiet murmur, 'It was the last piece he wrote for us. I couldn't print it. Libellous. We're a pretty hard-hitting rag but we have to draw the line at putting ourselves in personal danger. You understand?'

'Danger from who?'

'I'm speaking generally.'

'You had threats?'

'Threats? Where would I get threats from?'

'Threats from anyone cited in Lee Han's stories for instance.'

'Look, I've got a newspaper to run. We've got a phenomenal circulation. We do what we can to expose the shenanigans that go on, but I don't publish libel because we don't have the money to risk being sued. It's not a question of threats, it's a question of common sense, all right?'

'If this turns into a murder case, you'll have to answer questions in court.'

'Let's hope it doesn't.' He added, fast, 'For Lee's sake.'

'Where's this article now?'

'What article?'

'The libellous one.'

'Oh, the piece I wouldn't take? I never saw it. I heard the gist of what was in it. I don't want to know more than that. I guess you'd find it in Lee's files.' He half closed his eyes against the ribbon of ascending smoke. 'Haven't you found it?'

'We're looking.' Bright's mouth was a tight line. Maggie on the crime desk was looking. She hadn't found it yet. What would she do when she did?

'Listen, since his knee operation Lee's hardly been here, been working from home most of the time. Crabbe's in touch with him. Talk to Crabbe.' He made a last hard suck on his last inch of Camel and squashed it dead in his Coca-Cola ashtray. 'It was Crabbe that gave him his first assignment.' He led the way back through the workrooms, up the stairs, past his office to the first floor. 'Crabbe's the reason Lee's gone on working for us. I'd have – well, he's not that great at meeting deadlines, Lee, and that's nervous breakdown time for me. Yes, his work's good, but give me a little bit mundane and on time and I'm a happier man. So – course I don't wish the poor bloke any harm. Course I don't. But . . .'

'Course not.' Bright kept his voice flat. 'Who's Crabbe?'

'Deputy editor. See if he's in.'

They stood in the doorway to a narrow room with a window on the street and a window at the back. Five desks were crammed into this space barely big enough for two. 'That's him. Desk by the window. Crabbe? Someone to talk to you.' He said to Bright, 'See you later,' and disappeared.

The man at the desk side-on to the window struggled to his feet. 'Yes?' he said.

Like a lot of overweight people, as you got closer he got younger. At a distance fat and fifty, close up he was thirty and then possibly not even thirty yet. His hair was wispy and thinning. His shirt might have been clean on that morning but you couldn't say for sure; sweat had stuck it to his flesh here and there, transparent, like another skin. On his crowded desk was a box of Mars bars.

Bright said, 'John Bright. Kentish Town CID.'

Crabbe squashed himself back into his chair, picked up a can of Coke and put the hole in the tin to the hole in his face. He glugged then wiped his mouth. 'What can I do for you, Mr Bright?'

'You know Lee Han.'

'Yeah. Poor old Lee, eh?'

'He came to work here through you.'

Fatman hesitated, just a breath. 'That's right.'

'How come?'

'Well, I don't know. He was just a guy I knew.'

'Knew how? Knew from where?'

'Well, it's hard to say. I'd see him in the pub sometimes, you know, around and about. It started with his pictures. I took the occasional picture off him. He's not a bad photographer. He wanted to get into journalism, the writing side, so I suggested him submitting a piece. Some hard-hitting topic – that's what we like here.' He winked, and slid the other eye towards Priest's office.

'Why would you do that?'

'Well, why not? Do a mate a favour.'

'He didn't have any kind of a hold over you then?'

'Eh?' He rubbed his head between the sparse hairs, looked like getting up from his chair but thought better of it.

'No special little favour you were repaying, no debt you owed, nothing like that?'

'What? No! No. I said. It was just something I could do for a mate, that's all. We're not all kicking each other into the water, you know. Some of us are helping each other into the lifeboats.'

'See you're on the writing side.'

Fatman let out some air. It would have been a laugh if he'd been feeling better. 'Yeah, well . . .'

Bright got more matey. 'When did you last see Lee?'

'Oo, hell. Now you're asking.'

'Yes, I am.'

'Well. Er . . .' Fatman was thinking hard, you could tell, scratching his head, pursing up his mouth, sucking air in through his little teeth. A bit of over-acting never hurt. 'I think,' he said eventually, 'but don't quote me on this, okay? I think it was Monday.'

'Monday.'

'Yes.'

'Monday was yesterday!'

'Yes.'

'The day it happened. The attack.'

'Yes, er, I know, yes, it would have been.'

Bright spoke patiently. 'And what time was this?'

'In the morning. Around nine?'

'Where?'

'At his place.'

'You were at Lee Han's place at 9 a.m. yesterday – Monday – the day he was attacked?'

'I just dropped in on my way to work. To return a video he'd lent me.'

'A-ha? A video.'

The guy was sweating. 'Yes. I er, I didn't go in. Just chatted on the doorstep. He said he was glad I'd got him up because he was expecting his gardener.'

Bright let a little pause elapse. 'What was the video, Mr Crabbe?'

Fatman blushed under the runnels of sweat. His eyes were pathetic. 'Er . . . sorry, can't remember the title. *Delightful Dykes* or something. Girls doing it to each other. You know.'

'A-ha.'

'No, it was class stuff. Funky. Indonesian girls. Quite artistic, not just your usual hardcore. You know.'

'Lee running a little business, that what you're saying?'

Sweat stood out all over Fatman's shiny face and dripped into his collar. 'No! Someone had lent it to him, that's all.'

'Who?'

'I don't know, he didn't say! He was laughing about it in the pub, that's all. All right for him. Not a laughing matter for some of us.'

'Does all right for girlfriends, does he?'

'All right? Christ. Pussy Galore we call him.'

'He got a steady girlfriend at the moment?'

'Very private, Lee. Never would say. Secretive. He said in the pub, night before—'

'Sunday? You saw him Sunday?'

'Right.'

'Which pub?'

'Prince of Wales. He said—'

'Who else was there?'

'Who else? Half of Kentish Town. It was packed, man!'

'He said what?'

'He said, Jason—'

'Jason? That's you?'

'Not my fault. My parents both did classics. He said, Jason, I think I'm in love.'

'Did he?'

'But he wouldn't say who it was. Wouldn't even give me a clue.'

'Why?'

The flesh shook in a shrug. 'Dunno. He was always like that. Scared of Chloe finding out probably. Ex-wife. Phew.' He rolled his eyes. 'I wouldn't have let her go if she'd been mine. They're separated but there's a kid. Lee's crazy about the kid so he doesn't want to do anything to annoy Chloe, see.'

Bright folded his arms and watched him a moment. Crabbe

watched back, like a dog watching its master. Bright said, 'Lee was investigating the gangland case—'

'Yes. Yes. He wrote some good stuff on that, proper investigative journalism.'

Bright leaned in and lowered his voice. 'Priest says too good, says he was finding out too much. That right?'

'Well, we wouldn't print anything libellous. We're always absolutely scrupulous about that. Our lives wouldn't be worth living otherwise.'

'You see his last story? The one Priest wouldn't print?'

The fat man's body collapsed in the middle like someone had punched him in the gut. 'Er . . .'

'Priest says Lee talked to a copper.'

Crabbe's eyes swivelled, looking for escape, or scared someone in the room would hear. Reporters can hear the grass grow.

'Did you read this story?'

'I – I glanced over it. I got the – you know – the gist. I gave it right back to him. I said I didn't think we could print it, not in its present form.'

'When was this?'

'Sunday night.'

'Where?'

'The pub.'

'Christ. I was gonna ask were there any witnesses. You already told me, half of Kentish Town. Any particular half?'

Misery ran off the fat man like sweat. His tongue came out to lick his upper lip. His voice wasn't working right. He managed to say, 'No.'

'You receive any threats after that? Anyone lean on you?'

The big wobbly face just for a second went still. Again he just managed to say no.

Bright's nasal South London rasp softened to an intimate

murmur. 'A good journalist never reveals their sources, right? Must get to be a habit – not revealing things.'

'Well . . .'

'Only, see, in a case like this, where Lee might not survive and we're looking at murder—'

'Might not *survive*?'

'A-ha.'

'You're kidding?'

'No, mate. 'Fraid not.'

The big fat hands picked up a pencil, rolled it back and forth. 'I didn't realise.'

'See, you know what it used to be like, the drugs wars round here. Someone getting too big for their boots put in their place, villains attacking villains, all kinda self-contained. The villains had their rules. They weren't my rules or yours but there was a kinda code. Now it's different, it's changed. They're just – businessmen now. When innocent witnesses get shot before they can testify, that's not just the old local stuff – well, you know all this – you know more than us most of the time – for some reason people would rather talk to you than us – can't think why. This paper's got a great reputation for investigative journalism. Now, I know how you feel about revealing your sources, but . . . if I was in on some of Lee's information, I might be able to stop these bastards.'

The pudgy hands sweated on the pencil but Crabbe still said nothing. Bright tried another tack. 'Look, Lee's been attacked – maybe by someone he was getting too close to. Lee yesterday – could be any of you tomorrow. No use shutting your eyes to it. See—'

Priest put his head round the door. He said, 'Crabbe? Oh. Sorry to interrupt. I thought you'd be finished. Thing is, I need him. You can see how busy we are. I have deadlines to meet. We all have deadlines. It's the name of the game. We're sorry about

Lee but he didn't even work here much the last few months, you know. What he did off his own bat can't be laid at our door, we're obviously not responsible. Now, can we just get on with our work? It's press day tomorrow.'

Bright started to speak, then stopped then started again. 'I understand your problems, Mr Priest. But—'

'Then if you do, you'll leave now and let us get on with our work? Anything specific we can help you with, you've only to call. Always glad to help the law in the pursuit of its duty. Come on, Crabbe, need to talk to you about this piece.' He sprayed a professional cold matey grin round the room and waited. Crabbe picked up a notebook and squeezed himself to an upright position.

Bright blocked his way. 'I want three things from you. I want a list of everyone you can remember being in the Prince of Wales on Sunday night. I want a list of everyone you can remember ever seeing with Mr Han. And I want your fingerprints.'

The fat man gasped. 'What for?'

'Lots of fingerprints in Lee's flat. You're a mate. I know you visited him a fair bit – be surprising if yours weren't there. It would eliminate one set, see?'

Crabbe's head wobbled. 'I see.'

'So if you wouldn't mind dropping round to the station? Any time. One of my team will look after you. Here's my card. Thanks a lot, mate.' Bright put the pencil from Crabbe's desk absent-mindedly in his pocket. Passing the editor in the doorway he said, 'Thanks for your help, Mr Priest.' And then, as an afterthought, from half-way down the stairs, 'Oh yeah, Mr Crabbe – Jason – the flat upstairs from Mr Han – the vacant flat – you ever been up there?'

The big face shook from side to side: no.

'You sure?'

'Yes.'

13

Bright turned off the high street into Holmes Road and parked between the ugly station house and the back of HQ. He sat in the car and thought about what Priest had told him.

A copper had told Lee Han something that would incriminate someone? So some copper somewhere had information crucial to Bright's investigation into the gangland shootings. Why had this copper spoken to a journalist and not to a superior officer? Or had he spoken to a superior officer and no action had been taken? Or was he scared to speak to the superior officer because he knew that officer was bent? This was a possible inference. And Ken Priest knew that. Priest had swiftly covered his tracks. But Bright knew in his gut that Lee Han's last, unpublished story was crucial, not just to the gangland investigation but to the burning as well. He felt a hollow place in his stomach that he recognised as fear. He slowly got out of the car.

He couldn't go back to his desk. Not just yet. He needed a break. He needed to think. He checked his watch. Ten minutes wouldn't hurt. He strolled out of the car park, crossed Kentish Town Road and turned right at the Iranian corner store.

A wide peaceful street. He passed the little school with the nice houses opposite, small, Victorian, semi-detached, with unusual decorative stonework. Then the railway in a deep cutting crossed under the road at an angle, and the whole street changed. Either a bomb in the war, or Camden Planning Department, or maybe just the building of the railway in the nineteenth century had created a lot of wasteland. On this side of the road the wasteland had lately blossomed into a garden centre, and a fifties council ghetto; on the other side, a car repair place. Then the nice old houses started again. Next to the car repair place a three-storey little Victorian villa with a studded front door up five or six steps. Where the gardener lived, according to Cato's report.

Checking out the house from the other side of the street he realised he was being watched. There was someone behind the venetian blinds in the ground-floor window. He just caught a movement. Not of the blind but behind the blind. There it was again. He crossed the street and ran up the steps to the front door.

He rang and he waited and he rang again and waited again. Whoever had been watching was lying low. His hackles quivered. They'd had a lecture last month from a criminal psychologist who told them the occupational hazard of coppers was that they got so they suspected everyone, even the innocuous and the innocent. The psycho was paid a lot to tell them that. Bright could have told him for nothing. All right for those guys. They didn't get their hands dirty. Still, he told himself now, it's anyone's right not to open their front door.

He went backwards down the steps keeping a watch on the windows. No movement now, not a flicker, but he knew he hadn't imagined it.

She was coming towards him up the street, healthy-looking, freckles and curly red hair. He got that shock again at the sight of her. She wore a grey cotton dress today that blew in the breeze. As she approached he saw that stretched look round the eyes that comes from not sleeping. She didn't beat about the bush. She said, 'You've come to tell me Lee's dead.'

'Not yet, no.'

'Oh . . . Just let me sit down a bit.' She took the heavy bag from her shoulder and sat on the little wall. 'I'm sorry,' she said, 'I keep crying. If you knew what he looked like—'

'I've seen a picture.'

'Have you got any clues?'

She asked this like a child who'd seen cops on the telly. He shook his head. 'It's early days yet.' He said it like a million cops on the small screen. But it was true too.

She looked at him and discovered nothing, stalled by his impenetrable hard brown eyes. 'So why were you knocking at my house?'

'Wanted a word with you.'

'I told you everything I know last night.'

'Sometimes you don't know everything you know.'

'Is that your speciality? Finding out the things people don't know they know? Is that why they sent you?'

'No one sent me.'

'So . . . ?'

'I'm what's laughingly known as the boss. Of this investigation.'

'Oh, I'm sorry, I don't know anything about ranks and things. Hierarchies. Male things.'

'Are they?'

'Well, I think so, mostly, don't you?'

He gave her this sharp squinting look she couldn't decipher. She felt an inner shiver, hackles up, danger. Just as she had at the police station. This man, on the small side, wiry, restless, in his scruffy old bomber jacket, seemed insignificant at first, but he had this laser beam attention that he could turn on and off. When it was on, even for only a second or two, you felt it right in your middle. *Don't mess with him. Take care.*

She returned his look, steady, calm, but she feared he saw through that. She said, 'When something like this happens you feel guilty even though you're not. When a policeman questions you you feel as though you'll be arrested any minute and carted off to jail. Even though you've never broken the law in your life.

Well – parked on the odd yellow line . . . See? I'm jabbering. Come in and have a cup of tea.' She escaped his hard eyes, running up the steps. 'I'm surprised,' she said, getting out her keys, 'that Dan's not in.'

'Your husband?'

'He's an architect. He works at home. Oh of course you know all that. I suppose it might be simpler if you tell me what you *don't* know. Dan?' She called out in the cool hallway. Nice deep green walls and white woodwork. No reply. She shrugged.

Bright followed her downstairs and stood at the french windows while she put the kettle on.

'Looks like you could do with a gardener.'

'I know. It's a mess. I'm always knackered when I get home. I keep meaning to set aside some time.'

'I was joking. It's nice.'

A train went by, juddering the house. 'How do you stand that?'

'We've got used to it somehow. I think I'd miss it now.'

'Like the toothache?'

She made the tea and they sat down at the garden table.

'What did you want to ask me?' she said.

'I dunno.'

'You don't know?'

'Er . . .' He pulled at his right earlobe. 'Anyone ever visit Lee Han while you were there?'

She didn't want to answer. She looked upset.

He said, 'We'll find out anyway.'

But she still didn't reply so he put a question she couldn't get out of. 'What about the ex-wife? Chinese girl. Chloe.'

'I only saw her there once. Weeks ago. They're separated now but they still see each other. There's a little boy. She has the child but he adores Lee and Lee adores him—' Her eyes filled up again. 'Oh shit.'

'Bit of an acrimonious separation then?'

'In a nutshell,' she said reluctantly, 'yes.'

'Over another woman? Another man? What?'

'Look, this is none of my business. I'm not sure it's any of yours. Why don't you just ask Chloe?'

'You ever speak to her?'

'No. I just saw her once. I was down the end of the garden knee deep in rubble. She was on the terrace with Lee. I wasn't introduced.'

A tabby cat bounded over the wall and trotted towards Jude. He stopped at the sight of Bright, sniffed the air, decided Bright was okay and came on, the light of love in his eyes. Jude bent to stroke his head and he purred like a Rolls Royce. He made a light leap on to her lap, turned round three times then flopped. She held him lightly. 'This is George,' she said. 'He usually flees from strangers, especially blokes.'

'P'raps you'll see me with new eyes now.'

'Cats are terrible judges of humans. I wouldn't trust George's judgement an inch.'

'Does he like your husband?'

'Yes,' she said, just a bit too quick.

'As much as he likes you?'

'No. He likes—' She was going to say he liked her best but thought that would sound presumptuous. 'He always likes women best,' she said.

'Does your friend Lee always like women best?'

'Oh yes! There's nothing—' She broke off, some colour coming then going under the freckles and the tan. 'Well, as far as I know, that is. I don't know that much about his life.'

He let that go – for now. 'So you never saw anyone there except Chloe?'

'Not that I can recall. But when I'm busy in the garden, you know – I might not see someone who came to the flat.'

'Ever see the fat man?'

'Fat man?'

'Friend of Lee's. He was there yesterday morning.'

'Sorry, no.'

'He ever mention Crabbe to you?'

'Crab?' She floundered at this wild change of subject.

'Fat man's name.'

'Oh!' She smiled in a tentative way. 'No.'

'Lee ever discuss his work with you?'

'His photography, yes. He's been taking pictures of the garden. Work in progress.'

His pictures. That was a thought. 'But not his writing?'

'Not really, no.' She had a guarded look.

'What does that mean – not really?'

'Well, he said one day he was on to something really extraordinary. He was sort of – exalted. But he said he couldn't talk about it.'

'When was this?'

'About a week ago?'

'You read his stuff?'

'In the local freebie? Yes, always. He seems very good, to me.'

'But not his – like – rough drafts? Or his computer printouts?'

'No.'

'Investigative reporters have to mix with some funny types to get all that inside gen,' he said.

'I suppose they do.' The look in her eyes changed. 'Do you think it was one of those people who did it then? The criminals he writes about? The bandits, he calls them.' This idea seemed to afford her some relief.

'So. He doesn't confide in you. Especially.'

'He's a client. You know.'

'He's a friend as well, isn't he?'

'Well . . . Sort of, yes, but—'

'I suspect a lot of your clients become friends. You're a friendly girl. That's how it strikes me.' He was getting there, under her skin, just lifting the edge. 'You can't help being friendly,' he said. 'That's how it seems to me.'

'Not specially.' She held the cat for safety or her hands might have shaken.

'You didn't have to give me a cup of tea for instance. But you did.' He stood up and came close to her. 'It was good. Thanks. Just what I needed. What shall I do with this?' He waved the cup. She indicated the kitchen. He went in and rinsed it under the tap. She stayed outside with the cat on her lap. She had her back to him but sat still like she'd forgotten how to breathe.

He knew now for certain she'd been knocking off this Lee. He knew that was the thing she didn't want anyone to know. Especially her husband. It possibly had nothing to do with the case but it was something to bear in mind. He weighed it in his hand like a cool round heavy ball. Knowledge. It gave him power. Power felt good. But the pity that sometimes went with it felt bad. Really bad. Like he was the robber, not the cop.

He went out again. The cat, from the safety of her arms, warily allowed him to stroke his head. Bright said, 'Your husband ever get jealous of your clients?'

She thought for a moment. She was very still and quiet. And full of anguish. She said, 'We've been married a long time. More than twelve years. If we were jealous of each other's clients, our life would be pretty untenable.' She was running out of breath, and of words.

He took pity, the pity that went with power. He said, 'Did you do it? Set fire to Lee, I mean.'

She looked so amazed he could have laughed. 'No,' he said, 'I don't think you did. Your van's in the clear. So are your swabs. Did you help anyone else to do it?'

'Of course not!'

'But you think Chloe did it.'

She was shaking her head but he interrupted.

'Not used to keeping your mouth shut, are you? It's natural for you to blurt stuff out, you're no diplomat, stands out all over you. And you're keeping a secret. A bit of advice. Let it go. Let it out. Whoever it is that should know – tell 'em. Might be me; might be – well, someone else. Just think it over. Secrets aren't a good thing if they don't come natural. Know what I mean? And they don't come natural to you. And this is a very dangerous type did this. So don't mess with it. Okay? Tell whoever it is whatever it is they should know.'

She watched him with these wide-open eyes, the whites all blue with health. She was getting imprinted with him like a little duckling, he knew that look. She was bright but she was simple, she couldn't hide a thing. He felt like stroking her, like she was an animal, the way she was stroking the cat. But he didn't. He said to the cat, 'See you, George.' And to her, 'Don't come upstairs. I'll let myself out.'

Very quiet, he crossed the hall. Very quiet, he knocked on the door to his left. He listened. He didn't hear a thing. Very quiet, he opened the door.

The husband's workroom, big tables with drawings, easels with ground-plans, rolls of paper and racks with those cardboard rolls to protect drawings. He felt a twist of envy. What a job. What a life. Your own master. A gift. But all jobs had their drawbacks; even this one must have. No one in the room. But the venetian blind on the window was the one that had moved when he was out in the street. So the husband – or someone – was still in the house. Bright would have known if someone had gone out.

He closed the door silently and left.

When Dan came downstairs he found Jude and George still on

the terrace. She didn't turn to look at him. She said, 'I knew you were in. I could tell. Why didn't you come down?'

He said, 'I got a strong whiff of policeman. I didn't want to speak to them again. Want a scotch?'

A small pause. 'Yes please.'

When he gave her the drink she said, 'He's a strange guy. I can't make head nor tail of him.'

'Looks more like a crook than a policeman.'

'He doesn't think I did it.'

'He told you that?'

'Not exactly but—'

'I thought you were their prime suspect.'

'I don't think I'm his.'

'Well, that's big of him.'

'Unless he's just playing me along.' She took a sip of scotch. 'He's dangerous.'

'What do you mean?'

'I don't know.' Her eyes looked tired. 'Oh Dan . . .'

Dan put his hand on her head, stroked down her springy hair, just as Bright had wanted to do. She let her head fall back into his hand. She looked at him with a face that was all questions. She wanted to speak but in the end she couldn't.

'Shall I do some food?' he said.

Jude shook her head. 'I can't eat. I'm going to lie down. I just can't stand up somehow. Come on, George, let's go to bed.' She plodded up the stairs, George hanging in her arms like an old reticule. She rubbed her cheek on his head. 'Oh my George,' she said, 'what would I do without you?'

Dan watched them from below slowly disappear from his sight.

14

He deliberately went past the junkyard where his witness got shot a year ago. Even though it was out of his way.

The place was just a pair of big garage doors in the high garden wall that opened on to a square of concrete, with makeshift sheds full of old fridges and wartime wardrobes, terrible stuff you couldn't imagine anyone buying. The old guy who owned the place dozed in a 1940s Ercol chair and his Jack Russell sat on guard at his side. Bright didn't know why he had to go past the place. Like tonguing an aching tooth.

He continued down to the long straight street of high houses where a couple of the Snakeheads had lived. They didn't live here any more, thanks partly to him. He crossed Kentish Town Road into Anglers' Lane. The River Fleet ran underneath and the narrow lane followed its curving path. The anglers had fished from its banks in the old days; urchins dangled their feet in the water from just here, beneath the pavement he was walking on now. But that was history. And the dickheads who changed the name of the Anglers' Arms last year to something trendy and incomprehensible didn't know and wouldn't care.

He turned off at the ornate Victorian red-brick Kentish Town baths. He liked these narrow streets of small terraced houses with the names of the battles of the Crimea. More history. He found himself outside Lee Han's house. No crowds there now, just the blue and white police tape and notices asking for witnesses to come forward.

The house looked horrible, the front window a blackened

mouth of rotten teeth. He didn't know what he was doing here either. He could have sent someone else for what he wanted. He said hello to the PC on duty and went through to the back. He put on the inevitable plastic glove. A few years and the human race would be doing everything in plastic gloves. From cooking to sex. Well, come to think of it . . . He hunted. Opened the drawers, the cupboards. In one cupboard he found a folder with sheets of negatives in cloudy paper holders. At the back two small black cylinders with bright green plastic lids. Exposed films? He pocketed those.

He found it on the floor of the front room, the bedroom, the burnt-out room, in a dank corner, on the floor. It was fused into a distorted black lump of annealed metal. He picked it up and gave it to the duty PC. 'Bag it up, mate, there might be a film in it.'

The PC said, 'No film could survive that, sir.' But handed him the camera, bagged up.

'Worth having a look, just in case.'

He couldn't delay any longer returning to HQ.

He took the fat man's pencil down to the fingerprinting room. He had Lee's camera and the rolls of film sent off to the lab. He wrote his report and went into the CID room.

Atkins had visited the property company in the city. 'Looked fine, guv, all above board. Middle-sized company with a lot of properties, some here, some abroad, some big, some small. A posh office in one of them modernised warehouses near Bank station. Very nice receptionist. Just my type. Tits on her like battering rams. Excellent.'

Bernard was working through his list of prospective flat buyers from the estate agent. 'Five people taken to view it last three weeks, boss. No one's been given keys though.'

'The last tenant?'

'Left without giving notice. Forfeited his deposit. But as he didn't pay his last month's rent they broke even. No forwarding address of course.'

'References when he moved in?'

Bernard waved a short-hold tenancy agreement. 'I'm looking him up. All dodgy so far. Dodgy address. Non-existent referees.'

'How interesting does this make him to us?'

'Dunno. Estate agent says it's par for the course.'

'What did he look like?'

'Ginger-haired. Irish. Thirties.'

'The one Jude Craig saw at the window.'

'Oh, yeah, wicked!'

'Keep at it, Bernard. See what you come up with.'

Passing the crime desk on the way to his office, almost without pausing he said to Maggie, 'Have a word?' and walked on.

A minute later she opened his flimsy door. The walls of his office might have been cardboard for all the privacy they gave. He spoke in a casual voice, searching through the papers on his desk. 'How you getting on with Lee Han's files, Mag?'

She was a big girl with a muscular Girl Guide's body. She'd been a good copper, got a medal for bravery after being attacked with a knife in an alley in Camden Town, and after that she'd applied for a desk job and gone on a course. She was the best in the station at the computer stuff – duck to water. 'He's a bugger, guv,' she said.

'Eh?'

'Hacking in – it's not easy.'

'A-ha? So you haven't found anything yet?'

'John! It takes time! Specially going through the deleted files.'

'What? You mean deleted files are not really deleted?'

'Not unless you're really serious about getting rid of them.'

'Christ.'

'But I'm getting there.'

'Any idea when?'

'Might be tomorrow, that all right?'

'Have to be, won't it?'

'Can't have everything yesterday, you know!'

'On my desk. Crack of dawn. Or you're fired.'

She laughed. 'Oh well, if you put it like that.'

'Seriously. Straight to me, Mag, quick as you can.'

'Sure.'

Atkins was in the bog, putting on a clean shirt and a psychedelic tie.

'What's this in aid of, Tommy?'

'Orders is orders, guv – I'm going drinking.'

'Shit.'

'What?'

'I met him,' Bright said. 'The fat man. He works at the local freebie with Lee Han.' He couldn't let Tommy Atkins loose on Crabbe. Not till he knew a bit more. 'I need a few more words with him. I'll take over drinking duty, now that I've put in the groundwork. You can go boozing purely for pleasure, how about that?'

'Wicked!' Atkins didn't like Bernard because Bernard was black. But he picked up the West Indian street talk. And he didn't even know.

The fat man looked like he was a fixture. He spilled over a stool at the bar. He wouldn't have fitted in a chair. The pub was fullish. Noisy. Bright had a personal interest in a section of the clientele. He knew them and they knew him. He'd sent a few of them down one time or another, one for GBH, two for car theft, another two for drugs. All small time, but on the edge, straddling the straight world and the bent.

'What you having, mate?'

The fat man jumped and turned. 'Oh, shit. You.'

'Pint?'

'I can't tell you any more.'

'Two pints. Thanks. Yes you can.'

Crabbe groaned.'Not in here.'

'You didn't come round my nick to have your fingerprints done.'

'I'm going to. You can't force me, can you?'

'No, mate, goodness of your heart.'

'Well then—'

'Don't worry about it.' Bright didn't tell him he'd pinched his pencil; journalists knew their rights. He'd checked the prints against the lab report, no question one set was Crabbe's. 'Cheers.'

Bright walked him back to his place, a council flat in Raglan Street. 'Just a few streets away from Lee then?'

'Yes.' Walking winded the fat man. Fit he was not.

'How long you known him?'

'Just after he came here. Year and a half maybe?'

'The libellous story will be in his files.'

'Don't bank on it.'

'What d'you mean?'

'He'll have deleted it. If he's got any sense.'

'And you haven't got a copy, right?'

'I told him to delete it.'

'You had a copy. What you do with it?'

'Flushed it down the lav.'

'Think up something better. A piece like that – in your possession – that's worth money.'

'Blackmail? You kidding? I got a good job. I like it. I got an okay life. I like that too. I don't chase trouble.'

'Lee does.'

'He does, yes. And look what's happened to him.'

'This story. Was it worth doing that to him for?'

Crabbe stopped and sat on the low wall in front of a house, just like Jude Craig earlier. Bright moved too fast for people; it was how he worked. 'Look.' Crabbe was sweating and gasping. 'Maybe. Listen. I didn't read it closely. I didn't want to know.'

'Was it implying a bent copper?'

The big plump fingers rubbed across his lips. He nodded, then shook his head. 'Not necessarily. No.'

'Implying. That's all I said.'

'Maybe. If you read between the lines. With prior knowledge.'

'Did it name names?'

'You kidding? Even Lee isn't that mad.'

'But he must have had proof to back it up.'

'I didn't ask. I told you, I flushed it. I don't remember what was in it.'

'What could make you remember?'

'Nothing! Okay?'

'You got my card, Jason. Anything comes back to you, ring me. And when I say me I mean me. No one else. Sleep well.'

Light on his feet, Bright loped across the road and slid in through the metal gate to the Regis Road trading estate. He jogged round the curve of the soulless private road past the car pound, the council salvage dump, in through the back way to the police HQ car-park. It was dark now. He drove off without being seen. Back to his one-room pit in Tufnell Park. Again he felt as much the robber as the cop, hounding and hounded, both.

15

She woke and again Dan wasn't by her side. She listened for a few minutes. No sound from the bathroom. He hadn't got up to pee then. She crept out on to the landing. Half-past five. A blackbird jabbing a tuneless rhythm into the smooth lilac sky, like a psychotic banging his head against a wall. She crept downstairs.

She opened the door to Dan's study and the crack of light showed his tousled head on the day bed. They used to make love on those brown velvet cushions. In the days when they used to make love. She didn't whisper his name. If he was asleep she didn't want to wake him. If he was pretending, he had his reasons, and just at this minute she didn't want to know them.

George wove his warm body round her legs. She picked him up and he flopped in her arms while she carried him downstairs. Down in the kitchen, while she made tea, he crossed in front of her on the worktop, over and over, butting her chin with his forehead, caressing her face with his tail. 'My sweetheart,' she said.

He chirruped, jumped to the floor and made for the french windows where he stretched up, reaching for the door handle. He turned his head to give her his eager *let's go out* look.

'Okay,' she said. 'Just a minute.' She took the tartan rug off the couch and pulled it round her shoulders. They went out into the dawn garden.

George trotted ahead of her to the apple tree. The apples were swelling, reddening. The coal tits and blue tits flitted among them. No sparrows these days, the commonest bird, the city sparrow, now all gone. Jude still found their absence hard to believe.

No such questions for George. George's life consisted of the present and the immediate future; no past regrets for him. He looked up into the branches. His teeth chattered in anticipation, perfectly audible to the birds, who stopped trilling and gave their warning *tink tink tink*. He leapt at the lowest branch, and the birds flew up and away. Thwarted again, he crouched, shoulders up to his ears, glaring as the birds escaped him. He was no danger to them. He lacked the killer instinct.

'Better luck next time, George.'

He always detected her false notes. His eyes slid off, disdainful, to a distant view. He sat, lifted a hind leg and casually licked his outstretched foot. She was suddenly reminded of John Bright. He possessed the killer instinct all right, he'd wait for the moment and go for the throat. It would be quick; he wasn't cruel. Just efficient. He'd time it to perfection and get it right. 'Not like you, eh, George?'

It was good, this hour of the morning. No trains. No cars. Apart from the silent surreal procession along the top of the wall. No clouds. Just the lacy white moon fading away into the violet sky. It was going to be a heavenly day. She didn't know if she could bear another heavenly day.

For the first time in her life Jude was suffering from depression. It had never happened to her before. But she knew what it was, she'd read about it: persistent negative thoughts, lack of energy, lack of interest, lack of feeling, even; just the desire to curl up and sleep, for everything to go away and leave her alone. *Everything except you, George.* She wondered if a pet might prove a better cure than Prozac in cases similar to hers.

She heard Dan in the kitchen bashing about. She had to deal with the problem of Dan. With the secrets that had entered their lives, burrowing like a worm into the apple of their happiness. Then she wondered if it had been happiness, whose heart could so easily be eaten away. She barely had the energy to pursue the question. Reluctantly she went into the house.

He looked tousled, about twelve years old, with his crumpled boyish sleepy morning face. She stood watching him trying to remember how to fill a kettle, just emerged from the deep dream world of sleep. She felt a throb of tenderness like a thump in the chest, and her eyes, as they did all the time now for hardly any reason, filled with tears. 'I made tea,' she said. She nudged him out of the way. 'I'll do it.'

He leaned in the doorway. He said, 'George is trying to burrow out again.'

Jude laughed and blew her nose. 'All that energy just to bury his shit. He's so scrupulous.'

'He's the obsessive neurotic type.'

She stood close to him and took his hand. She felt as far distant from him as if they were in separate worlds. They were in separate worlds. She looked at his hand then put the teacup into it. 'Dan?'

'What?' He put his arm round her shoulder. He did not look at her. He drank some tea, kept his gaze on the garden.

She forced herself to go on. 'Yesterday. The inspector who came – John Bright – the man in charge of the case? He said it's bad for me to have secrets.'

'Incredible powers of deduction, eh?'

This sardonic rejoinder slammed a door in her face. She wanted to stay on the other side of this door. But she had to push against it. She had to force it open, break through it. Breaking barriers, forcing issues? This was not her way. She'd never had to do it before. She was clumsy, foolish, without the necessary skills. She said, stupidly, 'Have you got any secrets, Dan?'

He turned very slowly to look at her. He drew silence down

into himself as a sponge draws water. He said, 'Secrets? Me?' Very flat. 'Why are you asking me this?'

'You don't talk to me. I mean we don't talk. We've stopped talking. We live here in this house, we're around each other a lot, more than most married people I should think, but the days go by and we don't seem to talk.'

'This is talking, isn't it?'

'No. You know it's not.' She gave him a pale smile. 'It's talking about talking, though, and that's something.'

'And something is better than nothing, you think?'

'Don't you think something is better than nothing?' she said.

'It depends.'

'On what?'

'What the something is compared to the nothing it's replacing.'

She wanted to say, *I've been going to bed with Lee.* She said, 'Have you ever – had an affair – since we've been – together?' She quailed at the power of her cowardice.

He smiled, still in his sardonic mode. He said, 'How would you feel if I did?'

She said, 'I don't know.'

He withdrew his arm from her shoulder. 'I know how I would feel if you did,' he said, still leaning there in the doorway with the cup of tea.

'How?'

'Well, let's put it like this,' he said, still smiling. 'I'd kill you, I think. Probably. And then I'd kill myself.'

They exchanged a long look. His eyes and hers were both veiled, as a cat's eyes have a white veil of skin over them, the inner eyelid, when the eye is in danger or the animal is sick.

'You don't mean this literally, do you, Dan?'

He did not smile or change his expression. 'Actually I don't know what I'd feel or what I'd do. Impossible to predict our behaviour, isn't it? We can sometimes surprise ourselves.'

Does he know or doesn't he? Does he suspect or doesn't he? Now I can never tell him. I'm burdened with this secret for ever. What if Lee were to die? Then there'll be no secrets any more. I'll be forced to tell everything. I don't want the burden of this secret. But, oh, I don't want Lee to die. She said, 'I've got to get ready for work.'

'Where today?'

'Kate Creech.'

'Shouldn't you take the day off?'

'Just some tidying up. Nothing strenuous. I'd rather be busy. What will you do?'

'I'm going to Essex.'

'To see your client?' Her face glowed, all gladness, all hope. 'You're going to talk to him after all?'

He spoke slowly, still with the slight smile. 'I'm going to talk to him. Yes.'

'Oh, Dan, I'm so glad. I'm sure that's right. I'm sure it won't be as bad as you think!'

'Well, Jude, as long as you're sure, that's all that matters. Shall I ring the hospital?' Without waiting he picked up the phone. While he dialled and waited he watched her face but in an absent way as though he couldn't see her. 'Thanks,' he said.

She knew Lee was dead. She was certain.

Dan put down the phone. 'No change,' he said. '"Sorry to tell you, Mr Craig, Mr Han is still critically ill."'

'I'm free this afternoon. I'll go and see him. If they'll let me.'

'No visitors, they said.' Dan sounded suddenly uninterested. He turned the tap full on to rinse his cup. Water splashed everywhere. 'Shit,' he said. 'I'll get some breakfast at Liverpool Street.' He went past her in the doorway. Their bodies did not touch.

She fed George. She ate some muesli, standing at the window. She heard Dan leaving. She ran upstairs but he was gone. He hadn't called goodbye.

She took a shower. In the shower she suffered vivid images,

physical and visual, of the last shower she had taken with Lee. She dragged some work clothes on and went downstairs again.

She'd left her good spade at Lee's. She couldn't face going there to get it. She'd use Kate's inferior one. One day maybe she'd be able to face driving her contaminated van. Not that she'd have driven to Kate's anyhow, a couple of streets away.

She kissed George's hard forehead between his soft ears, and left the house.

16

But she only worked half the morning. She could think of nothing but Lee. At eleven she stuffed all the ivy and rose prunings into black bags and piled them in a corner of the terrace to take to the dump. Sometime soon, she was going to have to get back into her van. Avoidance techniques were new to her. Or were they? Maybe not as new as she thought. But thoughts of Lee she couldn't avoid. She went home and changed.

It wasn't like an English hospital. All space and white light in the vast atrium, art on the walls, sculptures, cafés, shops, an aquarium. Trees even. Two escalators zoomed up to the first floor. There were three banks of lifts all in stainless steel and a staircase either side of the central concourse. This was the sort of architecture Dan admired, the sort of work he should be doing. She went up in the lift to the burns unit and a male nurse took her to the observation room.

She expected a horrible sight; she was braced for it. But Lee was not precisely a horrible sight. He lay unconscious, unmoving, suspended above the bed, his limbs held apart, on a pulley arrangement. A sheet hovered over him, not touching him. A gauze mask covered his face. A machine breathed for him, a plastic tube fed him, and another at the other end drained him. It might not have been Lee at all.

She asked the nurse, 'What does he – actually – look like? Under all that?'

'Well, the skin's mostly burnt off, you know.'

Jude swallowed. 'Can they . . . ?'

'They might be able to graft some skin from his back, and his thighs, to do plastic surgery on his face, but . . .'

'But what?'

'Well, he has bad damage to his airway. See? He's got a line into his trachea. We've got him sedated. So he won't thrash about and that.'

'You mean he's *conscious*?' The idea horrified her.

'Well, just about.'

'Is he in pain?'

'No pain with full depth burns.'

'I see.'

'*He* can't, love, I'm afraid.'

'What do you mean?'

'He'll most likely be blind. If he lives.'

Jude's eyes filled with hot stinging water. The nurse gave her a box of tissues. She blew her nose and wiped her face. 'How much chance does he have?'

'Are you a relative?'

'No, I'm—'

'Oh, of course not, what am I saying? He's Chinese, isn't he?'

'I'm just a friend. I'm his gardener, actually.'

'Ohh . . .' The nurse gazed at her in a motherly way. 'Does he have a garden?'

'Yes.'

'I'm not supposed to say this and anyway no one ever knows for sure, but I'd give him 80/20 against. Best odds.'

Jude's inward breath choked her. She coughed.

The nurse went on. 'All this . . .' He sadly indicated the elaborate life support. 'I just don't see the point sometimes.'

'But you're in the business of saving lives.'

'Mmmm.' He made some notes on a clipboard then stared

at Jude. 'You think he should live then?'

'I think you'd have to ask *him*.'

'Which we can't.' He hugged the clipboard to his narrow chest.

'How can you do this job?' Jude asked him.

'I can't, sometimes. I'm always saying I'm getting out. Do a computer course or something.'

'No such dilemmas there.' Jude gave a faint smile.

'Exactly.' The nurse nodded at her with pursed lips and went out. Jude heard him say, 'Oh, sorry, love, I didn't see you there.'

John Bright was standing in the doorway.

Jude stammered, 'I didn't know you were there either.'

'I'm good at that.' He approached and stood next to her, watching the suspended unrecognisable object that had been Lee Han.

Jude said, 'You heard what we were saying?'

'A-ha.'

'Do you agree with the nurse or me?'

'If I was that object hanging there? I wouldn't see a lot of point going on. But I'm not him – you hit the nail on the head.'

'No one has the right to take that decision for us?'

'A-ha.'

'Not in any circumstances?'

'Listen, love, I'm a copper. What d'you expect me to say?'

I couldn't take a life in any circumstances, she wanted to say. But she couldn't. She was the last to see Lee before the attack, she was seen leaving just before the fire: *so I would say that, wouldn't I?* She blushed. She felt it. Maybe under her summer tan it wouldn't show. She turned away and shook her head, looking at the thing hovering above the bed, that had once made love to her with such childlike joy. 'I'm sorry. I keep crying like this. It's not like me. It's sort of – physical – like a reflex. I can't seem to control it.'

'You should go to the doc.'

'I'm not the doctor type.'

'Don't like them much myself. But you got depression.'

Jude's tears stopped in astonishment. She blushed again. This man made her blush. The metallic points of light in his small brown eyes, the suggestion of a squint, so slight you were never sure where he was looking, but you knew he missed nothing, and the air of cockney matiness, putting you at your ease, lowering your guard, then shifting the chat into a different gear. He was lethal.

He said, 'You saw Lee's wife Chloe one day at his place – when did you say that was?'

'It was – it was sometime in my second week there. I think.' *I know exactly when it was. The Monday of my second week. Because when Chloe left I comforted Lee and we kissed and that was the day we first made love.*

'You sure you never spoke to her?'

'Never.'

'But he told you she was violent to him?'

Jude paused to find a way to put it. 'I never saw that happen.'

'The day you saw her. Was he upset after she left?'

'Yes. Look, I don't want to give an opinion about their relationship—'

'Don't worry, I can read between the lines.' He regarded her with his amused squinting gaze. His face did not move. He did not smile. Just this light in the eyes.

Then Chloe came in.

He kept his eyes on Jude. His look of amusement intensified, hardened. Jude had nearly drowned once when she was six. She felt like that now. A red tide of guilt flooded her face.

Chloe stood in the doorway, suction pump eyes drinking Jude in.

Bright said, 'Hello, Chloe, this is Jude Craig.'

'Who?' she said in this flat little dry little voice.

Again John Bright gave Jude what with him passed for a smile.

Jude burbled. 'Sorry, I'm Lee's – I've been working on the garden. I was there one day when you came but we weren't introduced.'

'I didn't see you.' Chloe spoke without a spark of interest. She looked through the observation window at Lee's floating wired-up body.

Jude didn't know what to say. Bright folded his arms and leaned against the wall watching them both, waiting. 'Well, I'd better go,' she said.

Chloe didn't react.

Jude backed towards the door. 'Well, anyway . . . I hope they can – I hope he – I just hope.'

Chloe didn't turn to look at her. She said, 'I bet you do. If he dies you will be accused of murder. You were seen leaving the flat just before it happened, weren't you?'

Jude turned gasping at the door. Her wide gaze was on John Bright. He held her eyes for a while. She couldn't read the message there, if there was one. She hovered paralysed between fight and flight but he said nothing. She tried to answer Chloe but she couldn't. So she simply left.

She didn't take the lift; she went down the stairs, white space all round and blank white space in her mind. All the way to Earls Court Tube she saw nothing, heard nothing, thought of nothing. But standing in the crowded swaying sweltering Circle Line train she grew more and more agitated: if she didn't get out she'd suffocate; she couldn't stay on till King's Cross. She jumped out at Great Portland Street and, outside, she ran, as if running would help.

She ran across Euston Road and into Regent's Park. She ran across the vast beach of flat grass past the big stone animal sculptures. She did not stop till she reached the zoo enclosure, where, close to the railings, a pony the size of a big dog chomped on the hay in his manger. Here, she rested, bent over, till her heart stopped pounding and her lungs stopped aching.

She crossed the bridge over the canal then went down the steps to the towpath. It was peaceful down here, quiet. The sun on the water. And on her. London could be miles away. People sitting out on their longboats, dappled shade on the gardens that backed on to the canal. Ducks bobbing on the surface. And suddenly she sat down against the wall.

Chloe hates me. Chloe is trying to implicate me. Does she really believe I set fire to Lee? Or did she do it herself and wants me to get the blame? I ought to feel afraid but I don't; I feel relief. Why? And all at once she knew: *I've been suspecting Dan.*

She covered her face and crouched, staring into the dark hollow of her hard gardener's hands. She had been filled with this fear and now she felt it emptying out of her, liquid out of a jar, and as it emptied, for the first time she could examine it. Ask herself on what it had been based.

She lifted her head. She watched the ducks in their cheerful aimless circling and counted on her fingers. *One: Dan came in after me that day and he has never said where he'd been. Two: ever since, he's found some reason to sleep on the sofa in his office. Three: he's been depressed for months and now he's giving off the smell of suicidal despair. But Dan has this tendency. It's always been my function to keep him cheerful, to keep his head above water. When did his latest bout of despair begin? After or before my affair with Lee? Connected or not?*

The only way to find out is to ask Dan, and this I absolutely cannot do. I can't bear the thought of adding to his despair. But Lee is lying there in the hospital on the line to the vanishing point, and this is a police inquiry and might – oh God please not – become a murder inquiry. The truth is creeping closer to the cold light of day. Dan is inevitably going to find out.

But no – hang on – Lee will surely recover. The police will find the culprit. No one but myself and Lee can know for certain what went on between us. Lee is no macho kiss-and-tell merchant compelled to show off to the lads. He would never tell a soul. Would he? No! Come on, you know he wouldn't. He understands me, he understands about me and Dan. Jude clasped her strong hard hands between her breasts. *Oh God, please.*

The ducks had gone. The trees shadowed the glassy water. She got up. Her legs were stiff. Yet again she had come to no conclusion. *I won't tell Dan. I can't tell Dan. Not yet.* Walking on, she realised: *I've only examined the question of my own guilt again; not Dan's.*

She was in danger of becoming as full of despair as he. *Guilt does that to people. Makes them despair.* She stopped. Her breath stopped for a moment. *Guilt does that to people. Guilt did this to Dan? Is that what I mean?* Then quickly thoughts jumbled and crammed and fell over each other headlong to deny, to qualify: *other things also create despair – your beloved mother dies, your partner deserts you, your wife becomes successful and fulfilled, your coupling incapable of producing a child. Your wife – Oh God.* Her thoughts had come full circle. No way out. Jude pressed her forehead against the grimy bricks under the bridge and tears ran down her face. Again. She wiped them away and began to walk on again. *I can't believe Dan would take that kind of revenge. I can't. The most likely person is Chloe. She's the vengeful one . . .*

Chloe stood looking at Lee for twenty minutes without speaking. She was impenetrable. Impermeable. You'd need to be a surgeon, open her up, to see what was going on inside of her. Bright needed to know more about her. It was possible that she held all the threads of this case in her manipulative little hands. He knew she was waiting him out, having a little contest with him. So he didn't speak to her. He just stood behind her, watching her. Till at last she gave up and decided to leave.

She turned and went out of the observation room without giving him a glance. He followed her. She ignored him. They were the only people in the lift. She ignored him. But he walked at her side across the vast atrium to the exit, and outside, in Fulham Road, he said, 'Chloe?'

'What?'

'I'd like to talk to you.'

She didn't say anything, just walked on like he wasn't there, like he was some kerb crawler trying to pick her up.

'Can I buy you a drink?' he said.

'You're a policeman, aren't you?'

'So?'

'So I could get you into trouble just for asking me that.'

'I could take you to the station for questioning instead of offering you a drink and an informal chat.'

'I could accuse you of blackmailing me. Threatening me.'

He had no excuse for formal questioning: she was alibi'd up to the eyeballs. He sighed. 'Forget it, Chloe. Life can get too complicated.'

'Yes.' She walked off, legs like willow wands, perfect little body all dressed in black.

Bright said, 'Chloe?'

She turned. 'What?'

'Where's your kid?'

'That is none of your business.'

Bright felt tired.

17

Lee's rolls of film had given them nothing: shots of a housing development, maybe for an architectural journal. He called the fat man at the paper. They said he wasn't in. He called him at home. He wasn't answering and his answerphone wasn't on. He wanted to see his place and knew he had no grounds for a search warrant. He walked round and into the flats and up to the second floor and along the balcony and rang his bell. There was no reply.

He looked through the kitchen window. Surprisingly neat, not a thing out of place. Except an empty bottle of scotch on the draining board and one unwashed glass. He looked through the flap of the letterbox. He couldn't see much, but the rug was rucked up. That didn't fit with the obsessively neat kitchen. Put it down to the scotch. Maybe.

He called, 'Jason? Mr Crabbe? Hello there? Can I have a word?'

An impressive silence.

He rang at the flat next door. A girl came to the door. She looked sixteen. Baby in her arms, fag in her mouth. She said nothing. Just looked at him. Those dead eyes. Dead youth. Contradiction of the way it's supposed to be. It was starting to get to him. 'You know the bloke that lives next door?' he said.

She lifted her shoulders in a *maybe I do maybe I don't who wants to know* kind of way

'I'm a bit worried about him,' he said. He didn't want to say he was police; she'd shut the door in his face. 'I was in the pub with him last night, I said I'd pop round today but he's not there apparently. You see him go out?'

She shook her head and yawned, shifted the baby to the other shoulder.

'Anyone else been round to see him?'

'They was partyin' last night.'

'They?'

'Jason's place.'

'Who?'

'Didn't see. Music was real loud.'

'Who was there?'

'Kept him awake.' She indicated the baby, threw the cigarette butt down and left it smoking on the concrete balcony.

'Who was there? Anyone I know?'

'You a copper?' she said, straight in the eye.

'That obvious, is it?'

'What you after him for, then?'

'Nothing. I told you. I'm worried about him.'

'I di'n't see nobody.'

'No.' He sighed.

'I di'n't! But – like – Jason don't usually make that much noise.'

'Haven't got his key, have you?'

The dead eyes gazed at him a while. She turned round and went into her kitchen. She came back holding two keys on a ring.

'Sure you can trust me?'

'I clean for him.' She gave Bright the keys.

Bright opened the door. He smelled booze. And something foul.

The girl said, 'What's that awful smell?' She was behind him in the hall.

He said, 'Stay there, love.'

She did as she was told. The baby burbled away in its own

language as Bright went down the corridor, loo on the left, separate bathroom, undistinguished, clean. A small bedroom, pitch dark. He found the light switch. It came on infra red. In the eerie red glow he saw the room was fitted up as a darkroom. His hackles rose. Lee Han was a photographer. There was no darkroom at his place. This was the darkroom Lee Han would use. Must be.

Developed reels of film hung from a line of string. Dishes of chemicals lined up along a work bench. A decent-looking enlarger at one end, a shallow blue plastic sink at the other, with one tap. A four-drawer filing cabinet on the other wall. The window blacked out with a square of cardboard, taped with duck tape to the frame. The smell of chemicals sharp in the nose was not sharp enough to cut out the foul smell of the rest of the flat. He backed out into the corridor, shutting the door.

Across the passage the living-room door stood open. The rug concertinaed in the doorway. The smell. He went in. He saw the fat man lying on his sofa. A sheet of blackened foil and a teaspoon on the coffee table. A syringe on the floor, his fat left hand hanging close to it. Blood in the syringe and a trickle from his arm. His eyes were open but they weren't seeing anything. He'd shat himself. That was the smell. Crabbe's other arm was across his body, caressing his big belly, a peaceful pose. Bright touched his neck. A formality.

'What's the awful smell?' The limp voice again from the corridor.

Bright went out to her.

'Is he all right?' the girl said. 'Smells like he shit himself.'

'A-ha.'

'S'not like Jason. He likes everyfink spotless.'

'He's dead.'

'Oh fuck oh Christ.'

He took her arm to steer her out on to the balcony. He shut

the door behind them. He got Cato on the phone and gave him the news. 'Take it from here, Cat. I'll meet the guys when they arrive. Send Atkins. You and Helen get round to the newspaper office.' He took the girl into her own flat. 'Did he drug?'

'Jason? No!'

'Sure? Never?'

'Everyone round here's into everyfuckinfink, you know what it's like, but not Jason, never, no!'

'The music last night? That was unusual, right?'

'Right.' Her teeth were chattering. The baby watched this curiously, then put his hand into her mouth. She took his wrist and gently held his fingers. 'It's all right, Dwane,' she said. Dwane went on trying to poke his fingers between her teeth.

'When were you last in his flat?'

'Yisday. Round four o'clock. Two hours I do. Kitchen, bahfroom, toilet, livin'-room; he don't let me touch the darkroom, keeps it locked.'

'Does he?' It was not locked now. And the key was not in the door. 'And you're sure you didn't see anyone coming or going, last night? This morning, early?'

She shook her head.

'Hear anything? Door opening, closing? Voices?'

'Honest, no!'

'Just the music, right?'

'Yeah!'

'What time it start?'

She thought. The baby was making grabs at her hair now. Again she gently held him off by the wrist, disentangling strands of her hair from his small plump hands. 'Dwane woke up goin' on half one. Don't know how long it been goin' on before that.'

'And it was loud? Louder than Jason'd normally play it?'

'He never played no music, far as I know.'

'Okay. What's your name?'

'Sharon.'

'Nice name.'

'Oh yeah? Come off it. Common as muck. Like our mums fought you weren't allowed to call girls anyfink else. I got two best friends called Sharon.'

Her teeth had stopped chattering, but Bright couldn't stop her. He shepherded her into her own flat, sat her down and let the uninflected stream flow on. She suddenly started to cry. But the baby got a worried look so she stopped. 'He was good to me, Jason. He di'n't need me to clean for him, he just done it out the goodness of his heart, know what I mean?'

Bright winced. He too knew Jason had no harm in his heart – just fear, and something to hide. Anger came up from his gut like a fist. At himself as much as the benighted fag-end of the universe that had to wipe out the likes of Jason Crabbe to protect their stinking little corner. At himself worst of all. He'd talked to Crabbe in the pub. There were scum in there that knew bigger scum. He knew that. Crabbe seemed so harmless. How could he – an experienced copper – have been so thick? He could have talked to the poor slob anywhere. All he'd got out of it apart from this stupid cruel death was a little bit of knowledge. He knew now for sure that Lee – and Crabbe – knew something, or had something, that was so dangerous to somebody that it was worth killing for. And he was pretty sure he knew who that somebody was. And just for now he had to keep this knowledge to himself.

Ants have a whole squadron devoted to collecting their dead and carrying them back to the nest. Were they called funerary ants? He couldn't recall. But the human funerary squadron started to arrive. The police doc did his stuff, pronounced Jason dead, said unofficially he'd died no less than five hours ago, no more than ten, and turned the scene over to the socos. When they'd finished with him the mortuary van arrived and carried him off.

Bright caught the police doctor on his way out. 'Was he a habitual user?'

'Couldn't find any other needle marks. But I might at the mortuary. Could have been taking stuff other ways. Can't tell till I do the PM, John.'

Then Bright was stuck there, pacing round outside while the scene was dusted for fibres and fingerprints. They would find nothing of significance. They'd pronounce it a suspicious death. The coroner's verdict might even be suicide. But it wasn't suicide. Bright knew this as clearly as if poor old Fatman had cried out to him. It was murder, no question.

He went next door to Sharon. She made him a cup of tea. She said, 'You get a lot of this then?' and she didn't mean tea.

'Second in three days,' he said.

'Second murder!'

'Don't know if it's murder yet, Sharon. Let's say suspicious death for now, eh?' Then, Hang on, he thought. *Second?* He was talking about Lee Han. But the poor guy wasn't dead this afternoon. Not quite. Hanging there in limbo land. He called the hospital.

While the hospital was telling him *No change*, big Roger Gould turned up. Bright groaned. 'Thanks for the tea, Sharon. Gotta go.'

Gould was all over the scene, poking around. 'Oh, there you are, John.'

Bright said, 'How come they let you in and not me?'

'How come I'm working for the Area Major Incident Pool and you're not?'

'Area Major Interference Pool? Not for me, mate.'

Gould gave a good-humoured laugh.

The socos were on their way out. In the exhaustive search no one had come across the darkroom key. The duty officer side-mouthed to Bright, 'Sorry, guv. The AMIP bloke barged in just as they were finishing up. I couldn't stop him.'

'Anything I should know?'

'Have a gander at the darkroom.'

'Thanks.'

Big Rog was in there ahead of him, craning his big neck round sideways to see what was on the developed strips of film. 'Mmm,' he said. 'Quite interesting.'

'What are they? Girls with their legs open?'

'How did you guess?'

Bright started on the filing cabinet. Print after print, sad models in sad lighting and crude colour, sometimes one alone, sometimes two together, sometimes two girls and a bloke. Quite imaginative postures, quite inventive. Something caught his attention, stopped him in his tracks. He stopped flicking through the pictures for just one second.

Big Rog crowded him, peering over his shoulder. 'Well, it's easy to see why he'd want to kill himself, poor sod.'

'Why's that, Rog?' Bright swiftly resumed his search.

'Well, this is pathetic stuff, isn't it? Pathetic.'

'A-ha? Why'd he do it last night, Rog? Why not any other night of his pathetic life?'

'Well, it's pretty simple. He was depressed at his mate's – injuries. His mate Lee Han. He didn't have many friends. They never do, this type.'

'He'd never jacked up before. No other marks on him, not on his arms, not anywhere.'

'Well, that's just it, isn't it? He's obviously been imbibing in other ways before. First time he injects he ODs and dies.' Roger liked the sound of that so he said it again. 'ODs and dies. He wouldn't be the first to do that, would he, John?'

Bright said nothing. He moved on to the next picture in the filing drawer – a dark-haired girl with fine glowing eyes lying looking at the camera with her hand between her legs. Gould said over his shoulder, 'She's got something. She's really got something.'

'A-ha.'

Bright didn't say *Whatever she had when this picture was taken she certainly hasn't got it now.*

Gould said, 'I wonder who she is . . .' and he held out his hand for the picture.

Bright ignored the authoritative gesture. He held on to the picture, and he didn't say he knew who she was and he didn't say he knew where she was.

He handed over the filing cabinet to Atkins. Then he sat in Crabbe's pathetic flat and filled in his forms. He felt a bit sick. Someone had opened the windows. The smell had gone. But there was a stink to this death that was worse than the smell of human faeces and this one hung around longer. This one was on his conscience. This one was bad.

He rang Ken Priest, the editor of Crabbe's paper. 'I can't give you any details, Ken.'

'Give me something, Mr Bright.'

'We're treating it as a suspicious death.'

'I don't believe he did it on purpose.'

'Nor do I.'

'Can I quote you?'

'Not by name, mate. Not yet.'

'You think someone else might have been involved?'

'I'm not ruling anything out.'

'Christ, why? Who'd want to kill harmless old Crabbe?'

'No reason you can think of?'

'Is this connected to the fire at Lee's place?'

'You tell me.'

'Weird coincidence, isn't it?'

'A-ha.'

'Listen, maybe it's porn? Lee's a photographer, a good one. Crabbe – well – he was a bit of a porn addict, poor bloke. Is there any way the two of them could have been up to something illegal?'

'Nothing to justify being killed for, far as I can see.'

'Well, what then?'

'I don't know, Ken. If you or anyone at the paper think of anything, let me know before you tell the great British public, would you, mate?'

'Believe me, you'll have all our co-operation, Mr Bright.'

'Different when it's one of your own. Right, Ken?'

He went back to the darkroom. Gould and Atkins were going through the prints. Bright picked out a few, different girls. 'I'm taking these.'

Horsy noises from Atkins.

'Yeah yeah. Just so's I'm not accused of removing evidence from the scene, all right?'

Gould gave him a sharp sideways look. 'Have you ever been accused of that?'

'Not as far as I know. Have you?'

'Lord, no. Where are you off to, John?'

'Back to the station, Rog. Call me there if you want me. Be in touch.'

He got round to Holmes Road in two minutes. He ran up the stone stairs to the CID room. Caught Maggie's eye. 'Anything?' he signalled. She signalled *No* with the slightest shake of her head. Llewellyn was there. 'Taff? We're going visiting. Your car?'

Outside in the car-park he waited for Llewellyn. He looked at the top picture once more. His stomach muscles tightened. So did the hard line of his mouth. He bounced on the balls of his feet. The blood speeded up in his veins. Anger made great adrenalin.

18

'Where we going, guv?'

'Keep straight on up Highgate Road. Take the first left after Gospel Oak.'

'Oh no,' Taff said.

Cops were right to be wary entering these flats. Dignified red-brick Edwardian buildings right on the edge of Hampstead Heath, they looked like des res for the middle class. And some of them were. But the council had made a couple of them dregs res, filled them up with benefit-livers, in bed all day except signing-on day, cashing-giro day, awake all night, on whatever turned them on, to musical accompaniment, all night long.

They sat in the car waiting. Kids, nine, ten years old, with hard grey faces, sauntered by calculating, smelt right away they were cops, as a fox smells right away it's the hunt. They sauntered on. But not far. Even a cop car is fair game left unattended. A car radio, a bit of change, can score a few tabs or a wrap.

'One time a neighbour would tell them you should be in school, where's your mam? Where I come from they still might.'

'They got away, Taff, the kids. They got out. They're feral now, mate, jungle animals, they got their own life now, jungle rules.'

'Yeah. No one dares. Even us most the time. Just like you wouldn't with a tiger, a wolf.'

'Just not worth the hassle.'

'Where their bloody mothers?'

'On the game.'

'Or out of their skulls.'

'Sure. Kids – who are they?'

They sat in the car till the front door opened to let someone out. Bright was out of the car and into the building before it shut again on automatic lock. Taff, as guard dog, stayed with the car. The kids hovered at a distance like little birds of prey, ready to strip it to the carcass if they got the chance.

Bright took the stairs two at a time, light on his feet, quiet as a cat, and rang the bell on the fourth floor. He wasn't even panting. Didn't know how he stayed so fit, he didn't work out like half the lads, he downed a fair amount of booze. Just lucky that way.

He rang again. The building was silent this time of day. No one got up in here till seven at night. That's when the music started, *bam didi bam didi bam didi bam*, till seven next morning when they all went to sleep. Not great for the two or three tenants in the place who got up at 7 a.m. to go to work to earn their bread.

He admired the heavy Edwardian door. It used to have nice stained glass panels; now it had hardboard windows. He didn't expect anyone to answer his knock, so he was taken aback when the girl opened it. He hadn't seen her for a while and the photographs had showed her in more prosperous times.

She was grubby, white-faced, the hair dyed black, dead-looking, the mascara smudged under the eyes. She was in a long T-shirt, her skeletal legs bare. She saw right away who he was and shut the door on his foot. Bright was good at this – long service, good training. She couldn't keep him out. She let go the door and he followed her down the passageway. She didn't object, still half asleep, still more or less out of her skull on whatever she'd been on the night before. The nights and nights and nights before.

'How many here today, Joanne?'

She coughed, pushed the stiff dead hair out of her eyes. 'What time is it?'

'Time you were up.'

'Want – coffee?'

'I'll make it.'

She collapsed like a doll on to a kitchen chair, sighing.

'Last time I was here there was no furniture. You must be doing all right.'

She yawned and started to scratch herself methodically all over, as though only this way would her body wake up, become real to her.

While the kettle boiled he went into the other room. No furniture there, just a few tatty cushions, a camp bed, some blankets. A low table made from a pallet held some candles, matches, foil, a biscuit tin lid, all the gear. Three blokes, thin, grey-skinned, one maybe fourteen, the other two in their thirties, rings through their noses and lips, their ears and their eyebrows, snored fully clothed, on the cushions. The smell was doss house mixed with charity shop, the smell of old unwashed clothes and skin and hair, of people destroyed. No point waking them.

The bedroom was better. She made an effort here. She would; it was her place of business. A mattress, even a duvet in a cover. A curtain of sorts over the window, a bit of old black velvet she'd stuck silver paper stars to. It would make you weep. Kid's drawings pinned to the wall over the bed.

She was still at the kitchen table. She had a fag going now. She stopped scratching when he put the coffee in front of her. She took a mouthful, looked sick a minute, like she might throw up, but she swallowed.

'Where's the kid these days?' Bright said.

'My mum's got her. She goes to school now. She's clever.'

'I saw her drawings. Nice.'

'She's all right.'

'How often you see her?'

'She's better off without me.'

'How often?'

'Fuck off.'

This meant she saw her kid when she wasn't either smashed out of her head or trying to score. But she loved the kid. Or felt the emotion of love. If that counts. And yes, that counts. Because that hurts. Born when she was sixteen. Christ. 'Well,' he said, 'I'm glad she's doing all right.'

'Yeah. What you want?'

'Neighbours complaining.'

'What's new? Fuckin' piss arses.'

'A-ha. Dealing going down on the landing. People yelling up from down below, all hours.'

'Bell's broke. Been broke for yonks.'

'Fights, all the usual,'

'Don't like it they can ask for a transfer.'

The other flat on her landing had been sold off during the Thatcher sell-off-the-council-flats bonanza, and now the couple who'd made the mistake of buying the place couldn't sell it for love nor money. She knew this. And he knew she knew. She gave what passed for a grin, a gruesome sight. Her teeth had got worse since last time. Nearly 2001, and this was living at its most primitive, like the human race was racing backwards. Ought to be a new event at the Olympics: I'm running backwards for my country. For my species. Who can get back to the starting point first? He said, 'Joanne. You know a geezer called Lee? Chinese bloke.'

'Reporter.' She spat the word – almost as bad as cop; except when you wanted them on your side.

'You know him then.'

'Come here nosin' about.'

'When?'

'Weeks ago. He wanted to hang out here, see what was going down.'

'You let him?'

Her bloodshot eyes met his and slid away. 'Couldn't stop him, could I?'

'He pay with money, or what?'

'Pay?' she said, not even attempting innocence. They both knew; things did not always have to be said.

'What'd he wanna know, Joanne? Who was he asking about?'

She smiled, another ghastly one. 'Any more coffee?'

'Okay, so Lee came here—'

'I know he got burned,' she said.

'How?'

'Gets around, dunnit?'

Oh yes. They liked it to get around. He gave her his cup.

She gulped the coffee down. 'He deserved it. He was stickin' his nose in. You don't do that you got any sense.'

'Brennan been round lately?' Bright asked this with a vague expression, real casual.

'Passed me on, love.' That came out pat. 'I'm too much of a junkie for him now.'

'That what he said?'

'Don't need to say, do he?'

'So who comes round now?'

She gave him her blank look, and sighed.

He brought the pictures out of his inside pocket and laid them on the table. She stared at them a long time. Finally she said, 'I looked good in them days.'

'You could again.'

Her eyelids drooped over her eyes, full of contempt for his optimistic lies. 'What you want?' she said again.

'Who took these?'

'How do I know?'

He placed a picture of Crabbe on the table. She touched it. Her expression became what passed with her for soft. He said, 'You know him?'

She nodded.

'He brought the Chinese bloke here, didn't he, Joanne?'

She nodded again.

'This guy's a reporter too.'

'I know.' She sighed.

'Pay well, did he?'

'You fuck off. He's all right, poor old Fatman.'

'He's dead.'

'What?' She was nonplussed. 'You're joking me.'

'Found him an hour ago.'

'Where? How? I don't believe you.'

'In his flat. Heroin overdose.'

'OD? Jason? Bollocks!'

'He didn't partake then?'

'Jason? He couldn't stand the stuff. He's worse'n you, always tryin' to get me off of it.'

'He was killed then.'

'Ah, fuck . . .' She put her hands over her eyes.

'I think we both know who did it to him. Don't we? Same people who burned Lee Han nearly to death. Have you got anything to tell me? Anything! I need you, Joanne. I'm begging you.'

She'd never tell him. None of them would ever tell. No one would ever speak. You get the bastard banged up, he gets out – no evidence against him – the evidence shot dead in a junkyard less than a mile from here. Still, he had to push it as hard as he could. He said, 'Look, you give evidence, I'll protect you, I swear I won't let them get to you.'

She'd have laughed if she hadn't forgotten how. 'Think I'm barmy?'

'He'll be banged up. For life.'

'He was banged up when that poor sod got shot in the junkyard – your witness – right? It don't make no difference, John, bangin' them up.'

Bright's feeling precisely. He was sick of making empty promises.

'I've got a kid,' she said. 'Think they don't know where she is? They know everything. They're worse than you lot. But at least with them it's quick. Bang bang you're dead.' Her upper body collapsed on to the table, covering the photographs, of her in all her glory, and of Crabbe.

He knew he'd had the best of her. He'd given her a shock. So she was already thinking about her next hit. No use to Bright now. She was too much of a junkie for him too. 'Here,' he said. 'Don't spend it all in one shop.'

It was only a twenty but she sat up and her eyes got a momentary spark. 'I ain't give you nothing,' she said.

He shrugged and went out of the kitchen. As he got to the door she said, 'That Lee?'

'A-ha?'

'He come here five times. He was writing this place up. He should've had more sense. I told him. Everyone that come here told him. But he was like a bloody crusader or something. He was getting revenge.'

'Revenge? What for?'

'His fuckin' girlfriend or something. She's a user. He wanted to get the guy responsible for turning her on. His baby was born a junkie. So what's new? They cured the kid, he's okay now, so why couldn't he leave it? Move on. Be glad he's not a junkie himself, got a nice job, cushy number. No. They always gotta ruin it.'

'And did you tell him who'd turned her on?'

'Fuck off. You got your money's worth. And more.'

'Come on, Joanne.'

She held out her hand and he put a folded fiver into it.

She said, 'Yeah, I told him.'

'So Brennan moved on to Lee's wife after you? We are talking about Brennan here, Joanne, right?'

She pulled up the T-shirt and slid the money between her skimpy pants and her bony hip, staring at him with eyes like marbles. That was all he was going to get out of her. They wouldn't squeeze out another drop if they brought her in and pulled out her toenails. If she did say more she'd deny it later. She'd given him a lot. More than she knew, maybe. More than he knew, maybe? He gave it one more shot, however, pushing his luck. 'Any coppers been around, Joanne, asking you stuff? Apart from me, I mean.'

'Fuck off!' She said it fast and she tried to shut the door.

'I'm serious.' He held the door open and waved another tenner, just out of her reach.

She looked at the tenner and her eyes were hungry. But there was no way she'd tell him this. Also, he'd given her enough already to get her where she wanted to be and keep her there awhile. She shook her head and gave her sad laugh. 'I don't shop coppers, John.'

'You sure?'

'I don't know any coppers. Except you.'

Bright laughed. He pocketed the tenner slowly. He said, 'Keep in touch, okay?'

19

He came into the CID room and saw Helen first. She looked at him with her special *I've missed you, good to see you* look. He had not given her a thought for days. Something had to be done about that. But later, later. Not just now. Maggie wasn't on the crime desk. 'You seen Maggie?' he said.

'She had to go out for an hour. She gave Cato some stuff for you.'

'A-ha.' *Gave it to Cato. Ah, Christ.*

'Reports on the Crabbe death, guv.' She handed him a folder.

He couldn't chase up Cato now. He had to go through this stuff. He sat down at the team table. The neighbourhood had been questioned door to door. No one had seen anything. No one had heard anything. Except loud music. No sign of forced entry. Surprise, surprise.

Atkins got Helen to go through Crabbe's photographs with him. Atkins' sense of humour backfired this time. Helen classified them into hard and soft, legal and illegal without turning a neat blonde hair. Atkins glumly stared over her shoulder down her cleavage. Tried to include Bernard in the fun. Failed. Bernard was on the phone, keeping out of it.

'Anything interesting?' Bright asked.

'Fascinating,' Atkins leered. 'Right, Goldilocks?'

Helen said, 'Nobody we know. So far. Quite a few oriental girls. We've kept those separate, just in case.'

Cato came in. He said, 'Can I have a word, guv?' and kept going, in the direction of Bright's office.

Bright followed him and shut the door.

Cato looked grim. 'What's up?' Bright said.

Cato handed him two sheets of computer print-out.

The first paragraph gave a brief summary of events: killing of small-time villain over a drugs debt, no witnesses, all the passers-by disappeared into the woodwork and who could blame them? Just one witness comes forward. Local gangland boss charged with murder on basis of his statement, in prison on remand awaiting trial. But then witness shot at point-blank range in junk-yard in Kentish Town, twice in the head, three times in the back. His statement disallowed, because the law says a witness has to stand up in court and be cross-examined. And a dead witness can't do that. Thus case against gangster thrown out. *The police were left with one vital piece of evidence. The same gun was probably used for both killings. Forensic experts agree on this. But the gun has never been found. Or this was what we all believed.*

However, rumours that the gun was found at the junkyard after the killing continue to circulate. It now seems possible that the gun was left at the scene, indeed was seen there by the first police officer to arrive at the scene but it subsequently disappeared and was never entered into evidence. If it could be proved conclusively that the gun was used for both killings, then even though the first alleged killer was in jail, it is likely that the second killing was done on his instructions. Without the actual gun, however, this would be unlikely to stand up in court. If the gun disappeared from the scene, who took it and why? And how could it be removed without the knowledge, indeed the connivance, of the police?

Bright skimmed through the rest to the byline: *Lee Han*. 'Jesus,' he said. 'Who did he speak to?'

Cato said, 'It had to be someone on your team at the time.'

Bright's voice came down low. 'When I got there with Barton – my sergeant before you, remember?'

'"Dick" Barton, yes. He got transferred to Colindale on the AMIP team soon after.'

Bright stopped a moment then went on. 'There was a uniform PC there, preserving the scene before we all turned up. But Barton was duty officer. When I got there the AMIP lot were already there. Roger Gould briefed me. It looked like he was gonna take the case off me. But he didn't because I'd been dealing with the Brennan case so long, got him banged up at last, about to face trial, no way I wanted to lose him now.' He looked at Cato hard, but Cato wasn't meeting his eye. 'There was no gun when I got into the scene, Cat. There was no gun. You think I'd have let Brennan off my hook after all that hard graft? You gotta know me better than that.'

Cato tapped his pipe bowl on his hand. Little brown spots spattered the pristine white of his shirt cuff. He didn't notice, even though he was staring at his pipe and not at Bright.

'If you think I got bent somewhere along the line, you go higher with it, go on, go now.'

That made Cato look at him.

'But before that, we gotta find the copper who talked to Lee Han. We gotta find him before . . .' Bright rubbed his face. 'Crabbe—'

'The fat man?'

'Lee Han's mate. He knew what was in this piece. He was killed for this.'

'Shit, John.' Cato sat down. He took out his leather pouch and started to fill his pipe. Bright forbore to mention the no smoking edict. Cato lit his pipe and pa-pa-papped to get it going. Then he said, 'The editor, Priest, wouldn't print it because it was libellous?'

'So he says.'

'So he knows what was in it too?'

'He says he never saw it. Didn't want to be tempted, he says.'

'But he's got to know more or less what was in it, guv. To that extent the story's in the public domain.'

'Not the same as knowing exactly.'

'You believe him?'

Bright shrugged. 'The PC who was guarding the junkyard,' he said.

'It's got to be him who talked to Lee Han, hasn't it?'

'He was there first. He was preserving the scene.'

'We got to get out the file on the junkyard shooting and look up the original report, guv.'

'Yeah. A-ha. You're right.' His hand rubbed his whole face downward from brow to mouth. 'It goes high, Niki. This goes high. If it didn't it couldn't have been kept quiet.'

'So who do we report to, guv?'

'Nobody. Yet.'

Cato's face not looking anywhere, not knowing what to believe.

Bright said, 'Tell me what I have to do to convince you, and I'll do it. But whoever we report to could be in on this. And yeah I would say that wouldn't I? Whatever I do or don't do, I look guilty.'

He waited. Cato didn't respond.

'Look – you write a report, okay? We go on with the investigation, and if at any point you start to believe I'm involved in this crap you can take your report to the top, but don't fuck this investigation up now for Christsake, Niki.'

Cato didn't answer, tamping his pipe with a little metal instrument.

'What do you say?'

'I could agree and then go behind your back anyway.'

A straight look stilled the air between them. Bright said, 'I don't think you would do that.'

'I don't want to be the only one to know, guv. It's too dangerous.'

'Who else can we tell? Atkins will go straight upstairs and snitch. Promotion's too slow for him, he'd take the leg up.'

'Bernard and Taff?'

'Too much responsibility for them to handle.'

'That only leaves Goldilocks.' Cato spoke slowly, tapping his little metal instrument on the desk. He lifted his eyes and gave Bright a glimpse of his anger. 'And she's hardly impartial, is she, guv?'

So they knew. They all knew. All this time, he and Helen creeping around, never exchanging an intimate glance or word, never meeting in public, thinking they had this big secret to keep. All their careful subterfuge just a joke. He felt a dark flush explode under his skin. How could he have been such an asshole? Hadn't he learned anything all these years? 'How long's that been in the public domain?' he said.

Cato was relighting his pipe. He shrugged. 'Let's say months rather than weeks.'

Bright nodded. 'See?' he said. 'It's not easy to keep a secret in the old HQ, is it? If I was any good at it I'd have kept that one better, believe me.'

Cato pursed his lips round the pipe stem to stop himself smiling. 'Well, I don't want to be the only one to know. It's too dangerous. So it'll have to be her.'

'Wanna get her in?'

Cato went out. Bright put both elbows on the table, and both hands into his spiky hair. He tried to think but his mind had stalled.

Cato ushered Helen in ahead of him and shut the door. She looked alarmed. Cato had moved into self-important mode; a part of him was enjoying this.

Bright didn't speak to Helen. He handed her the print-out. She read through it fast then lifted her face to him. 'Who knows about this?'

'Just us.'

'What about Maggie?'

Cato said, 'It's okay. She handed the wad of stuff to me, said, "Put that on the boss's desk, it's taken me twenty-four hours, that's a record, tell him." She hadn't read it, I promise you.'

'Can I sit down?' Helen skimmed through the print-out again, slowing at certain points to check detail, then put it back on the desk. 'Who's this DS Barton?' she said.

Cato and Bright swapped glances. 'Why?'

'He's not on your team any more. Did he get promotion after this?'

'He's working for AMIP at Colindale. He made DI.'

'John recommended him.'

'He asked me to. I did.'

'It's got to be Barton,' she said.

'I can't believe it. The bloke was straight as an arrow.'

'We can't talk to him for fear of warning – whoever it is if it's not him.'

'Who is it if it's not him?'

'Has to be someone who was there that night. Someone there before me. Someone high up enough to matter. Someone important enough for Brennan to target. Someone on to higher things, who'll stay in Brennan's pocket because he's in too deep to get out.'

'Christ, guv.'

They all knew who he meant. No one said his name.

'How can we get to him?'

'Investigate him. Keep stumm till we got an airtight case.' Bright shook his head. 'Makes me want to throw up, this shit.'

Cato fiddled with his pipe, not in his usual poser style, but like his hands needed something to do, something to hold on to. Bright said again, 'Get the report on the junkyard shooting. Start from there. You look at it first so I got no chance to nobble it. You hand it on to me.'

Bright's praying while he waits. He never knew till now how much the trust of his team mattered to him. How much *not being bent* mattered to him. He tried to keep quiet, give Cato time. He said, 'Cat, we've worked together two years—'

'Yes and you got me my promotion too, don't remind me.'

'We can go together to the superintendent, now. Wanna do that?'

Cato shook his head slowly. 'No. You're right. The fewer that know the better. But, guv, I got to tell you, I'll never take my eyes off you. You got to take me with you now wherever you go.'

Helen said, 'You could both be in it together and this could all be a bluff to convince me. But we can hardly go round in a threesome, can we?'

Bright gave a sort of smile. So did Cato. Bright said, 'I believe the fat man was killed for this. It's also the strongest motive we got so far for the attempt to kill Lee Han.'

'Are you saying a bent cop nobbled the newspaper?'

'Well, they didn't print it, did they?'

'Libellous, they said.'

'Priest says he hasn't received threats.'

'He's not likely to tell us, is he?'

'Or where they came from either.'

'Even if he's sure, and he might not be. Newspaper people are not naive; they know just what they can tell and what they can't.'

'This is Priest's way of telling us without telling us.'

'If he hasn't printed it, they'll think that means he hasn't passed it on.'

'But, guv, it'll still be in Lee Han's computer.'

'So we delete the file,' Helen said, 'get the print-out and the back-up disk and keep them under wraps.'

Bright looked at the two of them. 'That means talking to Maggie.'

Helen looked alert. 'Who might, in spite of what you say, have already read this.'

'She hasn't,' Cato said, a touch patronising.

'How can you be sure?'

'There'd have been some sign. I'd have picked it up.'

'How? Female intuition?'

'Get her in,' Bright said.

Cato looked taken aback but went. Helen gave Bright her true blue gaze, full of questions and commiseration. He couldn't answer the questions and the sympathy made him feel a fraud.

Cato came round the door like a sleuth in a movie, guiding Maggie in then looking behind him with an *am I being followed* air as he shut the door.

Maggie approached looking anxious. 'Is there something wrong, John? I had such a hassle hacking in. Isn't everything there, or what?'

'This is the lot, is it?'

'Yes! I mean—'

'Did you read any of it?' He spoke in a casual tone, but not too casual.

'I noticed the headings. Stuff about the gangland shootings, is that right? But I didn't have time to read it. You know what it's like out there, you all want everything yesterday. If there's a file missing or something I can hack back in and—'

'I want you to do a back-up disk and delete the files. And I mean seriously delete. And give the disk to Cato. Not to me. Can you do that?'

She looked shaken. All three of them waited, watching her.

'We've both been here a few years, Maggie.' Bright felt sick talking like this; he felt bent. 'In a short while I'll be able to tell you what it's about. Right now, I can't.'

She was all pink round the eyes. She said, 'I have to think about this, John.'

Everyone waited.

Bright looked only at Maggie though he spoke to all of them. He was in their power. It was not a pleasant sensation. 'I'm asking you to trust me,' he said. 'Like I'm trusting you.'

20

George was sitting in his military posture in the doorway of the cloakroom, back of the hall. He peered hard to make sure it was Jude, then trotted towards her. She threw down her bags and got on her knees to greet him. He kissed her face Continental-style, this side then that side. He slid down and over, stretching his full length. His eyes lit up. He gripped her wrist in his front paws and scratched madly with his back feet, claws retracted, biting her fingers, but softly. He could do her real damage if he wanted – on occasion he got overexcited and drew blood – but mostly he kept up the appearance of mad aggression while remaining in kindly control. *Just what most human beings are not so good at. In fact human beings work the other way round – keep up the appearance of kindliness while destroying each other in secret.* This thought killed her pleasure in the mock fight. She did not even look in Dan's room to see if he was there. 'Come on, George, let's go.'

He trotted down ahead of her, stopping every few steps for her to catch up. She stowed the milk in the fridge, the bread in the crock. She lifted the lid of a saucepan on the stove. Dan had put some vegetarian chili on a low flame to heat up. So he must be in. Or have been in. She measured out some rice into the sieve and ran the water to wash it. George crossed in front of her on the edge of the sink, messing her about. 'I'll feed you in a minute, George; humans rule round here, okay?' Then the doorbell rang.

She heard Dan come out of his room and open the door. She

listened but heard nothing else so she ran upstairs. When she reached the hallway Dan was standing at the open door and outside on the step stood Chloe Han.

Jude recognised her at once. She felt oddly breathless, threatened.

The girl's flat cold gaze swayed from Dan to Jude. Jude should have introduced her but didn't. Her eyes went back to Dan again. 'I'm Chloe Han,' she said.

'Yes?'

'Can I come in, please?'

Dan stood back to allow her in. Neither he nor Jude wanted to take her downstairs to their cosy sanctum, hearth and home. They both knew this without exchanging a word or a glance, even though he did not know of their encounter at the hospital. Jude found herself grateful for this silent communication, proof of something she thought they had lost. But then two against one was always easy; it made even enemies friends, joined in truce. Dan opened the door to his study.

'Oh. You have the whole house, not just an apartment. Shame it's next door to the car repair place. And those awful flats opposite.' Just then a train went by at the back and the house shook, objects on the mantelpiece trembling. Chloe's brows rose. 'Why don't you live somewhere better? You're not poor; you're an architect, aren't you? You could afford somewhere nicer than this.'

Jude and Dan exchanged a look of grim amusement. Dan said, 'What can we do for you?'

'What can you do for me?'

'That's what I said, yes.'

'Well, that's funny, because that is what I came here to ask you: what are you going to do for me?'

Jude could not comprehend the cool insolence of Chloe's tone. She felt she'd missed something, perhaps before she came on the scene. Dan appeared equally nonplussed. He just stared.

'No?' Chloe said. 'You don't understand? I'll tell you. You see, I was in the street when the flames came out of the window.'

'In Lee's street?' Jude said.

Dan said, 'Do the police know this?'

'Of course not.'

'So why are you telling us?'

'You left Lee's place—' she looked at Jude – 'just a few minutes before.'

'Yes. About a quarter of an hour before, apparently.'

'That's correct.' Her blank gaze slid across to Dan. 'But you were there when the fire started, weren't you? You were waiting down the side of the empty house opposite, weren't you? Watching.'

First Dan said nothing. He was pale. He was shaken. He was getting his mind under control. Jude knew his body language, she could get a degree in the body language of Dan. So she immediately knew that Chloe had spoken the truth: Dan had been there on the other side of the street when the fire broke out. *He knew then. He's known all along. About me and Lee. He set the fire? Intending what? To kill Lee? No! To make him so ugly no woman would ever want him again – condemn him to a life worse than death? Dan? Not possible. Surely not possible? But why would he be there waiting and watching after I left? There must be other explanations, there must!* These thoughts clattered together in her mind all at once, without sequence. She felt they had all been standing there silent an age, numbed. Playing for time, giving Dan time, she said stupidly, 'Would you like a drink, Chloe?'

Chloe gave her little closed-lip smile and shook her head. 'No. A drink is not what I want, thank you.'

She said this in her cold sinister manner but she suddenly looked ludicrous to Jude, acting the villain like some forties movie star, doing the femme fatale. Jude even felt sad for her. Not that Chloe would want her pity. Chloe liked to see herself as the snake goddess, everyone under her control. Jude said gently, 'Look, I'm sorry, but I don't quite see what it is you want. Are you accusing Dan of setting fire to Lee's place? Because I think that's a bit daft actually, don't you? Dan came to meet me after work but he got there too late, I'd already gone. Dan is an architect, you see. He's always interested in houses.' She addressed Dan without looking at him. 'I suppose you just went to the house opposite out of curiosity, to pass the time, didn't you, Dan?'

Chloe looked pitying. 'And you told the police that, did you?'

There was a pause.

Jude said, 'The police didn't ask.'

Chloe said, 'And I don't suppose you told them that you and Lee were at it like ferrets every time you finished doing his garden, either. Did you?'

'Oh don't be silly.' Jude knew her face was red and she was sweating, her palms slick and her armpits pouring sweat in a sudden torrent and smelling, she could smell it, it was the first time she had smelled fear and this was it, she recognised it and she could smell it off Dan too, like sweat only pungent, intensified, sharp, and she knew Chloe would smell it too so she moved away to the door and opened it. George was out there. He smelled this sharp odour at once. His ears went back in alarm. 'It's okay, George—' But he fled down the stairs. 'Oh Christ. Listen.' She turned to Chloe, speaking slowly, trying to be calm. 'I think you'd better go. We could obviously all make trouble for each other if we wanted to. I don't imagine you want us to tell the police you were there in Lee's street. And if you really think that Lee and I were – lovers – then you might have wanted to injure him. Just as you're now threatening to injure us. So I want you to go now, and stop trying to make trouble for us, and for yourself. If you go away and don't come back we won't try to make trouble for you.'

'Oh, I don't mind the police knowing I was there.' She was

dead cool, dead cold, dead calm. This blackmail talk seemed easy for her, natural, normal. 'I went there to visit Lee.'

Jude's kind thoughts about the girl crumbled. She had never dreamed that a real person could behave like this. Passion she could understand, jealous rage. But not this cold, staring detachment. She said with real curiosity, 'Why are you doing this, Chloe?'

Chloe shrugged. 'I need money. You need me to keep quiet.'

Dan said, 'No. We don't.' His arms were folded across his chest. He was breathing quite quietly. His extreme pallor had gone.

Chloe looked outraged. 'I saw you!'

'They would not believe you. They will think, as I do, that you are desperately casting around for somewhere to throw the blame. To tell this preposterous story you would be giving yourself a motive.'

'Oh yes? What would that be?'

'Jealousy of Jude. And your husband.'

Chloe laughed.

Dan went on. 'Your jealousy and violence, your vengeful temperament, are well known. And you will have to admit that you were there at the very time the fire broke out. You will be suspected of being involved. I don't believe you don't care about that. I'm sorry, you have come to the wrong place. Now please leave.'

Chloe rose like a little snake about to strike but heard the cool logic in Dan's words and in his voice. Floundering, she said, 'But she was screwing him. She's been screwing him for weeks!'

Dan said, 'I trust my wife. I can see that's hard for you to understand.' Jude knew he could not speak much more, he had used up his control. He said, 'Get her out of here.'

Jude did not move towards Chloe – she felt physical fear of the girl, so thin and reedy but with such contained power. She held the door open and gestured, in a rather melodramatic way, she felt. 'Do go now, Chloe. Please. I'm sorry we can't help you.'

Chloe looked round her, round the room. She saw the model of Dan's project – a beautiful thing made in grey and white card and clear perspex, the tower with its perspex top to let in light. She swung her heavy shoulder bag across it. The tower broke in two. The rest smashed flat as befitted a house made of card and, all in little pieces, slid towards the floor.

Jude cried out in pain seeing it crumple like that. She made a move to – what? – save it? Attack Chloe? But Dan said in a tired voice, 'Leave it. It's fine.' Jude looked at him astonished. He was smiling! Then he laughed. 'It's fine,' he said. 'It's absolutely fine. Now get out, would you please.' He moved one step towards Chloe. She sidestepped. She crunched the model underfoot with her smart new trainers, and walked over it, smiling back at Dan. They were smiling at each other! Jude couldn't understand. She was lost here. The girl swayed her whole body towards Dan as she walked by him, the whole side of her body like an animal stroked the whole side of him, arm, hip, thigh. Dan made no response. His eyes were on the crushed destroyed model on the floor, all the little pieces of card and perspex, and he was still smiling.

They heard the front door bang. Dan stood arms folded, looking down. Jude did not dare speak to him yet. She went to the cupboard in the alcove where he kept a bottle of single malt. She poured a good inch into two glasses. She handed him one. He took it. He did not look at her. They both gulped whisky as though from thirst.

She said, 'Were you waiting there, Dan?'

He said, 'Were you screwing him, Jude?'

'Yes,' she said.

'Yes,' he said.

They had not looked at each other saying these things. The

words dropped down to join the ruined model on the floor. The ruined marriage on the floor, Jude thought. The things she wanted to say were all clichés of the most insulting kind – *I didn't want to hurt you – it had nothing to do with us – it was just sex (as if it's ever just sex or just anything, and why do people never say it was nothing, it was just love – is sex less important than love? or do we just want to think so?) – I thought if you didn't know it would be all right, it would do us no harm – you're the only thing I really care about.* She could predict Dan's response to these protestations and so it was impossible for her to speak. She drank another mouthful of whisky; she held the burning liquid in her mouth; it anaesthetised her tongue, her gums, and the roof of her mouth, a pleasant numbness she wished would spread to her brain and her heart.

Dan said, 'Do you wish now you hadn't done it?'

She did not know what to say. Did he mean wish she had not slept with Lee? Or did he think she had set fire to him? No, he couldn't think that? She said, 'But I didn't do it, Dan.'

'I'm not talking about the fucking fire, you stupid bitch.'

'It depends,' she said slowly.

'It depends? On what?'

'On what it may have caused.'

'Oh, I see. I didn't like the prick screwing my wife so I decided to set fire to him, that's what you mean? How many times?'

'I don't know.'

'Too many to remember? Yes, they do blur, don't they, after a while? When did it start?'

'The beginning of my second week.'

'How did it start?'

'Chloe visited him. And when she'd gone he was upset. Really upset. About his baby and everything. I just put my arms round him to comfort him, and—'

'I don't want the gory details, thanks. I can imagine the rest.

I have imagined the rest. I knew the minute it began. You think I'm such an insensitive asshole I don't know when my wife has had some other man's dick inside her? You looked like you'd been reborn. You've been looking that way for weeks. You've been happy, for fuck's sake. And you hadn't been happy for a long time before that because I am a crock of shit and have been for a long time.'

Tears ran down Jude's face.

He said, 'Don't blame yourself. And don't flatter yourself either. You're just one thing among many.' He gestured at the ruined model on the floor. 'That's the last straw, not you.'

She knelt as though to try to reassemble it.

'Come off it, Jude. All the king's horses and all the king's men. The job's gone anyway. I told him if he didn't want the tower I had no further interest in working for him.' He drank all the scotch and coughed.

'When did you tell him?'

'I went to the site today. He told me weeks ago he'd gone off the tower. But I thought I might persuade him. I was kidding myself. I'm good at that.'

'Oh Dan, I'm so sorry.'

'Yes.'

'If I'd known—'

'If you'd known? I don't think it would have changed anything, do you, Jude?'

She couldn't stop the tears rolling down her face. They were hot and they stung her raw wet skin. They rolled down to her mouth. She licked them away and they were hot and salty in her mouth. Eating her tears. Consuming herself because Dan would allow nothing between them except this uncrossable space.

She said, 'Dan, I know you can't forgive me. I can't forgive myself either if that's any comfort and I don't suppose it is. But I think I have to know if – because I have to know what to say to the police. You say you *were* there opposite Lee's place, where Chloe said?'

'That is correct, my darling.'

'And you saw me leave?'

'Oh yes.'

'Well – You have to tell me, Dan – Did you – Did you go in there and do that to Lee?'

Dan was pouring another whisky. He smiled at her and held out his hand for her glass. She gave it to him. He poured whisky into both glasses.

She said, 'I can't believe you did. I can't believe that, Dan. I can't.'

He clinked his glass against hers and drank.

She said, 'You said this morning – was it? – that if I had an affair you would kill me and then yourself.'

'Did I? Oh yes, I believe I did.'

'You didn't say you would kill the person I was—'

'Fucking? No, I didn't. Isn't that odd. I had fantasies of course. Detailed. Usually involving an axe, chopping him up with an axe into smaller and smaller pieces till he disappeared completely into the earth whence he came. Satisfying in a way, except not satisfying at all, a bit like masturbation, once it's over there's a void, an abyss, nothing, nothing left to do. I even had dreams at night of the axe murder. That's why I laughed the other day when you said to George I wasn't the Kentish Town Axe Murderer. That was funny, don't you think?'

'But you didn't do it, Dan.'

'I had a dream of doing it one night so vivid I woke thinking I really had. And I was horrified. It took me ten minutes to start to realise it was only a dream. And I was glad. Relieved that it had only been a dream, that I hadn't actually killed – anyone. I realised I didn't want the bastard actually to die. I just wanted him never to have existed. Impossible. Too late. Thirty-odd years too late in fact. So in fact therefore I didn't want *anything*. Certainly not you, after this. That's when I decided to leave.'

'Leave? Leave me?'

'It's been a matter of time, that's all. How to go. Where to go. When to go. You know. These details. It's all in the detail.'

'Don't, Dan—' *Don't what? Don't leave me? Don't talk like this, think like this? Roll back time like a carpet, roll it up again, make its pattern invisible, out of sight out of mind. Wait. Wait till the pain goes away.*

'And then this happened. The cunt gets burnt in his bed. All my fantasies come true. Well, better than my fantasies. Better than an axe in many ways, don't you think? Incredible the way the flames came out of that window. The noise. The amazing explosion. The beauty of it. The violence. And then the police turned up here and it was clear that they did not believe it was an accident and that you were likely, being the last to see him, to be their chief suspect. So I thought I'd better stick around, just for a while.'

Jude turned her face to him, open to hope.

'And now we've got this little bitch leeching on to us. What have you done to us!' These last words he screamed at her and his face was not a face she had ever seen on him before, except in climax in the act of love – this tortured mask of tragedy with veins standing out on his forehead and sweat pouring out of his hair in rivulets like those pictures of Christ on the cross with blood rolling out of the crown of thorns and she thought hysterically *Dan is suffering for my sins* and she thought she might go mad, they might both go mad, that going mad must feel like this, and then she thought of George. George hadn't been fed yet. So she left Dan there and went downstairs and George came towards her with a little squeak of worried welcome and she got his tin out of the fridge and turned some fishy stuff on to his dish and he pushed his forehead up against hers in thanks and set to, eating and purring at once. And she thought, *This is all I can stand. I can't stand anything more complicated than this. Why can't human relations be simple like this and sweet and loving? Dan and I have turned our love into a weapon of destruction. How can this have happened to us?*

Dan said, 'Well as long as that fucking cat is all right, that's all that matters really, isn't it, Jude?' He was standing at the foot of the stairs. He had followed her down and she hadn't heard.

Jude said, 'Do you want some food? I'm starving.' She turned on the gas.

Dan laughed. It wasn't a nice sound. 'Good old Jude,' he said. 'Let's bring the whole thing down to earth. Let's sit on either side of the old kitchen table and eat, like nothing in the world was wrong.'

'We've been doing that for the last five weeks.'

'And for a good while before that.'

'So why not tonight as well? People do have to eat, Dan. Most people don't starve themselves to death. Even anorexics find it quite hard, I believe. I'm going to eat anyway.'

'Funny isn't it?' He leaned on the newel post. 'Here it all is, looking just the same. Same old cosy place. The dream house. The dream used to be the reality. They were the same. Now this is a façade. Has been for a long time.'

'No.'

'Oh yes, Jude. Admit it. I walked out on this years ago. You know I did. You've been propping me up, that's all. Your fallen fucking idol, that's me. You've just been refusing to admit it. Using all your strength to keep me upright, keep me thinking I wasn't the walking dead. We've managed all right, looked okay to the outside world. Almost looked okay to each other. Propping me up, waiting for the day I'd be able to stand up again on my own.' He laughed again. 'In all senses of the word. Only I knew I never would, Jude. I never will. I had it. The big promise. The big talent. I let it go. I let it be corrupted. I turned it to dust. I'd have ended it if I'd had the guts but guts was never my strong point. That was your department. Hanging on in there because you once made a promise—'

'No, Dan. It's not making the promise. It's love. That's the promise. That doesn't go away. That's never gone away. I've wished it would sometimes, but it never has. It never will.'

His eyes filled up with tears.

She moved towards him. 'Dan, it's your mother's death, all this. You've been ill ever since. You would never admit, never mourn, never grieve. It's turned you into a cripple. If you'd go now and get some help—'

'Oh yes, the great counselling age—'

'You always say that, but it might help, it might turn things around—'

'Turn things around to where? In a big circle back to here? What would be the point of that?'

'I don't know. It might be possible to start again. It might start to look possible to you?' Her voice was small like a child's voice, no breath to prop it up. 'Please, Dan?'

He shook his head and emptied his glass. 'You eat. I'll be fine with this.' He turned and went back up the stairs. She heard his door bang and the floorboards creak as he walked about and then silence and she smelt the food burning and cried into it, scraping the burnt bits off the bottom of the pan. She ate with George curled up beside her on the sofa with the television on without sound, watching the people mouthing and miming in their small silent colourful world twenty-four inches by eighteen, flickering in the dark.

21

Ken Priest opened the door himself. 'Come in. There's no one else in the office. I can only work at night. When it's quiet. That's why I never come in till noon.' He cleared a mound of papers off a chair. 'Sit down.'

Bright told him how they'd found Crabbe. And about the photographs. 'The poor bloke was obsessed.'

'Don't suppose he ever got a go at the real thing.'

Priest wiped his face with a tissue from the man-size box then flung it amongst the debris on the desk. He was drinking cold tea with a skin on it.

Bright said, 'I think he was killed for what was in Lee Han's article. The one you wouldn't print.'

Priest took off his thick glasses and wiped them with one of the used tissues. 'I never saw it. I told you.'

'You knew what was in it.'

'No.'

'That's your story and you're sticking to it?'

'Yes.'

'Has anyone else asked you about this?'

'No.'

'Has anyone warned you? Warned you off?'

'No.'

'Threatened you?'

'No.'

'Offered you money?'

The man shook his head with a violent movement from side to side. 'No!'

'If you are approached – bribed, threatened, warned – you tell me, you hear me?'

'Yes. Of course. For Christsake—'

'Okay, don't get in a sweat about it.' Bright stood up. 'Any other stories of Lee Han's you might just find lying around in here, I want them. Okay?'

'There aren't any, I promise you.'

'A-ha.' He looked at the mess on the desk and all round the room. 'You'd know, would you?'

'Chaos theory. I work better this way.' Now that Bright was leaving, Priest was recovering.

At the door Bright turned round. 'Any of my lot been round to ask you about this?'

'What?'

Bright spelled it out. 'Any other coppers?'

Priest shook his head. Slowly.

Bright said, also slowly, 'You'll tell me if they do. It's DI John Bright.'

Priest's hands trawled the shifting shoals of paper.

'Here's my card. Again. That's my personal number, right?'

'Sure. Thanks.'

'You need our protection. Don't kid yourself you don't. You'll be called as a witness at poor old Crabbe's inquest. Next week sometime. I'll let you know.'

The Goths and Visigoths were coming out of their holes. Rings pierced their skin, chains bound their limbs. Man is born free, my arse. They wanted to be in chains. This was a bad scene all ends up. And Camden Town at eventide might have a gruesome charm for the rag-clad creatures that came up from under the ground to roam its neon-lit avenues leafy with fast food litter and redolent with fast food smells, but for him it was a foretaste of Hades. He had to talk to Helen, couldn't leave it the way it was. But not here. He got on the mobile phone.

He parked in Portobello Road, laid waste like the scene of a battle. Litter blew round his ankles here too. But he liked the melancholy of abandoned markets. A few stallholders were still packing up. A few tourists straggled hot and weary up towards Notting Hill Gate. Helen was waiting for him at the entrance to the mews. It used to be good to see her. Now it wasn't. Hadn't been for a guilt-filled while. 'How long you been here?'

'Ten minutes?' she said. 'No sign of life.'

The iron steps creaked and shifted as they went up. The shadowy little mews shabbier than when the details were bleached out by the noonday sun. A cat shot past their feet and undulated down the stairs like a fall of black water. They both jumped. Helen laughed. 'Thought it was a rat for a minute.'

'Wouldn't surprise me.' Bright pressed the bell. The tinny sound rippled away. They waited. No one answered the door. Bright pressed again and again they listened. He got a jolt of anxiety. The silence in the mews, the dusk, the hollow emptiness of the flat. 'Shall I kick the door in? Wouldn't take much. Made of cardboard.'

'You think some harm's come to her?'

Bright shrugged. 'Chloe doesn't strike me as a victim. But I could be wrong.'

'Oh, really? I thought you were infallible.'

'Well, I am as a rule but don't go taking it for granted.'

'Oh, I don't take anything for granted.' She sounded suddenly serious. Bright's heart, already low, sank lower. He didn't want to have to deal with this. Not now. Not ever if it came to that.

'Come on, let's have a drink.'

'We're on duty. Sir.'

'Oh yeah, a-ha, so we are. You gonna report me?'

Their eyes met. No joke. Not any more.

He pushed the door of the pub. Smoke, noise. Always sordid, pubs with the last of the sun glaring through the window at the pools of liquid and the crumbs of crisps. The soggy ashtrays. She followed him in. But when he asked her she ordered a St Clements. And he didn't have the heart in him to comment.

He picked a table in the corner tucked away. You could keep an eye on the mews through the window. Its nice etched glass had long gone; now just the grime of ages obscured the view. 'Cheers.' They clinked glasses. His eyes scratched the surface of the room. This wasn't his patch but one glance picked out the villains, and the guys on the edge, straddling the narrow gap between outright villainy and the odd little dodgy deal. Get a lot of that round a market. The ones on the edge are the useful ones – got a lot to lose, a lot to protect. And they're scared. You can put the fear of God up them no problem. Pushovers mostly. That was the question with this lot in this case. Chloe, for instance. Was she right over or still straddling? She played tough guy but it was hard to tell. If she was in with Brennan she wouldn't be straddling long . . .

Helen said, 'Those two guys in the corner? That's a deal going down.'

'You're a real cop, constable.'

'I know I am.'

'Don't trust anyone.'

'That's right.'

'Not even your own mother.'

'My wicked stepmum? Specially not her.' She smiled at him.

He smiled back. Sort of. But he did his squint thing. He didn't mean to; it just happened. Only it was the thing he did with people when he didn't want them to see his thoughts. She got that. Not much slipped past her. Her smile went out like a light.

She said, 'You think this thing is a bit of mistake, don't you, John?'

'What thing, Helen?'

'Oh come on. This thing between us.'

'No. Not a mistake . . .'

'But?'

'It's a bit tough always being on your guard. At work, I mean.' Even to him he sounded like a dink.

'But everybody knows at work!'

'I didn't find that out until today.'

'And you don't like them knowing, do you?'

He looked at her straight a second. No good denying it. 'No.'

'Even before this awful business about the bent copper?'

'Is that what this is about?' he said.

She looked at him dead level. 'No. But it made me see.'

'See what?'

'It's an added complication, isn't it? Us. The Us-Thing. Makes you more vulnerable, see what I mean?'

A terrible thought grabbed him – *Vulnerable is right – is she blackmailing me?*

She flushed suddenly, her eyes inflamed. She knew what he was thinking. 'It's just about us!' she said.

'What about us?' He was keeping it low, a damage limitation policy he despised himself for. But he turned off his mobile, a gesture she recognised.

'It was okay when we were carrying on in Bristol, out in the sticks, that's all right, but not in your own backyard, that's it, isn't it? You just don't like fouling your own nest.'

'Hey hey, Helen—'

'Oh, God, I meant to be all rational like and cool only—'

'It's okay. It's my fault. I get into a case, I don't cope well with—'

'Distractions? Yeah, that's what I am, isn't it? A distraction.

That's all. I saw that today. It's not serious for you, is it? It never has been.'

'Serious? Christ, Helen—'

'If we were out in the open we wouldn't need to be on our guard. No secrets is best, right?'

'We couldn't work together any more either. The Met doesn't look that kindly on personal involvement.'

'You ever thought I might not *want* to work any more?'

He was shocked. Little alarms went off all over his skin. 'You kidding?'

'I don't know. I didn't know I was going to say that.'

'You're a real cop, Helen.'

'Yeah, I heard the first time.'

'You don't want to be saddling yourself with—'

'Forget it. I didn't mean it. I just want to say, if you want out, I won't make a fuss or anything. I'll go quietly, officer.'

He stared into his scotch for so long she said again, 'That's all,' just to interrupt the silence. And then she said bitterly, 'I've hardly seen you since I came to London anyhow. Saw more of you coming up from Bristol weekends than I do here. You keep saying you'll take me to see your mother but you never do. There's always some reason why not. It's just I start to feel like a tart or something, some guilty secret. I never felt like that before. I don't like it, John.'

'I don't think of it like that.' He felt sick.

'Yes you do.'

He was glad to see she wasn't going to cry. She was young enough and pretty enough to take refuge in lovely tears, but she knew better. Anyway, it wasn't her way. Underneath that soft blonde flesh there beat a steely policeman's heart.

'I'm not going to be anyone's victim,' she said. 'That's just not me.'

He said, 'Look, Helen. You're right. About me. The way I – I don't let many people under my skin. I'm not comfortable with it.'

'I got under your skin for a while. I know I did.'

He didn't contradict her. He'd used her. That was bad enough. He didn't need to rub her nose in it. He hadn't known at the time he was using her. But that was no excuse. He nodded. 'A-ha.'

'I was a holiday romance,' she said.

He was impressed with her version of events. It was close to the mark. She didn't know the complications, or much of his history, but she'd got the point all right. 'You're not as daft as you look,' he said. He fancied her rotten just at this moment, so much he was in danger of starting the whole thing up again. *Don't do that. She's given you the out. Take it. Thank your lucky stars for her gallantry.* He stood up. 'Want another Ribena?'

'I'll have a G and T.'

'That's going it.'

She showed him her watch. 'I'm off duty now. So are you.'

'I'll stick around, see if Chloe comes back. Want to check her story against Joanne's.'

'Everyone else finishes when the shift finishes – more or less. But not you.'

'A-ha. Is that a double?'

'On second thoughts—' she gave him a level look – 'I think I'll be off back now. I like work but I'm not in love with it like you are, I don't need to be doing it night and day. I'm not afraid of just living now and then.'

He winced. 'One more. Chloe's not back by then I'll give you a lift.'

'No thanks. I'll make my own way.'

He opened the door for her and they stood outside for a moment. 'Sorry,' he said.

She shrugged. 'These things can't be helped. I'll get over it. I'm a big girl now.'

'You're a better man than I am,' he said.

'You're right there, anyway, John. See you. Bye.' And she walked off. Into the gloaming. Up the litter-strewn road winding towards Notting Hill.

And he let her go. He had a strong urge to run after her, grab her in his arms and beg her to stick around. But it was marriage she wanted, she'd as good as said so. And marriage was not for him. He'd found that out early on. Five months his wife had lasted. Come to think of it, Helen reminded him of her. He'd never noticed that before. Soft but capable, all or nothing, wanting him to settle down before he'd settled anything. It screwed you up disappointing someone that badly. Never again. Only one woman he could have said till death us do part. Millie Hale. He shivered. A little cool air after the heat of the day, he told himself. Helen disappeared round the bend. He turned back towards the mews, expecting a feeling of lightness, being unencumbered now, and not getting it. He did not feel unencumbered. He felt weighed down with gloom and guilt. In the bloody gloaming.

He ran up the iron steps, looking lighter than he felt. That bad scene with Helen had screwed up his surveillance. He rang the bell and listened to its thin jangle fade away and then the silence. And then he ran down the steps again and got into the car. He put on a Motown tape. Aretha Franklin cried out, *You make me feel – You make me fee-heel – You make me feel like a natcheral womaahn* . . . He winced again and pulled his earlobe. He experienced his first fine quiver of relief. Of freedom. He would not now have to introduce Helen to his ma. He had been putting it off, Helen had hit it in one: his ma would have taken one look and known all. She'd have been nice as anything, kind as kind. And as soon as the poor girl had gone: 'A wee bit on the young side, John, maybe? She needs someone her own age, not a miserable old cynic like you.'

'Sinner you mean?'

'I do not mean. You're a good man but not for her, poor wee thing. She'd be running rings round you in no time. And it wouldn't be her fault. You just think on.'

Did everyone have this fatal ability to live through whole conversations with their mother, like they'd learned off by heart words which had never even been spoken? Trouble with his ma was she seemed as right to him now as she had seemed when he was ten. She thought he should hitch up with Kate Creech. But that would never happen now. The moment had passed. They had subsided into friends, him and Kate. He'd pop in to see her tomorrow. She'd cheer him up. He found himself smiling thinking of Kate. Aretha Franklin agreed with him: *When mah soul was in the lost-and-found – You came along and clai-aimed it.* He turned on his mobile phone. It rang immediately. It was Bernard from HQ. 'Lee Han, guv. He's started showing signs of life. I couldn't get through to you.'

'Christ. Thanks, mate. My phone was turned off.'

Lights were coming on all over London. Street lights, headlights. He had a pair full blast in his mirror as he turned into Fulham Road. But he found a place to park in a little street just across from the hospital. He got out of the car. And there, just crossing the hospital forecourt, was Chloe Han.

He stood by the car to watch her. She cut through the dim summer air like the blade of a knife, waking people out of torpor, turning their heads. The child in her arms made her twice as exotic – two male fantasies of womanhood, the profane and the sacred, in one. He wondered if she'd have that effect anywhere, even Hong Kong where she came from, where girls like her, for all he knew, were ten a penny. He suspected she would. He watched her go into the hospital. He crossed the road and followed her.

She was a fast mover all right. There was no sign of her in

the atrium. She wasn't on the escalator to the first floor. Both staircases were visible. Nobody on either of them. And she wasn't in the lift. He pushed open the observation room door. But she wasn't there either. Just a nurse with her clipboard.

'When did it happen?' he said.

'About an hour ago. I just popped in for a routine check. I was monitoring the drip feed and I suddenly realised his hand had moved. I asked him could he hear me. He moved his hand again. Like this.' She demonstrated the slightest of gestures.

'Can I question him?'

'Heavens no, it's much too soon. Anyway, you'll have to ask the consultant.'

'Where can I find him-or-her?'

She looked startled, indeed shaken. 'Oh, I'm afraid he'll be in theatre for at least another hour.'

'Can no one else give me an opinion?'

'No one of more consequence than me, I'm afraid.'

'Okay.' He gloomed at his watch. 'I'll wait.'

Through the observation panel, Lee wasn't moving now. Apart from the glug glug of the drip and the undulating lines on the monitor, he might have been a corpse.

The door swooshed open and Chloe swanned in. She barely gave him a glance. She stared through the window at the still form. 'He doesn't look conscious to me.'

'No.'

'The nurse said he was conscious. They rang me up.'

'He just moved his hand a bit – like that.' Bright demonstrated.

'Oh.' She stared through the window again. 'He still can't talk then.'

'Don't sound too disappointed, Chloe.'

She looked at him with her customary disdain. 'It will take him a long time to get well. He might not ever be able to talk.

That's what the doctor said.' Chloe turned her gaze again on unconscious Lee.

'Where's the baby?'

'The nurses keep an eye on him. Out there.'

'Which way did you come up here?'

She turned to him. 'The usual way. Why?'

'What's the usual way?'

'Up the stairs. Chico likes the mobile sculpture. Why?'

'I was right behind you coming in. I lost you.'

Her gaze resumed its opacity. He might have been invisible. How did she do it? She defocused somewhere just in front of or behind or to the side of you, like where you were was empty space. And she let her gaze comfortably rest there. It unnerved even him. Her gaze said, *Well, that figures. That's what you'll always do – lose me. That's how it is.* He felt stupid, humiliated. He did not feel these emotions often. He didn't like it. First Helen and now this cool cow.

She said, 'I went in the Ladies. I had to change him. I guess that was why.'

'Where's the Ladies?'

'The ground floor, near the back.'

Bright sighed. The crypto-corpse lay there just as before, no movement, no sign of life. The nurse came back. She said the consultant was still in theatre but would call Bright later. When he looked round Chloe was gone. He went through to the nurses' station. 'Chloe Han come this way?'

'Just now. Took the baby. Lovely kid. It's a shame.'

Quite what was the shame she didn't say. Everything you could think of round that kid was a shame.

'A sin and a shame,' the charge nurse said.

That too. Bright sighed.

Leaving the burns unit he turned left before the spacious landing and found that to get to the stairs he had to go through a small ante-room with lockers, then push open a stiff fire door. The white stairs hovered over a vertiginous drop where the immense sculpture of coloured leaves swayed gently, from the clear plastic roof to the stone courtyard six or seven floors below. Sure enough, there was a Ladies towards the back on the ground floor. There would be: Chloe's stories always panned out.

He went back up the stairs to the burns unit. The timing for Chloe was just about right. Maybe for once she was telling the simple truth: she had stopped off to change the baby; she had come up all those stairs for the baby's sake. It would make a first. But there was a first time for everything, so they said. He ought to follow her back home, question her again, talk to her about Crabbe's death, make her face a few hard facts. But he was weary and, like Helen had said, he was off duty now. Time to go home. Let the sun go down on another perfect day.

22

She woke up, alone again, but for George, curled up as usual in the crook of her knees. Dan hadn't come out of the study last night, passed out on the day bed, she assumed. She didn't knock as she passed his door, just carried on downstairs with George to make the tea and set out the breakfast things. The smell of last night's burned supper lingered, so, though the morning looked cool and grey, she opened a french window.

She sniffed the chill of autumn in the air; not here yet but coming – not long now. She shivered. The kettle was boiling. She debated whether to take a cup to Dan. She quailed. His coldness now didn't just depress her, it frightened her. What would she do if he left? At one time the idea would have been ludicrous, a question not even askable. And now?

She sat at the table with her tea. Burnt her tongue on the first mouthful, a pleasurable searing of the mouth. And she suddenly knew she was alone in the house.

She ran up the stairs and into the study. The day bed was rumpled but Dan wasn't in it. She went on up. Not in the bathroom, the bedroom, the spare room or her room. She looked out of the window. The car was there, just as he'd left it last night. She opened the wardrobe his side. No way of knowing if he'd taken clothes. Nothing seemed to be missing. She ran into the spare room and opened the cupboard where they kept the suitcases. Again, she couldn't remember how many suitcases they owned, couldn't tell if one was gone. But nothing looked disturbed.

She ran down again to his study and forced herself to stand still, listening to the silence to feel what it might tell her. She shut her eyes and slowed her breathing. *Dan, even now, wouldn't leave without telling me why, not leave as in leave, really leave. Dan wouldn't leave.* But she knew he had left. And without telling her where, or why, he had gone.

She opened her eyes, calmer, at least with a surface calm, like the smooth surface of water just before the sickening surge of the rapids. The wreck of his model house still littered the floor. He hadn't tidied it up. Even more of it was crunched into bits, walked over in the night. *I'm overwrought, imagining dramatic events. He couldn't sleep, he's just slipped out for a walk. His keys?* They were on the big table. She picked them up. His house keys, car keys and office keys. His old office, empty but not sold yet, nor let. She dialled the number. It rang four times then the answerphone kicked in. 'Dan, it's me. If you're there, pick it up, will you? Dan?' She waited till it clicked off and put down the handpiece. She knelt on the floor to gather up the pieces of the model. And from that position she saw that his rucksack had gone.

It wasn't a big rucksack, just a small silly thing, navy blue and red, enough space for a sketch book and a change of clothes. It had always lain there, hunched against the wall, under the table. Dan had always joked it was his getaway bag. But it had really been a joke, Dan being the last man to want to get away. Dan, the happy man. Well, the contented man. The suited man. Another joke: *I'll never have the kind of job where I have to wear a suit.* And he never had. His own man. His own place in the world. Her hand reached out to touch the paler square of carpet where the rucksack had lain.

Jude swayed from her knees on to her side and lay curled up there on the floor. Only George coming to touch her nose with his wet one brought her back. 'Okay, darling.' Her legs were stuck in the foetal position, pins and needles. Getting up, she almost fell. She hobbled down to the kitchen, George trotting ahead, stopping every few treads as he always did to wait for her to catch up.

She gave him his food. Drank down her own cold tea. Shuddered. Then as George's tail disappeared through the cat flap she did what she should have done last night after Chloe's visit, what she had not even considered doing then; she dialled the number John Bright had given her and asked for him.

She took him straight down to the kitchen. Just instinct. She felt safer there. She didn't want him to see Dan's room. She had the idiot notion he would sense Chloe's presence there, and he must not find out about Chloe.

'When'd you last see him?'

'Last night.'

'What time?'

'Oh God, I don't know. It was just starting to get dark. I put the telly on.'

'What did you watch?'

She blanked. 'I'm sorry, I've no idea. The sound wasn't on. I don't know.'

'You watched telly with the sound off. Why?'

'I – don't know.'

'You don't know. You and him were – talking maybe?'

'No. He wasn't here. I mean he was in. But he went upstairs.'

'You were down here; he was upstairs.'

'Yes.'

'What was he doing upstairs? Getting dark, you said – round about nine o'clock then. He was having an early night? Working? What?'

He was rushing her, she hadn't worked out carefully enough what she was going to say. So many things she didn't want him to know. 'I assumed he went to his study,' she said.

'Ground floor, right? That normal? For him? Go up there to work nine o'clock at night?'

'Well, he sometimes did.'

'But not last night?'

'I don't know.'

'And you didn't see him after that? You went to bed at some point, did you?'

'Yes.'

'What time?'

'Midnight. About.'

'Where was he then?'

'I don't know.'

'You didn't look in his study?'

'No.'

'Didn't hear anything?'

'No.'

'And he didn't come to bed, I take it.'

'No.' Her simple blue eyes were under water again.

'Look, I'm trying to find out if last night was just a normal ordinary night or something special happened to make him go off. Look, sit down, you're making me nervous. Why do you think he's disappeared and not just gone out early this morning, see what I'm getting at?'

'His keys are here, his car's here—'

'Were you going out?'

'Not till this afternoon.'

'So he's gone for a walk. You'd be here to let him in.'

'No!'

He made an impatient move towards the door. 'Look, I'm a busy copper, Mrs Craig, I don't have time to waste on this kind of stuff. Why have you got me here? You got something to tell me or not?'

'We had a row!' How inadequate could language get?

'A-ha?' He turned to her and waited, relaxed now she'd said it, giving her time. 'Gonna tell me what about?'

'Oh God.' She turned away and put her hands on the edge of the sink. She faced the window with her back to him. 'I was having a – Lee and I were – It was just a – It was just—' She came to a halt. She gave up.

'You were having a thing with Lee Han, right?' He didn't sound surprised, or shocked, his nasal crake softened to a subtle hum, intimate, kindly even. 'Well, I can't say I'm surprised.'

She turned to him, her street-kid freckled face open and amazed. 'No?'

'No, two beautiful people, sunny afternoons. And your Dan found out last night.'

'Yes.'

'How?'

Her face blanked again. 'How?'

'Why last night?'

She hesitated. 'I told him.'

'You told him. Why? Why last night?'

'He – I—' This man always asked the question you dreaded. She did not want to mention Chloe. *But what if Dan did set fire to Lee and he's gone to harm Chloe, to keep her quiet? I mustn't tell him that Dan was there just before the fire. During the fire. I mustn't tell him about Chloe.* She was paralysed with conflict, her mind an overloaded junction box. And Bright quietly waiting there for her answer. 'With this – awful thing happening to Lee and – everything. I just couldn't – I thought – I suppose – that he ought to know. It wasn't fair on him. That's what I thought. Only, now, I think I should have left it alone.'

'You telling me he hadn't suspected it before?' The small glitzy brown eyes squinted not quite at her, but into her, inside her head.

Her face blanked again. A clear sign she was lying. 'No. He hadn't,' she said.

'It'd come as a bit of shock then.'

'I didn't want him to know because – he told me – once – he'd kill himself if I ever – if I was unfaithful to him. And, you see, he's been very depressed the last two years. His mother died and everything else in his life just fell like dominoes. His partner, Martin—'

'Partner?'

'Not any more, and no, he won't have gone there. Martin pulled out of the partnership six months ago.'

'Why?'

'Because he felt Dan had become a drag on him. You see Dan – we met at college. He was the best student they'd ever had. He was really brilliant. But when he left college he just couldn't get work. He was remarkable but he was too way out. Clients turned down his ideas. They chickened out. See, it's not enough just to have talent. There are things you actually need more: powers of persuasion, the ability to sell yourself, not to shock people too much up front, bring them to accept your ideas gradually. So he set up with Martin. Martin was more kind of run of the mill, sound but not exciting. It looked for a while like that would be good for Dan, like Dan could kind of sneak his ideas into jobs that Martin got for them. It worked for a bit but then they'd lose clients because Dan got sick of compromising, he couldn't bear it. When I left college I joined the partnership and they got their first council project. Well, you can imagine the kind of thing. Dan called them the public lavatories. Every original or beautiful idea quashed because it cost too much. They had to tender low to get the jobs. The lowest tender always won. It was pretty soul-destroying. I couldn't stand it myself. I lasted a couple of years and then opted for garden design. But Dan kept hoping for a breakthrough. He did do a few lovely things but they were small-scale for rich eccentrics and you can't survive on those. Anyway six months ago Martin found another partner out in Suffolk, more congenial – well, dull, actually – you know – like an old dog that knows all the tricks and can hardly be bothered to think, just gets on with the job – same thing you did last time – as long as you come in on the price and on time that's all that matters. Well, Martin and Angela have got two kids. A lot of responsibility—'

'And you've got none.'

'Responsibility?'

'Kids.'

'Just never happened.'

'A-ha.' Bright nodded. For a second the squint totally disappeared, the small brown eyes with the sharp points of light locked with hers, gave her a shock that went through her body like electricity. Then the mask came down again. He got up and opened the french window. 'Come and get some air,' he said.

Standing on the terrace by her side, he said, 'You more successful than him?'

'Than Dan?'

'A-ha.'

'Well, I earn a living, that's all. Since Martin pulled out I've been keeping us, I suppose. Then, a few months ago, Dan got his first project in two years. A house for this really rich guy, made a lot of money in property and – you know – a really nice job. But just the other day the client decided against the bit that for Dan was the essence of the whole design. A beautiful tower with a glass top. It broke his heart.' Jude made a sound like the breaking of her own. She knelt on the grass and bent over, her forehead touching the ground. The red hair fell forward. Her neck awaited the final blow. 'Please find him. Please. I can't bear this, I just can't.'

'We'll find him,' he said. 'Don't worry. Got a picture? A good likeness? Recent? Doesn't have to be a work of art.'

She went back in and scrabbled in the dresser drawer. She

pulled out a folder with some colour snaps. 'I think that one's the most like him. He didn't like it.'

Dan screwed up his eyes in sunlight. His hair was thinning and his stomach bulged a little over his trousers. Apart from that he looked tall and strong and handsome. And his face was sad as hell. Bright said, 'Did he take his passport?'

Her face opened up with the possibility of knowing something, better than nothing. 'Why didn't I think of that?' She ran upstairs. 'It would be in his workroom.'

'Take your time.' He followed her.

When he reached the workroom door she was at the desk by the window, going through the drawers.

'It's just like before he went,' she said. 'The only thing gone is his old rucksack.'

'Describe it.'

'Twelve inches by eighteen, navy blue canvas, red trim. He always called it his getaway bag. I thought it was a joke. I must be a very stupid woman.'

He halted just inside the room. She felt him go stock still. 'What's this?' he said.

She turned from the desk. 'It's the model of his latest project.'

'When did this happen to it?'

'Last night.'

'During the row?'

She hesitated then nodded. Her face was flushed.

Bright said, 'You did this? In anger?' like he didn't believe it.

'No! No, it – just happened somehow.'

'It was quite a row then.'

The tears bubbled out of her eyes. 'Yes, it was.'

'This happened and then what?'

'We went downstairs and . . .'

'Rowed some more?'

'Yes. He wouldn't eat. He was drinking.'

'So I see.' Bright touched the empty whisky bottle with his toe. The glass and the bottle lay on their sides, both on the floor. 'Then you watched telly down there and he went on drinking up here and you went to bed and he wasn't there and you woke up and – etcetera. And you never heard him go out?'

'No.'

'And you went to bed at – what time did you say?'

'About midnight I think.'

'And you didn't look in on him on your way up.'

'No.' To her infinite regret, her expression said.

'Passport,' he said.

'Oh, yes!'

While she hunted through the desk he prowled the room. He stopped at the big work table and leaned over, studying some drawings. He said, 'This name on the bottom of these plans.' His voice had taken on the gimlet effect of an electric masonry drill.

She came to see. 'That's the name of the client.'

'Embrey is the name of the client?'

'Well, that's the name of his company, I think. It's a property company in the City.'

'It is, yeah.' Bright took out his mobile. 'Atkins? That property company, Embrey? Did you get a list of the board of directors? Well, get it. We need to check it out. Now.'

Jude Craig was watching him like a kid expecting a telling-off. 'You know this company?' she said. 'Is there something wrong with it?'

'Where's this house being built?'

'I don't know exactly. Near the Blackwater River in Essex.'

'And this—' he pointed at the crushed model – 'was the model for this?' He pointed at the drawing.

'Yes.'

'So he was building this for the geezer that owns this company?'

It was like someone had switched on a motor inside him. Energy started to hum out of him. 'What name?'

'I don't know his name.'

'He must have written it down somewhere!'

'Yes.' She went back to searching the desk.

'He never mentioned the bloke's name to you?'

'I can't remember!'

'Bloke ever come here? You ever meet him?'

'No. Dan would go up there to see him.'

'To Essex. Would he? When'd he last go?'

'Yesterday. He said.'

Bright heard the doubt in her tone. 'Why would he say it if it wasn't true?'

'I don't know.'

'You got some reason for not believing him?'

'No!' She turned to him with the passport. 'Here it is! He hasn't gone abroad then!'

Bright didn't look convinced. 'Where's he from, your husband? People go back where they came from sometimes.'

'He's a Londoner. His mother was actually born in Gospel Oak.'

'Gospel Oak?' His head came up. He was like a race horse in the starting-gate. 'Where in Gospel Oak?'

'Cleverden Mansions.'

'Cleverden Mansions?' He was looking at her like she might be taking the piss. She didn't know what she had said that had turned him into this quivering thoroughbred, poised for vertical take-off. 'What number Cleverden Mansions?' he said, his voice very quiet.

'Thirty-four.'

'Thirty-four.' He looked incredulous. 'He lived at thirty-four Cleverden Mansions?'

'She lived there all her life, his mother,' Jude said. 'She died there too. Refused to go to a hospice, said she wanted to die in her own bed.'

'And the flat? What happened to it?'

'It was a council flat. She was just a tenant. I suppose it reverted to the council?'

'Your husband buy it for her? Letting it out for a big rent since she popped her clogs?'

'Dan wouldn't do that.'

'A-ha? That right?' Bright got on his mobile again. 'Maggie? Check with the council. Thirty-four Cleverden Mansions, Gospel Oak. Do they still own it or has it been sold off?'

'Dan wouldn't have bought it. He doesn't approve of selling off council flats.'

Bright didn't respond, just watched her.

'He gave her furniture to Shelter or Crisis or something,' she said. 'He didn't want reminders.'

'Why? Didn't he get on with her?'

'Oh, the opposite. He adored her. He hasn't been the same since she died.' She swallowed an upsurge of emotion. 'She was ill for over a year before she— just waiting really. It was awful for him.'

'Did you get on with her?' His attention was not on Jude; his eyes jazzed round the room like a house fly, buzz, buzz, alighting here, buzz, buzz, there, buzz, buzz, moving on, buzz, buzz.

Jude went on anyway: 'I – tried. But she didn't like me. When Dan was around she seemed friendly to me. But if I was alone with her—' Jude shivered – 'she just didn't speak to me. I think she hated me. Well, she'd have hated anyone Dan loved, it wasn't personal in a way.'

Bright was prowling the room. His manner looked casual but wasn't. 'What did Dan think about that?'

'He never really believed me. Thought it was my fault. She had this reputation for helping everyone, everyone's mother-figure, you know? Salt of the earth cockney woman. The church was packed at her funeral. The police had to control the traffic in Lady Margaret Road. Just me she couldn't like. Maybe it was chemical. There are those things.'

Bright was standing close to her. 'Yes, there are.'

George came between them, brushing both their legs with his winding tail. Jude bent to rub his face with the back of her hand, breaking Bright's gaze, strange, concentrated, opaque.

Bright said, 'Where's his address book?'

'I've rung all the friends he might have gone to. He's not there.'

'They could be lying for him.'

'I didn't get that impression.'

'What's the address of this Martin bloke?'

Jude plunged. 'I don't think he'll have gone anywhere that I would think of looking.'

But he ignored that and she gave him the address and he wrote it down and then she found a battered old black book in the top drawer of the desk and handed it over.

Bright flipped through it. He stopped at a page, then at another, but moved on. He sighed. 'I'll take this with me, okay?'

At the door he said, 'Were you in bed with Lee Han the afternoon he was burned?'

Her face didn't show guilt, just sadness and weariness. 'Yes.'

'You went to bed, then you had a shower, to wash him off before you came home. Was he in bed when you left?'

'Yes. He was fast asleep.'

'You lied to me. You lied to the police in a murder inquiry.'

The innocent blue eyes dilated. 'I couldn't risk Dan finding out. I wouldn't have lied otherwise. I wanted to tell him before you did. And now look.'

George jumped on to the table and butted her with the top of his head. She held his head with both hands and stroked his ears with her thumbs. 'It's okay, George, don't fret.'

'A-ha.' Bright controlled the impulse to stroke her the way she was stroking the cat. 'You ever seen him?' He shoved a picture in front of her, a fat man with a sweaty sheen to his skin. 'You ever seen him?'

She shook her head.

'Your husband ever mention the name Crabbe? Ever?'

'No. You asked me about him before. Why? Who is he?'

'Nobody.' Bright sighed. 'He's nobody, poor sod.' He put the picture back in his pocket. 'Keep looking for the name of that client.' He pointed to the detritus on the floor. 'Ring me the minute you find it. And anything else you think of. You've got my card. Ring me. Okay?'

'Okay.'

'We'll find him. Like you said to George there – don't you fret.'

As a policeman – for what he might find out about Dan – he terrified her. But – the paradox – he was the only thing in the world just now – apart from George – that made her feel safe. It was bad seeing him go, so lightly, down the steps.

She put some food down for George. She fixed the cat flap so he could get in and out. She stood thinking a moment. She wrote a note and left it on the kitchen table. Then she went upstairs.

In the cloakroom she had a wee, brushed her teeth and picked up her bag. George was sitting at the top of the basement stairs with that astounded look he gave her whenever she unexpectedly went out. 'I won't be long, George, I promise. I'll be back tonight.'

23

Bright passed down the plastic-bagged exhibits – Dan Craig's passport and the photo Jude had given him. 'Get these finger-printed, and order some copies of the picture. Get them circulated.' And the address book. 'Go through this with the old fine fang comb. Methodical. Every single name. Any whiff of anything, check it out. Now listen.' He gave them the run-down: Jude Craig's affair with Lee Han, Dan Craig's long-term depression, the loss of his big project, and the row last night. 'So yesterday,' he said, 'was not the happiest day in Dan Craig's life.'

'Bit of a coincidence, though, isn't it, guv?'

'What?'

'Poor old Crabbe cops it and then Daniel Craig does a runner?'

'Any connection there?'

'We never even interviewed him over the Lee Han burning.'

'No one saw him at the scene. We had no excuse.'

'He had no alibi.'

'The only connection between him and Lee Han was his wife.'

'They were having it away – that gives him a motive.'

'She says he didn't know till last night.'

'She's been screwing this guy for weeks and he didn't suspect? Come off it.' He felt Helen's hostility like a fist in the face.

'Is she genuine?' Cato said. 'The gardener?'

'She's genuine.'

He caught the look that flicked between Cato and Helen. He said, 'Maggie? Did you ring the council about that flat?'

Maggie came over. She gave Bright a slip of paper. He read the message. 'Yes!' he said. 'Thanks, Mag.'

'Any time, boss.' She grinned at him in a reassuring matey way. He felt grateful. He also felt humiliated that for the first time in his life he needed these signals of trust. He held up the memo Maggie had given him. 'Four years ago,' he said, 'Daniel Craig bought his mother's flat off the council for twenty-five thousand pounds.'

'Twenny-five thou? You can't get a rabbit hutch for that!'

'His mother had lived there forty-five years. You get points for staying the distance.'

'Could he afford twenty-five grand?'

'I'm coming to that.' He took a piece of A4 paper and a big red magic marker and he wrote some words. 'You wanna talk about coincidence?' he said. 'This is what we call coincidence.' He lifted the paper and turned it to face them. Silence fell. Bernard and Atkins came closer to get a look.

At the top of the page he had written:

34, Cleverden Mansions

Cato took his pipe out of his mouth. 'Thirty-four Cleverden Mansions? Isn't that where—?'

'A-ha.' Under the heading, Bright wrote:

Jason Crabbe
Daniel Craig
Michael Brennan

Cato said, 'Okay, Brennan and Crabbe are linked to thirty-four Cleverden Mansions but how come Dan Craig?'

'That is the flat he grew up in. That is the flat he bought off the council.'

'You're kidding.'

'The same block where Brennan grew up?'

'Different block but it's all Cleverden Mansions, innit?'

'They're the same age just about, Brennan and Craig. Kids always know each other, place like the Mansions.'

'Craig's connected to Brennan? Jeesus!'

'For the last two years Brennan's kept one of his toms there. *That actual flat.* It's the centre for a lot of dealing, as we know. And quite a few of Crabbe's juicier pictures were taken there.'

'That could be coincidence.'

'How many coincidences turn out to be coincidence?'

'Think he's bought the place off Craig, guv?'

'Maggie? How long you gotta own an ex-council property before you're allowed to sell on?'

'Two years, isn't it?'

'Check with Land Registry. See if it's changed hands since Craig bought it.'

'Land Registry take forever. It all has to be done by post.'

'Goose them up. Tell them it's a murder inquiry; I need it—'

'—yesterday. I know.'

Atkins said, 'That Embrey Properties, owns Lee Han's place?'

'A-ha? You checked the personnel?'

'Brennan's name's not on the board of management. Not any of his usual nomdiplumes either.'

'What are they?' Helen said.

'Reynolds is one. Ryan . . .'

Bright's shoulders drooped. 'Ah, well, that woulda been too good.'

Cato said, 'Embrey! Em, that's M for Michael. B, R, E, that's the first half of Brennan and R, E, Y, that's the first half of Reynolds!'

'That would be just like him, put his fucking signature on the company but not be down as the fucking owner.'

'But—' Atkins said, 'you wanna know somink? The company lawyer is down as J. French of French, Son & Barber.'

'Yesss!' The muted cheer went right round the table.

Helen said, 'What's the significance?'

Bernard explained. 'Julian French is Brennan's lawyer. Gets him off of everything. Bent as a wire coat hanger.'

Bright looked breathless, blinded, like a searchlight was shining in his eyes. 'This house Craig was designing?' he said. He paused. They waited. He swallowed. 'His big project that fell through yesterday? Guess the name of the client he was doing it for.'

'Shit, guv . . .'

'You got it. Embrey Properties.'

'Jeesus . . .'

'No name of any individual to be found. And no address. But his wife told me more or less where it is.'

'And where is that, guv?' Cato was enjoying this.

'Near the Blackwater River. In Essex.'

They were all laughing now. 'God, that's original for a villain.'

'Must have been getting lonely in London now they've all moved out.'

'He can't have been there long,' Bernard said. 'We'd have known, wouldn't we?'

'That Triad shooting a couple of years ago up there. Wonder if he was there then?'

Bright said, 'Roger Gould mentioned that.' He caught Cato's eye.

Cato didn't move a muscle. He said, 'They didn't think any Brit villains were involved with that Triad business at the time.'

'Wrong,' Bernard said. 'They thought there was; they just couldn't get any evidence.'

'I got the files out, guv.' Cato dipped into a plastic stacking box and brought out a scruffy folder.

'The Chinks used to confine themselves to Chinatown. They were no bother in those days.'

'There's just no discipline any more.'

They all laughed. Except Bernard. And Bright, who was frowning down at the table, leafing through the folder Cato had handed him.

Bernard said, 'You got a theory, guv?'

'No. Just another little diagram.' Bright slapped the sheet of A4 on to the table. Under the heading *Embrey Properties* he'd written:

> *Lee Han/Chloe Han – tenants of Embrey Properties.*
> *Julian French – lawyer for Embrey Properties.*
> *Daniel Craig – architect for Embrey Properties.*

'I'm expecting a call from my old mate Superintendent Derek Cooper at Essex HQ.' Bright whipped through the file, reading a few words here and there, stopped a few pages before the end, slowed down and read a page again. They waited. He looked up. He said, 'At the time of the Essex Triad shooting, Brennan was reported having a meal at a Chinese restaurant in Colchester. He was with a C1 male, tall, well built, curly brown hair thinning on top.'

'That's Dan Craig, guv!'

'The curly-haired guy was Brennan's alibi. They were there all evening; other people eating there said so. The guy was not named or traced; Brennan wouldn't name him, said, "this is a legit guy, a respectable citizen, don't get his name mixed up with me, wouldn't do him any good." Essex CID thought that was a fair exchange for info Brennan supplied them with in connection with the Triad shooting.'

'What info?'

'Doesn't say. But it helped put them away.'

'Where they banged up? Here or China?'

'Here. Ex-Hong Kong Brit citizens, weren't they?'

'That right?'

'Like Lee Han.'

'And Chloe Han.'

'Call for you, John.' Maggie gave him the phone.

The buzz died down.

'Yeah. Hi, Del. Good man.' Bright listened. 'A-ha, a-ha. Thing is, we've heard Brennan's having a house built on your patch. Using one of his nomdiplumes probably. Know anything about it?' He listened. Made a fist, pulled the fist down hard, released a thumb, which he showed to the team. 'Del, you're a hero. Any time. Call it in. Be down to see you one day soon. Book a table, mate. See you. Yeah.' He cut off the phone, took his magic marker and to the bottom of the *Embrey* diagram added *Brennan!!!* 'Brennan, using the name Reynolds, acquired – acquired – this bit of land right on the Blackwater River a year ago. Nice wide bit of the estuary. Got his own mooring and a nifty cruiser. He's living in this old farmhouse while the new place gets built. No new house yet, but a team of locals clearing the undergrowth, bulldozers, mechanical diggers. Been going on for months. Very slow. And the architect is definitely Craig. My old mate Del Cooper has been keeping an eye out. Craig visited the site once a week or so last few months, till this last week. Word is Brennan dropped him from the job.'

'Your mate hasn't seen Craig the last few days then?'

'Hasn't been looking, has he?'

'He will now?'

'He certainly will now.'

'Has he paid Brennan a visit?'

'No, but he gets the word.'

'Anything going down?'

'Brennan's always got a few of the lads with him. And his oily lawyer Mr French. Del'd normally have a whiff of anything being set up. He says there's no word out. Just looks like the building work going on as normal.'

'You can dig a grave quite fast with a bulldozer,' Helen said.

Everything stopped. No ribaldry. No sly *there speaks the innocent abroad* grins. You could drive a bulldozer slow and steady through the pause. Bright said, 'Let's hope Brennan hasn't put Craig to an early rest . . .'

'Have we got enough on Brennan for a warrant, guv?'

'Vague connections with all the personnel in the case? Talk about circumstantial. CPS would laugh in my mush.'

'Maybe we could just be passing and pay him a call though, guv?'

Atkins came back in and started to pass round copies of Dan Craig's picture, the sad boyish face multiplied round the table.

Bright caught Helen's eye, first time since their painful chat. She turned away. He went to his office to check the reports on Crabbe. Cause of death: heroin overdose. No one had seen anything or anybody suspicious. None of the fingerprints from the scene were on police files. Poor old Fatman. His amateur porno pictures had given a bit of innocent pleasure to the many who had now viewed them. The one tenuous link between him and Brennan was Joanne, a tom, a user, and a snout, who would never give evidence in court because she knew the score.

Poor cruds like Crabbe were the casualties in the true meaning of the word: casually swatted, like you'd swat a fly, because it might become a nuisance. The inquest was tomorrow. The chance of getting a verdict of unlawful killing and bringing his killers to court was zero. But if he couldn't get them for Crabbe he'd sure as hell get them for something.

He checked his watch. His brain was pulsating with theories. He needed action. Sitting at a desk, waiting, was no life for him. He stuck his head out of his office to see who was still in the CID room. *Good*. 'Cato?' he said.

24

That afternoon the weather broke. Rain turned the windscreen into a waterfall. At the Blackwall Tunnel they turned off on to the A13. Not a bad road down along the river, maybe a mile inland. Not that you could see the river today. Driving through Dagenham you could hardly see Dagenham Motors. Even the blue and grey striped Ford factory, nearly half a mile of it, was almost invisible. But not unsmellable, the pollution rich, like a fist up your nose. And the trucks and tankers hurling spray.

Past Rainham Steel and suddenly they were in the marshes, flat, with hassocks of grass, humps of bramble bushes. The rain thinned to show a battalion of pylons marching through the mist, along the Thames, over to the right, and seagulls swooping on the fields in gangs. Approaching Basildon, Bright said, 'We want the A130 to Chelmsford.'

Not such a good road, this, only two lanes with a roundabout a minute, but quieter. A hand came out of a parked van and floated a food carton out on the breeze. 'That's a lay-by,' Bright said, 'where you stop to drop your litter.'

Not a sound out of Cato. He'd been silent all the way. Bright put on his CD of Marvyn Gaye. Cato took his pipe out of his mouth. 'I can't stand that stuff.'

'Can't stand Motown? What's the matter with you?'

'Just don't like it.'

'What you want? Beethoven's violin concerto?

'Wouldn't mind.'

Bright switched to Radio 4 and kept his mouth shut for a few miles. Trying to see through the swags of moving water was hard enough without trying to shout over the crackling newsreaders.

'Anyway,' Cato said, 'it's hardly the music of your youth.'

'No, it's my ma. She had it on all the time when I was a kid.'

'That explains a lot.'

Bright negotiated a tidal wave thrown over the car by a Triton truck. 'A-ha,' he said. 'I was brainwashed.' He threw Cato the map. 'We want the turn-off to Battlesbridge. Jude Craig said the site was somewhere between there and the Blackwater River and not that far from the sea.'

Cato sat up and studied the map. 'Can't see a thing through this waterfall,' he said.

'Oh, is it raining?'

'Don't take the piss, guv—'

'No, I gotta watch that these days.'

Cato didn't rise to that. 'Next exit'll be best.'

Battlesbridge looked like a bit of old Holland in the rain, a tall granary-type building, black wood, a bridge over the River Crouch, little boats, village green in front of the long low clapboard pub. The Barge Inn. It looked inviting, the Barge Inn, but they'd better carry on.

The roundabout outside Battlesbridge was an obstacle course, roads going off in ten directions. They had to go round twice, passing the railway station, its timetable stuck on a post. 'That's interesting, there's a railway.'

'With trains what's more.'

'Follow the railway, Cat.'

'Can't see Brennan coming down by train.'

'No, but it's – I dunno – for a city lad, know what I mean? Like a connection with civilisation.'

Cato thought he was nuts but he shrugged. 'All right, Fambridge next.'

Even the rain seemed quieter in the lanes. The battering eased up. Cato navigating, the road wound and wriggled, banks and hedges bulging with summer, weighed down with water, slapping the sides of the car. Outside Fambridge dinky pseudo cottages stood in small estates. 'They turned it into the suburbs,' Bright said. 'Not a likely spot for your friendly neighbourhood gangster.'

'Never know these days. You're probably not allowed to live here unless you're a gangster.'

'They probably have an entrance exam.'

Down at the river, ancient clapboard houses, boats again and an old clapboard inn. Black marsh and a little house right out on the marsh. It wasn't right. Didn't have the right feel. You could go no further, except into the river, so they turned back.

A couple of villages wavered through the veil of water. One had a village green and a pub painted white. 'This looks promising.' Bright stopped. 'Least they got real beer.'

'But no customers,' Cato said, looking at the empty car-park.

Low ceiling, knobbly beams, tongue-and-groove half-way up the walls, pictures of old Thames barges. A pint of Old Speckled Hen and the best cheese sandwich he'd ever had. Even Cato started to look a bit human. 'That's real Montgomery Cheddar, that is, guv.'

'That right?'

'That's the only cheddar still made with the traditional method.'

'Where d'you get it?'

'Know that healthfood place up Brecknock Road, the Bumblebee?'

'A-ha.'

'I get it there. Every Friday. Denise'd kill me if I didn't bring some home Friday night.'

Bright spread the map out on the end of the table.

The guy who'd served them looked over his shoulder. Slim, fair, designer jeans, chenille sweater, he didn't look the landlord type. 'Where you heading for?' he said.

'Lived round here long?' Bright asked him. Always answer a question with a question.

'No. Got out the rat race three years ago. Bought this place. Did it up.'

'How's it going?'

They all looked round the empty bar.

'It's worse today 'cause of the rain, but I couldn't say business was booming.'

'Why's that? Good ale. Great food. Nice old place. What more do they want?'

'They want lager and video games and plastic music. I thought there'd be enough people tired of all that. I'm beginning to think I was wrong. If it doesn't pick up in the next few months we're in deep shit. My wife already goes out to work. She's more or less keeping us at the moment. Computer skills. What you need these days.'

'What you do before?'

'Had my own building firm. Too much hassle. Still, seems to be one kind of hassle or another whatever you do.'

'Talking of building . . .' Bright said. 'Friend of mine – architect – been working on a project down here – on the Blackwater River – for this businessman.'

The landlord's face closed up, shut down. He picked up a cloth and wiped the spotless bar, then he turned away. 'Er, sorry, I think that was the phone, I won't be long—'

'Look, mate—'

'Now listen, I don't want any trouble. I told your boss—'

'Hey!' Bright shouted.

The landlord stopped in his tracks.

Bright waved his ID under his nose. 'We're coppers. Metropolitan Police, okay?'

'Oh Christ, I'm sorry.' He raised both hands and backed off. 'I thought you were—' He relaxed, shook his head. 'I came here to get away from scum like that.'

'Want to tell us what happened?'

'They came in here a few times. I've been around, I know their kind. They put it about they're legit, you know, good business types, but you can recognise them a mile off. Well, I can. But they're a bit of excitement to the locals. And they're a source of work. They've had a small army working on the site clearing the land, lads who've had no work to speak of for years. And he pays well, all cash in hand. Well, he came in here with a few cronies once or twice, fine, no problem, spent money, caused no trouble. Then he offered me some dodgy stuff. I'm in a fix, right? If I accept, I'm transgressing the law, and I don't want any trouble, new business, all that; if I refuse I'm putting myself in bad with the bad boys.'

'What you do?'

'I declined. Gracefully. No hard feelings, all that, but—'

'What was he offering?'

'Continental lagers, fags, spirits half the usual price, you name it.'

'A-ha. And when you refused?'

'All they did was – they were at that table, over there in the corner – all they did – they stood up. In the middle of their meal. I'm at the table taking orders for drinks. The boss guy stands up. They all stand up. They button their jackets. They don't say a word. Not a word. The boss guy looks at me. Never takes his eyes off me. Takes a big wad of notes out of his pocket. Puts it down on the table. Says that should cover it. Goes past me like that, like I have to step back. And they all walk out, dead slow, dead casual. Only, like, the place goes silent. They walk right the way across there to the door and out they go. That's all. No violence but I – well, I tell you I had the shakes for days.'

'They never come back?'

'No. But nor did anyone else.'

'That's how it works, mate, corruption. You don't have to use the power, you just have to show them you've got it.' Bright put Dan Craig's photo on the bar.

'I know him.'

'You do?'

'He came in here a few times. Quite a big guy but not a hard man, you know? Curly hair. About forty? Yes, that's him. Haven't seen him in a while.'

Bright put the photo away. 'When was the last time?'

'Weeks ago. Three weeks at least.'

'Ever see him with our gangster friends?'

The guy thought a minute. 'I'm not sure. I couldn't say for certain. If he was in here at the same time it'd be a few months back when business was booming. I couldn't say.'

'Carry on thinking about it, right? I need to know.'

'Sure.'

'And you're sure you haven't seen him for three weeks?'

'I'm sure, mate, believe me. He was my only customer for a couple of weeks before. Apart from the vicar. She sees herself as a Christian martyr. Sits in here drinking her half, thinking her flock will follow her example, ready to die for her faith.'

'What name's our friend the businessman using down here?'

'Reynolds.'

'Not inventive, are they, guv?'

'Not with names.'

'They'll know you've been in here.' The landlord looked sick. 'It's not like London. Everyone knows everything.'

'I'm sorry about that, mate. We'll go, soon as we know where to go. Gonna tell us where he hangs out?'

He traced the route on Bright's map. 'Out of here, turn right, keep on for a couple of miles, terrible road, turn right again and keep going, towards the river. It's round there somewhere. I've never been there myself but I know more or less.'

'Thanks, mate, 'preciate it. Here's my card. Get in touch right away, if anything—'

'I will if I can.' He put the card in his pocket without looking at it. 'Don't mention me for Christsake if you find him.'

'You joking?'

'Well—'

'You're not the only one who'd like to see the back of him.'

They turned out of the high street. Small Georgian brick houses gave way to Victorian cottages and then fifties, sixties and seventies developments. They passed the railway station. Then, just as the pub bloke had said, the houses stopped, and the road got worse. Cracks, fissures, craters, sudden volcanic hillocks. Just the kind of driving Bright enjoyed. Cato hit the roof. Literally. He held on to the dash after that, swaying and swinging and rocking from side to side. 'Pity there's no bends,' Bright said, 'just to make it interesting.' Straight as a die the road ran, out towards the sea. And flat, flat, flat. No hedges, no hills. One tree standing up, jumped out of the mist at them and was swallowed up again.

Then they came up against a big barrier gate, across the road cutting off their route. A board said *Private Road. No access without permission* in neat official-looking lettering.

'Funny,' Cato said. 'Doesn't show this on the map.'

'Maybe it's an old map.'

'Rubbish, it's well up to date.'

To the left a cart track traipsed across flat fields. To the right the road looked better than the one they'd come on. They turned right.

The road wasn't just better; it was good. Smooth, newly

surfaced, with neat margins. Bright got this prickling all over his skin, prickles like little icicles, all over. 'This is looking possible.'

Cato agreed with a glance at Bright. 'Bloody bleak, though,' he said. 'Who'd want to live here?'

'Like you say: who'd want to live here? That's the whole point, right? Place is like a desert.'

Another noticeboard loomed, up on a pole. Same as the last. Same words: *Private Road. No access without permission.* 'Can you do this? Just put up a notice on a public road saying it's private?'

Cato peered at the map. 'Definitely looks like a public highway to me.'

Half a mile of good road and a gaggle of biggish brown birds burst out of the field and dawdled along in front of the car.

'What are they?' Bright said.

'Pheasants, guv.'

'Pheasants don't look like that.'

'How d'you know what pheasants look like?'

'I've seen them hanging up outside the butcher's. They're bigger and they're coloured.'

'And they're dead.'

'No wonder! Out the way! Fuckin' idiots, want to get yourselves run over? If you kill one by accident do you get to keep it?'

'No, but the car behind can.'

'That's a good law. Hunt in pairs. One in front does the killing; one behind collects.'

A bigger bird with a proud tail in brilliant colour now ran out. 'Now that's a cock pheasant, see?' Cato shouted. 'That's the male!'

The females all huddled towards the side of the road now, pottering about in the stubble. Bright said, 'They haven't heard of women's liberation yet.' He drove on round a bend and they saw some buildings sticking up out of the flat empty land.

Cautious, he slowed down. A big old house stood on the left

of the road, with barns and sheds, and three white ducks walked in a line towards a pond. 'Romantic picture,' he said. 'Nice old-fashioned English farm.' He slowed to a snail's pace. 'No one about but the ducks.'

'Well,' Cato said, 'in this weather that's no wonder.'

'Maybe.'

Nothing happened. No one came out. No one even came to a window. He didn't even get that feeling he was being watched. Just this weird empty silence. But the house didn't look empty. A kid's tricycle lay on its side in the grass by the front door. If this was a nice prosperous farm, farmer, wife, kids, where were they all? Not even a curtain flicked. And why the official notices with the veiled threat? Didn't fit. Those cold pinpricks just under the skin, Bright got them strong again, driving slow through that farm and on round the bend.

The rain was easing off. You could see the blank landscape now, miles of it, and sense the river ahead. You couldn't hide in these lowlands. No hills, no valleys, no houses, no hedges, just flat black wet fields in all directions. 'I hate the bloody country,' Bright grumbled. 'Gives me the creeps. Don't they grow anything round here?'

'They've had an early harvest, all the sunshine. Bet they're glad they got it in before the weather broke.'

'You're not telling me you're a farm lad, Cat?'

Cato looked sheepish. 'My grandad. But my da gave it up. No money in it. No life. But that was up in the hills. Not like this. Couldn't live in this. You'd go mad. Christ, guv!'

'My God, a hill!'

They crested the sudden small rise and over it they saw trees. Not one tree on its own but a clump, not what you could call a wood exactly but definitely a copse, standing either side of the road, and in between stood a gate, a high wide metal barrier, and that notice again. Same white-painted board, same black lettering. *No access without permission.* 'Looks like we shoulda got permission, Cat.'

'That right, guv?'

They got out of the car. The barrier gate was not locked, just a square strip of metal looped over the side post. Bright lifted the loop and pushed. The heavy gate swung easily back. It did not make a sound. Not the slightest creak.

The rain had stopped and there was no wind. The trees sighed. A throng of seagulls screamed to a circling halt and landed on the field like stones. The silence lapped them again.

The feeling they got was of people watching. Hiders in the trees or farther off. The feeling a gun might go off. Accidental, like, a shotgun, just taking a potshot at a pheasant and missed. Two dead coppers from the Met. What a damn shame.

'Do we drive in or walk, guv?'

Bright whispered. 'Why you whispering?'

Cato laughed. A weird sound. Bright realised he'd never heard it before. 'Dunno, guv,' he said, normal voice.

'We drive in.'

'Wish this was a tank.'

'Wish we were armed.'

'Thought you hated firearms, guv.'

'I do.'

They got back in the car. Bright let the handbrake off and glided forward, free-wheeling, soundless, using the downward slope. The trees went on farther than you'd think, and they were thick, twined with ivy and brambles. Anything could be hiding in there.

The road still had the appearance of a public road, resurfaced recently. It went straight downhill between the trees and then they saw light ahead. And then they inhabited the light. A clearing. Tree stumps and cut-down undergrowth.

Clearing was the word. Five hundred square yards of

devastated ground. Like it had been shaved. White wood-chip litter and wet leaves, flat as a pancake, with a strip of trees left standing around the perimeter enclosing it.

There was no one about, just two machines, a crane and a digger thing – big metal mouth with teeth – both standing still. The rain. There wouldn't be anyone about, would there? A shriek shredded the silence. They both jumped and a crow flapped black across the windscreen and landed, lurching like an awkward bony old priest in a cassock, jabbing at the ground with its predatory beak.

Cato laughed again. 'We been watching too many horror movies, guv.'

'This looks like the chainsaw bloody massacre all right.' Bright turned the engine on now the ground was flat, but stayed in neutral, rolling quietly along. He drove beyond the tree rim and the road curved again. He rounded the bend and there stood the remains of a house.

It was a big smooth grey cube, the brick or stone concreted over. The slate roof was damaged at one end, ribs showing. It looked like someone had started to demolish the thing and given up, left one end caving in while the rest stayed solid as rock.

'Looks like a bunker.'

'Not exactly your seaside bungalow, no. I see why he'd want a new one built.'

No one came running. No one shouted to know their business. No one appeared at a window. Nothing happened at all. Bright swerved to the right and drove down the side, following a concrete wing that jutted out from the back, then a high wall thirty feet long. And then a high grass bank cut off the way, rising steep in front of them and stretching to either side as far as they could see. They could drive no farther. He stopped.

They got out, keeping their backs to the car. Cato stayed by the vehicle while Bright ran fast up the grass bank. He crested it and there on the other side, a silver shock, ran the river, a vast delta here. Also unexpected, a landing stage, thirty foot square, built snug into the grass bank. He walked out on to the thick railway sleepers. Heavy chain fence looped between metal rods on either side.

He went to the edge and looked over. It was a long way down to the water. The railway sleepers rested on thick round iron stanchions, pretty old, pretty grim, streaked with green slimy stuff, bedded in black mud with stones and broken bottles sticking up out of it. It wasn't nice down there. He shuddered and turned round to look inland.

From here he had a view of the back of the house. The high wall enclosed a courtyard nearly forty foot square. The courtyard was not your romantic cobbled job. No dinky French tables with sun umbrellas. This courtyard meant business. Then, maybe thirty yards beyond the house, along the river, he saw a boat that also meant business, moored to a long narrow jetty with a lithe and useful look. Bright wasn't that well up on boats, but the prow of this one jutted forth like the nose of a swordfish. It looked like it could put on a fair turn of speed.

Something caught him, made him look back at the house. A movement at a window? He saw no movement now. He could have imagined it. But he hadn't. No more movement. Dead blank windows. Not a soul stirred. Dirty grey gulls shrieked now and then, enough to frighten you out of your wits. That was all. A glob of rain landed on his face, then another, it was starting again. He went down the slope again to Cato. And that was when the man appeared. With the dog.

The dog was a pit bull on a thick leather leash. Straining, slavering, its good-humouredly mindless face looked forward to the next mouthful of raw flesh. It was hard to take your eyes off it. The owner on the other end of the leash was a country-looking geezer, shapeless but strong with big dirty capable hands. He wore a parka, and one of those hats with earflaps like a Canadian woodsman. He had a big florid face with small eyes like his dog. 'Private,' he said.

'Sorry, mate?'

'Can't you read?'

'What's private?'

'The road. Says so all along.'

'Er, 'cording to my Ordnance Survey map . . .' Cato reached into the car. The shotgun now appeared from under the man's right arm. It was aimed at Cato.

'Watch it, mate.' Bright spoke in his quietest nasal purr. The man didn't glance Bright's way, but the dog did. Bright didn't say anything else.

Cato turned round, slow, with the map in his hand. ''Cording to my map it says this road is a public highway, public right of way. I don't think you can just put up notices just like that declaring it private. Can you? You can't do that where I come from anyway.' Cato put on the Geordie real broad. 'Not very friendly, that, is it?'

'This land's private.'

'But look, mate, look at the map. The road comes right down to here and it says "ferry" like, just here. So it must be public if there's a ferry here. Course it must.'

'No ferry. Hasn't been no ferry for years. This land's private.'

'Sounds like this land's private, Niki.'

'That right? My map's out of date then? Oh, that's bad, isn't it? I'll have to get in touch with them, tell them it's all changed. You the owner then, are you?'

'Why?'

'Oh no, nothing. Just must be a nice place to have. Right on the river here. Nice views when you can see them. Terrible weather, though, eh? For the time of year like.'

'So you better get back on the road and get on your way.'

'So who owns it then?'

The man was surprised to see Bright so close. Cato's daft antics with the map had momentarily diverted him. 'Who wants to know?' he growled, showing his bottom teeth, just like his dog.

'Is it Mr Reynolds by any chance?' Bright looked relaxed, friendly.

The gun arm tensed. 'Who wants to know, I said.'

'Take it easy, mate. We're old friends of his from Gospel Oak. Well, I am. This is my cousin Nick from Sunderland. He fancied a day out so I said let's go and see old Mick Reynolds, haven't seen him in a while, heard he's moved out Essex way. So here we are. Well, that's if this is the right place, and I think it is – Niki here might look daft but he can read a map, know what I mean?'

The man's little eyes slid sideways and back, sideways and back, like metronomes. The dog's neck bulged with the strain on the leash. It grunted, its big tongue lolling, saliva frothing. Bright and Cato stood relaxed as anything, with amiable daft expressions, waiting. The man elbowed the gun and dug a fist into his pocket. Bright and Cato tensed but not so's you'd notice. The man brought out a mobile phone and stuck it between his ear and the furry earflap. He muttered, 'Yeah . . . S'right . . . Two . . . Gospel Oak? . . .' He listened and nodded, pretty serious. 'Woss yer names?' he said.

'John and Niki. He doesn't know Niki. But he knows me. We're old mates. I lived in Cleverden Mansions. Went to school with him. Come on, he knows John. Let me talk to him.' Bright stepped forward. The dog leapt. The man hauled it up on to its hind legs. He controlled it – just. Bright stepped back. The man muttered again into the phone and listened again, hard. He jerked his head. 'He says all right.'

He turned and plodded up the track the way he'd come, along

the length of the high grey wall. The dog kept jumping, nearly throttling itself to look back over its shoulder, snarling.

'It's got us marked out.'

'What for?'

'Its next meal,' Bright said.

'So has its master.'

'Which one?'

25

They said Suffolk was flat. They were wrong. The road rolled up and down, winding round fields of corn prostrated by rain. They also said modern farming had killed off all the wild flowers. Here too they were wrong. The banks were rampant with poppies and purple loosestrife and ten species of wild flowers she ought to know the names of but to her shame did not.

She achieved her last turning, a lane off a lane off a lane, then the entrance to Bede's Farm. A long drive with muddy ruts opened out to a big flat area where a smart jeep and a scruffy Renault Clio were parked. The long low house to the left, and a long low barn, joined to the house at a right angle, a door in the crook of the angle. Jude knocked

Angela came to the door. She was pregnant. Dan hadn't mentioned that. Two boys tumbled round her. Nice blond kids with that classy pale hair like silk, flopping over their brows. 'Hello, Jude.' Angela looked tired.

Then Martin emerged into the hallway from the barn. He looked worried and compassionate and he welcomed her in. 'Shut up, chaps, leave her to get her breath.' They went through a lovely room with floorboards a foot wide, polished dark oak. The boys slid ahead in their socks. The ceilings were low and low the windows, with small leaded panes, in thick walls with deep window seats.

The kitchen had an Aga, naturally, and a big farmhouse table and an oak dresser. The floor was brick, herringbone-pattern.

The window was a low oblong on to the weedy parking area where she had left the van.

She and Martin sat at the table while Angela made tea. The boys went yelling off up the stairs somewhere. 'Sorry,' Angela said. 'Normally they'd be out. They're going mad with the rain.'

'I'm sorry to barge in on you. He's lied to me about a lot of things and . . .' She shrugged.

'You thought I was covering for him?' Martin said.

'It seemed a possibility.'

'The police came this morning.' Angela's back was stiff. So was her voice.

'I'm sorry. That must have been—'

'A bit of a shock, yes.'

'What did they—?'

'They insisted on searching the house!' Angela's face swelled with indignation.

'They didn't insist, darling.' Martin turned to Jude. 'They asked rather politely if we minded.'

'We could hardly say no! What would it have looked like?'

'What on earth has he done, Jude?'

'Nothing, Martin. He's just disappeared, that's all.'

Angela came to the table with the tea. They both looked at her, accusing and puzzled. She wished she hadn't come. 'You feel – contaminated,' Angela said. 'Police crawling all over your house.'

'There's a priest's hole, you know.' Martin grinned. 'Just as effective now as during the Reformation when the house was built. The police didn't find it.'

'And don't worry – he's not in there.'

'We looked. After they'd gone.'

'You wouldn't have given him up then?'

'Not till we'd heard his side, no.'

Jude looked at Angela and saw that, for her at least, this was not true. 'When's the baby due?' she said.

Angela touched her belly in a protective way. 'Mid-October we think.' She was calming down on purpose for the sake of the baby.

'That's why we moved when we did. Dan didn't tell you?'

She looked at their puzzled faces. Another secret Dan had kept from her. Why? In case it upset her? Or because it upset him?

When the rain stopped the boys and Martin pulled on their wellies. 'Show you round,' Martin said. They went out of the kitchen into a big hallway with a wide oak staircase, panelled walls all the way up, and a low doorway with a wide warped oak door that opened on to a yard at the back with high hedges, beech and hawthorn. 'That's our neighbour's land over there. Grows cereals mostly. Very pretty. And we've got a big hay field. He cuts the hay and pays us three hundred a year. We think that must be a bargain for him as he hasn't mentioned it, but we don't mind.'

They moved round the house, Rupert pedalling hard at their side on a small tricycle with a trailer. He kept getting off to pick up something to put in the trailer, a stone or a piece of broken tree that caught his eye, then getting back on and pedalling hard to catch up. Archie had run on ahead and disappeared. 'They can run wild here. You don't have to worry about them.'

They rounded the corner of the house and came across a big pond, all overhung with trees. 'It's a positive lake,' Jude said.

Martin smiled with modest pride. 'Well, not quite.'

'Dad, can we take the boat out?' Archie was pulling at a long low boat resembling a canoe.

'That's a nice canoe, Archie,' Jude said.

'It's a coracle, actually.'

Martin said, 'I had it specially made. It hasn't been christened yet because of the drought. There hasn't been enough water in the pond. Not now, Archie. We need a bit more rain yet.'

'Ah shit!' Archie's face swelled with rage like a bullfrog, like his mother, spoiling his cool English beauty. He kicked the boat.

'It's not the boat's fault, Archie. And if you ruin the boat we'll never get to sail it.'

'It's not fair!'

'No, it's not.' Martin calmly walked on, leaving Archie to get over his temper in his own time. No fuss.

Jude thought he was the sort of father it might be nice to have. She said, 'I've been seeing you as a monster these last months, leaving Dan in the lurch.'

'I've been feeling a monster actually, Jude. Pulling out like that. But Angela couldn't wait any longer. It was always agreed we'd move to the country at some time. And this was the time, it was now or never. And this partnership coming up just at the right moment. I asked Dan to come too. I did put it to him.'

'I know.'

'He despises the sort of stuff I do now. Restoration, tasteful additions, civic development that fits unobtrusively into these Georgian market towns. He'd hate it.'

'I know. He knows.'

'And he got that commission. In Essex, wasn't it? He was given a really free hand! What happened to that?'

Jude sighed. She told him Dan's version, about the tower, and left out John Bright's discoveries.

'Is that why he's gone off?'

'I don't know, Martin. I thought you might be able to offer me a clue.'

He shook his head. 'He hasn't been right for a couple of years, not since—'

'Since his mother died, I know. It hit him hard.'

'It started before she died. From when she got sick really.'

'Yes, it was a terrible time for him.'

'And for you, I expect.'

'Well, I couldn't help him.'

'I hope you don't blame yourself for any of this, Jude.'

'What do you think, Martin?'

'I hope you don't blame me then?'

'We all fail each other.'

'Dan has failed us as much as – I mean—'

'Yes. Oh yes. But he – Yes. He has.' She sighed.

They walked on through the long wet grass, meadowsweet surrounding them with the thick scent of vanilla, bulrushes standing above the reeds, green velvet cylinders emerging from their carapace of leaves. The birds had started singing after the rain. A pair of ducks sailed with absurd dignity across the surface of the pond breaking up the reflection into scraps of leaves and sky. Jude felt scorched with envy. She wished she hadn't come.

She said, 'Martin, it's hard to say this. I don't know how to put it really. But is there anything – I mean – Did Dan say anything, do anything – Is there anything you know that he might have kept from me? Even if he made you promise not to tell. I don't think it's the time for keeping that kind of promise. Because I don't know if he's in his right mind any more. And he might do something, he might have done something, he might be planning something – I've got to know.'

Martin's eyes locked with hers then slid off and away. He called, 'Rupo, Archie! Be careful, it's slippery at the edge.'

'Martin?'

'Oh Christ, Jude.'

'Please.'

'He only – It's just – About six weeks ago I went to the office to pack up the last of my stuff. He met me there. He was in a funny state. I thought he was drunk but he wasn't. He was bumping into things, knocking things off the desks, cursing, mumbling. I said for Christ's sake, Dan, something about him getting pissed and he said – Oh Jesus, Jude—'

'Come on, Martin, you've started so you'll finish. Come on.'

'He said you were having an affair.'

'Oh. I see.'

'I told him it was rubbish, that you'd never – you know – but he insisted. He said he had proof, that—'

'What proof? How? Where? Who?'

'He said this guy had told him.'

'What guy? Who?'

'I don't know. Someone he knew well. Someone he grew up with. Someone he said wouldn't lie to him.'

'It was true.'

'No? Jude? Are you sure?'

'Martin!'

Even Martin saw the funny side of this. 'Of course you would be sure. Yes. Oh, dear.'

'You believed it anyway.'

'Sorry.'

'People always do. On the no-smoke-without-fire principle.'

Martin scratched his nose but couldn't deny this.

'And you told Angela and that's partly why she's so angry about this whole thing?'

'I only told her to show how absurd Dan was being.'

'But she believed it, as you did. And as it was true, well . . .'

She looked sadly into his eyes and Martin ducked his head and kicked a clump of thick grass like a kid.

'This man who told Dan. Why did he tell him?'

'Well, it's what mates do, I suppose?'

'You think?'

Martin sighed and shook his head.

'What was this proof he said he had?'

'Photographs.'

'Photographs? Of me with—? Photographs?'

'It's what he said.'

'Did he have them? Did he show you?'

'I don't know if he had them. I wouldn't have looked at them—'

'Oh yes you would. Anyone would.'

'No—'

'How could anyone get photos? It was only ever in the flat. We were alone, it's not possible. It can't be true!'

'I did see one, actually. Just one. I didn't want to look at it but . . . It was pretty blurred but . . .'

'What?'

'You were – you and this Chinese-looking guy – in a garden.'

'In a garden?'

'Kissing. That's all.'

'Kissing.'

'But it looked pretty – Well, I think anyone would have said you were pretty – well – close.'

'Well, it's a bit difficult to kiss at long distance, Martin. You do have to get pretty close.'

'You know what I mean.'

'Where was it taken from?'

'How would I know?'

'No, I don't suppose you were looking at the background.'

'Oh, I see. Hang on.' They walked on. The pond petered out here under thick willows to a narrow stream with a trickle of water in the bottom. It gurgled gently over stones. A little round apricot-coloured cat emerged from the deep grass and walked with them. 'It's Jemima,' Martin said. 'She came with the house.'

Jemima emitted a deep growl like a distant sheep.

'She always takes part in the conversation.' Martin stopped under a willow frond that splattered him with raindrops. He said, 'The house was in the background. I noticed some sliding glass patio doors that I didn't much care for. And a pile of dug-up earth and rubble.'

'So it was taken from the end of the garden. Maybe from the roof of the shed.' *Where a person could hide out so easily. Just as John Bright said.* She shivered and gave a small moan. The cat responded with another deep sympathetic growl. They walked on.

Martin said, 'Maybe he took it himself.'

'Can you see Dan doing that?'

They looked at each other, speculating. And neither of them could answer this question. About a person they had known intimately all their adult lives. Martin said, 'I can't see any reason he would lie to me. About that.'

'He would be ashamed to admit that he was spying on me.'

'Yes . . .'

The cat spotted an intriguing movement in the deep vegetation beyond the stream. She crouched low and quivered. Martin said, 'No.'

'No what?'

'It was in an envelope. The photo. The envelope had your home address on it. It was posted to Dan. Don't tell me he posted it to himself. That's more devious than I'm prepared to consider.'

'Yes. Me too. He was manipulated then.'

'They don't think Dan started that fire, do they, Jude?'

Jude looked at him.

Martin said, 'Oh Christ. It hadn't occurred to me.'

'It has to Angela.'

'She hasn't said so.'

'Only because Dan's your friend.'

'It can't be true, I don't believe it. That's just not like Dan.'

'Is it like Dan to disappear without a word to me?'

'If he was manipulated. If this person who sent him the picture—' Martin turned to her. 'If this person was a danger to you, say. Maybe Dan's gone to, to . . .'

'Yes?' Jude looked sadly at Martin. 'Fairy-tale stuff, Martin. Dan would go into despair, not vengeance.'

'Vengeance?'

'Anyway, he hasn't come to you.'

'Well, Angela, especially in her present state – she wouldn't stand for it, you know.'

'No. Well, I had to come and see. I envy you, Martin.' She shivered.

'Come in and get warm before you go.'

'No—'

'Just come and see my studio.'

They had come round the barn to the door. He discarded his green wellies in the hall and opened the door to his right. The medieval barn. Low ceiling, low long windows, curvy limed oak beams. A central working table almost filled the room. Plans and drawings were pinned to the walls. The afternoon light slanted in. 'You've made a lovely job of it, Martin. No wonder you're getting plenty of work round here.'

'Not bad, is it?' he said. 'For a working-class lad like me.'

He didn't seem to realise what he'd said. Dan too was a working-class lad. And what did Dan have now? Dan who had started out with more talent than the lot of them. She even managed to smile.

He said, 'Stay and have some supper with us.'

She smiled again, more amused. 'No, Martin, thanks. I'd better get back.'

They stood in the sunlight, all the raindrops glittering, like the place had been showered with gold. 'Remember the day we got married, Martin? Hampstead Town Hall. Just you and Angela. And us.'

'We had lunch at the Holly Bush.'

'We got pissed and decided to have a party. We rang up all our friends: hey, we got married this afternoon!'

'They all came.'

'We got one present. The Beatles. "Will you still need me, will you still feed me When I'm sixty four." An old single.'

'We gave you that. God knows where we got it.'

'Witty.'

'Angela's idea.'

'"Things fall apart. The centre cannot hold."'

'"Human kind cannot bear very much reality."'

'That's a fair description of Dan.'

'Eliot suits him better than Yeats. The elegiac tone.' Martin hugged her. The boys and the cat looked on.

Angela came to the door. Jude and she touched cheeks. This was a formality. Gone the days of affection and witty wedding presents. Martin gave complicated directions back to the London road. Jude got into the van and waved. They stood in the yard, two parents, two fine boys, one sweet cat, seeing her off. She drove off with this miniature idyll framed in her wing mirror fragmented by raindrops. She put her hand out of the window and rubbed it out.

26

The light off the water at the back gave an airy float to the room, like it might be a boat. Rough sections of plaster skin had been hacked off the walls, exposing innards of liverish brick. Strangely this added to the room's charm, its rakish, hastily assembled air.

The furniture, in bizarre contrast, was big business boardroom, two long low settees of teak, chrome and leather, a low square table of teak, chrome and glass. A drinks cabinet six foot long with sliding glass doors.

The man with the dog and the gun and the furry animal hat stood, uneasy indoors, shifting from wellie to wellie and coughing from time to time. The dog growled low in its throat and occasionally whimpered.

Bright and Cato stood as policemen stand, relaxed, casual, with their eyes going everywhere, sussing out doors (two – the one from the hall they'd come in by, and another towards the back), windows (one, huge, at the front, another, same size, at the back), window locks (elaborate), alarm sensors (three to each window, one to each door), fireplaces (one, this end, rose marble with an enormous empty grate). There would be no easy way out, not with Animal Ears and his cocked shotgun, unless you were prepared to try the chimney.

'Cool place,' Cato said.

'Wouldn't wanna take it on myself.'

'Why's that, John?'

'Too big, Niki.'

'Oh ay.'

'Musta cost a bob or two.'

'Yeah, need a bob or two right enough.'

Their voices rang in the high carpetless space.

'Plenty security, though, I notice.'

'Need a lot these days, John.'

'That's true, Niki – all the villains about.'

'Hah.' Cato was almost tricked into a laugh. 'Hasn't got much of a view, though. That big grass bank in the way.'

'No. Pity. River's nice just here if you could only see it.'

'Why is that, mate? That bank there? What's it for?'

'Floodin'.' Animal Ears spoke through clamped lips, eyes straight ahead. Didn't want to lose his concentration.

'Listen, will Mr Reynolds be long?'

No reply.

'P'rhaps you could go and see what's keeping him.'

No reply.

'What's he up to these days by the way? Haven't seen him in a while.'

Animal Ears stood mulishly silent. Didn't even look at them. Concentrating hard. He stared into the middle distance with a dignified expression. Scornful even. Perhaps he was concentrating on his scornfulness technique. It could do with some work. The dog squeaked then settled down, ugly head on his big front paws, staring shrewdly at them from his piggy little eyes. Bright sighed.

'Well, well. Mr Bright! Sorry to keep you waiting. If I'd known it was you— How're you keeping? Long time— Okay, Trevor, relax, Mr Bright is an old friend. Trevor's a good gamekeeper. Lots of poachers round here. Got to keep an eye out for them, haven't we, Trevor? See you later. Thanks for taking care of my guests.' Brennan closed the door softly behind Animal Ears and his charming pet. 'Better than a dog is Trevor. Not much brighter either, just enough to be useful. This a social visit, Mr Bright?

Just passing and you thought you'd drop in? Well it's nice of you, I'm delighted.'

Bright had forgotten how big Brennan was. No fat on him either. Lean, like the middleweight boxer he'd been as a lad. Thick in the neck from training. And the shoulders needed no padding, bulging inside the Armani suit. Apart from that he hadn't put on a pound. His clothes sat elegantly on him. He had the air of an animal prowling his territory barefoot. He prowled to the drinks cabinet. 'What'll you have? Don't tell me you're on duty, all this way off your patch.'

'Nothing for me, I'm driving.'

'What about you, Mr . . . ?'

'This is DS Cato. Niki, this is Michael – what is it down here, Michael? He was born Brennan but we know him by a few other choice names, don't we, Michael?'

'Choice names, that's good. Names of choice. There's no law says you have to call yourself one name from cradle to grave. Not if there's no intent to defraud.'

'And no one'd ever accuse you of intent to defraud, eh, Michael?'

He smiled. 'Absolutely not, Mr Bright. Mr Cato? What can I get you?'

Cato didn't reply. Brennan shrugged. 'Well, I'm trying to lose a pound or two myself so it's just as well.' He poured sparkling water from a green bottle into a tall glass, dropped in a handful of ice from a bucket and a slice of lime from a saucer.

Bright and Cato looked on, mouths watering. 'You never were a drinker, Michael, if I recall,' Bright said.

'Well, I like to keep my wits about me, I admit. Have a seat.' He lowered himself with graceful power on to the leather sofa. It sighed gently taking his weight.

Bright stayed standing. This way he felt just about on a level. Not many people made him feel like a short arse – he was fit, he was wiry, he was lean and light on his feet, he could take care of himself – but this guy . . . Every movement, even of his eyes, relaxed and under control. So much power he had no need for tension. So much power because he had no limits. He'd take you out soon as look at you. Copper or no copper. Like nothing could touch him. Bright had known a few real villains and this guy was the best. He'd only had him face to face once before, in an interview room, with his lawyer. He had everything sewn up. Everyone accounted for. Friends in high places, friends in low places, employees everywhere. There was the system, law and order, cops and robbers. And there was Brennan's system, watertight, shipshape. No one got out of line more than once. 'Animal Ears always keep his gun cocked indoors?' Bright said.

'He doesn't often come indoors, it's not his natural habitat. You should have told him who you were, Mr Bright. Not his fault if he took you for the ordinary trespasser.'

'Can't imagine your average trespasser daring to go past those notices, Michael.'

'Ah yes. It's the pheasants, you know. They're not too intelligent, you might have noticed, put themselves in the way of moving vehicles and poachers. They're the sort of birds that are just begging to be shot. So I had a word with the local police, they're a reasonable bunch and they do like to be invited to a shoot. They agreed the notices would do no harm. Even though they can't be enforced, of course. Round this way they understand these things. They're very reasonable. Mind you, I have always found the police very reasonable. On the whole.'

He let his navy blue eyes rest on Bright, baiting him. Bright concentrated on not rising to his bait. In spite of Cato's acute attention, in spite of his need to prove himself to Cato, Brennan must not know they were on to his police connection. Not yet.

Brennan drank the sparkly water. He lowered his eyelids. He kept his little smile. He was a handsome bastard and he knew it. When you come into the presence of a guy like this you feel all the aspiration of the human race, all advances in science, in intellect, in art, in any kind of endeavour, to be pointless; that this easy gift of physical superiority is the only gift worth having. Everything bows before it. Everything has to. It has the supreme right. It is an animal quality. And coupled to intelligence, which it rarely is, it is unbeatable. It wasn't often Bright felt defeat. He'd had this guy within an inch of a court case and the bastard had beat him. Bright kept still. In the jungle that's what the smaller animals do in the presence of the king of beasts and that's what Brennan was – the king of beasts.

'How did you know where to find me, Mr Bright?'

'You'd like to know that, would you, Michael?'

He shifted the smiling dark blue gaze to Cato. 'Mr Bright and I have known each other a while. Gives him the right to call me by my Christian name. In someone else it might look like he was being familiar.'

Cato stood with folded arms impassive, doing his stolid British copper act, like nothing could shift him.

With his eyes still on Cato Brennan said, 'I would be interested in knowing that, yes, Mr Bright. Which of my many acquaintances has given away my rural retreat. If only people couldn't talk. It would make life a whole lot easier. I look after a lot of people, Mr Cato. It's what a good Christian does. Helps his neighbour. I help mine. And what do they do in return? They give away my secrets. You know the hardest emotion for human beings to feel? Gratitude. You don't want to tell me, Mr Bright? I understand that. But believe me, I've become tolerant in my old age, I'm a pussycat now. I understand human weakness. I'm a merciful fellow these days.'

'You talk more than you used to, yourself, Brennan.'

Brennan sat forward, a slight movement, and dangerous. 'The name's Reynolds down here. You hear me? Reynolds.' He smiled.

'Come on, Mr Bright. It's easier for you to tell me who gave away my whereabouts than it will be for me to find out. But I will find out.'

'When did you last see Daniel Craig?'

Brennan sat back, sipped his drink, let his gaze rest on Bright. You could see where Chloe had learned the trick. Or maybe she didn't need to learn. Maybe they were just two of a kind, she and Brennan. 'Daniel Craig . . .' He spoke the name like it was hard to remember.

Bright got fed up. 'Cut the crap, Michael. You lived in the same flats, you went to the same school. Just lately he made the mistake of accepting your charity—'

'Mr Bright.' His tone was reproachful. He got up and refilled his glass from the green bottle. 'Sure you won't join me? I did not give Dan Craig charity. I gave him a job. I asked him to design my new house. Out there in the clearing. I asked Dan Craig because he is the best there is. I appreciate quality.'

'And when did you say you'd seen him last?'

'Dan Craig? Well now let me see . . .' He spoke into a mobile phone the size of a fob watch: 'Julian, join us, would you? Thanks.' He sat again. 'I like to have my lawyer present on occasions like this. We know how easy it is for one's innocent words to be misconstrued by the police.'

Bright groaned. 'Oh not the bloody lawyer. This is the guy I told you about, Niki. Michael keeps him on a leash, like Animal Ears keeps his bulldog. Hello, Julian,' he said without a pause as a man as tall as his master came into the room.

Julian French was fifty maybe? Smartly suited, urbane, ugly as sin but careful of himself, nice clean hands with lovely cared-for fingernails, and graceful poses. No Armani for him. Only Savile Row. Sharp navy pinstripe, and handmade shoes from Burlington Arcade. Bright hated him. Snakes like him were worse than the villains. Without them the villains couldn't operate.

Money launderers. Fact launderers. Justice launderers. They made him want to throw up. And this was one of the best.

'Good afternoon. Mr Bright, isn't it? How nice to see you again. To what do we owe your visit? Not quite purely social, I'm sure.'

'Mr Bright mentioned Daniel Craig to me, Julian.'

'Really?'

'Wants to know the last time I saw him.'

'I see.' Julian slid a hand inside his jacket, smoothing the cloth over his barrel chest like he was stroking a dog. A pause while he did not look at Brennan and Brennan did not look at him. 'Does this mean Daniel Craig has disappeared, Mr Bright?'

Bright waited. Just because someone asks you a question this does not mean you have to give him an answer. Everyone waited. No one knew what anyone else knew, what was going to be admitted here.

'Well, does it or doesn't it?' Julian's tone got an authoritarian courtroom edge.

'Why would you think Daniel Craig had disappeared, Julian?'

'I have no reason whatever to think so, Mr Bright, apart from your presence here. And the fact that you are asking when we last saw him could mean that you would like to know where he is. This place is not known to many of Michael's acquaintance. A retreat from the rat race, a place in the country to relax—'

'Yeah yeah—'

'Daniel Craig is one of the few who know of it. If he has disappeared you would have reason to search his papers and so on and thus you might have come by this address. Michael trusts most of his employees to keep his secrets.'

'A-ha. He's a trusting soul, we've noticed.'

'Dan promised me not to put this address anywhere in writing, you see, Mr Bright.' Brennan spoke very soft, very Irish.

'He didn't. Or if he did, not so's we could find it.'

'So he told someone where to find me.' Brennan unwound himself from the sofa in one movement.

'I found you, Michael. Without his help. From the very few clues he let slip.'

'Let slip to you? I don't believe it.'

'Cool, Michael, cool, keep cool.' The lawyer spoke softly too in his deep oleaginous resonant voice, like a ham actor playing the oily barrister he really was. 'Are you telling us Mr Daniel Craig has disappeared, Mr Bright?'

'I'm not telling you anything, Julian. I'm asking Michael when he last saw his architect friend. I don't understand why he should have any objection to that, only the question seems to have upset him a bit. First he calls you in to help him answer this very simple question and next thing you both seem to be losing your cool. Now why would that be? Why do you think that would be, Niki?'

'They seem to think he's disappeared for some reason, guv.'

'Oh there they go.' Julian's weary drawl. 'The amusing policemen playing their amusing little games. You know why you never win, Mr Bright – not you personally of course, far be it from me to suggest such a thing – but the CID in general? Because the police recruit from among the lower class of intelligence. And the CID recruit from the worst class of low intelligence – those who think they are clever. And you think you're so clever, don't you, Mr Bright? Because you are a tintsy bit cleverer than the others.' He left a dramatic pause here to let the dire insult sink into Bright's thick skin.

Bright's face kept its amused mask. No one could tell what went on behind it. The metallic points of light in his small brown eyes danced like light on night-time water, watching Julian's performance.

Julian went on, patient. 'Mr Reynolds commissioned Mr Craig to design a house for him. A week ago – would it be a week? –

thereabouts, anyway, they had a – disagreement. An aesthetic disagreement. Things got a little – heated? Threats were made. On both sides, we have to say, Michael. On both sides. You know how it can be when old friends fall out.'

'Now what could Daniel Craig possibly threaten Michael with?'

'It is more interesting, I believe, to inquire what Michael could threaten Daniel Craig with.'

Bright went still. Cato recognised one of those moments, when Bright stood up like a hare in grass, inwardly quivering, ears cocked, listening. 'Well, it's pretty hard to imagine Michael threatening anyone with anything. That would be most unusual, wouldn't it, Julian?'

The lawyer's lips drew into their thinnest line. They didn't like to be mocked, these upper-class gits. They did like to keep their dignity. They loved their dignity. Their dignity was their fur. You stroked it, and they wagged their little tails. But their vanity was their Achilles' heel. Before he could speak, Bright addressed Brennan. 'What could you have over on a bloke like Daniel Craig, Michael? He's not whoring for you. You're not his pimp. He's not into illegal substances. He hasn't had his hand in anyone's till.' Bright paused. 'Has he?'

No reply. No reaction.

'And I get the strong impression even his life's not that valuable to him the last few years.'

Brennan smiled. 'Since his dear old mother died. No.'

'And he bought her flat, didn't he, Michael? For twenty-five thousand quid. Now where would he get twenty-five thousand? You lend it him, did you, Michael? Out of the kindness of your tender heart?'

The lawyer piped up again. 'A perfectly legitimate transaction. Perfectly within the law, and, what is more, in conformity with government policy at the time.'

'Oh, I would never dream of suggesting that Michael would ever be caught doing anything against the law. Let alone against government policy. No way. Eh, Michael? So what you had over on him was nothing to do with the sale of his mother's flat.'

Bright and Brennan regarded each other. Both let the silence hang. Bright shifted his gaze to the lawyer. He watched them both for a reaction. It was like watching a rock face. Two rock faces.

Bright said, 'For the last two years that flat has been used for immoral purposes. Prostitution and drug dealing.'

'Yes?' Julian said in a puzzled way. 'I fail to see in what way this is anything to do with my client. I hope you are not suggesting that Mr Reynolds would have anything to do with either activity. The flat is surely not in his name.'

Even Bright had to smile. Then he wiped the smile and speeded up. 'Another journalist has died in Kentish Town. In very suspicious circumstances. Certain dodgy photographs connect him with that flat.'

This one they were ready for. Julian replied, smooth as the silk he was – you couldn't see the join. 'Again, I fail to see the connection with my client. I see so far only a connection with Mr Craig. His mother owned that flat, you say, and he bought it. And his wife was rather closely connected with the Chinese journalist who was in that rather gruesome fire, I believe.'

'You brought that up, Julian, not me.'

Julian gave him a bland smile like a frog on dope. Brennan also said nothing. Blank face but for the amusement flickering at the corners of his eyes and mouth. He sipped his drink. Cool as the ice clinking in the glass. The lawyer raised his eyebrows, what there was of them, as pale and thin as his lips. 'May I have a drop of that delicious single malt, Michael? Thank you so much.'

So Bright knew one thing. They knew about Jude's affair with

Lee. And they wanted him to believe that Craig knew of it. Because that gave Craig a motive. They wanted him to think that Craig had set fire to Lee. From jealousy. And because they wanted him to think this, Bright was now as sure as he could be without a shred of evidence that it was not the truth.

While Brennan was pouring the whisky into a nice piece of Waterford crystal Bright went to the window at the back. He felt wired up. He looked out at the big square yard, concrete and high walls, spectacularly empty, in the far left corner a big garage with a small door. The big doors would be on the outside of the wall, on the side of the house where the boat was moored. He'd give a lot to have a look inside that garage. He'd give even more to get a shufti round that boat. He said, 'That Triad shooting coupla years ago. That was round here somewhere, wasn't it?'

A little hiatus followed this remark. No ice clinking on glass, no tinkle of whisky being poured. This told him a big fact. Gave him a big connection. He didn't know how he was going to use it. Not yet.

Then, like the smooth continuum had never been suspended, Julian said, 'I believe it was,' and lifted his glass. 'Your health. Yes. Strange to hear of such a thing outside Chinatown.'

'Not so strange as all that. Not these days. The days of the godfathers are over, so they tell me.' Bright let his sparky gaze rest on Brennan. Brennan gazed back unsmiling. His unsmiling face had struck terror into the bravest of hearts. But Bright liked it. He liked wiping the smile off Brennan's face. 'The animals are breaking out of the cage. There isn't the loyalty there used to be. That's what they tell me. Nice boat you got out there, Michael. Bet it can put on some speed when it wants. Would you like to show it me?'

'Another time, with pleasure, Mr Bright. It'll be dark soon. Much better in daylight.'

'Why don't you ask your guests to stay the night, Michael?'

Brennan's face expressed surprise without moving. Like Bright, he had that knack. His eyes swept slowly over the two coppers. Bright felt like they were two scruffy kids about to be left with their wicked stepmother in the woods. 'Well, why not? Would you like that, Mr Bright? Mr Cato? We could continue our conversation at leisure.'

Cato looked at Bright. He saw Bright was tempted. 'I think we ought to be getting back, guv.'

Bright considered. It was getting dark. It would be useful to spend a bit longer here. It would be fun anyway to call their bluff, these self-satisfied bastards, though he knew he had to watch that, rising to the challenge, taking the bait. So far he had nothing except some hints and a feeling. He would get nothing more; in fact, if he stayed he might end up giving away more than he'd got. At the moment they didn't know how much he knew. They thought they had the upper hand. He said, 'What do you reckon, Niki? Not often we get out of the smoke. And I'd like to have a drink with our old friends here.'

A glance passed between the villain and his lawyer. It expressed surprise and the slightest degree of alarm. For just a split second no one knew what to do.

'Just kidding,' Bright said. 'More than my reputation is worth. One night under this roof and I'd be tarred with your brush for ever. Wouldn't I, Niki?'

Cato got the point. His face screwed itself into a complicated grimace.

Bright turned back to Brennan. 'No thanks, mate. Kind offer but we'll be on our way.'

'The law is not the most flexible of friends.' Julian gave an oily smile.

'Not for the likes of us. Different for you, Julian, eh? Well, we'd better be off. Nice to see your place in the country.' He turned in the doorway. 'Your little retreat's blown wide open now, Michael. What will you do?'

'Oh, I'm sure Michael will think of something, Mr Bright.'

'A-ha. I'm sure he will, Julian. Or you'll think of something for him.'

'What's happened to Dan Craig, Bright?' Brennan's smooth slightly Irish lilt took on a hard North London edge.

'You want to know, Michael?'

'He's my friend. We go way back. I take care of my friends, like I said.'

'I don't know where he is. He hasn't been seen for twenty-four hours. He knows where you are. You don't know where he is. That's interesting. He knows a lot of your business, Michael. He has more on you than you could ever have on him. He's led a pretty respectable life as far as the law is concerned.'

'Oh has he? That's all you know.' The face was pale, the eyes dark. You could see the two lines that would run from nose to chin when he got older and the muscle went. You could just get a glimpse of when the strength would go and the strongest young male would take him on and win. You just got a glimpse.

'That is all I know. You know more? You wanna tell me, Michael?'

Brennan nearly went on. Just a look from the lawyer was enough to stop him. 'See them out, will you, Julian. Take care on the road, Mr Bright. Look out for my pheasants.'

The Barge Inn in Battlesbridge was swinging this time of night. Great place, room after room, low beams, pictures of Thames barges, looking like Holland, on the delft tiles. Those were the days of real trade up and down the Thames. A river of commerce and industry. He guessed it was a river of commerce again. For some. For Thames barge read racing yacht. Read Michael

Brennan-stroke-Reynolds and his natty boat and his land and his big house and his tribe of slaves.

'I might have put a lot of people in danger, Cat.'

'How?'

'We've blown his cover. We've surprised him in his den. He'll be looking for someone to blame.'

'He won't give a toss about that.'

'Oh yes he will. That location was his big secret.'

'Someone would have grassed it up sooner or later.'

'A-ha. Yeah, true, I guess.' Bright swallowed a mouthful of Adnam's bitter. 'Christ, this is good stuff. Goes down like silk.'

Two piled platefuls of liver and bacon arrived, with fresh veg and nice little spuds on a separate dish.

Cato said, 'You weren't really thinking of spending the night, were you, guv?'

Bright speared a Jersey potato and popped it into his mouth. 'A-ha. Yup. Just for a little minute I was tempted there.'

27

'Hi, George! It's me! I'm back!' Jude put down the shopping in the hall and took off her wet things in the cloakroom. Why had she stopped off on the way back to shop? Why couldn't she come home without a carrier bag full of food? Especially now there was only herself and George to feed. It was a displacement activity, it must be.

She didn't call out for Dan. She was superstitious. If she didn't call out or look for him, she would walk down the stairs to the kitchen and find him there at the old kitchen table, reading the *Architectural Journal* or the *Standard* or even the spaghetti packet. He'd put out an arm and pull her close to him and squeeze her arse and she'd hold him round his neck and stroke the side of his face, his ear, his eyelids, his nose, and he'd kiss her fingers and say Ah the hoary smell of the soil and she'd say Who are you calling whory? And then. And then, and then . . .

Sitting on the loo she lowered her head so her hair made a chestnut curtain between her and the world or at least the part of the world encompassed by the cloakroom carpet. She felt sick. And as she pulled the chain she thought, *Anyway that was the old days, the old Dan. It hasn't been like that for so long I can hardly remember.* And then she got a memory of Lee and herself together, so sharp it made her weak so she had to lean on the door jamb. But it passed. She picked up the shopping, listened at the door to Dan's room – silence – and went downstairs.

Funny, George not coming to greet her. Normally he'd appear

right away, peering round the banisters, or trotting down the stairs. He must be out. 'Where are you, George?' Not in the kitchen anyhow. God, it was a nice room. The garden through the window, the red Le Creuset pots and pans on the shelf, the big deep blue American fridge, the old scrubbed table, the mismatched chairs.

She just glanced into the cosy bit at the front of the house with the old sofa and the telly. She knew for certain just at this moment that Dan would be there, sitting under the lamp with his feet up on the coffee table. But no. No Dan. She switched on the lamp for atmosphere and the telly for human noise. She stowed the surplus-to-requirements food in the fridge.

Then she opened the french door and called, 'Come on, George!' with the note of mock exasperation he usually came running to. 'George? I'm home! Come on!' No George. A new dread crept into her stomach. She prayed. 'Please not George. I can bear a lot. I am bearing a lot. But not George.' She told herself she was being daft. Only so many bad things could happen. But she knew of old that bad things bear worse things on their shoulders. That's how life was. Things had to get pretty bad – worse than you thought possible – before you reached a corner and turned it to rediscover the broad flat plain of the good life.

She searched every inch of the house, all the hidey-holes, in the cupboards, under the beds, even inside the washing machine. 'Please, George. Don't do this to me.' She went out every half an hour and called him. She had to call quietly, she felt such an idiot. A lost child, they'd sympathise, but a cat? You couldn't expect them to understand. But George was her friend, her dear good loving faithful friend, for years now, all through her bad years. Dan had changed towards her but George never had. He loved her for no reason, just as she was. 'So why are you doing this to me, you little bastard?' she whispered into the night.

Just as she had not opened the door to Dan's room or looked for him upstairs, so she did not put the ladder against the wall to look over it for George. She saw him in her mind impaled on rusting metal, chewed by a fox – foxes roamed these days along the railway, in and out of gardens – or run over by a train. The phone rang and she ran to it.

'Jude? It's Kate Creech.'

'Oh. Oh, Kate. Hello. Yes.'

Not the police. Not Dan.

'Are you okay?' Kate's deep strong flexible sympathetic voice. Jude felt the usual suspicion of actors – were they pretending? But look at other people – they were so sincere? They could be trusted? She knew Kate of old. Kate had never let her down. Gave her work when she was just starting out. Got her clients just by talking her up. Ready with sympathy. Ready for a laugh. She'd had her own share of troubles – like anyone, only more so – and life had turned the corner for her – lovely flat, nice work, new lover, precarious happiness.

Jude told her that George had gone. 'He never stays out this late, not without popping in to say hello and have a bite to eat. He never has.'

'Talking of a bite to eat, have you eaten yet?'

'Yes, oh yes,' Jude lied.

'Cats do these things, Jude! A friend of mine, her car was vandalised and her cat disappeared the same night. Stayed away three days till things had calmed down.'

'Is that true, Kate?' Clinging to any little thread.

'Yes. They don't think like us, apparently, cats. The house must feel different with Dan gone and you all churned up and I guess it's just too disturbing for him. His nerves won't stand it. You know how sensitive they are to atmosphere. He'll be back, Jude. He will.'

Jude did not believe this but Kate sure could do conviction. She decided to hope. 'Yes. I'm sure you're right.'

'Do you want to cancel tomorrow?'

'Oh no, Kate. Gardening's the only thing that's saving me at the moment. I'll be there at nine. With my bucket and spade.'

'Okay. And Jude? Take a sleeping pill. Don't wander round all night looking for him, okay?'

'Okay.'

At 3 a.m. she went out to the garden one last time. At last she did climb up the ladder and shine the torch among the rusting metal carcasses of piled-up cars. She called in a whisper so's not to disturb the neighbours or all the bogeymen lurking in the rusty cars waiting to pounce. She listened for some answering squeak. None came. She moved the ladder to the end wall and looked over to the railway, deep down there in the cutting. Trees and brambles and God knew what. Trains anyway. But George had lived here all his life and never come to harm before. This was his world, his urban jungle, he knew how to handle it. Why would he suddenly succumb to its perils now? She climbed down the ladder. Kate was right. She should have just taken a pill. *Worrying never helped anything*: her mother's voice – the worst worrier in the world. It certainly never helped her. Strangely, towards her death she stopped worrying for the first time and became cool and serene, even happy. She got them all through her dying like that; you just couldn't be sad for this person who was so content. Normally Jude let her thoughts glide away from this tricky little hiccup in her life. But every loss brought back the memory of all previous losses and tied them together in the parcel of one big loss.

Now she stood in the night garden and asked her mother to give her George back safe and sound. It had rained all day. The garden was wet, smelled wet. Her feet and the hem of her kimono were wet. Wet grass squeezed between her toes. She whispered, 'Be safe, George, wherever you are. Just you fucking well be safe, okay?' And went in. Leaving the cat flap open and food there close to it. And then she knew there was someone in the house.

It wasn't precisely a noise she had heard. She'd just felt something. Hope leapt up like a tiger and clawed her despair. But no, it wasn't George; George would know where she was and come running to say hello. This intimation of a presence was of a human who did not mean to be heard. She had not set the alarm, because she had not gone to bed, just lain on the sofa and kept going out to call George. *Oh Christ. What shall I do?* How had they got in? Out there in the garden in the night she'd have heard nothing, all her nerves strained just for George. She'd have dismissed a car crash as irrelevant, a mere interruption to her listening.

Her heart hammered so hard it made a noise, in her chest, in her ears, in her brain; she couldn't hear herself think, she couldn't think. She had to think. And she had to breathe without being heard. Two listening presences, hers and the person – or people – upstairs, all keeping still, all waiting. *I imagined it, I'm imagining it. No, I'm not. I'm like George, I know this house, I know when it's empty and I know when there's someone lurking, I know—*

Suddenly a picture of Dan came into her mind, so strong she forgot her fear. *Dan* creeping through the house. *Dan* letting himself in with a spare key, creeping about so's not to wake her, suddenly hearing the french door close. Standing up there, like her, not daring to breathe, not knowing if it was she down there or an intruder. *But why would Dan think it could be anyone but me?* No, the breathing presence up there was not Dan.

This scrap of certainty gave her back a spark of rational thought. She should pick up the phone and call 999 or she should grab the broom and charge up the stairs roaring and open the front door for escape. She couldn't use the phone without alerting the intruder. And somehow she didn't think this burglar was a kid after drugs money; this whole horrible business had taught her not to believe in coincidence. Her husband disappeared, her cat disappeared. If there was someone in her house, it was connected, it was a part. It was significant.

And she couldn't move. She felt she'd been there for hours just standing in the dark, thoughts in collision, then scattered, scraps and shards.

She heard something. A creak. The small creak of the floorboard in the hall outside Dan's room. She moved. She picked up her mobile phone. She grabbed the broom from the corner. She didn't creep, she ran, up the stairs, not roaring like she'd imagined, but pressing 999 on her mobile. There was a light in Dan's room. She gingerly pushed the door ajar with the end of the broom and saw the mess, file drawers spilling, papers everywhere, but no one in there now, and the front door was open, and the street was as still as death.

'Ambulance fire or police?'

'P-p-police. P-p-please.' Shivering on the doorstep in the silent street.

It was the uniform branch who came. Two nice young guys, gentle with her. A bit humorous till she explained that her husband was missing and the circumstances – some of them. 'Inspector Bright is the one in charge, I think.'

They looked at each other then and the senior one spoke on his radio but he kept his back to her so she couldn't hear what he was saying, while the other one distracted her attention, asking if there was anyone who could spend the night in the house with her.

Jude said, 'No, I can't think of anyone actually. No one I could ask to get out of bed at this hour.' And she thought how curious that was – that she'd always had Dan to look after her, and now she didn't have Dan, and she didn't have anyone else either.

'Is there anyone you could go to, then? Just for the rest of the night, anyway?'

'I can't go anywhere,' Jude said. 'My cat's missing, you see.'

'Your cat?'

'If he came back and I wasn't here, I couldn't forgive myself.'

The policeman looked incredulous.

'Anyway—' she shivered – 'they've gone now, haven't they? They're not going to come back tonight.' She was amazed how detached she sounded, rational, objective, cool. In fact the tears were dammed up behind a face so stiff she could barely speak. But no one would have known.

The other policeman shut down his radio and came back. 'The CID will be along later on to talk to you and have a look round. In the meantime we've got to freeze the scene. That means we put a seal on this door, your husband's office, right? So you're not to go in, okay?'

Jude nodded. She said, 'How did they get in?'

'Looks like with a key, love.'

She had been afraid of that. It was Dan then? Come in, searched for something, not even woken her, left without even speaking to her?

'There'll be a path up to the door, we'll use that, and you use it an' all, okay?'

Then she recalled: 'My husband left his keys behind.'

The police exchanged a look. 'He'd have a spare, wouldn't he?'

'I suppose he might, yes.'

'Was the alarm on?'

'No. I was awake. Because my cat's missing.'

The senior policeman took notes: where she was, what she'd been doing, what she'd heard. The other one went up the stairs to look round. He came down shrugging. 'No sign of disturbance up there. Will you come up with me, love? Walk on this side right behind me.'

She followed him up the stairs, squeezed next to the wall. They stood in the bedroom doorway together. 'Well?'

So stupid – she felt relieved that she'd thrown the duvet over the bed before racing off to Suffolk, so it didn't look too much of a mess. 'It looks just the same as I left it this morning.'

'Sure?' He took her round the other rooms, the bathroom, her workroom over the front door, the spare room at the back. All undisturbed. She hoped, absurdly, to see George shoot like a meteor from under her bed or behind a door. But she knew he wasn't there. She could always tell. 'I'm sure,' she said.

'Where had you been, by the way, during the day?'

'Suffolk. Visiting friends.'

'Anyone know you were going?'

'No. Spur of the moment.'

After they left she was numb, the tooth out, the gum anaesthetised, but another visit to the dentist tomorrow: more police to come, crawling all over her house, fingerprinting, footprinting, asking questions. And Dan was the cause of this. The hairy beast inside her leaped into her throat and roared. She beat the wall with her fist. She wanted to kill Dan. She wanted to claw his face and get a knife and stick it into him all over, and over and over and over again until— Her breaths sounded like sandpaper on wood, grating out of her angry throat, choking her. All the anger – for his betrayal, for whatever he had done to make him leave like this, for leaving her in the lurch, in the shit. So she'd had an affair with a beautiful young man – so what was she supposed to do when Dan didn't want her any more? It wasn't his fault he'd had this crisis in his life. But it sure as hell wasn't her fault and her life was scorched earth now because of him. She was the one who should have left. She'd hung in there, waiting and hoping, building him up – for this.

She sat on the bottom stair and knew. The only thing that would make Dan do this. Leave like this. She knew now for sure. He was the culprit. He had set fire to Lee. And if Lee died Dan would be a murderer. But then what had he come back for?

Why would he do that? Something important he had forgotten? What could be important enough to risk discovery for? So she realised it could not be Dan who had got in. It was another person. An unknown person. And this unknown person had a key. And if the alarm had been on as it would normally have been? This person knew the code for the alarm? Only Dan could have provided these things. The code, the key. Dan had arranged for someone to burgle his house? Her house? So that he would not be discovered? He would put her at that risk to keep himself safe? The old Dan would have protected Jude from anything. But the new Dan, she accepted at last, was removed from her as fully as by death. He no longer existed. He was inhabited by an alien soul. And not a soul she cared for any more.

She shook with this new feeling. It was new to her. Hate. It was a big thing, as big as love. You would die for love. You would kill for this. What Dan had done to Lee she would do to Dan. She would avenge his revenge. If Lee died, Dan would die.

She let her neck muscles loose. Her head drooped. She laughed and wiped the tears off her knees. Ludicrous. As if she would ever, could ever – daft old, soft old Jude. But she could never live again with Dan. Never. It was over now.

28

The phone woke him at 6.45 a.m. It was the duty officer at Kentish Town.

'Ah Christ,' Bright said. 'Don't tell me. When?' He sat on the side of the bed. The beer last night. The drive in the rain. His brain was sticking to the inside of his skull. *I shouldn't have gone to Essex. I was tempted and I fell. It's not a coincidence they chose tonight.*

'Who shall I send?' the duty officer said.

'Tell Cato to meet me there.'

The morning traffic starts to build up at seven. It took him three quarters of an hour to get to Fulham.

Cato met him in the big white atrium: 'The nurse on the morning shift found him. His life support had been switched off. Normal procedure had not been followed. Definitely a suspicious.'

'Ah shit. Ah shit.'

'What shall I do, guv?'

'Get Chloe. Take her to the station. Don't send Taff.'

'Sorry, guv, he's already gone.'

'Gone where?'

'Chloe Han's place.'

'Ah shit.'

'You found him what time?'

'A quarter to six.'

'What did you do?'

'I paged the duty houseman.'

'You didn't tell anyone else?'

'The nurse on duty with me.'

'You didn't think to call us? You knew he was the subject of a police investigation.'

'We didn't like to inform the police until the doctor had seen—'

'A-ha, I see.' Every profession stuck in its hierarchical loyalties like pigs in – mud. 'Where is he, this doctor?'

'I'm here. Dr Chris Morgan. Who are you?'

Bright had no time for power battles; he flashed his ID. 'What time did you arrive on the scene?'

'5.55 a.m.'

'What did you do?'

'I heard what Janet had to say—'

'What was that?' Bright turned to the nurse.

'Well I . . .' She struggled between embarrassment and truth. 'I told Dr Morgan I thought we should phone you.'

'I went in to check the patient myself. I discovered that his life support system had indeed been switched off and there was no report to say when or why. I was puzzled by this.'

'You realise you contaminated a possible crime scene?'

'I'm a doctor. My first duty is to my patient.'

Bright sighed. 'What did you do next?'

'I called my consultant. He suggested I phone you.'

The nurse said, 'I gave your number at the police station. They said you weren't there. Another chap turned up.'

'Chief Inspector Gould,' the doctor said.

Bright paused. 'Inspector Gould is here?'

'He came and inspected the, er – scene? And he made some calls and then all these forensic people turned up and—'

'Where is Inspector Gould now?'

'How would I know?'

'How long was he here on his own?'

'Again, how would I know?'

Bright looked at the nurse. 'Janet?'

'I suppose about – quarter of an hour?'

Bright was speechless.

The doctor said, 'I also contacted the charge nurse from the previous shift.'

'Did Inspector Gould question her?'

'Him.'

'Did Inspector Gould—'

'I don't know!' The doctor's exasperation was getting out of control.

'Where is he now – the charge nurse?'

Janet said, 'I'll page him for you.'

'Thanks, love.'

'Do you need me any longer?' the doctor said, 'because—'

'No. Thanks. You can go. Look like you could do with some sleep.'

'Sleep – now what is that? Remind me.'

Poor sod, a young tired know-all at the end of his third night-shift this week; Bright wanted to throttle him.

The room was cordoned now and swarming with socos. Bright turned to Janet, the nurse who'd found Lee dead. 'The other charge nurse?'

'He's on his way.'

'What's his name?'

'Adam.'

'How long between Adam going off and you coming on?'

'No time. You never go off duty until the next shift arrives.'

'So you were already here when Adam went.'

'Yes, but I didn't check on Mr Han right away. A little girl came in in the night. An RTA. She's not as bad as Mr Han. I mean as Mr Han was. But she needs more nursing care, if you see what I mean. She's new. New to me. So I went to check on her first, you see.'

'How long would you be with her?'

'Oh . . .' The girl looked bewildered and flustered and worn out. She was young, looked no more than eighteen to Bright, but was probably mid-twenties. Pure clean skin like a baby; not like someone who spent her life in a hospital. 'Maybe twenty minutes?' she said. 'I'm not sure.'

'Show me.'

She took him along the corridor. A small body lay there, limbs supported, floating above the bed in a form of levitation. 'Her skin mustn't touch anything. We have this pulley system.'

The child's eyes opened sleepily and closed again. Her face looked fine.

'It was her back got it mainly,' the nurse said. 'She's had a big operation. They've taken skin from her thighs and inside her arms and grafted it. We have to see if it takes. There'll be a few more operations before she's through.' She looked at Bright. His face had an expression people didn't often get to see. 'She'll be all right,' the little nurse said. 'We can fix her up.'

The door swung open. Roger Gould looked in. 'Ah there you are, John, there you are. Sorry to miss you. Jim Beresford, chief administrator, has been giving me a tour of the hospital, just getting an idea of the layout, ways that unauthorised personnel could have entered and so on. Sorry, got to run, leave it in your capable hands. I'll call you later. Fill you in. By the way, I've already contacted the victim's mother – in Hong Kong, you know. Very shocked, very shocked. Bad business, this, bad business. Changes everything. Have a good day, John.' And he disappeared.

Even if there'd been room to get a word in edgeways, Bright would not have trusted himself to speak.

The nurse led the way out of the observation room into the

corridor. Bright rubbed a hand over his face. 'Okay. So you came in here first. You were here say twenty minutes. Then you went where?'

'I just went along to each patient from here.'

'How many before Lee Han?'

'Four.' The girl looked ready to drop. 'If I'd only gone to him first.'

'Might not have made any difference. Whoever pulled that plug it only took them a minute. They just had to wait till you were in one of the other rooms. It's not your fault.'

She nodded unconvinced. 'You get used to losing them if it can't be helped. But . . .'

'Can someone get us a cuppa tea?'

'Oh – yes.'

'And ask this Adam to come and talk to me.' Alone for a minute, he called Chloe's number. No reply. He cursed.

'Inspector Bright?'

Slim, supple, narrow-shouldered, he had approached silently, startling Bright. 'Scuse the language,' Bright said.

'Oh, nothing shocks me. You see it all in here.'

'Adam?'

'That's right.'

'We met before.'

'Oo, you've got a good memory.'

He was one of those motherly gay men you'd trust with your life, Bright could see at a glance. Immense experience. More knowledge of the hospital and its workings than the consultants or the administrators. See all, tolerate all. 'Poor thing,' he said. 'Just when he was showing signs of life. Now that's a mean trick.'

'You think he'd have lived?'

'Not for me to say, is it? Could have gone either way. At that stage you just can't tell. But, you know – there was just that hope, wasn't there? Have they told his family?'

'His mother's been told.'

'What about his ex-wife? She comes in every day.' Adam stopped and looked at Bright. 'O-oh,' he said.

'Oh what?' Bright's squint held Adam fixed.

'Oh nothing.'

'What time of day would she normally come?'

'Could be any time – unpredictable I think we'd call her, don't you? Visiting up here is 2 to 8 p.m. – says so clear as day on the door, but she took no notice. I've seen her here all hours. Nine at night, ten in the morning.'

'But not this morning?'

'Doesn't strike me as an early riser. Does she you?'

'But if someone had seen her they wouldn't be all that surprised?'

'Don't get me wrong – I'm not accusing anyone of anything. But she's the only visitor he had apart from that nice big girl – his gardener, she said she was. She was more upset than the wife if you ask me. But you can't tell, can you? It's not just Chinese people who are inscrutable, is it? The older I get the less I know what anyone's really thinking underneath all the blather.'

'Know what you mean.'

'You too? Mmm . . . Is that it, then? Can I go now? I need my beauty sleep, death or no death, or I'll be no use to man nor beast.'

'What time do the doors open to visitors?'

'Oh, love, this is a hospital. I mean security's one thing but anyone can get in if they really want to. We're all too busy to be noticing. You know what it's like. All I can say is I didn't see a thing that was peculiar on my shift. And when I left everything was hunky dory. And Mr Lee Han was definitely alive, poor thing. I said good morning. He moved his hand. Just a little bit more movement than the day before. I said we'll be having you on meat and two veg before you know where you are. Poor bloke was probably a vegetarian. Maybe that's what killed him. Oh dear, sorry, you won't be used to the – well – what goes by the name of humour round here. I shouldn't have said that. Foot-in-mouth disease. Discretion is *not* my middle name.'

'Okay, mate. Off you go. We'll be in touch.'

'Will I have to give evidence at the inquest? I've never done that before.'

'Not sure yet. See how it goes.'

'Oh God . . .'

Bright tried Chloe's place again and this time got Llewellyn. 'Where's Chloe?'

'No sign of her, guv. Looks like she's done a runner.'

'You inside the flat?'

'The girl she shares the flat with came round and let me in.'

'I'll be there in twenty minutes. Keep her there.'

29

The girl was tall, with close-cropped hair, pure Afro, not straightened. Her tight red dress was just long enough to cover her crotch. Her legs were longer and thinner than Chloe's, and she wore red high-heeled shoes to match the frock. The red against her dark chocolate skin was spectacular. She put out a languid hand to shake Bright's. Her voice was as deep as a man's. 'Hi. I'm Shelley.'

'Any idea Chloe was going?'

'I told him, no. I let him in 'is mornin', it was like this.'

Clothes thrown around, drawers open, one baby's shoe on its side under the window.

'You had no warning?'

The girl moved her beautiful head from side to side so her silver loop ear-rings swung. 'No.'

'When'd you last speak to her?'

'Yes'day.'

'Time?'

She shrugged. 'Noon maybe. Yeah. Round twelve noon.'

'Here?'

'On the phone. I think she was on her mobile. I think she was down the market.'

'Why?'

'Donno. The noises, innit? Shoutin' an' that.'

'What she say?'

'She wos goin' out, be back late.'

'She tell you that so you could use the flat?'

The girl shut her lips. They were painted, glossy scarlet, the colour of the dress, the shininess of the shoes. She gave Bright a look.

Bright said, 'This is about to become a murder inquiry. I'm not about to prosecute you for turning a few tricks, am I, Shelley?'

'Murder?' She stood up. She was as tall as Llewellyn. Three or four inches taller than Bright. This case was making him feel smaller and smaller. He was sick of dealing with these magnificent creatures. 'Sit down.' The nasal tree-saw effect.

She was gasping. 'I got azma, I need my puffah.' She gestured at her bag, on the chest of drawers near where Llewellyn stood. Llewellyn picked up the bag, goatskin dyed to look like tiger, opened it, had a good look. 'Woss he think?' Shelley wheezed. 'I'm tooled up? You gotta be jokin'.' Llewellyn sheepishly handed her a blue asthma inhaler. She breathed out hard, then closed her shiny red lips round the thing, took a sharp intake of breath, released a puff of the medication into her mouth, held her breath for a few seconds and breathed out again. She coughed. She looked better. But she still wheezed a bit when she spoke. 'Who's been knocked off then?' she said.

'Chloe's ex.'

'Lee? My lovely little Lee? Oh no, man!' Her eyes filled with big tears that shook on her lower lids then rolled down her face. 'I'll kill her,' she said. 'I'll kill her, I will.'

Bright glanced at Llewellyn who looked a bit white round the gills. 'Kill who?'

'Well, why she disappear, man? What else she got to run for? He paid her a allowance. He love her kid. He never was unkind to her. I don' believe he was unkind to anyone.'

'They say he knocked her about.'

'He never! She the one done the knockin'. Maybe he slap her face one time she drove him too far, but tha's it, man. He call the ol' bill cos he scared he goin' kill her, but he never touch her. She couldn' handle the stuff, she be out of her head, the baby cryin', then she have a go at him. Wass he suppose to do? And now she kill 'im. Ah shit!' She was pacing the room like the walls were too tight to hold her. The long red nails looked dangerous. Bright was glad not to be in Chloe's shoes.

'You wanna watch what you say, Shelley. We don't know it was Chloe. We've reason to believe there's a few people would like Lee out the way.'

'Who? That bastard—' She stopped, wiped her face with her hand, went to her animal-stripe bag and got out a handful of tissues. She dabbed her face.

'That bastard who, Shell?'

'I'm not saying. You the one say I should be careful, innit?'

'Are we talking Brennan here? Michael Brennan?'

'We not talkin' anyone.'

'Are we talking at all?'

She looked out of the window. At the innocent street. People going about their innocent-looking business.

'Lee was your friend?' Bright could make his voice purr like a cat, soothing, suggestive, reassuring as a stroking hand, *oh I'll wash you in milk And I'll clothe you in silk.* He said, 'Lee's got no one to speak for him, Shelley, and he can't speak for himself, can he? He likely wouldn't have spoken again even if he'd lived, poor sod. But someone couldn't take that risk.' He waited. She turned round. She didn't look at him but she stood there at the window waiting for more. He said, 'You're in here with us. Whoever it was will know that. Whether you talk to us or not, they'll think you have. We'll give you protection—'

'You lot? Protection? You couldn' even protec' a poor sick bastard in a hospital, man—'

'It's a murder now. We get more resources. DC Llewellyn here will be on your case. Twenty-four hours a day.'

Taffy looked pained. He wanted to be out – looking for Chloe.

Shelley looked him down and up like she was thinking of buying him. 'Him and who else?' she said. 'He gonna stay awake twenty-four hours a day? Oh yeah! What is he? Fuckin' Superman?'

'Well, not just him, obviously. Three shifts. But DC Llewellyn will be in charge. He's one of my most reliable officers. I trust him to do a good job.'

'I'm a workin' girl. How can I work with a crowda old bill on my tail day an' night?'

'I told you—'

'Yeah you tol' me. I been tol' lossa things.'

'I promise you. You got my word.'

She looked at him. Her look would smelt metal. Not for the first time in this case he wondered about spontaneous combustion. He looked back, not saying a thing. She said, 'Sometimes you got this squint, sometimes you don't. How you do that?'

'I dunno, Shelley. One of those things. At school the teachers couldn't tell where I was looking. They could never accuse me of anything – *I wasn't looking at you, miss!* You know.'

'Iss a good trick.' She was working him like a john. She was promising him a very good time.

He said, 'I don't trade, Shelley.' He said it soft, not a rebuke, not a put-down. 'I promise you something? I deliver.'

'Yeah? You the only man in the worl' tha's true of then.'

'Talk to me, Shelley?' He had moved closer to her. She didn't back off.

She sighed. She leaned her beautiful tight ass on the back of the settee and looked at her shiny scarlet toes. 'No names,' she said.

Bright looked at Llewellyn. 'Okay. For now. No names.'

'Guy who got her started.'

'Chloe?'

'Chloe! Yeah! Who else we talkin' 'bout?'

'Got her started on what?'

'Everythin'. The hard stuff and then bein' a workin' girl. You know him. You know how he work. He got girls all over. Start you off high class, good money, high-class tricks, then the hard stuff get you and it gets lower and lower class and then you no use to him any more, he stop supplyin'. I seen it all over. Girls goin' down the fuckin' tubes for that bastard.'

'How about you?'

'My little brother was a junkie. Ten year old. We couldn' do nothing. Eleven year old, he sellin', innit? Stealin' an' sellin'. Three hundred a day habit. Then he got put away an' they got him in detox. After detox he was a little kid again. Like they give him his soul back. I'm on'y fourteen, right? But I say then never, I will never touch that stuff, never!'

'So what happened?'

'I met that bastard. I wos fifteen. He seduce me, man. You gonna ask me how come I'm so stupit? Everyone wos tellin' me, but he so beautiful, so smooth, so rich, he seem like so legitimate! His nice car, nice suits. He was like, I'm really in love with you, Shell, I really want to marry you, I ain't never felt like this about no one before. Says I'm gonna be like, this model, have an international career, he can do all this for me. Then it was like, Just this once, Shell, just to please this real importan' client of mine? He likes three in a bed, so what? Where's the harm? Like, come on Shell iss only this once just to please me? And then the nex' time and the nex' time. And he got me hook the same way. Come on, Shell, it'll cheer you up. Jus' this once. I love you, I wouldn' let you get addicted, Shell! And when he drop me, I di'n't care what happen to me. Only, that year, my little brother came out. He so ashame of me. He make me go col' turkey. He sat with me, he hold me, he bath me, he wipe my vomit, he hold me while I'm having convulsions. So I got clean. I'm clean.'

'How long?'

'I know what you sayin'! How long before I go back? Well I'm not goin' back, right? I been savin'. I work for myself.'

'Who pays the rent on this place?'

'I'm off his hook. That bastard. But he don't know that. Not unless you lot tell him. You gonna tell him he don't own Shelley no more? One more year, I got enough saved and I'm out. I'm leavin'.'

Bright nodded like he believed her, tried not to let his sadness show. 'You could be a model now. Straight up. Why wait a year?'

She gave him an old-fashioned look. 'I heard that once I heard it a million times. Forget it.'

'So he got Chloe the same way?'

'No. She think she's usin' him. She ain't; she's just usin'. She thought she could control it. She think *now* she controllin' it. She's wrong. She got no heart. She wa'n't never in love with no one. 'Cep' maybe Lee. Once upon a time. When they was kids.'

Llewellyn shifted like his back itched. Bright gave him a warning look. He coughed. He went to the window and looked out. Bright said, 'Where will she have gone?'

'She'll go to him, innit?'

'This no name bastard we're talking about?'

'She need him, man. He's her supplier, innit? She can't get away from him. She got no way out. He an octopus. You think you got away, this big arm come round you neck and you hooked in again. On'y way you get away is if he want to drop you. Then you drown, man. Tha's it. He got her to pull the plug on Lee? He'll drop her. But he got to keep her quiet first.' Shelley's face went into an astonished stillness, hearing what she'd said.

Llewellyn's face looked the same. If Chloe had pulled the plug on Lee – if she had done it at Brennan's instigation – there was nowhere she could go to hide. Or her baby either. Bright wondered if Brennan drew the line at babies. He suspected not. 'Why would he want to pull the plug on Lee?'

'Lee was writin' all this stuff. He just got hold of this big thing. He wouldn't say what. Just a big thing was goin' to blow the bastard's kingdom sky high. I tol' Lee, Stop, man, you gettin' in danger water. But no. Lee had to get the bastard. It was revenge, innit? Not just Chloe. His kid. His little junkie baby that nearly die.'

A great sigh filled the room. It was a shock hearing it. It came out of all three of them at the same time. Bright said, 'Well, we know who we're talking about, Shelley.'

'I'll never testify. I'll never go to court. I'm not gonna be a witness. I know what happen to witnesses. I'll never do that.'

'Can you go in the other room a minute, Shelley?'

They watched her into the bedroom. They shut the door.

'Think Chloe's gone to Brennan?'

Llewellyn's eyes stared out of black pits. 'She wouldn't go to him. She's not stupid.'

'Well, maybe she was clever enough to broker a deal. Get paid off up front.'

'That's assuming she's done it. We can't assume that.'

'Why else would she disappear, Taff? She clears out of here last night and this morning we find Lee's copped it? Bit of a coincidence, you got to admit.'

'She could've known Brennan was going to do it – have it done – and cleared out before we got to her.'

Bright's squint narrowed. 'A-ha. Yeah.' He sounded as convinced as he could. 'I'll leave you here with the panther. I'll get you replaced soon as I can organise it.'

Llewellyn looked hungry, sick. But he nodded. A good cop doesn't argue with his superior officer; a good cop obeys orders.

Then the door banged back on its hinges and Shelley stood in the doorway like an avenging angel. She panted, she could barely speak. 'Iss gone! Iss gone!' She held out a tin box, used to hold Oxo cubes, sort of thing you bought in the market on the stalls selling shabby kitsch. The tin was empty.

'What was in it, Shell?'

They followed her back into the whore's boudoir. The cheap exotic finery, the satiny scarlet slither. The bed had been pulled to one side. A floorboard had been lifted.

'All my savin's, man. She's took it, that bitch.'

Taff said, 'You don't know Chloe did this.'

'I didn' know the bitch knew it was here.'

'When you last see it?'

'Las' see it? Yes'day mornin'.'

'Anyone else here then?'

'No.'

'Sure?'

She rolled her eyes. Shrugged, not a languid shrug, ferocious, like her shoulders might lift the roof. She threw the tin box on to the bed. Taff picked it up with a tissue. Bright said, 'We'll fingerprint it. How much was there?'

Big tears rolled down. 'Five thousan'.'

She should have saved more. But the five K would have been scraped off her secret johns, her bit of private enterprise, after Brennan had taken his cut. She said, 'Five *thousan*', man.'

'Anyone else could have known it was here?'

'You never leave a john alone in the room, right?'

Bright's mobile rang. The duty sergeant at HQ said, 'A Mrs Jude Craig is at the front desk. Wants to see you. No one else will do.'

'Jude Craig? Tell her to go home. I'll see her in half an hour.'

'You see?' Llewellyn said. 'Chloe Han's not the only one who's done a runner.'

Bright paused on his way out. 'You're right there, Taff. And who went first – Dan Craig or Chloe?'

30

She knew as soon as she saw him it was bad news. She was watching at the window and had the door open before he rang the bell. She couldn't find any voice. She whispered, 'Dan?'

He shook his head.

'Not Dan?' she said.

'Lee Han.'

'Lee?' She couldn't understand at first. She backed away into the hallway, her hand out as though to push the bad news away. 'Lee's dead?'

Bright came inside and shut the door.

'Lee's dead.' Her mouth formed the words but her voice did not back them up. 'Ah, no.' She sat on the lowest stair and covered her face with her hands. The tears crawled through her fingers and down the backs of her hands, snaking down the insides of her arms.

'Looks like he was killed,' Bright said.

'Killed?'

'Looks like someone pulled the plug on him. Early hours this morning.'

She stood up, startling him, and walked to the back of the hall where the sun came blinding through the cloakroom window. She turned on the tap and splashed cold water on her face. She groped for the towel and he handed it to her. She held it to her face for a few minutes, breathing hard, then she took it away, folded it neatly and hung it on the rail. She turned to him. 'Did Dan do it?' she said.

'Fuck me, Mrs Craig, you don't mess about.'

'Did he?'

'Why do you think he might have done it?'

She started to speak then stopped. Then pulled herself together and started again. 'Chloe came here,' she said. 'That's why I wanted to see you. That's why I went to the police station. To tell you that.'

'Chloe was *here*? *When?*'

'Night before last. Evening. Early. The night before Dan left.'

'Why didn't you tell me this before?'

'I couldn't.'

'Why?'

'I was trying to protect Dan.'

'You've lost me.'

'She accused Dan.'

'Accused him? What of?'

'Setting fire to Lee.'

'Christ.'

'She said she saw him. Dan. Standing in the garden of the house opposite. Hiding. Waiting. Watching. After I had left. Before the fire broke out.'

'He deny it?'

'No. She told him I was having a thing with Lee.'

'You deny it?'

'Sort of. Yes.'

Jude looked at him, waiting. The opaque stare. The strange inward-focused eyes. 'What did she want?' he said. 'What she want from him? Chloe's not known for her devotion to law and order. She blackmailing him?'

'Yes.'

'What for? Money? What?'

'Yes. Money. She thinks we're rich.' Jude gave a sad laugh.

'So what'd he say?'

'We both said if you saw Dan, it means you were there

too and the police would like to know that.'

'A-ha. And?'

'She said she didn't care if you knew she was there.'

'Oh, did she now?'

'She was furious. But she went.'

'She been in touch since?'

'No.'

'You hear from her or see her, you call me. Right away. Okay?'

'Yes. Yes.'

'Or your husband either, come to that.' He was looking at her with this sad angry gaze, like she'd done something bad but he was trying not to blame her.

'I'm sorry. I know I should have told you right away. And now I've betrayed Dan anyway. Now you know he was there. At Lee's place.'

'You ask him what he was doing there?'

'Yes.'

'What was his story?'

'He wouldn't tell me. He sort of implied it was just – jealousy.'

'Spying on you?'

'Yes.'

'What'd he tell Chloe?'

'Nothing. I made an excuse for him. I told her he had come there to meet me. I even gave this mad explanation for why he'd be loitering in the garden opposite – I said as an architect he's always interested in empty houses. I mean, it's true but—' She stopped, pushed the piles of chestnut hair up off her forehead and gave a choking sound – a sigh or a laugh or a sob – hard to say which. 'So we sent Chloe off, in a terrible rage. And then of course everything came out about me and Lee. Dan had known from the start, he said. He blamed himself. But he was blaming me really. I said he'd never recovered from his mother's death and he needed help and he stormed off upstairs and I haven't seen him since. And now—' here she broke down – 'now he's gone and Lee has died and George has disappeared and I can't bear it, I can't . . . I've lost everything in the world I ever cared about and it's all my own fault.'

He wanted to put his arms round her. He wanted to wipe the mascara off her face, all smudged round her eyes like a panda. She was big but she was about the only big bugger in this case that didn't make him feel a midget, made him feel protective even.

'He's dead too,' she said. 'I know he is.'

'Your husband?'

'George.' Then she stopped sobbing. She looked at Bright, these flowery blue eyes, ringed with wet mascara, smears of mascara all over her freckled face. She said, 'Dan? Dead? No? Is that what you think—?'

'No!' Bright handed her the face cloth from the sink. 'I'm not paid to think; I'm paid to investigate.'

She rubbed the cool damp cloth over her face. She was obedient with him. She handed it back to him. Like a child.

He said, 'Why don't you think something bad has happened to your husband?'

'I don't know.'

'You said he was depressed.'

'Yes.'

'Why do you assume he went of his own accord?'

'His getaway bag. I told you. He's always had it. Under his desk. Packed. Toothbrush, shaving gear, change of underwear. No one else would know about that. Only me.'

'A-ha. Okay.' She could see he wasn't convinced. He bounced on his toes, hands deep in his pockets, jangling his change. She could feel this febrile energy coming off him, making the atmosphere jagged like broken glass. He said, 'Money.'

'What?'

'What's he doing for money?'

'Well, he'll have his credit cards, cheque book—'

'He wants to disappear he won't use those.'

'Oh. I see.'

'He take any money out of the bank?'

'I haven't checked. Just a mo.' She rummaged in the drawer and found a letter from the bank. She dialled the number. An electronic voice said, 'Welcome to our customer services. If you wish to make an inquiry about opening an account with us, press 1.' She groaned. She let the options run out and waited for a real person to speak to her. The real person asked for her password. 'Password? Oh God, I don't know! I can't remember.' She looked at Bright like a woman drowning. 'Hang on a minute. I must be able to remember. I must!' She closed her eyes. '"George"?' she said.

The bank person said thank you, and then something Jude could not believe.

'Excuse me,' Jude said. 'Could you repeat that, please?' She listened to the repetition, picked up a pencil and wrote down what the woman told her, then asked, 'When was this?' and the woman gave her a date. 'I see. Thanks.' Jude put down the phone and looked at the paper.

'So what was all that about?'

'There's been no withdrawal,' she said. 'I just don't understand.' She passed him the piece of paper. 'That amount was paid into the account on Wednesday.'

The day Crabbe died. Bright took the paper and looked at it. 'Fifty thousand quid?'

'Yes.'

'Who paid it in?'

'Dan's signature is on the paying-in slip.'

'Was it a cheque?'

'It was in cash.'

'Fifty thousand? In notes?' He whistled. 'How much is usually in the account?'

'Around a thousand if we're lucky. Just enough to pay the bills and live on for a while. A lot of the time we're on the overdraft.'

'Any other accounts, building society, anything like that, he could have transferred it from?'

'We have got a building society account. But we never had *that* much in *any* account.' She scrabbled through the papers and bits of string and spare keys in a bottom drawer of the desk. 'Here it is.' She handed over the book.

Bright checked the last figure. 'Seven thousand four hundred quid. No withdrawal since last May. No payments since two thousand quid on the fifth of June.'

'That was my last major job, before Lee. We've got no other accounts.'

'As far as you know.'

'Dan and I had no secrets,' she said, then moaned and covered her eyes.

'This client – Embrey – paid him off then.'

'Yes, that must be it.' But her face was full of doubt.

'Would it be that much?' Bright said. 'In cash? That normal, is it?'

'I don't think so. And anyway I thought Dan said the cost of the job was round two hundred thousand. So Dan's ten per cent would be twenty thousand. But it was Dan who broke the contract. I don't think he expected to get paid.'

'His mother left it him then. He's had it in a secret account, or he's had it under the mattress; he put it in the current account for you to use now he's – while he's – gone.'

'His mother never had that sort of money. She had nothing to live on but her state pension. And us.'

He looked at her, speculating, ruminating, wondering. 'Dan

did buy his mother's flat,' he said.

'No.'

'He did. Four years ago. We checked the council records.'

'What with? We had no money. None to spare.'

'He only paid twenty-five grand.'

'But – even that's a fortune to us, and . . .' She shook her head from side to side, trying to apply some rational thought.

'We went to see Mr Reynolds yesterday.'

'Reynolds?'

'The tower house client.' Bright stared at her, little hard chips of light in his eyes. 'Reynolds is one of the names used by a local villain. He was at school with your husband. Lived in the same flats.'

'Cleverden Mansions?'

'Dan never mentioned him?'

She shook her head: no. She said, 'Are you saying this Reynolds lent him the money?' She wasn't slow. 'To buy his mother's flat? Four years ago?'

'I think it's possible. Don't you?'

Again she didn't speak; just shook her head.

Bright said, 'We've since been informed by the Land Registry that the flat is now owned by a property company that is probably owned by Reynolds. The name on the plan here – Embrey Properties.'

'Since when?'

'Since just under two years ago.'

'And you think this fifty thousand is for the flat?'

'Let's say I wouldn't be surprised.'

She said slowly, 'Those flats sell for a hundred and fifty thousand now.'

'That's why we think this – Reynolds – might have something over on your husband. Can you think of anything?'

She shook her head, her heart clutched tight by dread. She

whispered, 'I can't think of anything Dan ever did wrong.' *But I know now he lied and lied. To me. About so many things. He's made our life – my life – so hard – by refusing to tell me what was wrong. But that's because he was ashamed. Ashamed of something he'd done? Something that had been done to him?* 'Perhaps it was just that,' she said. 'The deal over the flat – this gangster giving him the money.'

'Reynolds has had one or other of his whores in there for a couple of years. A lot of drug dealing. It's known to us.'

'Well, there you are! Dan would be ashamed at that! It would make him feel terrible! He disapproves even of selling off council flats. It's against his principles.'

'The gangster's real name is Brennan,' Bright said. He was watching her for a reaction but the name meant nothing to her, he could see. She'd never heard of Brennan. People could live round here year in and year out, the biggest criminal families in London operating all around them, and not even know. Two parallel worlds. Going on side by side. Never meeting. And when the bad life impinged on her life, picked it up and shook it loose like this, it was like she was being hit by another species, from another planet. He really longed, just for a minute, to shake her and make her see. Or better still, to work and live among her kind. The unconscious ones. The good ones. The pure ones. The innocents. The ones who didn't know. 'Michael Brennan,' he said.

She said, 'Michael?'

Bright's breath left his body real slow till it was all gone. All he'd had to say – Michael. And if he'd said it at the start—

'Michael?' she said. 'Dan's friend Michael? Michael's not a criminal! A gangster? It can't be the same Michael.'

'You know him?'

'I've only met him once. At Dan's mother's funeral. Two years ago.'

'What's he like? Describe him.'

'Tall, very good-looking, very charming, obviously well off, quite sort of – cultured. I mean, he's read a lot and likes – you know – nice buildings and pictures and – things. He has a slight Irish accent. I was surprised, because he was brought up in Gospel Oak like Dan. But he said he spends a lot of time with his family over there, so I— I was surprised that Dan didn't invite him again. I liked him— Oh God. It's him then? Yes.'

'A-ha. It's him.'

'Michael! Dan really loves him. He used to look out for Dan when they were kids. Dan was a couple of years older but Michael was bigger, stronger. He fought Dan's battles – Dan never told me he was a—' She walked about, she couldn't keep still, getting this into her head. 'Dan's boyhood friend Michael is this Reynolds? They're one person? And this person is a criminal, a real criminal like you read about in the papers?'

'You got it.'

'Was Dan really designing a house for him?'

'Brennan/Reynolds says so. The land's cleared but there's no sign of any building.'

'You've seen him then? Asked him—'

'Yesterday.'

'And Dan's not with him?'

'I'm pretty sure he's not.'

'And you think he has some hold over Dan?'

'It's possible.'

'And because of that he could make Dan – do things – against his will.'

'It's possible.'

'Even – really bad things.'

'A-ha.'

She said, wondering, 'My whole life has been a sort of lie. A fairy tale that I've been making up as I went along. The only real thing in the last ten years has been George. Animals don't pretend or lie. They can't. Animals are better than people.'

'Well, they don't have the possibilities, do they?'

'It's my fault of course.'

'What is?'

'Dan getting into this trouble, whatever it is.'

'How's it your fault?'

'Being blind. Staying blind. Living my fantasy life. The good life. He didn't want to spoil it for me. He was my hero; I couldn't believe he would do wrong: how could he tell me? If he had, I could have helped him. I could have told him what to do.'

Bright said, 'It's not your fault. People do what they do. He's the one done wrong. Not you.'

'What wrong?' She looked at him. The same look. A lot of action going on behind those childish blue eyes. 'Buying his mother's flat with money borrowed from a friend? Even if the friend is a gangster. That's not so very wrong. Is it? It's not even against the law exactly. Is it?'

'No.'

'You think he's done something worse.'

'I hope not.'

'But you can't find Chloe Han.' Her eyes closed. She put a hand out to the wall like she was dizzy. She opened her eyes. It was better with her eyes open. The world stood still again. She had to put it into words. 'And someone killed Lee.' She felt her face dissolving like wax but she would not cry till she'd said what had to be said. 'You think Dan could have set fire to Lee. When that didn't work he had to – pull the plug, as you put it. And he had to get rid of Chloe because she could give evidence against him?' She shook her head. This was outlandish. This was not Dan. 'No.'

'I agree with you. I'd take bets your husband has not killed anyone. But there's a lot of people in this case with quite a lot at stake. So if you get word of him for Christsake tell me pronto because bad things could happen to him, worse things than getting arrested, believe me.'

'I don't believe Dan could kill anyone. I suppose they all say that – the wives and mothers and girlfriends?'

'A-ha.'

A long sad look passed between them. His eyes lost the hard metallic specks. Just small brown eyes with the slight strabismus of a Siamese cat. For a wild moment she thought he was going to put his arms round her. She nearly stepped forward into his arms. It would have felt natural. Normal.

'Will you be all right?' he said.

The moment was over. She caught her breath. 'Sure.'

'You shouldn't be on your own.'

'I've got a job this afternoon. Should have been this morning but – all this. A garden in Lady Margaret Road. Kate Creech. I think you know her.'

His expression made a complicated adjustment. 'A-ha. I know Kate.'

'So I'll just go there and get on with my work. As though everything were normal. I can't think of doing anything else, I don't like leaving the house for a minute. Just in case— But I've got my mobile. If one of your blokes finds my cat – or my husband – perhaps they could give me a call?'

'A-ha. Sure.'

She said, lightly, 'Alive or dead.'

31

And just before five that afternoon a call came through to the CID room. Cato picked it up.

'Guv? Call from BA. Girl seen on BA flight to Hong Kong. Answers Chloe's description. Different name: Mun-yi Wong. With a baby. Six months old. Hong Kong passport. Purpose of journey: return home from visit to relatives in London.'

'Tell them to hold her at Hong Kong airport.'

'Plane arrived already in Hong Kong. Girl passed through airport authorities there, no problem. Not searched.'

'How does she do it?' Bright ran to the DCI's office, shoved the door open without knocking. 'I gotta speak to someone in the Hong Kong police.'

'You have to go through Interpol.'

'Shit, yeah.' He phoned the Interpol office at Scotland Yard. They would speak with the Interpol office in Hong Kong. The guys on the ground, the ones doing the hard graft, never got to speak to each other at all, unless they clawed a tunnel from both ends through the geological strata of hierarchy. It was called Improved Communications.

A posh bastard answered. 'We'll get in touch with the relevant authorities in Hong Kong. It shouldn't take too long.'

'Don't give me this shite, mate. I haven't got time. I need to communicate now!'

'They're all in bed there at the moment, Inspector Bright. Hong Kong is seven and a half hours ahead of us.'

'Get them up! This girl, if she is Chloe Han, could bust open the biggest rats' nest in years. This is connected to a very big case, mate. If you go slow now it'll mean bad consequences later.'

The voice lost just a millimetre of its patrician drawl. 'We'll do our best, at least to get them to start background checks there. What is the suspect's name again?'

Bright did not sigh, did not groan. Abide in patience, his ma had told him all his life. He gave Chloe's details as far as he knew them, filled in the background to the case.

'Why isn't AMIP handling this, excuse my asking?'

Bright silently ground his teeth. 'This has been our case for two years now. AMIP are keeping a watching brief.'

'Oh . . .' A lingering tone of puzzlement. 'Which officer in particular?'

'DCI Roger Gould.' Bright made his voice flat as a chapati.

'Oh, Roger, I know him well. We've attended conferences together. And he's just keeping a watching brief? Hmm . . . I'll have a word. I assume he's up to date with this latest development.'

Assume what you want, mate, Bright did not say. He did say, 'How soon am I going to get to speak to someone in Hong Kong?'

'Is there anyone in the Hong Kong Police Bureau you've ever had personal contact with?'

Some hopes. 'Nah,' he said, but politely.

'I'll do my best, Inspector.'

'Thanks.'

He put a call through to Roger Gould who wasn't there. He left a message with the secretary. He'd have preferred an answering machine.

Cato came to his door and waved a piece of paper at him. 'Guv? Address of the relatives this girl Mun-yi Wong's supposed to have been visiting in Chinatown.'

Bright grabbed his old leather jacket off the back of his chair.

'Anyone from Hong Kong or Interpol calls, get me on the mobile!' He ran down the stairs and out of the building before anyone could catch him.

The address was a narrow street off Gerrard Street, away from the golden dragons and glitz, past the small Chinese medicine shops, not far from Manzi's where he used to eat in the old days before they fixed it up for the tourists.

He walked in the road, forced off the narrow pavement by the bulging black garbage bags, the wooden pallets and piles of polystyrene packaging. A garbage truck took up the middle of the street, holding up a honking line of cars. Bicycle messengers dodged between and around, terrorising the pedestrians. One nearly took Bright's foot off just outside the address he was looking for.

It was a small fishmonger's. A young man was laying out a rainbow of fish in his tiny window. Bright stood and watched. The shop was only big enough to take one customer at a time. Bright went in. The young man ignored him.

'You the owner here?'

He did not look at Bright. Nor did he answer. He rang a bell on the door at the back of the shop. 'Mr Kwan will come,' he said. He returned to his fish.

Bright watched him take a knife like a small scimitar and with lethal expertise open up a sea bass. He slit the stomach from gills to tail, then sliced out its innards which he squelched in his hand and threw into a wooden tub. Then he took a knife worn down to a long curving bodkin, lifted the fish by its tail and in three lightning sweeps sheared off its scales. Silver shards of mica scattered over his marble block. With one stroke of the knife he swept them off into another wooden tub.

A door opened at the back of the shop, breaking Bright's mesmerised concentration. A small thin Chinese man came out of the shadows. The young fishmonger said something in Chinese without looking up from his work. The older man said nothing; he stood waiting for Bright to state his business. He was smooth-faced but something about the lines from nose to mouth said mid-fifties at least.

'Mr Kwan?' Bright showed his ID, then a picture of Chloe. 'Do you know this girl?'

He shrugged. His face showed nothing. Bright had this problem with the Chinese. He'd always had it, even with Chinese waiters. He knew racial stereotyping was out of order but inscrutable was right. Mind you, *he* could talk; he specialised in inscrutable himself. He knew the value of the blank face. 'She's not your niece then?'

'No, sir.'

The fish slitter raised his eyebrows at Chloe's picture and made a silent whistle. But he too said no. 'Who is she?'

'Name Chloe Han mean anything to you?'

The two men shrugged and shook their heads.

Bright said, 'Your niece has been staying with you?'

'Yes. Two week. Go back Hong Kong.'

'Got a picture of her?'

The man called something in Chinese up the stairs.

'When'd she go back to Hong Kong?'

'Yesterday.'

'You go to the airport to see her off?'

'No. Taxi came.'

'A black cab? Or a minicab?'

The young man had stopped his work. The two men did not look at each other but they were communicating all right. Bright caught the young guy's eye. Blank. He went back to his fish, sliced the green and bronze belly of a bream wide open.

Mr Kwan said, 'Minicab.'

'What firm?'

'Don't understand.'

'What minicab firm did you ring to fetch her?'

'Ah. Niece ring cab.'

'How? Someone gave her one of those cards that come through the letterbox? What?'

'I ask wife.' He called again in Chinese up the dark wooden stairs. A woman appeared, short flat grey hair, small face, wiry body in black trousers and black silk blouse. They spoke together. She went through her pockets. She brought out a handful of cab advert cards and fanned them out like playing cards.

'You can't remember which one you called?'

'Ah no. I gave cards to niece. She call cab.'

'Are you sure?'

'Sure I'm sure.'

'Your niece speak enough English for that?'

The fish slitter spoke without looking up. 'She speaks better English than them. You get a decent education in Hong Kong.'

Bright turned his attention to him. 'Were you here when their niece left?'

'Yes. She's my cousin.'

The middle-aged couple conferred then the woman handed Bright a colour snap of a Chinese girl with a baby. The baby was plump. The girl had long shiny hair like a black waterfall to her shoulder blades. She was pretty. But she was no Chloe Han. However, judging by the height of the windowsill she was standing next to, she'd be about the same height and build.

He spoke again to the fish slitter. 'No one went to the airport with her?'

'No. Too busy. Long journey back here. Expensive too.'

'What about the baby? She manage all right by herself?'

'Sure, why not?'

'You've no idea what cab firm they used?'

'No.'

'Did you see the cab?'

'Sure. Big maroon car. A Ford maybe? Not so clean.'

The guy was now proffering a bit too much information. Not quite in character. Bright's ears went up. 'Notice the driver?'

'Paki, wasn't he?'

The parents did not reply.

Bright asked them. 'You remember?'

A pause then the woman said, 'Not Paki. White man.'

'White man? That it?'

No response.

'Oh well, I guess we all look the same to you.'

The fish slitter did not smile. 'They're usually Paki or blacks,' he said.

'So – no name of firm, no description of driver, no particular make of car. I suppose one of you definitely got the registration number?' No smiles. Nothing. He sighed. 'A-ha.' He waved the picture of the niece. 'Can I keep this?'

'Yes, sir.'

The fish slitter said, 'What's this about anyway?'

Now he asked. Now that was strange. None of them had asked. They might think kidnapping, plane crash, pile-up on the M4? Or the girl arrested for something? Or the baby sick maybe? But not a single question. Not one. He showed the picture of Chloe Han again. No reaction from anyone. 'This is definitely not your niece?'

'No, sir.'

'You never saw this girl?'

'No, sir.'

'And as far as you know your niece caught her plane at Heathrow for Hong Kong yesterday?'

'Plane round two o'clock. Yes.'

'And have you heard from her since she arrived in Hong Kong?'

They looked at each other: which of us is going to answer this one?

He waited. He tried to be really inscrutable too.

Finally the woman said, 'No. Big time different. Jet lag. We hear today maybe?'

'A-ha. Maybe.'

'She okay?' The fish slitter again did not look up. Well, maybe it was wise not to look up while you were slitting fish. 'Something happened to her?' he said.

Bright hesitated a moment. What the hell: 'We're not sure the girl who travelled on your niece's passport was actually your niece. We're not sure your niece went back to Hong Kong.' He looked from one face to the other.

No reaction. No reaction at all. But all movement stopped. Just for that instant. Bright waited. You wait long enough, generally somebody speaks.

The fish slitter said, 'But that's crazy. A girl with a baby? I mean—?'

'A-ha. Well . . . You think of anything that might be useful, you let me know, okay?'

Fish Slitter wiped his bloody hands on his bloodier apron. He took a cab card from his mother's small narrow hand and a pen stained with dried blood from his shirt pocket. He wrote a few words and said, 'Her mother's phone number in Hong Kong. My auntie.'

Bright took the card. He wanted so much to call this number now, in person. But he knew a hasty action at this point could get him in deep shit. He had to deal through Interpol; he had to play by the book. He called the Interpol office.

He gave the number to the posh sod he'd spoken to before. 'They tell me it's Mun-yi Wong's mother. We need to know if she arrived. Has her mother heard from her? You'll want a Chinese interpreter.' At least while he was here in the fish shop, these people couldn't be calling her to warn her of events.

He reached in his pocket, took out some more pictures, fanned like the woman's hand of cab cards. He chose one. 'You know him?' he said. 'Ever seen him?'

Fish Slitter got the picture first. Bright watched him go dead still. 'No,' he said. Again he looked at no one. 'Who is he?' and passed it on to the woman.

The man and woman looked at it together. Said no together. Just a second too fast. Handed it back.

The picture was of Brennan; not a police mug shot; he was in an expensive suit and tie, night-club ambience, smiling, charming, urbane.

Next he passed a picture of Julian French, Brennan's oily lawyer. They were ready for that one. They all in turn shook their heads. 'No,' said the man. 'Sorry,' said the woman.

Bright tried another one. 'How about these guys?'

Fish Slitter took the photo with his right hand, fish blood in the fingernails. His other hand, resting on the counter, moved like a startled crab, just once. Then bunched to a fist. His face had no expression. His voice had no expression. 'No,' he said. He was lying.

The parents looked at the picture together. Together they shook their heads. The man said, 'Sorry, can't help you, sir.' His voice had no expression but when he handed the picture back there was sorrow in his eyes. Bright saw it. The picture showed the Triad man who had been shot dead in Essex two years ago and, standing next to him with an arm round his shoulders, smiling, a known Chinatown crime boss.

Taking back the picture from Mr Kwan he said, 'Thank you,' with more gratitude than they could know. He slid this picture into a plastic envelope. They all watched in silence. He considered briefly. He said, 'My name's John Bright. You can help me to put an end to some bad stuff. You know what I mean.' He saw the blank faces but the eyes were no longer blank to him. He knew misery when he saw it. He'd seen a lot of it. He was seeing a lot of it here, now. He was also seeing hopelessness. He'd seen a lot of that too. He didn't like it. 'And I can help you, but only if you tell me how.'

He knew these people would never tell him anything. They couldn't. He had no grounds for questioning further. And no grounds for a warrant to search the flat upstairs. And even more certainly he would never be invited in. He gave the woman his card. She seemed to be the card collector of the family. 'If you hear from your niece, will you tell me right away?' No one replied so he turned to go.

32

He walked, slow, out of the shop, down the street, to Newport Place, lined with classy Chinese food shops and little restaurants selling Peking Roast Duck. He salivated. It was going-out-for-a-meal time. But not for him. He called HQ on the mobile. 'Cato? It's shifting! Brennan is definitely connected to the family of the girl who may or may not be Chloe who was on the plane to Hong Kong, and this family is also connected in some way to the Triad shooting two years ago in Essex.'

'Is this info usable, guv?'

'No.'

'Oh.'

'But I know. For sure.'

'I believe you.'

'That's big of you, Cato. Do something else for me?'

'Sure.'

'Is Maggie on lates?'

'Yes. She's here now.'

'Get her to have another look at the file on the Essex Triad shooting. I want a print-out. I want to know the gun that was used. Was it found? Where is it now?'

'You got it.'

'And tell her I want it yesterday.'

'Er, guv? You want me to call Inspector Gould?'

Bright's voice was bland. 'I tried him earlier. He'd already gone home. I left a message. So I don't know if we need to bother him with this right now. Do you?'

'I might leave another message. Just to call you when he gets in?'

'That's a good idea, Cat.'

'De nada, guv.'

Cato greeted him with a wad of print-out on the Essex Triad shooting. 'Look at this!' His pipe was clamped so hard in his teeth he could barely speak. He'd underlined certain passages. He compared these to highlighted passages in the Kentish Town shooting report. He said, 'It's the same gun! Fuck, guv, why didn't we know this?'

Bright had seldom before heard Cato swear. He read the passage about the gun used in the Essex killing. It too had not been found at the scene. But the details about the bullets were identical. His hands screwed into fists, crunching the paper. He pulled down both fists hard. He said, 'Yes! Yes! Yes!'

He spent ten minutes with the team. 'No connection was made between the shooting in Kentish Town and the shooting in Essex because at that time, and until we talked to Jude Craig on the Lee Han case, we didn't know Brennan had a place there. Now I don't have any hard evidence, but I am as sure as I can get of a connection between Brennan and the Triad guy that got shot. And we've now established that these two shootings were done with the same weapon.'

He detailed Cato and Helen to watch the Chinese fishmonger's. 'Follow the young guy. He's the only one likely to take any action.'

He brought the DCI up to date. 'Get me clearance for a phone tap.'

'Fat lot of good. They'll use a mobile.'

'You never know. We might get something.'

He spent an hour pacing, adding notes to his report. It was the first time in his life he enjoyed doing a report. He would have liked to write it in letters of fire. Then his phone rang.

'Hello, this is Albert Choi, Detective Inspector of the Hong Kong Police Bureau.'

Albert? Bright was taken aback. They had names like Albert there?

'You needed to know if a Hong Kong national by the name of Mun-yi Wong arrived yesterday morning in Chek Lap Kok airport on a BA flight from Heathrow.'

'I do.'

'A person with a passport in that name passed through customs with her baby.'

'A-ha? And?'

'She did not arrive at her mother's house.'

'And?'

'Her mother has not heard that she had arrived in Hong Kong.'

'She seem worried?'

'She says her daughter phoned her yesterday, four thirty our time—'

'What's that our time?'

'Er . . . 9.30 a.m.? – said she was staying on in London. Someone was helping her.'

'Who?'

'The girl wouldn't tell her.'

'The mother's worried now then?'

'Not unduly, I'd say.'

'A-ha. Interesting.'

'Yes. I think so.'

'So what now?'

'We are doing background checks, of course.'

'A-ha.'

'And I have taken some preliminary steps.'

'What steps? Can you tell me?'

There was a sigh. 'You know how it is. I need Interpol

clearance.' There was a pause. 'This is not an official call.'

'Christ, mate, I appreciate this.'

'What else can I do for you? Before I go back to my bed.'

Bright delivered it like peas out of a shooter, bam, bam, bam: the Chloe Han connection, the Brennan connection, the Triad connection. Albert Choi stopped him once or twice to clarify but he wasn't slow on the uptake. They chatted awhile, what you might call an exchange of ideas. Albert Choi said, 'Let us hope by tomorrow our conversations will be official.'

'You mean they'll let us talk person to person? That might rock the boat a bit.'

Albert Choi made a slight noise that might have been a laugh.

The DCI came into the CID room. 'Well, you got clearance! You go to Hong Kong, identify the suspect. If they can find her. Put extradition proceedings in progress. Jammy bastard, aren't you?'

'Wasted on me, guv. I can't stand abroad.'

'Typical. Who're you taking with you?'

'Think I should take Niki Cato.'

'Why?'

'He's involved – been involved from the start.'

'I could do with a trip abroad myself. It might be a good idea to have someone of higher rank, to smooth your passage?'

Bright felt like telling him what he could do with his own passage but controlled himself. Leave things alone they sometimes go away.

This didn't. Ten minutes later his phone rang. 'Hello, John?'

'A-ha. Sorry, Rog, been up to my eyes—'

'Yes, yes, of course, of course. You're going to HK then!'

'A-ha—'

'I'll come along.'

'Look, Rog, that's a great idea, only—'

'Yes, I heard you want to take—'

'Cato knows the case, knows the girl—'

'But I have the international expertise, you see, John. Been to Hong Kong before on official business. You'll need someone with a bit of international clout, if you don't mind my saying so. Plus of course AMIP want to keep an eye on the progress of the case. Afraid you're stuck with me. Ha.'

Ah, shite. Bastards. The old boy network at it again.

'Oh, well,' the DCI said, 'he's just going along for the jolly.'

But Bright knew better.

He barely slept that night. He feared flying. He feared abroad. He'd only been to France once for a day trip with the school. Twenty-odd years ago. You don't speak the language, there's no jokes, and that's no joke. He'd hardly been able to wait to get back to South Norwood where he knew how things worked. He didn't like going fifty miles up the M1, never mind off the island altogether.

And next morning he did get the jokes. And that was no joke either.

'Don't worry, guv, Roger'll see you right.'

'He'll give you the benefit of his international experience.'

'Long as you don't drink on the flight, you'll be okay.'

'Don't drink? Spend twelve hours with Roger the Bodger sober?'

'Relax, guv! Big Rog'll travel business class. You won't even see him till you get there.'

Bright's face lightened. 'Is that right?'

The phone rang. 'Hello, Inspector Bright?' A pleasant woman's voice. 'Chief Inspector Gould's PA here. Just to tell you he's had you both upgraded to business class.'

'Oh. Great.'

'Yes, he thought you'd be pleased. It's so ghastly in steerage, isn't it?'

'I wouldn't know, love.'

'Oh, well, take it from me. It's awful.'

'Great. Tell him great.' Now even he was saying things twice.

He sorted his desk, put relevant documents into a folder and with a hollow feeling in his stomach slipped across to Islip Street.

Jude was outside, pinning a notice to a tree, a photocopy of a picture of George so black you could barely see it and *MISSING, George, large tabby cat, one chewed ear, ten years old.* With her phone number and *REWARD* in big black letters. 'I used Dan's printer and photocopier. I'm not brilliant at it. But everyone round here knows George. And I know he can't be round here or he'd have come home.' She took a magic marker out of her pocket and added *PLEASE LOOK IN GARDENS AND SHEDS. HE MAY BE HURT OR TRAPPED.* 'I should have put that on to start with. I'll have to add it to the next one.'

'There's no news of your husband.'

'There won't be.'

'Why d'you say that?'

'He's left me and he's run away from – the consequences of his own actions. So he won't be found.'

'I thought you'd have more faith in him.'

'So did I.'

'So why don't you?'

'I've believed in him for a long time. It's been hard. I'm tired. Lee's dead.'

'Did Lee want you to leave Dan?'

She hesitated. 'He thought he did. He asked me to.'

'Would you have?'

'Left Dan? No. Never.'

'A-ha?'

'Never, never, never.'

'Even though you were in love with Lee?'

'I wasn't!'

He'd managed to shock her out of her misery. Just for a minute. 'Yes you were,' he said. 'You might not know it but you were.'

She shook her head. But he knew he was right even if she didn't. She couldn't admit it, that was all.

He said, 'I'm going to Hong Kong. We believe Chloe's gone back there.'

'You're going away?' She looked pale, her skin seemed to shrink round her freckles. 'When?'

'Tomorrow.'

'How long will you be gone?'

'No more than a week. Probably. It depends.'

'This means you think Chloe killed Lee?'

'She's a suspect. Her doing a runner indicates—'

'Dan did a runner first. You don't think he did it?'

'I can't follow Dan. I don't know where he's gone. Chloe was seen on a flight. Different name but identified by BA cabin crew. Had the baby with her.'

Jude sat on the low garden wall like a big rag doll left out in the rain.

He said, 'My team will find your husband. He hasn't left by any plane, train or automobile. He's still in the country.'

She lifted her wan face, sceptical. 'If Michael Brennan is what you say he is—'

'And more.'

'If he is protecting Dan, you won't find Dan. And if he has harmed Dan you won't find Dan alive.'

He was taken aback at her cool logic. 'You don't beat about the bush, do you?'

'I can't afford to. I'm in the middle of a tornado. There's nothing to hold on to except my mind. There's nowhere to hide. So don't think you have to soften things for me. I've got nothing to do except think. Gardening is good for that. Traipsing round pinning up notices is good for that too. Think I ought to add a picture of Dan – "Oh by the way my husband is missing too"?'

'Hey hey hey.'

'I'll miss you,' she said lightly, facing sideways on to him.

'I'll miss you too.' It was out before he thought. He hadn't meant to say it. Hadn't meant to say a thing.

'Yeah,' she said, 'I'll bet.'

He looked at her with this odd expression. They stood without speaking a moment, she with a sudden astonished question in her face, he with a wince like he wanted to take back what he'd said. Too late.

She smiled. The smile emphasised the sadness of her expression. He smiled too. His wide tight mouth didn't move much when he smiled, but she got it.

'Bye then.' She put out her hand and he took it. Their hands were the same size. Hers was harder than his. Both warm, dry, practical, capable hands.

He nodded. Didn't say anything. Their hands parted. He trudged off towards Kentish Town Road, like he was leaving his ma for his first day at school.

She spent a couple of hours trawling the neighbourhood putting posters on trees and lamp-posts, leaflets through letterboxes. She understood now why criminals and con men used sniffer children to stick their noses through letterboxes to smell out the houses where old people lived. Some of these oblong cavities, like gaping mouths, released a gust of warm damp air, some smells of cooking, others unspeakable odours she didn't even recognise. She hoped her own letterbox might be cool, neutral, emitting no heat, belching no fetid hot breath at the hand that opened it. She also wondered why some people had a letterbox at all, so hard they made it to get a hand inside: stiff brushes that gripped you like teeth, old bits of curtain that stroked you with their limp soft touch, inner flaps, stiff hinges, swift backbites that nearly took off your fingers. You needed a different technique with each one, requiring intimate knowledge and much experience. She met the postman, a small man with a red face and ginger hair. She felt sympathy with him and a new respect. She gave him a leaflet about George.

'Yes.' He screwed his face into a knot of sympathy. 'Seen your notices. Haven't seen him but I'll keep an eye out.' And on they trudged, she in one direction, he in another. She did not ask him if he had seen Dan.

The young blonde policewoman interviewed her in the afternoon. Jude gave her photographs, even a video of Dan and George fooling around in the garden, one Sunday with Martin and his wife and kids, two years ago, before it all went apeshit and life turned slowly upside down.

Dan's disappearance – though not George's – was on the evening news. In the absence of John Bright Cato was the police spokesman. Cato loved being interviewed. His Geordie accent had nearly gone; he was quite posh. He'd trimmed his beard to a neat point. They showed the pictures of Dan. And bits of the home video. She didn't cry watching Dan lift George above his head. She sat surrounded by loss, pictures scattered where they'd lain since the afternoon. She felt like the sole survivor of a battle, sitting up like that picture of Britannia on an old penny, devastation all around. And John Bright on his way to Hong Kong. She turned off the TV and got ready to go out, put up more posters, call George in corners where cats gathered, on waste ground, in gardens, outside lock-ups and garages, feeling no hope. He had never run away before. He had always been steadfast. If he could come home, he would. She sent him messages: *Hang on in there, George. Bloody well come home*. But she had no belief he was receiving them. Sometimes she thought that Dan had taken him as an act of revenge.

In Montpelier Gardens she suddenly got tired and sat on a bench. There were too many people around now for George to show himself, dog-walkers chatting in groups, parents pushing children on the swings. She watched all this normal life going on around her and felt removed from it. And then Dan called to her. That moment, as clear as if it had been his actual voice from the trees over there, he called, 'Jude!' One call. Dan's voice. Inside her head.

She had no belief in the supernatural. The natural covered a wide enough spectrum of experience. Human beings communicate on all kinds of levels. But she didn't know how to interpret the call. Dan in danger? Dan dying? Dan now dead? Dan saying I'm alive, hang on in there, like she was saying to George? What?

33

He was actually scared in the airport. He felt like a lost kid. He wanted his mammy. He did not want Roger Gould who bore down on him near the BA ticket desk. 'Oh bad luck, John. I'm so sorry, they can only upgrade one of us. And I'm afraid as I need a little bit more leg room than you, ha ha, I hope you don't mind but I've taken the upgrade. Sorry. Bad luck. Hope you don't think I'm pulling rank.'

Well, life even at its worst wasn't all bad. 'You, Rog? Pull rank? Never.'

'Good, good. Well, you go there to check in and I go to the fast desk. 'Fraid they'll fast track me through to the VIP lounge.'

Bright was cheering up by the minute. 'Fast track, eh? Well, that'll make a change for you, Rog.'

'What? Hey? Oh yes. Ha. Well, see you later, John.' And off he sailed, big head and shoulders above the crowd.

Bright handed the limp notebook of ticketry to the girl in the smart little uniform behind the desk. She asked him if anyone else had packed his bag. And whether he wanted to check his luggage. He had four shirts and a spare pair of jeans, a few underpants and socks, and shaving tackle. 'No,' he said.

The noise in the airport was that echoey high-pitched jangle that stimulates the nerve endings the way aluminium foil stimulates the fillings in your teeth. He went to the bookshop and bought a John Grisham. He needed a story to hold his attention, and he liked Grisham's passion for justice. He kept looking up at the little TV screens that showed the times of flights and their gates.

He went to the chemist and wished he had a prescription for sleeping pills. He couldn't see any other way of getting through the next thirteen hours. He looked at another hanging TV and there was his flight. He checked with his ticket. Again. It was definitely his. He set off for the gate.

Bubbles of nausea kept rising to his throat. He sweated. Then, going through the metal-check, he set off a pinging. He felt like a criminal. This SS guard of a woman frisked him. It was his keys. You were meant to sling them into a saucer. He didn't know the form. He hated not knowing the form. He sweated worse: fear and embarrassment combined.

This side of the line was better. He'd have come through sooner if he'd known. Brighter lights, less nerve-jangling noise, smarter shops, even a caviar bar, for fucksake. He'd never had caviar, he could have tried it, and now he didn't have time. They were calling his flight.

He couldn't believe the distance you had to walk. Miles. On moving walkways to nowhere. Then a long sit on the rows of benches. Then another neat girl in her neat little uniform snatched his ticket, kept it, and gave him a little insignificant bit of card. Then they walked some more, down a tube like a package of Smarties, discharged into the plane. Too late to go back now. Captured by more nice uniformed ladies. 'Good afternoon, sir.' Telling him how to find his seat number. And him a detective.

The size of it. The number of seats. The number of people. It looked like a refugee camp, hundreds of them crammed into this metal box, stowing themselves, their luggage, their babies, spilling into the aisles. And his seat was right in the middle of the middle. If anything happened he was trapped. He wished Jude Craig was with him. Earthy, he thought. Of the earth. She's a gardener and she earths me. Funny to think of her at this moment, like she'd been lurking in the back of his mind for some time.

He scrabbled around for three minutes trying to find the ends of his seat belt. He fastened it. Immediately the seat in front shot backwards into his face. The arms of a big African bloke stretched up above it then rested with one big hand over the back of the seat even more in his face. He wanted to kill. He tried to breathe slow. He was going to have to put up with this for twelve and a half hours? Even Big Rog might be preferable.

Then the stewards started the pantomime of safety precautions. He checked out his emergency exit, then thought, Fuck it, if I gotta go, I gotta go, no use fighting it. Saw his body turning over and over in the sky then plummeting into the sea. He'd be dead before he got there, wouldn't feel a thing. This paradoxically helped him calm down. And then a passing stewardess told his invasive forward neighbour to put his seat upright for take-off. The African took a long long time to understand this request, then reluctantly obeyed. Bright's panic receded, the stewardess moved on. And the seat shot backwards again into his face. He no longer wanted to kill, he wanted to die. He couldn't wait for this ill-conceived machine to rise into the sky and blow itself to smithereens, just finish the whole thing fast.

Then the build-up to take-off began. The rocking, the jolting, the roaring. And then the speed! His white knuckles gripped the seat arms. They were up. They were blasting through the sky! He couldn't believe it. And suddenly, unexpectedly, his heart raced with exhilaration. It was *worth* dying for this!

Everyone round him did this every week, you could see, all arranging their stuff like happy campers, their books, their medication, their magazines, their little computer toys, settling into their nests, taking it for granted, but he felt wild with excitement like a kid on the Big Dipper. If he got down alive – which he doubted – he was going to learn to fly: pilot's licence here I come.

Exhilaration did not last. The food, all sealed in foil or plastic, impossible to open, and Mr Africa bouncing cheerfully back and forth, soon brought him low. Even two miniatures of scotch and a couple of chapters of John Grisham couldn't help. The captain announced the rugby score between France and Scotland. No one gave a damn. What did it matter up here, thousands of miles above it all? Later he told them. 'It's 1 a.m. in Hong Kong. Adjust your watches and then we'll leave you in peace.' The trays were whisked away, the lights were dimmed, and Bright went to find the loo. He waited in a queue for ten minutes. Some blokes were drinking in the bar area, jolly jocks, preparing to make a night of it. The loo was all stainless steel, very clever, a place for everything, only he couldn't figure out the miniature toothpaste they'd given him. He unscrewed the top but could get no further. He had to rinse his teeth with water and go back to his seat, frustrated and woolly-mouthed.

He wrapped himself in his blanket and tried to avoid Julia Roberts' dazzling smile up there on the screen. Mr Muscle of Africa jerked backwards once more. Bright kneed him sharp in the small of his back. The guy turned, very surprised, but saw Bright sleeping. He didn't straighten his seat-back, but he did move his big arms back over to his own side. This small victory gave Bright enough satisfaction to allow him to fall asleep for real.

But only for five minutes. He awoke to another radiant Julia Roberts smile, clamped the earphones on and gave in. He watched this terrible movie, like scenes from the ten worst sitcoms shuffled together and presented at random, the whole thing based on the premise that a big American movie star was going to make us little English hicks wee in our pants from sheer gratitude that she had landed on our shores. But at least Mr Africa was snoring away and keeping his big fat fists to himself. Bright was praying for sleep but, like all the prayers he'd ever made, it wasn't answered. Sleep? Forget it. He imagined Roger replete with champagne or whatever they got up there in first class, the nectar of the gods, gently subsiding into slumber, plump thighs spread and big feet splayed, and Bright grinned with relief. Things could be worse. He could be awake and sitting next to Big Rog.

The second movie he missed, though he'd swear he hadn't slept. The third, set in wartime Italy, was full of jolly English actresses, hiding an Italian boy from the Nazis. At least it looked like a movie, not a blown-up sitcom. The breakfast coffee was drinkable, the croissant unfrozen. He even worked out how to penetrate the miniature tube of toothpaste, a triumph of detection. But he felt shaky, as you do after a night without sleep and, in Hong Kong airport, way out of his depth: what was he supposed to do now?

The customs and passport officials were meticulously thorough – how had Chloe slipped through their net? Their queues were interminable. He attached himself to the end of one, then caught a glimpse of Roger's head, happy and beaming. Now there was a man who had slept. Roger waved. Let's face it, Bright thought, for once I need the bastard. He left the queue and made a beeline for him. And stopped in his tracks, watching as Roger was whisked through the checks with a flash of ID by a solid-looking Chinese man in a dark suit. Bright's queue was now even longer. He rejoined it, too defeated now even for indignation.

'Inspector Bright?' A slim handsome Chinese guy, mid-thirties, also in a dark suit, touched his arm.

'A-ha. That's me.'

'I am Inspector Choi. Albert.'

'Albert?' Maybe things were looking up. They shook hands. 'Er— right. I'm John.'

'Okay. Your senior officer? Roger?'

'Roger? He'd like that.'

'Oh. What should we call him?'

'I think he'd prefer Chief Inspector Gould.'

'Oh dear. Too late now.'

''Fraid so.'

'Well, Chief Inspector Roger and my senior officer from the Customs and Excise Bureau have taken an official car into Hong Kong Island. To the hotel in Central District. I don't know if you would like to go by car or to try out our new fast train.'

'What do you think?'

'I think your girl with her baby? I think maybe she would take the train. More anonymous?'

'So let's take the train, Albert. Let's go the way Chloe would go.'

Albert had a quiet word with the customs man. Bright showed his police ID and they were passed through to a broad marble concourse with cafés and smart boutiques under a high roof of white metal and glass. They glided from the marble floor straight on to the train; that was Bright's impression. Porters lifted luggage into the train with a pleasant manner, and the train slid away silently. Little TV screens in the backs of the seats showed a choice of programmes: touring, shopping, landscape, hotels, and even French comedy, also silently.

'I'm impressed, Albert.'

'We are quite proud of it, the train and the new airport too.'

'There's a lot of money here then.'

'There is a lot of money, in a small place. And also a lot of people.'

The train was cool. Outside the sun shone. Cone-shaped grey hills rose up in misty distance and in the foreground these Chinese boats with one big sail rocked on sparkling water.

'Nice,' Bright said.

'The sampans? Until recently many people lived on these boats, like a trailer park in the water. But now the boat people have been housed by the city.' He indicated a phalanx of buildings all along the shore, rows and rows of them, that shinned up the hills and thrust into the sky. Though the sun was bright and the water sparkled the sky thickened as they approached the city.

'Pollution,' Albert said. 'We have some of the best in the world.'

'And crime?'

'Well, it's like anywhere. We play cops and robbers just like you. If we catch them all you and I are out of a job, right?'

'You learn your English here?'

'Oh yes.'

'You mind being taken over by the mainland?'

'No, it's fine. Nothing much has changed. We run things well here. They respect that. They leave us alone. We are the shop front. The retail outlet?'

'So far.'

'We don't feel anyone breathing down our neck.'

'So what's the set-up here for this visit?'

'You mentioned a drug connection in your conversation with our Interpol department. So they have assigned our liaison team: one Customs and Excise Bureau, one Narcotics Bureau, that's me, and one Hong Kong Homicide Bureau to co-ordinate. I take you to your hotel in Central District near the police headquarters. You can go to sleep and recover from your journey. After lunch we will have a case conference to tell you what we have achieved so far.'

'What have you achieved so far?'

'I'm afraid we haven't found Chloe Han for you.'

'Oh well. Early days yet.'

'She has not as far as we know made contact with anyone since her arrival here.'

'If it was her who arrived.'

Albert shrugged. 'Sure.'

'And my other girl – Mun-yi Wong?'

'She has not surfaced either.'

The train slid to a silent stop, the doors swept silently open. They got out and rose through the station to the concourse of a huge office building-cum-shopping mall with marble floors and pillars, to a small bus station and on to a small bus. 'This is a shuttle. It goes from hotel to hotel.' The bus filled up and moved out into the city.

'Christ.' Bright had felt small from the start of this case, dwarfed by huge blokes, tall women. Now he was dwarfed by buildings that punched and soared and leapt and sailed into the sky. They went up further than you could see, craning to look from the window of the bus, all styles, all shapes, all colours. Traffic roared between them on the vast width of pollution-filled road, four, five lanes a side. In small gaps between the skyscrapers you caught glimpses of steep green hills, pushing the city down and forward towards the harbour. The buildings were crammed into this narrow line between hills and water, facing mainland China, nowhere to go but up, defiant fists thrust into the air.

The bus stopped outside a smart hotel, black glass and marble and brass. Albert got up and took Bright's small bag. Bright followed him off the bus. Between the air-conditioned bus and the hotel door came a close wet blanket of heat, producing instant rivulets of rolling sweat. He gasped. 'Christ. I'll need more than four shirts here.'

Albert grinned. 'You need a bit of a rest, John.'

'I need a cold shower, Albert.'

Albert led the way through the glass doors past a bevy of uniformed flunkeys. He spoke in Chinese to the dapper bloke on the reception desk. Bright signed a piece of paper. Albert took him to the lift, more black glass and brass and pale oak. 'I will call you at three. I will pick you up here at three forty-five and take you to the police building for a short case conference. Then if you like we will have dinner. Or maybe you would rather be alone till tomorrow to get your bearings?' He saw Bright's dazed expression. 'No hurry. We'll work it out later.' They shook hands. The lift doors closing on Albert shut Bright off from his last vestige of security. He rose imperceptibly to floor twenty-eight in silence. Silent lift with silent doors, thick cream carpet in the corridor silencing footsteps.

The room was not palatial, but it was smart. The tiles in the bathroom shone. The air-conditioning wafted freezer-cold air. There was a safe, a minibar, a Teasmade, a basket of exotic fruits with the compliments of the Hong Kong Police Bureau. He could just see the Met providing figs and kiwi fruit for visiting inspectors. Some hopes. 'But how would I know?' Being no traveller he'd stayed in few hotels – maybe this was typical? He suspected, however, that this was the luxury side of normal, that he was only getting the treatment because he was accompanied by Roger. Where was Roger? He didn't know and he didn't care.

He thumped the bed to try it out. Firm-to-hard, with plenty of pillows. He lay down on his back. Not bad. Should be able to sleep tonight. Not now. He was too wired, too worried, too impatient, too raw. Shit: he hadn't asked Albert about Lee Han's mother, the amazing woman in the photos. Where was she? Did they know? *I'll look up Albert's number in a minute. Call him.*

He slept.

34

Jude had lived in this house for nearly ten years, but she had not known her neighbourhood till now. The streets in the dark. The streets at one o'clock in the morning, at four o'clock in the morning. She found that the noise of the city never stopped, the howling of sirens, the continuous throb of traffic. Calling 'George? George?' outside the lock-ups behind flats, outside garages, at doors in garden walls. There was never silence enough to hear if he replied. Four thirty in the morning was the quietest: a break in the noise for half an hour before the birds began their deafening choir practice at five.

She returned to shower and eat breakfast then went to work for Kate Creech; Kate, being an actor and used to unsocial hours, did not recognise Sundays. Jude was replacing her trellis today. She took a bag of posters to put up on the way. The whole neighbourhood was plastered with George, George sitting up looking battered but military, and irrepressibly cheerful, George sellotaped round lamp-posts, drawing-pinned to trees.

Her mobile rang while she was hammering in the last post for the new trellis. 'Are you the lady who's lost the cat?'

'Yes!'

'I've seen a big tabby in my street. I'm in Leighton Grove.' Leighton Grove wasn't that far but it was on the other side of the railway from Jude's street and that seemed an awesome journey for George to make. 'He was outside number twenty-six. He's gone now but . . .' The woman's voice had a droning sameness, all on one note. She moved on to general information about lost cats of the neighbourhood. At this rate Jude would be on the phone for an hour while George moved inexorably out of sight. She tried to keep her voice calm but failed. 'You will have to get off the phone now so that I can come round and look for him!'

'Oh, yes!' the woman said, surprised and sweetly apologetic.

She left the trellis swaying. Kate came with her up Lady Margaret Road. They cut across into Falkland Road, a dead end, and made a quick left into Montpelier Grove. A quiet street, no through traffic, four-storey handsome Victorian houses mostly divided into flats, backing on to the little park where Jude had sat yesterday. Off the beaten track. A good street for cats. They saw five or six – ginger, white, black, tortoiseshell – some of them big, some of them small. None of them George.

They crossed the little park and emerged into Leighton Grove. The woman who had called Jude came out of her house. Jude recognised her voice. 'This is not a good time,' she intoned. 'The best time is just when it's dark in the evening and then at one o'clock in the morning. There's definitely a new tabby around. He's been round here about three days now.'

'George went missing three days ago!'

'I know, it's on your notice. I know all the cats around here. I feed the feral cats on the Regis Road Trading Estate. You know it? I go there round midnight. I'll see you there tonight if you like. Show you where they are.' There was something sweet and diffident in her manner in spite of her insistent tone.

'Thank you. Yes.'

On the way back Jude said, 'Do you think it's like this being a detective? You get a call; you follow it up; it comes to nothing; you file it for future reference; you start again. You search the streets by night. You never look where you're going, your head always turned to the side, looking for the one significant thing.

You live by night. You live separated from other people, with different aims.'

'Detectives get paid for it.'

'And they go home at the end of the day. Leave it behind.'

'Some do,' Kate said. 'Some don't.' Jude glanced at her. Kate had an odd, private expression. She said, 'I've got a friend who does the pendulum.'

'Oh no. I don't believe in all that stuff, all that mumbo jumbo. I really hate it.'

'Me too, but it works for her. She's found a few lost cats. I could get her to try.'

'All right. I'll try anything. If it works I'll even believe in it.'

'What about Dan?'

'She could swing a pendulum and find Dan?'

'I don't think she's so good at finding husbands.'

'Oh?'

'She hasn't found one for herself yet anyway. And believe me she's looking.'

Jude laughed. The first time for days. 'They do seem easier to lose than to find. It'll take more than a pendulum to find Dan, I'm afraid. The whole of the Metropolitan Police hasn't managed it yet.'

Nailing up the last section of trellis, carefully tying the Nelly Moser clematis back up to it, Jude felt her mind had split like an apple sliced in two. One half concentrated on Dan: *Wherever you are, whatever you've done, come back to me, come back and talk to me. Whatever it is we can work it out.* And the other followed George. Her first and abiding image was of George thrown in the air by a fox, his back broken. She shut this image out. Then she saw him trapped, down a hole he couldn't get out of, or in a shed with a broken leg. Sometimes she simply saw him wandering lost, trying to find his way back home, taking the wrong turning again and again. *Just you hang on in there, George, you can make it, I'm here, I'm waiting, just don't give up, come home, come home.*

Sometimes she saw Dan, like George, injured, hurt, dying, dead. Again she shut her mind's eye and pushed these glimpses away. She'd had that one call from him and no other. And that had only been inside her head. Not another sound, imaginary or real. Did this mean he was dead?

Kate brought out some tea. 'My niece calls these the serious biscuits.'

Jude bit into a crisp savoury biscuit covered with a fine skin of black chocolate. 'God, I see why.'

'They cost about a quid each. But you're worth it.'

'You know John Bright.' Jude had not meant to say that. John Bright must have been lurking in her mind.

Kate turned to her, deep surprise in her face. 'Is he in charge of—?'

'Yes. He seems good to me.'

'He is. He's like a terrier, gets a problem in his teeth and worries it till it's solved. Won't let go. Won't give up. He's fine. He's so fine. He seems mean at first, but he's not. Believe me, Jude, if anyone can find Dan, he will.'

'Did you have a – thing with him? Excuse my asking. I wouldn't normally. Only when I mentioned your name—'

'Yes. Oh yes. I thought he was going to be the – you know – the love of my life and all that, unlikely though it seemed. But he was just working through something that – Sorry, awful psycho-babble language. Unfinished business, you know. And so was I, I think. We got together briefly. It brought us both back to life. But we went in other directions almost immediately. Amazing really. I met Rupert. He met Helen—'

'Helen? Helen Goldie?'

'Yes. She's CID now. Working with him here.'

'I know her. He's left her sort of in charge of me, I think.

She's nice.' Jude sounded sad.

'Yeah. Far too young for him. Far too pretty too. And nice with it, yeah. The cow.'

Again Jude laughed, but sadly. 'Where's Rupert by the way?'

'Ireland. Filming. Don't know what he's up to but at least I know where he is.'

'He's the faithful type.'

'Is there any such thing?'

Jude's face flushed. She looked away. No. There was no such thing. Nowhere in the world.

'There are those who try and those who don't,' Kate said. 'That's all. Even being madly in love is no guarantee. Because being in love turns you on – to everything! In the immortal words of Samuel Beckett: nothing to be done. It's how we're made, Jude!'

'I was having an affair with Lee.'

'I guessed.'

'He's dead.'

'Oh God. I didn't know.'

'Dan killed him.'

'No!'

'For revenge.'

'No, Jude. No.'

DC Helen Goldie came to see her again that evening. Jude saw her in a new light. She and John Bright were lovers? Well, what did it matter? What did anything? Three reported sightings, she told Jude, none of which turned out to be Dan.

Have faith, Kate had said. And Jude did. She would not give up on either of them – Dan or George. Both of them had to come home. Even if she and Dan should ultimately part – and she thought this inevitable now – they had to sort things out first.

Later a call came. 'You're the lady who's lost the cat?'

'Yes.'

'Well, it's not good news, I'm afraid. Do you know Lupton Street?'

'Yes.'

'Well, I saw him. Just in the road up there.'

Jude kept her voice, and her mind, quite flat and without emotion. 'Where exactly?'

'By a red car. I think it's a Metro.'

Jude took a deep breath. 'Is there a more – permanent sort of landmark?'

'Oh, just by the school.'

'You're sure this was a tabby?'

'I think so. I didn't look that close. I mean, it – well, it wasn't a pretty sight. I mean, it – well, it was – it was, well – dead, basically.'

Even in this extremity hysteria filled Jude's throat. 'I'll come now. Right away.'

She walked. A better pace for cat-hunting than the van. It took her a quarter of an hour. An elegant black girl, hair extensions threaded with beads, and a large white woman stood over the body. It was the white woman who had phoned. Jude recognised the voice.

It was hard to tell the original colour of the cat, matted and broken as it was. But it wasn't George. It wasn't. This cat was smaller. And might once have been white. Several boys wheeled round on bicycles shouting and joking. The large woman said, 'They stoned it to death.'

Jude said, 'That can't be true.'

'My husband seen them.'

'When?'

''Safternoon. Then I seen your notice.'

Lumps of concrete bigger than cricket balls lay in the gutter, close to the cat. These were the stones? The cat wore a collar that had once been blue. Jude did not think; she ran at the boys. 'You cowardly disgusting miserable mean godforsaken little pieces of shit. Couldn't you pick on something your own size to stone to death?'

They wheeled round her on their bikes laughing, hooting. The biggest one, the leader of the pack, came close enough for his wheel to brush her skirt. He shouted in her face, 'Have you got a bum'ole?' They all laughed. 'Have you got a coconut up it?' She stood in the middle of them as they wheeled round her. 'I'm gonna shove a coconut up your bum'ole, darlin'!'

The black girl shouted, 'Leave her alone, you little bastards! Get out of here!'

'Fuck off, black cowbag, fuck off back where you come from.' The ring-leader wheeled threateningly close to her. He held his hand sideways and straight up like a blade, making chopping motions in time with his words, shouting in a violent manner. 'You don't shut your fuckin mouth in one minute I will beat the fuckin life out of you. You don't fuckin belong here, fuckin cunt. I do.' He was perhaps eleven years old.

The black girl took out a mobile phone and pressed numbers. The boys hooted. 'Ooo, she's phoning the police. Ooo!' Chanting and whooping and laughing they wheeled around and rode off toward Ravely Street.

Jude said, 'I'm sorry. I brought that on you.'

The girl shrugged. 'The kids round here are bastards. Anyway,' she said, 'at least you know it's not your cat.'

But it was somebody's cat. And these were somebody's kids.

Jude trudged home. She went out to the garden and called George. She tried to make it sound like her customary call to him, bracing, welcoming, cheerful, but even to her own ears she sounded hollow.

She reported the stoning of the cat to the RSPCA. They said such incidents were not uncommon.

She sat shivering on the sofa warming her hands round a cup of tea. She was cold with fear. The world was a different place to the one she had imagined all her life.

She went out again at midnight with her torch and a tin of George's favourite food. It was a dark night tonight, a thick cloud-blanket under the moon. She crossed the road and went over behind the flats calling him. She crossed Leighton Road, went up the alleyway to the dead end of Falkland Road. An empty converted pub, several houses littered with builders' stuff, being made over. A little yard with spears of blue metal fencing. She shone her torch in its empty corners. A black cat ran out when she called, sniffed her hand politely, and sped on, up over the wall into the back gardens of Leighton Crescent. Being only human, Jude had to take a longer way round.

At the side of the church in Lady Margaret Road she came across a group of teenage boys, one of them in urgent talk on his mobile phone. 'Come on, man, you're late, you said you'd be here hour ago, where the fuck are you?' As she approached one of them said, 'Shh, shh.' A drug deal going down; something illegal anyway. The boys had a desperate look. They acted nonchalant as she passed. But, as Kate always said, real human beings are such bad actors: they watched her go by in silence, convinced she was a policewoman, a spy, suspicion and defiance coming off them in waves.

Wandering the streets in the night, shining her torch into people's front gardens, she was vagrant, homeless, equally detective and criminal, on the wrong side of everyone's line. She was grateful that it was summer. Though even now there was a chill coming on the air. The chill crept into her back and stayed there, down Leighton Road, across Kentish Town Road, into the Regis Road Estate. Big wholesale outlets, headquarters-buildings, on one side of the curving deserted road; on the other the car-park of the police station enclosed by a high brick wall. John Bright was not there. John Bright was in Hong Kong. She came to the council dump and the car pound, busy even at this time of night, with victims redeeming their bounty-hunted cars.

She heard the voice of the cat lady across the road near an island of undergrowth – 'Puss, puss! Puss, puss!' – high and carrying, different from her normal deep sombre tone. There she was, thin and tall, wheeling her bike with a basket on the front filled with tins of cat food. She was ladling the stuff out into plastic containers. 'I save these from the supermarket. They're just the thing.' Jude made her pathetic contribution – one small tin. And cats came from everywhere, a bold macho black one, a cosy feminine tortoiseshell, a take-it-or-leave-it marmalade, and a timid tabby that didn't dare to come close. The timid tabby was not George.

Jude stayed, marvelling that so many cats lived on the edge of the human lives, eking an existence, forming a society, a loose-knit family, like the homeless humans, the winos on the benches by the Tube station. A different life.

She hung round for an hour with the cat-woman, impressed with her knowledge, her commitment, her dedicated life-by-night. Jude asked her name.

'Themis Stefanoides.'

Jude thought she had misheard.

'Themis,' she repeated. 'Themis was among the most ancient of the goddesses, the goddess of law and justice. The lady with the scales over the Old Bailey? That's me.' Themis had more knowledge of the neighbourhood and its inhabitants, feline and human, than Jude would ever have. She felt shame, learning too fast that she had led not just a sheltered but a blinkered life.

On the way home her mobile rang. A woman who had found a cat in the gutter in Ravely Street, just round the corner from

Lupton Street. 'Run over, I think. My kids found him. They're sure it's your cat.'

'Oh, thank you but I've already been there. It's a little white cat. George is a tabby.'

'This one's a tabby.'

Oh, no. She went back up there and searched and searched, but the cat had gone. *Even dead cats disappear before I get there.* And not having seen him she told herself he couldn't be George. Why would George put himself in such danger? Surely these boys though cruel and violent were not so cunning as to lure an animal with food in order to get it into a good position for the kill? Then she started to think about hunting, fishing, factory farming. The methodical unthinking cruelty meted out to animals kept for human food or scientific experiment. What was the difference between those boys and all that? If there was a difference it was too subtle for her. *People are cruel, that's all. Cruelty is perhaps the strongest human characteristic. Worse than any other animal in creation, people are cruel. Cruelty weighted Themis's scales too heavily on the side of evil ever to put it right.* All her life, thirty-four years, she had hidden this cold fact from herself. She had blindfolded herself. Like Justice in that at least.

When she trudged up her steps at 3 a.m. her front door stood slightly open. She knew she had locked it when she went out. Should she go forward or back? Should she call out or stay silent? She pushed the door but stayed outside on the top step. She called quietly, 'Dan?' then louder: 'Dan?' A strong hand grabbed her wrist in the dark and pulled. But Jude was strong too. She pulled away hard, and turned her wrist to loose it. A pain and a crack. She howled loud. The pain weakened her a moment, her body folding itself around the injured wrist. An arm came round her face, shutting in her noise. She tried to bite the arm but her teeth closed only on cloth. Her mouth filled with cloth. She gagged on cloth, no breath to scream. A large male body hard as iron, smelling of expensive perfume, pulled her inside. The door was kicked shut. The night world shut out. She was in her house, in the hallway, in the dark, with a broken wrist and a man's iron arm round her face. The man did not speak. His sleeve filled her mouth. She bucked like a horse. His right leg came round hers, tripping her off balance. She fell forward and sideways on to her knees. On to her side. Then he dragged her into Dan's room.

35

He woke to his alarm clock ringing. He flailed an arm but failed to connect. If only the thing would stop and let him sleep on. He opened his eyes on a strange room. The room rocked round him. The bed rocked under him. At once he knew this was Hong Kong. At once he knew it was the phone that was ringing. And that the rocking motion was the blood in his veins still rocking to the motion of the twelve-hour flight.

'Hello, John, I'm sorry to wake you. This is Albert. I'll collect you in three-quarters of an hour.'

'Not possible, mate.'

But after a shower he felt good. Power showered. Powered up. He picked up the leather-bound folder with the name of the hotel embossed in gold. *Room service*, it said on page three. He dialled the number and asked for a BLT. 'Yes, sir. Right away, sir. Ten minutes.'

In ten minutes he was dressed, cool in his first clean shirt. A smart Chinese boy came with his sandwich on a large oval plate with salad and crisps. Bright felt like a kid, wolfing this somehow party food all on his own. He felt more optimistic. He felt almost capable. Albert was good news. He and Albert could cut the crap, sideline the Rogers. Albert was skilled at this. Bright knew an expert when he saw one. It takes one to know one.

He came out of the lift to the reception floor, black glass, black marble, businessmen and other expense account travellers at low tables. Waiters served them drinks. The men wore dark suits. The women wore red or black fitted dresses, with chunky gold jewellery. He caught sight of Roger Gould. Roger bent over a woman and lit her cigarette. From the back the woman appeared to be Chinese. Slim, dressed in black. No gold. Before Bright could take evasive action, Roger saw him and waved. Ostentatiously. The woman saw him wave; who could miss it? But she did not turn to see who he was waving to. Gould returned her lighter to her, joined Bright, took his arm and turned him towards the escalator.

'Fast work, Rog. Who is she?'

'What did you say, John, sorry?'

'Who's the lady?'

'Lady?' Roger was mystified. Then he managed to recollect. 'Oh! God knows, John, God knows. She asked me to light her cigarette. Unfortunately I did not have time to investigate further, ha ha.'

'What is this place, a high-class knocking shop?'

'Of course not, John, of course not, I was joking, I'm sure the lady as you call her genuinely needed a light.'

He probably was attractive to women, the bastard, with his big blond head and his big bulging shoulders, and his deadly dependable dialogue.

They sailed down the escalator to street level where a black Mercedes waited. Albert sat in the front with the driver. Bright had no choice. He got in the back with Roger.

'Ah, Chief Inspector Roger.' Albert turned to shake hands. 'Chief Inspector Vincent's sorry not to come and meet you, but he is arranging the case conference at the police building, he hopes you will forgive him.'

Roger, after a brief panic attack at being addressed by his Christian name by an inferior rank, albeit in a foreign police force, decided to be generous. 'Yes, yes, of course, of course. No problem. Er – Albert.'

The car glided through a gateway under the building into a private road system that doubled back on itself several times, and dropped them at an unobtrusive entrance under the police building. They took two escalators up to the reception level.

Albert took a card from his pocket, smiled, waved at the man on the desk, and led them to a sealed glass booth. He pushed a button pad, the glass slid back. They entered the booth and the glass closed behind them. Albert stuck his card in a slot and a red metal turnstile slid open. They went through the turnstile. Again Albert pressed a button pad and the second glass door slid back, releasing them into a blank hallway lined in grey unpolished stone, whence they rose on another escalator to a line of windows over the city. Skyscrapers soared up in front of the hills, and around a hilly park. 'This is Central District,' Albert said. 'The harbour is over to the left, you see?' They craned round and could just glimpse sun on water, small craft, large craft, little green ferries like toys.

He led the way round a corner to an office. The plate on the door said *Senior Superintendent Lawrence Tsang Weh* in English and Chinese. Albert knocked, and pushed the half-open door. A tall man was practising a golf shot on his carpet. 'Ah, hello, gentlemen.' He stood the golf club in the corner and came to shake hands. 'Roger, I believe. And John? I am Lawrence. I am the dedicated liaison officer with the police department, heading this inquiry. Welcome.'

Roger looked mollified at being on first name terms with the senior superintendent, even if everybody else was too.

'May I offer you some tea?' Lawrence bent to a small kettle on a ring. Chinese teacups were arranged on a tray. He poured a straw-coloured liquid into them. 'Please sit down. How is your hotel? I hope it's okay?'

'Fine, fine, er – Lawrence.' The cup looked tiny in Roger's hand. 'It's fine.'

'Pretty ritzy, Lawrence,' Bright said. 'Thanks.'

Lawrence shot him a sideways glance. 'Good. They usually do us proud. And they are close by.' He handed Bright his tea. 'My colleague from our customs liaison team, Chief Inspector Vincent Pang, will be with us in a moment.'

Bright tasted the tea. It was good, tangy, light. It put the stuff at Peking Garden, Kentish Town Road, into the shade.

'When Vincent arrives we will tell you what we've got and how we are progressing and with your help we will outline our future strategy. Ah, Vincent, welcome.'

The man who had escorted Roger through customs came in, short, solid, heavy, carrying kilos of paper under his arm. The dignity of his office came with him like a street band. He had a pompous worried look, the effect of peering ahead and looking over his shoulder at the same time. Bright got the impression of a bloke promoted just one step beyond his abilities but determined to get level with the game. Vincent declined tea with a single movement of his hand. He laid out his papers on a table under the window. Albert shut the door and sat.

Lawrence put down his teacup. 'Okay. We have opened a file on Chloe Han. We have done background checks on her and her known associates. Her family, the Tiu family, was well known here. Her father made TV commercials. Her mother appeared in them. The mother left when Chloe was young – three, four years old? Chloe herself left Hong Kong six years ago with Lee Han. Her father died fourteen months ago after a stroke. Chloe flew over for the funeral. It was just a four-night trip, a special cheap offer on BA. She went to the funeral and presided over the, er, reception afterwards, held in the offices of her father's TV company and organised by them.'

'What else did she do?' Bright said. 'Who did she see?'

'She visited her husband's mother. Eloise Han.'

'Oh?' Roger sat up. 'That's strange.'

'Why strange?'

'There's no love lost between them, to say the least. Well . . . that's the impression I got from you, John?'

'That's the impression I got from Chloe.'

'Exactly.'

'But—' Bright flicked a glance at Lawrence – 'maybe that's the impression Chloe wanted us to get.'

Lawrence considered Bright's point. 'Yes. But our intelligence is that these two women are implacable enemies. Eloise did not want Lee to marry Chloe. She made him choose – Chloe or her. He chose Chloe. They went to London. As far as we know, Lee has not been in touch with Eloise since.

'Clement Han was one of our biggest shipping magnates. One of the biggest ship owners in the world actually. A big power in Hong Kong. Eloise took a part in the business from the first. She was not content to be just a pretty face. She was his PA as well as his wife. A very intelligent woman. Very clever. Very charming. When she wants to be. Eloise Han is a powerful woman here.

'You will see on your trip down Victoria Harbour the section where the docks used to be. Now it is a typhoon shelter; the boat people occupy it. The big ships have gone. Until the last ten years it was a thriving port. Now it's the biggest container port in the world, but not ships.

'When the docks began to die many ship owners simply went bust. Not Clement Han. Eloise saw that though the shipping business was down the spout he had something pricelessly valuable: his expertise, his knowledge of the trading routes, of the ports all over the globe. You know? You stop one container on a border and it can cause a traffic jam that can last for weeks! So searches are not undertaken lightly, without good intelligence. Han would know where searches were likely, which port authorities might be more – accommodating. He had detailed knowledge of the personnel et cetera, et cetera. She decided he would become a broker. Brokering deals, smoothing the passage, you understand.'

All the men sat up. Except for Vincent who nodded wisely.

'Clement died seven years ago,' Lawrence said.

'A year before Lee left,' Bright said.

'A heart attack in fact and he was gone. Eloise took over the business and it is doing well.' Lawrence sat forward. 'Okay. Let me outline our strategy so far. Since we got word that Chloe Han might be in Hong Kong we have been keeping surveillance on Eloise Han and her associates twenty-four hours continuous in case Chloe makes contact. Of course, she could have made contact before we were informed. There is no one else we know of that Chloe can have come here to see. Han Enterprises have many properties. We have these places under observation but I am not allowed enough personnel to keep up the twenty-four-hour surveillance on every possible location.'

Roger said, 'Chloe won't personally meet Eloise, surely. She will know that you will have her under observation.'

Lawrence poured more tea. 'One of my officers believes he may have seen Chloe Han in the vicinity of Eloise Han's house near Repulse Bay.'

The room stirred like a breeze had blown in through the window.

'He can't be sure it was Chloe,' Albert said. 'He was some distance away and the target was in a car.'

Bright asked Lawrence, 'Have you questioned Eloise Han?'

'Not formally. Not possible. Not until we have some good reason. She is not suspected of anything. Even if Chloe contacts her, Eloise is not breaking any law. I went personally to see her. Albert accompanied me. She says Chloe has not contacted her. She had no knowledge of Chloe's arrival in Hong Kong. Of course.'

Bright clasped his hands together and shook them up and down between his knees.

'I'm sorry, John. I understand your frustration.'

'Yeah. I'm a bit too hands-on for this game.'

'We can exchange intelligence, co-ordinate our arrest operation. Undercover, you can assist with normal intelligence gathering, of course. But you cannot be present at our interview with a suspect. You would cease to be the investigating officer and become a witness.'

'A-ha, I know.'

'We had no reason to disbelieve Eloise Han. We may indeed have been used to inform her of Chloe's arrival. If we locate Chloe we will bring her in, question her along the lines agreed with you, and institute the extradition process—'

'What does that entail at this end?' Roger said.

'A hearing before the magistrate, then detention in the women's remand facility, Lai Chi Kok, reception centre in Kowloon, until the process is complete. Now Vincent will take you through the customs and excise end of things. More tea?'

The tea slipped down pleasantly while Vincent, at some length, explained the intricacies of the drug traffic through Hong Kong, trotting out reams of statistics. 'Golden Triangle remains the main supplier of drugs to Hong Kong, coming in via mainland provinces, for instance Yunnan and Guangdong, Nigeria for herbal cannabis, Nepal for cannabis resin. Cocaine comes from South America. Mainland China however is the source of methylamphetamine – ice. Ephedrines, Chinese herbs, used to be the source. Now they use synthetics, which are sent to labs in Thailand to be processed. This is now the biggest trade. Last year our officers seized eighteen kilos of methylamphetamine.'

'And that is only the tip of the *ice*berg,' Lawrence murmured.

Puns were beneath Vincent's notice. He continued. 'Psychotropic drugs – ecstasy et cetera – come from Europe and the mainland.' He listed details of enormous seizures at airports, container ports, and from small craft.

Bright glanced out at the river crowded with all its little craft ploughing up and down and back and forth. Lawrence missed nothing. 'The small boats division of our Customs and Excise Bureau, as Vincent will confirm, has draconian powers of interception and boarding rights.'

Vincent drew himself up and stuck out his chest. He detailed operations to close down heroin-attenuating centres and money-laundering operations.

'Money-lawyering,' Lawrence said. 'Whoever we catch, the lawyers mysteriously get richer and richer.'

Roger smiled thinly. 'Yes, strange, that, isn't it?'

For the first time a little thread of warmth passed from Lawrence to Roger. Bright's hackles rose. He knew Gould's power to ingratiate.

'Our department attaches great importance to international co-operation,' Vincent went on. 'We made the biggest haul of cocaine – 142 kilos – stowed inside an aircraft tyre at the airport last year.' He read out from his bureau's annual report seizures of enormous amounts of heroin and other substances. All impressive stuff but Bright longed for someone to tell the guy to cut to the chase.

At last Vincent put down his wad of paper and clasped his hands. 'We have developed excellent co-operation with other drug enforcement agencies all over the world. But I assure you there is very little traffic to or from the UK. We would be surprised to discover such a traffic.'

'How about a UK, er – businessman? – buying into the business?'

'I'm sorry?'

Lawrence said, 'I think John is saying, if the Han Corporation is involved in the brokering of drug shipments, is it possible that a UK – syndicate? – has moved in to take a share.'

'You got it.' Bright leaned in to Lawrence.

Vincent picked up a wad of papers. 'We have investigated Han Enterprises three times since 1993 on suspicion of brokering illegal shipments. We have never been able to bring charges. In fact we have never been able to prove a connection between Han Enterprises and any illicit traffic. The firm appears to be above board.'

'Of course, we are dealing with clever people here.' Lawrence smiled.

Roger stirred. 'Thank you, Vincent. Very convincing. I think, you know, John, that on the basis of Vincent's very thorough assessment, we can forget the possibility of Brennan's involvement. Sorry, Lawrence, an internal matter, not necessarily connected to this case.'

Lawrence gave Bright an inquiring look. Bright managed to say nothing. 'Very well,' Lawrence went on, 'this is what we have so far. The name the girl travelled under was Mun-yi Wong with an address in Kowloon. There is such a girl. She went to visit her mother's family in London two weeks ago. Albert?'

'Yes. I visited the mother's address yesterday. The girl was not there. Her mother told me she was still in London. That a rich man was helping her to stay there – presumably with false papers et cetera. The girl on the BA flight, who may have been Chloe Han, with Mun-yi Wong's passport and her return ticket, claimed to be travelling innocently back from a fortnight's holiday in London.'

'Maybe,' Roger said, 'this girl was really Mun-yi Wong.'

'It is a possibility we do not ignore. We are still checking out all the places her mother thinks she might be. No luck so far. The relatives in London swear she was with them for two weeks and left for Heathrow in a minicab, you call it? at 11 a.m. on Thursday to catch her plane.'

Bright outlined his theory: 'The girl wanted to stay in London.

British immigration policy since the hand-over doesn't make that too easy, right? Not without some dodgy help. A businessman, unnamed, promises the girl a British passport and a new life, in exchange for her own. I interviewed the family. They say the girl who left in the minicab is the same girl who'd been staying there. Their niece. And the neighbours confirm their story.'

'But . . .' Lawrence shrugged and smiled. 'English neighbours . . .'

'A-ha, you all look alike to us?'

'John, precisely.'

'Only this is Chinatown, sir. The neighbours are Chinese.'

'Ah?'

'And they might be lying. Just like the family might be. Only I don't think so. I think Mun-yi Wong did leave in this so-called minicab.'

'Has the cab firm been traced?'

'No chance. Not much chance of tracing the car either. Maroon Ford. C1 male driver. Anonymous.'

'So, she leaves in the cab and there is no further trace of her.'

'That's it. Until this girl and her baby are seen on the plane.'

Roger spoke up, in a not altogether friendly way. 'And we don't even know if the girl on the plane was Chloe Han or this Mun-yi Wong.'

Albert said, 'And if the girl on the flight was Chloe Han, what's happened to the other girl?'

'A-ha. That's it. If there was a switch, where was it made?'

'All we've got is a Hong Kong girl and her baby. On a Hong Kong passport. Who presumably didn't attract any particular attention in the airport here?'

'She was not checked more than any other Hong Kong citizen returning here, no.' Vincent looked hot.

Roger persisted. 'Excuse my asking, but why was that? She was spotted on the plane by a BA steward who reported to us in London. According to him, he also informed someone at the airport here.'

Vincent sat impassive as a soapstone Buddha. 'We can trace no report. The airport customs and excise personnel are being questioned. We still do not know where the break in communications occurred.'

Lawrence intervened. 'We have some video footage we can show you without, I believe, infringing rules of evidence.'

'Let's see it,' Bright said.

'Roger?'

Roger nodded, sighed, and folded his arms. Lawrence put the video into the machine. A spoiler gave the date and time in English and Chinese. Lawrence said, 'This is an airport security tape. Vincent's department.' They watched fuzzy people jerk across the flickering grey screen to join a queue. 'Now. Here come the girl and the baby.'

The film slowed. They all sat forward. Except Roger who maintained his upright posture, arms folded across his chest. The girl jerked from the top corner of the screen – now you see her now you don't – in and out of the crowd, carrying the baby. The baby in every clip had its back to the security camera, and the baby's head obscured the girl's face. Even at the passport check the girl lowered her head to speak to the child, now in a trolley with the luggage, so that her hair fell across her face. The hair was long, unlike Chloe's. Hardly a factor. Hair can be bought by the yard. The kid looked small, sad; he sat in the trolley with his back rounded, his head drooped.

They had all been sitting forward, tense. They sat back disappointed. The video flickered to a stop. Roger shook his head and unfolded his arms. 'Inconclusive,' he said, 'is hardly the word.'

'What do you say, John?' Lawrence said. 'You of all of us know Chloe's appearance best.'

'Can you rewind to the bit by the passport control?'

The figures jerked speedily backwards. Bright said, 'Stop?'

Vincent put the machine into slow mode. The people jerked on in slow motion to the point where the girl leaned over to speak to the child. They watched the hair swing forward hiding the girl's face. Bright again said, 'Stop.' He sat forward staring. He said, 'It's not Mun-yi Wong's kid.'

'Oh come off it, John!' Roger spluttered. 'It's a six-month-old baby. How could you possibly tell?'

'Mun-yi Wong's kid is fat and cheerful. This miserable little shrimp is Chloe's. No question, mate.'

'It's a back-view of a baby! You cannot categorically say—'

'Sure. I know that.' Bright turned to Lawrence. 'Look at the photo of Mun-yi Wong with her baby.' Lawrence took it and passed it round. They each studied it then compared it with the blurred little grey child on the screen. 'I'm talking off the record here,' Bright said. 'And God knows I'm no expert. I can't say for sure it's Chloe's kid. But I've seen Chloe's kid close up. He's little. He's thin. And he's miserable.' He pointed at the screen. 'He's just like that kid there.'

The five men, professional investigating officers all, gazed with faces as sad as dogs' at the small human being slumped in the luggage trolley like there was no hope in sight. They all nodded slowly. Only Roger shook his head, exasperation simmering.

Bright said, 'Have you got the security tape of Mun-yi Wong leaving for London two weeks previous?'

All the Hong Kong men lowered their heads. Nobody looked at Vincent, who said in a specially dignified way, 'We have not been able to locate it.'

'We know there are always bent airport staff.' Albert did not look at Vincent. 'Otherwise there would be no illicit traffic at all, in people or any other dodgy commodities.'

Vincent sighed and nodded. 'Oh yes. This is true all over the world. At Heathrow also, I think so.'

'Oh yes, mate. You bet.'

Roger said, 'I suppose there won't be any video of your interview with Eloise Han—'

'Eloise Han? I'm afraid not. Her lawyers would blow us out of Victoria Harbour.'

Bright looked fit to be tied.

Lawrence said, 'But believe me you will get the most detailed possible report of our – discussions – with her.'

'And her lawyer.'

Lawrence smiled.

Bright took a file out of his battered briefcase. He gave it to Lawrence. Roger stood, towering over the rest. 'What is this?'

'It's the file on my drugs-war murder, the shooting of my only witness, the subsequent dropped charge. It might be of interest to you, sir, er, Lawrence. As background.'

'Oh surely—' Roger blustered, 'we don't need to burden Lawrence with this kind of detail.'

'My suspect may also have been involved in a Triad killing,' Bright said.

Roger interrupted. 'There's no proven connection between the two cases.' Bright watched his big hand itching to snatch the file back.

But Lawrence murmured, 'No, no, this will be of great interest. I'll glance over it this afternoon. Thank you, John.'

In the front of the folder Bright had placed pictures of Brennan and of his lawyer, stapled to their files. Lawrence contemplated them with a gentle concentration that looked idle but was not. He said, 'And now for the next two days – sightseeing. Enjoy Hong Kong while we proceed with our inquiries.'

Roger hovered in the room as if for a private word with the senior superintendent, but Lawrence appeared not to notice. A deferential Albert waited at the door and the stodgy Vincent was at his elbow. Roger had to follow them out and join John Bright in the corridor.

36

She couldn't see him. She couldn't see anything except the outlines of things, sturdy table legs and the spindly ankles of a high stool. The shadow of a branch outside groped across the moonlight in the room. He said, 'Where's your husband, Mrs Craig?'

She shook her head to say she did not know. His sleeve no longer filled her mouth. He had taped her mouth dumb. She concentrated – breathing in through her nose on a count of four, then letting all the breath out of her lungs on a count of eight. Yoga breathing. It slowed her heartbeat, her pulse, and calmed her panic. It took a hard effort of will. She refused to be frightened by this man, whoever he was, whatever he wanted.

A hand with a gold signet ring on the little finger placed on the floor in front of her an Oxford pad and a pencil. He held her right arm behind her back, just hurting enough, not unbearable. He seemed to be an expert, calculating pain like an adding machine, knowing how much to add, how much to subtract, to get the result he wanted. She wasn't fighting him. She saw no point. Not yet.

She wrote, in the mad writing of her left hand, *I don't know where Dan is.*

He pulled a little harder on the fulcrum of her twisted arm. She wrote, *Dan has left me. Three days ago.*

He increased the pain. She made a little noise. She wanted him to know he was having an effect, in case he thought he wasn't and hurt her more.

Hearing her moan, he didn't slacken off but he didn't increase the stretch either. He calculated to the millimetre. Though he seemed fuelled by a rigid state of rage, he also seemed supremely cool, rational, even just. She knew who he was. And the strength did not surprise her. She recalled his handshake.

And the voice. Camden with a wisp of the Irish. Forward in the face like a singer, reverberent, resonant even like this, a soft, caressing breath on her ear. He said, 'I will hurt you till you tell me what you know. I will go on hurting you till you tell me where your husband is.'

She wrote, *Just before Lee's death, he left.*

'You think he did it,' the voice vibrated against her ear.

Dan would not kill. Her left-handed writing was developing a strange style of its own.

He said, 'Dan has killed before.'

'No!' she cried out against the clamp of tape. Her throat hurt, he twisted her arm tighter, she screamed in her hurt throat.

'Oh yes,' he said, 'he has.'

He let go of her and she fell heavy and awkward. Her head hit the edge of a metal filing cabinet, she felt blood trickling. Now both her arms were free. He moved. She heard him lock the door. Then his shadowy figure seated itself in an old metal and leather chair, Heal's circa 1965, a classic, a favourite of Dan's. She had bought it for him second-hand out of her first commission. This crook was sitting in it.

He said, 'Take the tape off your mouth.'

She pulled with her left hand, tearing all the fine face hair with it. Water came out of her eyes. It wasn't just the pain; it was him sitting in that chair and the whole sorry mess and what he'd said about Dan and trying not to believe it, not to believe him. She fought for control.

'Ah, don't cry,' he said.

This made her angry. No way was she about to cry. 'Dan is not a killer.'

'Why do you think he can't fuck you any more?'

She winced with shame and shock and the cool evil of this man and, worse, at the fact that Dan had told him.

'It's the old Catholic guilt, Jude. Wouldn't let him get away with it.'

'He stopped being a Catholic when he was eighteen.'

'The guilt, Jude. They can't stop the guilt. It eats them up.'

She said, 'Okay then, who did he kill and why?'

'Ah now that would be telling. I'd never grass up a friend, would I now?'

'You must have made him do it.'

'Oh now that's harsh.' His arm came round her from behind. His hand stroked across her right breast and squeezed her left, hard, sharp, so that she shouted with the pain. 'I don't like people to say things like that.'

'You made him buy his mother's flat!'

'I persuaded him it was a good idea, sure. Give her a bit of security, peace of mind. In case she had to go into care, the rent from the flat would pay for it. Dan saw the sense.'

'Can't you let him go now?'

'He knows too much about me, Jude, that's the thing.' He smiled, she saw the gleam of his teeth in the dark. 'And when people know too much about me, I have to take precautions.'

She said, 'Did he set fire to Lee? Did you make him do that?'

'It didn't take much pressure,' he said. 'I told him what you and Lee were getting up to these lazy summer afternoons. It's called lighting the touch paper.' He laughed softly. 'All you have to do then is stand back and wait.'

She believed him and she didn't believe him. She said, 'There's no evidence that Dan was ever there. Inside Lee's place.'

'Oh, my people never leave evidence,' he said. 'That would be foolish and I'm not a fool. But he was there all right.'

'No.'

'Listen, love.' He crouched close to her. 'Don't contradict me. Don't feel clever round me. There's people who get their O levels and their A levels and their BAs and their MAs and their fancy law degrees. Where do they end up? I sussed it early on. I worked it out for myself. They can keep their degrees, their little medals, their prizes. Their little rewards. They're on my payroll. They've been on my payroll since I was twelve. They're pack animals. I'm the pack leader, me. It's natural selection. That's the law I live by. The law of nature.'

'I don't know where he is,' she said.

He said, 'You've lost your cat. That's sad. I saw the notice on the trees. And these.' He picked up the posters from the photocopier where she had left them. She did not like his hands on them, touching the picture of George. Her throat closed up so she could not make a sound.

'A husband and a cat. That's a bit too much. I'm sure you'd like to get your cat back again, wouldn't you?' She saw his teeth shine again. 'You tell me where Dan is, and who knows? I might be able to do something about that.' He brushed his trouser knees and walked towards her. 'I can do something about most things. I keep my promises and I'm good to my friends. You get it? You understand? You only have to tell me where Dan is.' His feet in beautiful handmade shoes stood next to her hand on the floor. 'Deal?' he said.

She wanted to flinch but she didn't. She said again slowly and as clearly as she could with her mouth full of a tongue that seemed swelled to twice its size, 'I don't know where Dan is. I thought he had gone to you.'

He hit her casually, the back of his hand to the side of her face, she heard her neck crack and the clang of the filing cabinet as her head hit it. She fell with the weight of the blow. She lay there hearing him leave the room. And she lay there after he had left. And she heard him leave the house. And she went on lying there.

37

They were tourists. They did the Hollywood Road, a mile of antiques and not so antique antiques, squeezing through a crowd of smart young estate agents on their mobile phones outside the Man Mo Temple. There must have been twenty of them, with little gaggles of people clustered round each one, and a long queue of people on the pavement opposite. 'What's going on?'

'That building has just been converted to apartments. There's big competition for apartments here, space is at a premium. The estate agents are making appointments to view.'

The heat was close and wet but not much sun got in between the cliffs of buildings.

They went up in the Peak Tram, glad of the air-conditioning, up through the strip of jungle between the rail track and the buildings, travelling almost vertical.

'The Peak Tram was the first public transport in Hong Kong,' Vincent said.

'Which means it's the oldest,' Bright said.

'Believe me it is very, very safe! It has never had a single accident since it was built!'

There's always a first time, Bright thought.

At the top it wasn't any cooler, but the air felt fresher and the glint of water in the distance gave hope of cool somewhere.

'Drink?' Albert said.

They crossed the road to an old Chinese house and entered the air-conditioned chill. The place was a restaurant, surprisingly big, that opened at the back on to a terrace above the jungled hills. From the terrace they looked down to the sparkling bay, islands like blue shadows, blades of gold light rippling over the water.

Vincent settled them at a table on the terrace and Bright went off to find the Gents. He finished washing his hands and in the doorway sidestepped a Chinese guy built like a Sumi wrestler. 'Sorry, mate.' Bright stood back. The man did not look at him, just plodded past. The back of his head was flat and broad, with a small pale circle of flesh in the middle of his close-cut hair.

Back at the table, Vincent was preaching statistics at Roger. Roger's eyes were hooded with polite boredom. Albert gave Bright a smile, hardly moving his face; he just employed one eyebrow and a sideways slide of the eyes. Economical. Roger was sipping white wine. Bright ordered scotch. Vincent drank tea. 'Sensible,' Bright said. 'I haven't got the sense I was born with, as my dear old ma says.'

'You are attached to your mother?' Albert said.

'She's in a wheelchair these days. So I have to keep an eye on her.'

'Mothers are important,' Albert said. Did Bright imagine a significant glance?

'Yeah, well, she's on my mind a bit. She'd like to have a gander at all this. Wish I could've brought her.'

'You can. You see now how easy it is.'

Roger looked puzzled at the banality of their conversation. Vincent waited for his attention. Roger's eyes returned like the eyes of the rabbit to the headlights. Bright and Albert turned slightly away to look at the view.

Bright lowered and muffled his voice. 'Speaking of mothers—'

'Yes. Lee Han's mother, Eloise.'

'A-ha?'

'Lee was always under her thumb,' Albert said. 'She wanted him in the business. Lee wasn't interested in the business but he was going along with it.' Albert leaned forward, studying the distant view, and lowered his voice further. 'Eloise also wanted him to marry Chloe.'

'Eh?'

'Oh yes. In order to keep him here. Then Lee announced he was not going into the business. At that point Chloe got pregnant.'

'Great timing.'

'Yes. Lee did the right thing, but instead of staying and joining the business, he took Chloe off to London and married her there.'

Bright's eyes got these metallic specks of light. 'So it wasn't just Chloe getting pregnant ticked him off? What happened? What did he find out about the business? Why then?'

'The precipitating factor? There has never been a word of explanation, not even gossip. The story that it was a choice between his mother and Chloe has stuck.'

'Why don't you believe it?'

'Lee was a friend of mine.'

'You're kidding.'

'So it is quite important for me to find out what happened to him. He was a nice man with no harm in him.'

'Who's close to this Eloise? How can we get to her?'

'Close?' Albert moved his eloquent eyebrow. 'Close is not the point.'

'What is the point?'

'You don't step out of line with Eloise Han.'

'Lee did.'

'Yes. Lee did.'

'She's his mother,' Bright said. He saw the charred lump of flesh brought out on the stretcher, he saw it suspended between life and death in the IC unit, then severed from its lifeline;

dropped without ceremony into death. This is what happened if you got on the wrong side of Eloise Han?

Leaving the restaurant, Albert went ahead with Vincent. Roger caught Bright by the arm. 'How can I get this customs man off my back?'

'You can't.'

'Did I hear you mention Eloise Han?'

'A-ha.'

'Yes? And?'

'Oh . . . nothing much. Whether maybe her and Chloe are closer than they'd like us to think, that sort of stuff. Just speculation.'

'Not likely, is it?'

'Doesn't seem like, nah.'

They caught up with Vincent and Albert at the entrance to the Peak Tram station. Making the precipitous descent, Albert said, 'I expect you would like to have a quiet evening now in your hotel?'

'Yes,' Roger said eagerly. 'Yes, yes. I think so. Don't you, John?'

Albert gave Bright the slightest movement of an eyelid. Bright said, 'A-ha. Yeah. Me too.'

'Yes, a spot of room service and catch up on some lost sleep,' Roger said.

A hard cold shower and the soothing hum of the air-conditioner. Bright wrapped himself in the fluffy white hotel bathrobe and lay on the bed. He did catch up with some sleep. Then his phone rang.

'John? It's Albert.'

Bright groaned.

'Yes I know, I'm sorry. I have a helpful person in the hotel. He tells me that Roger has ordered a taxi.'

'You're kidding.'

'I'll be outside the hotel in a grey Nissan ten minutes from now.'

'You're on.'

The nondescript Nissan, no distinguishing marks, lurked in a group of smarter cars just over to the right. Albert opened the door and Bright slid into the back seat.

A taxi drew up ahead, at the entrance. Red with a silver roof like all Hong Kong taxis. A flunkey came out of the hotel with Roger. Bright huddled down, peering between the front seats. The flunkey opened the taxi door. Roger bent double and stepped in and the taxi drew out. Albert purred out after it. 'Stay down, John.'

'Yeah, yeah. Which direction is this?'

'East. Towards Wan Chai District.'

'What does that mean?'

'You've heard of Susie Wong?'

'Oh God, he's not going to a cat house?'

'I doubt it.'

Bright was thrown sideways on to the floor as the car began steeply to rise. The road swept round in sharp upward curves. He was flung one way then the other; he couldn't see a thing. 'Come on, Albert, give us the guided tour, mate.'

'We are now level with the tops of the skyscrapers and rising.'

'Is the taxi in view?'

'You're criticising my driving?'

'A-ha. I'm thinking of hailing it.'

'You can have a look.'

Bright pulled himself up by the door handle and raised his head. He was looking down on roofs with swimming pools forty floors up. This place played hell with your sense of perspective. 'Rising to where?' he said.

'I suspect we are making for the private villa of Mrs Eloise Han. It is on the road to Stanley, overlooking one of the most beautiful bays on the island.' Albert made a sudden swing right that flung Bright to his left. 'Get down.'

'I'm down. Jesus.'

'Yes, I thought so.'

'What?'

'He is going to pay a call on Eloise. This is interesting.'

'I don't like to think what it means.'

'It means you have to tread rather carefully, I suspect.' Albert had slowed down.

'What's happening?'

'He's paying off the taxi. The taxi is driving off. Roger is looking around.'

'Shit a brick.'

'A car is coming up behind me. I'll let it overtake, I think.'

Bright hunched lower as beams of light filled the car and swept like arc lamps over him. Albert switched off his headlights as the car passed, then he pulled in and stopped. Darkness returned.

'What now?'

'The door of the house has opened.'

'See anyone?'

'Not much light. He hasn't looked this way – that car distracted him. He's going in now. The door has shut.'

'What now?'

'We wait for him to come out?'

'Bit dangerous, Albert.'

'Especially for you, John.'

'No. For you. You live here, work here.'

'The arms of corruption are long. Their embrace is tight.'

'Bloodyell, Albert, don't get poetic on me.'

Albert laughed softly. 'Lawrence has it in Chinese calligraphy on his wall. It ends, "These arms can hug you to death."'

'Quite a warning.'

'Roger has not heeded it perhaps.'

'Well, he can't read Chinese, can he?'

Albert laughed. 'And now you're going to tell me what is going on?'

'It's a can of worms that's had the lid on for a long time, Albert.'

'And Roger is—?'

'One of the worms, mate.'

He didn't know how long they waited; long enough for him to tell Albert what he needed to know. At some point he must have sunk into sleep, foetal position on the back seat. He woke up stiff with a dead right arm when Albert hissed, 'John.'

A black limo nosed out of the garage and purred down the road. A man was driving. A bigger man sat in the back. The man in the back was probably Roger though they were not close enough to be sure. Albert made no attempt to follow. They looked at their watches. 3 a.m. There were no lights in the front of the house. This did not mean there were no eyes. Bright said, 'I'm going in.'

'You are not. You will break the rules of evidence. You will completely screw up your case.'

'Big Rog has already done that. You think he's going to snitch? His word against mine. He wouldn't risk it. I can blow him sky high.'

'You can be silenced pretty permanently before you do that.'

'But you'd know what happened, Albert.'

'And the only way I could tell them what I know would be to admit I had aided and abetted you and that would lose me my job. Is that what you want?'

'No one knows you brought me. You just saw Roger go in and

come out. You haven't seen me. I get out of the car now. You drive off. You don't know where I am, what I'm doing, anything about me.'

'I will not leave you here alone. I will not lie. I will not let you screw up this case.' Albert started the engine and drove off down the hill.

They didn't speak till the car slowed down. 'Where are we?'

Albert was cruising along almost at a stop. 'Wan Chai District.'

There were many old, low-rise buildings here, filthy, crumbling under the pressure of the sleek glass sky-needles shooting up all round. Air-conditioning units dotted their outside walls like acne.

'That is the Han headquarters,' Albert said.

A wide solid nineteenth-century brick building, it was only eight storeys high and not particularly smart. It had an old-fashioned green-tiled canopy all round at first-floor level and a pair of goggle-eyed green lions guarded the entrance.

'Not all that posh,' Bright said.

'Ostentation is not Eloise's line. She has kept the office very much as it was in her husband's day.' Albert drove a little faster. There was little traffic now.

In Central District the buildings were lit like carnival, embroidering the sky. Albert drove off the road and made elaborate turns ending in an underpass. He drove dead slow, making sure they did not catch up with the black limo. 'Your hotel.'

Bright made no move to get out.

Albert said, 'You want me to inform Lawrence?'

'Screw up my case? You kidding?'

'What are you waiting for? Roger's presence is not valid here now. He has interviewed a witness.'

'We don't have proof of that.'

'Our testimony will be enough to have him taken off the case.'

'I want more than that, Albert. I want proof. I want the guy exposed. And I want the Brennan empire brought down with him. I want the lot, mate.'

'You want the fame and glory?'

'No. I've been close to that. It's a nuisance. It's a millstone. It's a mirage. I don't want it.'

Albert gave his invisible grin. 'Okay. I believe you.' He turned round to look at Bright. 'I hope I'm doing the right thing.'

'Thanks, mate.'

They shook hands.

38

Her face hurt, she could not move her jaw without exquisite pain, she could not even turn her head. The strange light in the room must be dawn – a bird chipped away at the unearthly quiet. It was a blackbird's alarm call. That could mean a cat in the offing.

She pressed her hand on the floor to lever herself up. The pain tore up her arm to her shoulder and into her neck. She was helpless. She managed to roll on to her back. Her other arm had been trapped under her for many hours. A swarm of bees buzzed around inside it. She waited, gasping, for normal feeling to come back. The bird's insistent alarm call stopped. No cat now then. She didn't have to get to the window after all. She could just go on lying here on the floor.

The ceiling was a beautiful blue like a Mediterranean sky. Dan's ceiling. Dan's office. Dan. Dan had killed someone for this criminal and put himself in his power. And perhaps because of that he had also killed Lee. And now he had gone. She saw him in a B&B somewhere, a horrible room with brown linoleum looking out on a gasworks. Our imaginations are filled with clichés from movies that take the place of experience. She knew that. In this room of her imagination he was lying on a narrow bed with a candlewick bedspread. He was lying on his back. He was dead or asleep. He was thinking of death anyway. So was she. She shut her eyes.

He wasn't in a room now; he was crouched in the Essex marshes. A V of ducks flew overhead; dawn was opening the sky. He was observing a beautiful half-built house without a tower. He was waiting for a posh car to appear, approaching the house. He had a gun, a shotgun. When the car came round the bend he was going to shoot the gangster. She liked this scenario better and she decided to believe that Dan had left not in order to escape from trouble, or from her, not to cease upon the midnight with no pain, but to stalk the evil and exterminate it. Yes.

But then what? The man who had threatened her and hurt her so effortlessly last night would not allow himself to be killed by an innocent like Dan. Dan wouldn't have a chance.

Her left arm felt almost normal now. She rolled on to her front, pain in so many bits of her she couldn't count. Then she used her left arm to lever herself along, pressing her hand on the floor, pulling her bruised body along after it, the way an earthworm moves, curling and lengthening. Worms did it faster. Worms got more practice.

She reached the phone and pulled it down by the wire. Then she remembered – John Bright had gone away. She got a cold feeling in her stomach, as though he were the only one in the world she could trust and without him everything would go wrong. Go wrong? How much wronger could it go?

She pressed 999. This was no emergency surely? Which service would she ask for? Not fire anyway. She asked for ambulance, hoping ambulance people would be patient and hear her out.

They were, and they did. While they examined her injuries, they listened. They called the police. They wanted to take her in for observation, but she said no, she'd be okay, she had to stay at home in case her – Here she broke down.

She was lucky, they said. The cut on her head was not too deep. A few lumps but no sign of concussion. They cleaned the cut and dressed it. Her wrist was swollen purple and black. She could barely move it. A bad sprain they said but not fractured. They strapped up her right arm. They got her to move her neck and jaw: painful but she could do it. 'Nothing broken,' they said, 'but you're going to have a nasty bruise or two.' They gave her a sedative and told her to go to her doctor today. She said, speaking with difficulty, 'You have to make an appointment two weeks ahead to see my doctor. Which planet did you say you were from?'

They grinned at least. 'Tell them you're an emergency; we said so.'

A young policeman arrived and took a statement. He asked her to describe the man. She said it was Brennan and that Inspector Bright knew all about it. 'We all know all about *Brennan*,' the young policeman said. He didn't quite believe Brennan had been here in this room, she could see. But he'd make a dutiful report. He was worried about leaving her but she said, 'He's not going to come back today. I'll be all right.'

She felt hideously lonely when they'd all gone. But she pulled her forces together. She went downstairs to find the arnica. She was surprised to find a pair of limbs that worked. Her legs when she had first woken up on the floor had been useless, from being bent under her all night. They were fine now.

The little bottle of arnica was still on the table. She emptied two into her mouth. She'd take a couple every ten minutes, ten doses, to heal her shocks as well as her bruises. She'd be all right. She had to be all right if she was to find both George and Dan and get them back again. Fear like nausea filled her stomach and rose into her throat. She heaved with it, bent double. She'd never get them back. She'd lost everything. And the worst man she had ever met was just biding his time to trace Dan back to her and destroy them both.

She curled on the sofa in the snug and pulled the green tartan rug up over her. The room was shimmering with golden light, but Jude did not see it. She was asleep.

* * *

'My God, you look a sight.'

She knew it – one side of her face swollen, dark blue and crimson, with a penumbra of green and yellow, her right arm in its sling. 'Thanks.'

'You won't be doing my garden today then, Jude?'

'Don't make me smile. It hurts.'

'What happened? I just came over to see if you needed some help with your George hunt. I didn't expect an accident victim.'

'No accident, Kate.' The jaw was so swollen now it was like speaking with a whole doughnut in her mouth. She felt a bit mad. The sedative had made her light-headed.

Kate was a better listener than the police. She made tea and sat round-eyed on the other side of the kitchen table like it was *Jackanory*. The tea was good also, and Jude began to sense that to feel better might just sometime be possible. She told Kate everything, even that, according to this man, Dan had killed someone.

'It's not true,' Kate said. 'I don't believe it. And nor should you. He said it to scare you into telling him where Dan is. I mean, who's he supposed to have killed?'

Jude looked at her forlorn, and then out at the garden. She hated looking out there, always hoping to see George at the window looking in. And he never was.

'Not Lee?' Kate said.

Yes, he could have killed Lee. He could have set that fire. Yes. Because Michael Brennan has such power over him. And I helped to give him that power. 'I played into Brennan's hands,' she said.

'You? How?'

'Going to bed with Lee.'

'You didn't know.'

'No. I didn't know.' Weary, she stood up and opened the french window, looking up and down for George. She said, 'He even mentioned George. Brennan did. As if he – Oh God.' She shook.

Her legs shook, a rigid shaking that stuck her to the spot.

Kate put her arm round her and dragged her across the terrace to the bench. 'You have to shut your imagination down. I know it's hard but you have to. Seeing awful pictures does you no good, and Dan no good, and George no good. You have to assume that they're both alive and well. That man was just bluffing to be cruel to you. Cruelty's his hobby as well as his job. He's a lucky man, obviously chose the right profession. Well, more of a vocation really, I suppose.' She kept on talking till Cato and Helen Goldie arrived, to take a detailed report. Helen and Kate greeted each other with a wary politeness. Cato asked for a description of the man.

'I can't describe him really, his face, I never saw it, he made sure I didn't. But I know it's the same man I met a couple of years ago, Dan's old school friend Michael.'

'How do you know?'

'Well, the things he said obviously. But . . . his voice and . . .' She knew there were more tangible things but they hovered on the edge of her mind and would not come any further.

'Take your time,' Helen said.

Cato said, 'You didn't see his face – what bits of him did you see?'

'His hand – Oh.'

'Yes?'

'A signet ring, a gold signet ring on the little finger. I remembered that. From when I first met him, I mean. The nails very manicured and this ring with entwined initials. Like this.' She drew on a sheet of Dan's paper an M and a B intertwined in a complex design, and the shape of the oblong of flattened gold on which they were engraved. It was easier to draw than write with the wrong hand, but still the sketch wobbled and shook. It might have been done by a small child.

The police looked at each other a little hopelessly. 'Thanks,' Helen said. 'That's great.' She forced a smile.

Cato, whose eyes had been whizzing round the room taking in the details, suddenly said, 'You're sure Brennan was here? You're sure it wasn't your husband that did this to you?'

'Dan?' She gaped at him. 'But Dan's—'

'Yes, disappeared, we know. But what if that's just a story? What if you're protecting him?'

'Oh Christ, I don't need this.'

'Come on, Mrs Craig, don't take offence—'

'And anyway Dan wouldn't hurt a—'

'He certainly wouldn't hurt Jude,' Kate said.

'Keep out of this, Miss Creech, please. Nobody's questioning you.'

'Sorry, but it's absurd actually to think that Dan—'

'Yes, yes, thank you.'

'Could you leave the room please, Miss Creech.' Helen looked like she might take Kate out by the arm. Kate made a sideways shift to avoid her.

Jude said, 'Thanks anyway, Kate.'

'I'll be down in the kitchen,' Kate said.

They were most intrigued that Brennan did not appear to know where Dan was. They took Jude over and over her story, till they could see she had had enough. Cato fastened his snazzy blazer. 'All right, Mrs Craig. We'll talk to you again in the morning when you're feeling better. Phone us the instant you hear anything.' He opened the front door on to the sunny street. Some boys were hanging about in front of the Peckwater Flats. They whistled at Helen as she went down the steps, sidemouthed cracks to each other then laughed.

Jude said thickly, 'How's Inspector Bright? Have you heard from him?'

Cato, a bit taken aback, said, 'He's fine, thanks. Arrived safely in Hong Kong.' That was all he was going to tell her. He went off down the steps after Helen. The whistles and catcalls stopped.

The flat-dwellers all knew Cato. Their existence was different from Jude's; the police were a constant in their lives. The kids stared over at her. She shut the door.

Kate was preparing a scratch meal. Bread and cheese and a salad. She said, 'Did Dan take any food with him?'

'Food?'

'Food, yeah. Like tins of stuff or anything.'

'I didn't look.'

'Nobody asked you?'

'Nobody asked me and I didn't look.'

With her okay arm Jude opened the dresser cupboard. She squatted in front of it. Kate knelt beside her. 'Well?'

Maybe there had been more tins of beans? Maybe there had been more tins of fruit? She couldn't tell. 'Sardines!' she said.

'Yeah?'

'Dan loves sardines. He's always buying them, as if they're an endangered species. Which they probably are.'

'There are none in here.'

'Look in the other cupboard. There's always at least two cans.'

'None.'

The two women stared at each other, kneeling face to face. 'What does it mean, Kate?'

'I think it means he went with an intention.'

'The Essex marshes with a shotgun then.'

'What?'

'Rather than the bottom of the Thames with stones in his pockets.'

'Revenge, you mean?'

'Yes.'

'Revenge. On . . . ?'

'On Michael Brennan.'

'Not on you?'

'Oh, on me, obviously. Just going away without telling me is revenge on me. And there's what he'll do after whatever he does to Brennan. What he'll do to himself.'

'What's he avenging exactly?'

'His own corruption. The destruction of our marriage. My infidelity even. He'd blame Brennan for all that.'

'He wouldn't blame himself?'

'Oh yes, he blames himself more.'

'So if he kills Brennan, then he'll—?'

'Oh yes, he will. He was always an escapist, Dan. Always looking for a way out.'

'Where will he go looking for Brennan?'

'Essex. That's where he lives.'

'Not the flats where they both grew up? You said Brennan had tenants there.'

'Yes. Brennan keeps a prostitute stroke drug dealer there apparently. In Dan's mother's old flat. But I doubt if he'd set foot there himself.'

'He would if Dan called him.'

'Called him out?'

'Exactly.'

'This is all just conjecture, you know.'

'I know. Eat! as John Bright would say. And then we'll think.'

Before she ate, Jude called the police station and told Cato about the sardines.

'Why didn't you tell us this before, Mrs Craig?'

'I didn't think of it. I didn't notice.' Cato always made her feel like a criminal, like she was in collusion with Dan, and even with Brennan. So her ideas about Dan's intentions she kept to herself.

39

Roger stuck to his side like butter to bread. They'd spent the whole damn day sightseeing – first Aberdeen Harbour, constantly importuned by old ladies in coolie hats: 'Sampan ride? Round Bay? Only forty!' A few words shot out of Vincent's small mouth like bullets, and the sampan touts melted away.

But they took the shuttle ferry from the pier across to the floating restaurants. Vincent led Roger to the far end of the ferry, pointing out the sights of the harbour. For the first time in hours Bright was alone with Albert. Without shifting his eyes or changing his emphasis he said, 'Who's he?'

He liked the way Albert caught on fast. After a second or two gazing over the water, he turned slowly, Bright with him, and they faced the other way. Albert said, 'You've seen him before?'

'Yesterday in the restaurant. Is he one of yours?'

Albert slowly shook his head. 'I apologise. I should have spotted him.'

'Who's his owner then?'

'Han Enterprises, I imagine.'

'Think Rog has seen him?'

'I think perhaps he may know he's there?'

They climbed off the lolloping ferry at the landing stage where this floating pagoda flamed, scarlet, gilded, curlicued, dripping with dragons and blossoms, its green-tiled roof with wide deep eaves, curled at its four corners, also tipped with gold.

They went in, up the wide staircase to tinkling Chinese music, through palatial spaces, to a vast hall. Pillars embossed in scarlet and gold held up a ceiling thick with gilded blossoms, and everywhere hung scarlet banners and the ubiquitous oval red paper lanterns.

Portly Vincent led the way to one of the round tables overlooking the harbour. On a platform at one end attendants dressed people up in ancient Chinese royal robes, made up their faces and gave them fans to hold while they posed for photographs. An American woman was posing now, holding her flowered fan in front of her made-up face, not looking as daft as you might expect, looking almost like the real thing, living proof that it's the clothes that maketh the man.

'We will eat female crabs. Great delicacy,' Vincent announced. 'You will enjoy this experience.'

'We do have the odd Chinese restaurant in London,' Roger smiled.

Vincent deflated a little. 'You have eaten female crabs in London?'

'Well, no actually,' Roger said. 'Not female crabs as such.'

Bright turned away to hide his grin, and the man from the ferry and the restaurant on Victoria Peak strolled in. He sat the other side of the room, not even facing their way. Bright was getting to know the back of his head, broad and slightly flattened like he'd been hit with a frying pan. If they were any good at this surveillance lark he should have been replaced by now. Unless—? Of course they were good at it. If they had not wanted this man to be seen, Bright would not have seen him. They wanted Bright to know. They were warning him off. He had felt clever spotting this needle in the teeming Hong Kong haystack. *Shit.* A little cold trickle of alarm shivered down his throat: *Be ever on your guard against vanity.*

Several men and women pushed trolleys from table to table. They had the air of not belonging to the restaurant, not being employees, but small trundles of private enterprise. 'Dim sum,'

Albert explained. Each time a trolley stopped at their table Albert and Vincent argued in Chinese – their words pounded out ba-ba-bap like missiles – and the table began to fill with little dishes of largely weird-looking foods.

Vincent said, 'Tuck in, please.'

Bright balked at nothing except the crabs, whose orange meat tasted nastier than anything he'd eaten in his life.

'After lunch,' Vincent pronounced, 'we go to Albert's home town. Tsim Sha Tsui.'

'Kowloon,' Albert said.

Roger looked tired. He closed his eyes. But they sped back to Central District in the chauffeur-driven limo by way of Happy Valley. Roger slept or appeared to.

Albert said innocently, 'Poor Roger is tired.'

Bright was disturbed at the difference between the rich districts and the poor, at the miles of public housing, great walls of China stuffed with battery humans. Worse than in London or any other city he'd been. The limo drew up at the Star Ferry landing stage in Central District, and he was shocked by the beggars. Even after the way London had got since the eighties, he was taken aback. There was one without legs or arms who levered his way along on his stomach. Bright dropped a note in the tin, he couldn't help himself. Roger looked sick. Vincent made no comment. 'Star Ferry,' he said. 'Very old. Very famous.'

Albert bought tickets at the little booth and they went through the turnstile, following the crowd along the tunnel, down some stairs, then a sloping walkway with wooden ribs to the gangway, and on to the boat.

The boats were nineteenth-century, painted apple green, with an upper and a lower deck. Rows of wooden benches on metal supports, the smell of diesel, a crowd of well-behaved people, some out in the open at the front end, some in the glassed-in section in the middle.

He was struck by the elegance of the girls, mostly dressed in black as black as their shiny hair, neat, stylish, up to the minute. And slim! If you stood them sideways you'd hardly see them. How did they do it? Was it this good food they had here or did they starve themselves, or were their bodies just different from Westerners'?

Suddenly latecomers raced down the gangway and a metal portcullis came down to close them off. The gangway was raised with a terrible screeching noise. 'Needs a drop of oil,' Roger said.

'One of our biggest problems,' Vincent said. 'Red diesel. It is coming from the mainland. Huge amounts. Polluting the island and the harbour. We make big hauls, big arrests, big penalties, but it goes on.'

'So what's new?' Bright sounded lugubrious. 'You got bent officers in every department everywhere.'

Vincent looked affronted.

'No offence, mate, I'm talking every country, every city—'

'Speak for yourself,' Roger said, affronted on Vincent's behalf. 'John's an old cynic,' he said.

'There's corruption everywhere, Rog. There's big temptations. The more high-up you get the bigger they come. You'd know about that.'

'Yes, yes,' Roger groaned, cares of the world on his honourable shoulders. 'It's vile, vile. You have to be strong. You have to be very strong.'

'That right?' Albert gave Bright a sideways glance. He ignored it. 'You ever been tempted then, Rog?'

'Haven't we all, John, haven't we all?'

'But never stooped, eh?'

'Once, actually – in confidence.'

'A-ha?'

'Yes. A call girl, I'm afraid. Very high class. In return for services rendered I kept her out of a case in which she was peripherally involved. Peripherally, only peripherally.'

'Oh, the women.'

'Yes, yes. It's always the women that get you.'

'They touch the parts that money can't reach, eh, Rog?'

'Ha, ha, yes indeed, yes.' Roger, pink in the face, laughed his mirthless laugh.

The ferry forged a track across the glittering blue water. Bright looked back, at the little boats and the big boats plying the waters. And at the amazing skyline of Hong Kong waterfront. 'Manhattan, eat your heart out,' he said.

Vincent looked gratified.

The ferry pulled up. Bright was sorry to lose the cool breeze, the light on the water, the gentle movement of the boat, and the pleasure of baiting Big Rog, with Albert for audience keeping stumm. But then there was Kowloon.

The cliffs of buildings towered up, just as they did on Hong Kong Island. But over here, at second-storey level, banners reached across the narrow streets, advertising in Chinese and English *Very Good Canton Restaurant, Choi Gems, Ching Fat Necktie, Adam's Apple Topless Bar*; their neon dragons and girls in bikinis, twinkling in and out, lit up the place like a fairground. People thronged the streets, strolling, shopping, eating, happy, relaxed, friendly. There was no sense of danger. Shopkeepers plied their wares from their doorways: *I make you good suit by tomorrow, good cloth, I train in Savile Row, blouse for lovely wife.* They walked down a street full of wedding shops where girls tried on their European princess wedding dresses attended by shopgirl acolytes, then into Han Fook street, full of common-folk little restaurants.

He didn't come back to himself till they were sitting at the table. He actually felt a jolt like he, whatever 'he' might consist of, had dropped from a great height and rejoined his body. He thought, It's the effect of that long flight, lack of sleep, body clock screwed up, all that. But it wasn't. It was like being fucked by the best lover, it was like dying and coming back, and he knew it wouldn't happen again. You could never repeat this at will. Not unless you went and lived in an ashram on the top of the Himalayas for forty-five years. But he'd had it this once without trying. He'd been there. And There, he discovered, was Here.

Albert said, 'What do you want, John?'

'Nothing, mate.'

'You're not hungry?'

'Oh! Food? Yeah! You order, Albert.'

The restaurant was a small simple joint with formica-topped tables, filled with families, three generations, people still in their work gear, no tourists except for Bright and Roger Gould. The waiter brought a big pot of tea. Albert had a serious discussion with him; he didn't speak English. When the food came – *Shrimp Sweet & Sour* (huge juicy prawns), fluffy steamed rice, vegetables tasting like they'd just been picked – it was like his tongue had new tastebuds, tingling, expectant, innocent. It was years since he'd felt like this. He'd been off his form for a long time. He knew it but couldn't get back on again, couldn't care enough. Couldn't care. Losing that witness had been a blow, a shame, a sorrow. He still sent money to the poor guy's widow and kids, but never went to see her, couldn't face her. He knew only now how jaded he'd been all this time.

He looked at Big Rog across the table, covertly checking the chopsticks for cleanliness in this low-class dive. This was the bastard responsible. Not just for the murder of that witness, but now for Lee Han, for whatever had happened to Daniel Craig, to the girl whose passport Chloe Han had travelled on, her and her baby, for poor old Crabbe, and for what might happen to Detective Inspector John Bright if he didn't put a stop to him first. Bright was going to put him away. He didn't yet know how, he didn't yet know when. But he was going to get his revenge.

For all the lives this dignified Detective Chief Inspector of Garbage had defiled one way or another, John Bright would exact the just revenge.

Later Albert took them to a small square near the harbour. A cube-shaped man in a tuxedo stood outside a bar. Over the canopy naked neon ladies flashed on and off between the words *topless dancers* in English and Chinese. The Cube greeted Albert as an old friend, took them through a dark lobby into the bar.

Chinese and European girls gyrated to Europeanised Chinese music in dim lights that strobed on and off. A girl with neat small breasts and a bow round her neck brought them drinks. Bright tried the Tsingtao beer. It had a powerful kick. And the Cube bent solicitously from what must once have been his waist and offered, through Albert, God knows what in the matter of extras. Albert kept laughing and shaking his head.

'What's he offering?' Roger asked.

'The usual type of thing. You know.'

Vincent with pompous tact went off to the Gents while Albert gave Roger the details. Roger laughed his pompous laugh, red in the face, not committing himself.

Albert said, 'Unfortunately it is against the law. He doesn't know I am with the police.'

'But you don't work for the Vice Bureau, so . . . ?'

Albert demurred. 'I think, Roger, you might be better off . . .' He produced a small card and wrote a name on the back of it. 'One of the staff in your hotel, very – discreet. He will arrange anything you—'

'Oh lord, Albert, just joking, you know, just a joke, lord, I'm so jet-lagged I can hardly keep my eyes open, let alone . . .' He pocketed the card. 'In fact I'm knackered. Had enough of this, John? Shall we go?' He stood up and drained his G and T. Subtle as a Sherpa tank.

Bright didn't stand up. 'Listen, mate, I'm not going back to the island tonight. I like Kowloon. Albert will find somewhere for me to stay. Won't you, Albert? Just for the night?'

'But – but—' Roger was flushed, flustered, revealing that part of his deal here was to be sure where Bright was. Now he didn't know what to do.

Vincent returned. Albert, who, though he had drunk as much as anyone, appeared smoothly sober, swiftly arranged for Vincent and Roger to return by car through the tunnel to Central District while he found a suitable hotel for Bright.

They came out into the square: bright lights, music, people, the proprietor still inviting the punters in. A shiny black Mercedes came to a halt. A uniformed chauffeur got out and opened the passenger door. Bright, himself not wholly sober, said, 'Well, Rog, looks like you been Shanghaied.'

Roger said, 'Yes.' He could say no more. Vincent pushed him in and the car rolled sleekly backwards out of the square. Bright and Albert strolled after it and watched it disappear in the traffic down towards Nathan Road. They then took a narrow street inland. The man with the flat head leaned out from a tree in the square and sauntered after them.

It could have been any hour of the day or night. The air had cooled to a pleasant warmth. The narrow streets still thronged with people, the garbage collectors, frail old women pulling carts with wicker baskets, shovelled the litter. Not that there was much of that. This place made London look like a slum. 'Why's no one drop litter, Albert?'

Albert shrugged. 'Just tradition. We like to keep the city clean. Also—' his teeth shone green in the neon light – 'there are very big fines.'

Again Bright felt two inches of air under his feet. This was life the way it used to be back home once upon a time, all these little shops and the easy happy crowds, and the matiness, and the personal way the guys tried to sell you stuff, good-humoured jokey chat when you turned them down. Life down any street market. In spite of the buildings shooting hundreds of feet into the sky, it was human life on a human scale.

Albert said, 'You'll need things for the night.'

'I'm not going to sleep tonight, mate.'

'Oh yes you are. Case conference in the morning. I will collect you. You are my responsibility.'

Bright meekly followed Albert into a pharmacy where he bought toothbrush and paste, then into a small cluttered clothes shop where he bought three cotton shirts, a pack of three Y-fronts and a pack of three pairs of socks. The shop people spoke, at best, only a pidgin English. 'I thought with it being part of the Empire and all, all those years, they'd all be chattering away in cockney.'

'Only the educated.'

'Like you.'

Albert took him up Carnarvon Road, a narrow winding lively lane with the all-night street-market buzz, across Cameron Road, streets with Brit names where no one spoke English. 'Flat Head's still keeping us company,' he said to Albert.

'Shall we ask him to join us?'

'Don't think so, Albert, don't think he's our type.'

They went up a steep narrow alley between a building site and the torn side of a building maybe twelve floors high, low-rise in this context, bamboo scaffolding all round. They came out into Kimberley Road and Albert led the way into the foyer of a hotel, up the usual two escalators to the reception level where sleepy men clutched drinks in the dimly lit bar and a piano tinkled out hybrid tunes.

Albert had a word with a tall scholarly young man behind the desk. The young man grinned at Bright from behind his serious spectacles. Bright signed a paper. Albert said, 'You have to pay a deposit. That's the way here. It's normal.' Bright handed over several hundred Hong Kong dollars. Seemed a lot till he worked it out in his head. Fifty quid maybe.

Albert took him up in the lift to floor eight. 'Eight is the lucky floor. Eight is the luckiest number. Numbers are very important to Chinese.' He pushed a card into a slot in the door. The room number was eighty-eight. The lock clicked and Albert opened the door.

The room was not as luxurious as the place in Central District; it was half the size and the air-conditioning made a racket. But it was big enough, the windows set at an angle to take the dressing-table and the TV. The bathroom was clean as a hospital scrub room, and a white towelling robe hung on the back of the door. 'This'll do me,' Bright said.

Albert sat in the chair. 'Okay, John. What are you up to?'

'I'm having a good time, mate.'

'You don't trust me.'

'I'm getting Roger off my back. I can't stand the geezer, I'll be straight with you.'

'You are not being straight with me. I tell you what you are doing. You are inviting them to make a move on you. But I'm not sure you quite understand their style—'

'Don't understand their style? I saw the charred remains of Lee Han being carried out on a stretcher, mate! I smelt it!'

'Okay, okay—'

'I gotta do something, Albert! I'm going crazy being a fucking tourist, pardon me, both hands tied behind my back, led around like a fucking puppy dog. Sorry, mate, I don't use foul language as a rule. So look – I'm not doing anything, okay? I like Kowloon, I feel like I shoulda been born here, I'm just having a night on the loose. Let me off the leash.'

'If you get in trouble, I get in trouble.'

'I will not get in trouble.'

Albert got up, walked round the room; that is, he walked round the periphery of the bed, with his hands in his pockets, frowning. 'Okay, look. The guy on the desk downstairs, Kim. He's my brother-in-law, okay? He will look out for you. He will let me know if anything happens. This is his mobile number. This is my spare mobile phone.' Bright took the small light instrument that flipped open and closed in his hand. 'This is my pin code, okay?' Albert keyed it in. 1122 came up on the display. 'I'll write it—'

'I got it.'

'What?'

'The code. First three letters of your name – A equals 1, L equals 12, B equals 2.'

Albert gave his quiet grin. 'Maybe you should come and work here.'

'Wouldn't mind.'

'If you survive long enough.'

'A-ha.'

'A-ha.' Albert repeated Bright's exact intonation, and shook his head. 'What will you do now?'

'Have a shower. Watch the box. Bound to be a movie.'

'Case conference at ten-thirty tomorrow morning. I'll pick you up here at nine-thirty.'

'And if I'm not here?'

'Where else would you be?'

'Thought I might pay a courtesy visit.'

'No, John.'

'She's not a suspect, Albert.'

'Who are we talking about?'

'Come on! She's not a suspect in my murder case.'

'That's true.'

'And *you* can't question her.'

'That's true. My senior superintendent said so.'

'And it's a free country, mate.'

'Well, it's a relatively free city anyway.'

'I mean, is there any reason why I couldn't pay her a courtesy visit? In the morning? If nothing happens to me tonight?'

'To commiserate with her in person on the tragic loss of her son?'

'I mean, that would be only polite, wouldn't it, Albert?'

'And you are a very polite man, John.'

'Polite? It's my speciality. I'm known for it.'

Albert shook his head again and went to the door. Then he took a card from his wallet and looked at it awhile. Then he came back and handed it to Bright. Bright read, *Eloise Han Director Han Enterprises* with the office address and phone number and her own private line.

'I did not give you this, John.'

'You got my word, Albert.'

40

'What we'll we do is, we'll go up the street and down the street knocking on doors, ask if we can look in the back gardens.'

Jude turned round from the window. 'But that will take your whole afternoon.'

'I've got nothing better to do,' Kate said.

They found several women at home, people Jude had never seen, though they lived in the same street. She and Kate were welcomed in with sympathy – 'Oh, yes, I got your leaflet' – then left in peace to search. Jude looked under bushes, in tiny spaces between walls and sheds, lifting bits of wood, logs, buckets. Inside a tiny shed, right back in a dark corner she moved a small tin can to look behind it.

Kate said, 'Not even a cat could hide in that little space!'

Jude didn't reply.

'Jude, I wish I hadn't said that.'

Jude said, 'A cat can hide anywhere. Especially George. It's his greatest talent.'

'Yes.'

'And a cat's body could be hidden anywhere. I think things shrink when they die.'

Kate looked sick. 'Jude, I'm so sorry.'

Jude thought, I've changed. I've started to be ruthless. I'd never have said these things before.

The men who worked at home were different from the women. They were cautious, unwelcoming, wary. One man's tiny garden was crammed with old window frames and doors, piled against the back wall. Perfect hiding places for a lost or injured cat. But the man would not leave them alone to search. He stood over them saying again and again, 'He's not here,' emphatically, in an overbearing voice.

'He might be,' Jude said. 'He could be.'

'Nonsense. I would have seen him.'

'Not necessarily. He's such a great hider.' Jude couldn't go on. She was about to burst into tears and couldn't do that in front of this aggressive, unlistening man.

Kate said to him, 'Look, he won't come out if he smells us here. Could you and I go inside and leave Jude out here in peace? Just for two minutes?'

But he wouldn't go in. Like he thought they were casing the joint – for what? – to steal his rotting old window frames? It was hopeless. Jude said, 'Sorry to have annoyed you.' This was all she could manage to utter. She went out through the house very quick with a straight back and tears running down her face.

In the street outside Kate said, 'Stupid bastard.' But that was no comfort to Jude. Ruthless? She should have made that man go in and leave her to search. She was a coward, failing George out of sheer feebleness. She thought her heart was going to break. She could actually see her heart. She saw it when she closed her eyes. It was bright crimson with a jagged black crack down the middle of it. They gave up on the gardens after that. Instead, they crossed Kentish Town Road and went where Jude dreaded, round the corner of Willes Road towards the burned-out flat where Lee had lived, where Lee and she . . .

They stood outside the blackened wreck. Old Gregor came out and stood with them sighing and shaking his head. 'Poor guy, poor guy.'

A man in his twenties came out of the house over the road,

where Dan had been seen by Chloe. He had long hair in a ponytail and wore a soft white Indian cotton top and tattered jeans.

Jude said to Gregor, 'I thought that house was empty.'

'He come back.'

'Was he here when the fire—?'

Gregor shrugged. 'I donno. Maybe. He don' talka me.'

They said goodbye to him and went on through the little streets named after the battles of the Crimean war. Jude shone her big torch into more dark corners, deep areas to empty basements, mounds of bulging black garbage bags, braced to find any unspeakable thing. But found only the detritus of people's chaotic lives, piled in forgotten heaps. At six o'clock she was tired out.

Kate said, 'I'd kill for a cup of tea.'

They went back to Jude's place. No George. No Dan. No intruders. Jude phoned the police station. She got Helen Goldie and told her about the boy who appeared to live in the house opposite Lee's. Helen sounded pleased. She said thanks, they'd follow it up.

After tea Kate had to go home. 'I'm filming tomorrow, they're picking me up at the crack of dawn. I have to prepare.'

Jude felt crazily sad.

'Spend the night with me,' Kate said.

'I can't. Either one or the other or both of them might come back. I've got to be here.'

Kate looked dubious. 'Okay then, but call to tell me if you're not all right. I'll be here in minutes.'

She hugged Kate with her left arm. 'Thanks, thanks, thanks.' But after she shut the door she knew what it was to be alone. The house was enemy territory now and for the first time she wanted to leave it. *But if George doesn't come back I can never leave because then he'd have no one to come back to.* She put the TV on but found herself listening for noises and had to turn it off. She heard doors surreptitiously opening and closing. She heard footsteps creaking. She heard George's pathetic worried mewing. She investigated every noise. Every one was a mirage. She was always alone.

At ten that night the phone rang. 'You found your cat yet?'

'No.'

'Only I seen the notice on the tree. And I think I seen him.'

'Where are you?'

'I'm on the Peckwater Estate. He's a big tabby with one chewed ear, right?'

Jude had no breath. 'Yes, he is.'

'Right, well, I seen him on this bin-housing by the medical centre, know where I mean?'

'Yes. What sort of time?'

'Well, he's there now. I can see him from my window.'

'I'm on my way. Thanks, oh thanks!'

Before George's loss she'd seldom gone into the estate because the place felt like a ghetto. If you weren't a resident you felt noticeable there. And not welcome. But she grabbed a torch and a bag of George's favourite dried food and ran. She ran down the side road which was part railway bridge, between the garden centre and the estate. Near the back entrance to the stylish new medical practice she slowed down and, silent so's not to scare him off, entered the estate and approached the place where George had been seen.

She saw the bin-housing right away, an open brick shed with a concrete slab roof and open metal mesh doors. Inside stood five or six big cylindrical metal bins. She waved the torch under the bins into the dark corners and whispered George's name. No cat lurked there. She was sure. No cat. Not on the roof either, not in the grass, not on the tree. And not, when she crept closer, in the shadows at the foot of the tree.

Then she saw there was a space about a metre deep between the bin-housing, and the high wall behind. She shone her torch down there. No. No cat. Beyond the high wall loomed a row of Victorian warehouses with broken windows, their scabby bricks draped with a lace-work of barbed wire. She called, 'George? George? Where are you, George?' as much as possible the way she did at home when there was nothing wrong, so's not to alarm him.

'What d'you want?' A wild angry voice. A thin man in a grey raincoat and a woollen hat appeared suddenly from nowhere, from among the parked vehicles, like he'd been lurking there.

She was really scared. Her experience last night, not to mention her injuries, made her vulnerable. She said feebly, 'I'm looking for my cat.'

'There's no cats here. The caretaker wouldn' allow it!'

How would the caretaker prevent it? She didn't want to know. 'Someone saw him here, my cat, they phoned me—'

'Saw him? Who saw him? There's no cats here! Over there there's cats, loads of 'em.' He pointed to the warehouses and the small building site next to them.

'In the building site?' Jude said. There was a small housing development over the other side of the high wall where the warehouses left off. Little half-finished flats in pale yellow lavatory brick with mean windows. The sort of thing Dan despised.

'Estate on the other side, over there! Over there!' He waved a violent arm in her face.

He was angry, shouting, but she stood her ground. She tried to make herself heard. 'What time do you see them there, these cats?'

'Night-time! Night-time! I only go out night-time!

She didn't ask him why only night-time; again she didn't want to know. She said, 'I go through there most nights. I never see them.'

'Well you must be blind. There's no cats here! They're over there.'

She dutifully plodded off. To stay would only provoke him. She understood his violence: he was afraid of her. *She* had frightened *him*. What a joke. He watched her out of the slip road, she could feel him watching, she must not turn round to look at him. So she did not see the man who hung back in the shadows of the concrete garages. The shadow man waited till the angry man had gone grumbling into his block of flats, then padded after Jude unseen.

She went out into Bartholomew Road, passed the house of the caretaker who was sinisterly able to rid the estate of cats, then she cut along behind the other flats. But she didn't see the cats the man had told her about. She called at every lock-up and listened to the traffic that never stopped long enough for a cat-cry to be heard. Behind the din she heard the anxious little squeaks that George made when he needed to get out. There came a few seconds' pause in the traffic. She listened hard, heard nothing, and knew that she'd imagined George's sounds. She moved on. The shadow man softly came after, hanging back behind a gatepost at the entrance to the backyard of the flats.

At the end of Leighton Place, a little cul de sac, converted warehouses one side, small 1920s houses the other, two cats came out of the shadows. One black and white, the other tabby. Her heart jumped into her throat. The tabby was George! It was! The same size, the same big feet, the same tigerish stripes. She stopped still, hardly breathing. Slowly, slowly she squatted down on her haunches. She shook some food out on to the pavement under the lamp, to tempt him out, to get a better look at him.

The black and white came out cheekily, purring and munching. The tabby hung back, timid. Jude retreated, to reassure him. The tabby ventured out, sniffed the food, went purring mad, and gobbled up the little pellets like he was starved. He was smaller than George. His face was flatter. And both his ears were intact.

He allowed her to stroke him. He kissed her hand over and

over, chirruping thanks for the food and hoping for more. Then, also like George, he forgot the food and went for the loving instead, rolled on his side inviting her to stroke his stomach, wrapped all his legs round her hand and bit the side of her palm softly in an amusing way. She spent a long time saying goodbye to him.

She turned at the end of the road. She did not see the shadow in a warehouse doorway that squeezed itself deep into the deeper shadows. She just saw the cats, both still sitting there at the end of the cul de sac, under the lamp, watching her. Then she went home. She did not see the shadow peel off from the deeper shadows and follow her.

She ran home. She would 1471 and speak to the woman who'd phoned, she'd ask her to keep looking out, not to give up. She ran up the steps. The door was shut. It was still locked. She opened it and stood still, listening to the house. She expected a strong arm to come round her neck and drag her down. She felt terror but she heard nothing.

She shut the door behind her and went on in just as if she felt fine. She trod through the house as through a battlefield, delicately, not stepping on mines, expecting anything, fire, explosion, why not? The shadow watched from the shadows over the street as the lights went on then off all over the house, signals to the outer dark.

No Dan. No George. No roughneck to manhandle her. No Lee Han. No John Bright. She 1471-ed. 'Number withheld.' No number either. Just Jude. Hey Jude . . . Take a sad song . . . Well, she might not make it better but she couldn't make it worse, could she? She put food for George just inside the cat flap. She put the tartan rug imbued with his hairs and his dusty velvet smell on the floor by the french window where he could see it, smell it, from outside. She said, 'Just come home, George.'

* * *

She often dreamed she was travelling. It was always dark in her travelling dreams. She was always engaged on a mission that got endlessly delayed. She was always diverted, into one parenthesis after another, never reaching the final goal, losing the journey's original intent. She checked her pocket for the mobile phone. She never did that in the travelling dreams. She had never had to work out how to drive with her arm in a sling before either. So maybe this was no dream, maybe this was real. She turned on the ignition with her left hand. She leaned her strapped-up arm on the steering wheel, to control it while she put the van in gear. She started up the van and drove off.

She did not see the shadow dart across the road to the line of parked cars, tear open a car door and jump in. She had turned the corner and gone by then.

41

The phone rang. It was not 7 a.m. yet. He knew instantly where he was. 'Albert?'

'Some people start work at seven fifteen. It's cooler in the mornings.'

'Thanks, mate.'

A quick shower, then he put on his nicest shirt, and ran a comb through his hair which stood up in shiny black spikes. He felt excited, like he was going on a date. He cleaned his already spotless fingernails. He went to the window, bounced on his toes, rattled the change in his pockets, looked at his watch. Seven fifteen. 'Yes!' He flexed his hands and picked up the phone.

Her voice was like water, cool and ripply. 'Yes?' she said. Slight accent, charming, not heavy. 'Oh, Mr Bright, how kind of you. By all means come. I can make myself free between seven thirty and eight. Then I have a meeting. I look forward to seeing you.'

Yes! He clenched his fist, then opened his hand and made a short sharp movement, shattering an invisible brick.

Wan Chai District was heaving with activity. Vans unloaded bales of food into restaurants and shops. Chinese shouted at each other – good-humoured bullets of sound that ricocheted off the walls. The first trams came rollicking down the lines, rounded at both ends, dark green or scarlet with Chinese lettering all over them. This was a weird place, modern as hell but it kept all this great old stuff as well, trams from way back and those Toytown ferry boats.

He paid the taxi, had no idea if he was cheated and didn't care. The Han Building looked deserted. He peered through the glass strip at the side of the embossed copper door. A guy sat at the reception desk reading a newspaper: vertical rows of Chinese print, and pictures of people with their faces shot off, in colour.

Bright rapped on the glass and the guy looked up, shoved his newspaper under the counter and came to let him in. Bright showed his ID. The guy waved it away, 'Mr Bright, yes. Madam is expecting you.' He pressed the lift button and they waited in silence. The guy gazed upwards like they were expecting the chariot of the gods. Bright gazed at the guy. He was smart as paint in his natty suit, grey shot with mauve, like a wood-pigeon, smoothing his tie down inside his jacket. The tie was kind of lilac and silver. But he looked like he worked out. Like the suit was a disguise. Bright was just determining how he'd handle him in a fight when the lift rattled down and its doors opened.

Inside it was all gilt mouldings topped with black-spotted mirrors. Bright stepped in. He watched the smart guy's face till the doors closed and never caught his eye. But something gave him the feeling the smart guy would know him again.

He went up past seven floors. The lift doors opened at the eighth, not on to a landing but straight into a room. The room was big, longer than it was wide, and six huge windows gave on to the river. Glass in the roof distilled more dazzling light. A woman came from behind a big old-fashioned desk to greet him.

Bright couldn't say what it was about her. She was small, not plump but not exactly slim. She had large breasts for a Chinese woman but she wasn't top heavy. Her face was squarish with broad smooth lips, and her eyes were almost black, with a bloom on them like polished plums. Her forehead was wide and smooth. There was no way to say what age she was. Not a girl, but he doubted she had ever looked like a girl, even when she was one. Her hair was shortish and well cut in a European way, swept back from her face and curving into her neck. Her expression was grave. She was dressed in a simple black frock with a high Chinese-style neck and short sleeves. Her arms were rounded, smooth, pale brown, hairless. Bright had this extraordinary urge to touch them. He couldn't recall ever being turned on by a woman's arms before.

'Mr Bright?' She took him by surprise, stretching out her hand to shake his. 'I am Eloise Han.' Her hand was small, smooth and malleable with a grip of steel. She held on a second longer than normal? He wasn't sure. He was wrongfooted. Before he could speak she had turned and was walking away, not back to the big desk but to the other end of the room where there was a big deep sofa and a long coffee table with a thick glass top. Reflections of roof-lights and sky in the table dizzied him for a moment, the world turned upside down. She motioned him to sit on the sofa. Correction: in the sofa. He sank with the sensation of being ingested by a big soft mouth.

She sat at the other end of the sofa, but she was wise to the thing, she perched on its edge. 'It's so kind of you to come to see me,' she said. Everything she did, with her voice, her eyes, her movements, made this seem like a tryst instead of a formal call.

He'd had enough of this beguilement. He struggled out of the clutches of the sofa and rearranged himself on the edge, like her. He was there to tell her about her son's murder for Christsake. 'It's the least I could do,' he said. 'Seeing how you were too busy to get over there yourself to see him before they finished him off.'

'They? You know who they are then?'

'We're not far off. The bloke behind all this won't have pulled the plug on your son himself. He gets other people to do his dirty work. Until I can trace things back to him, I don't want anyone else taking the rap for him.'

'I understood that you were here to trace my daughter-in-law.' No one could accuse her of not going straight to the point. Once she decided to cut the crap.

'We need to question her, a-ha.'

'Because you suspect her of cutting off Lee's life support?'

'She's a key witness.'

'I have not seen her, Mr Bright. I am the last person she would come to see.'

'She told us there was no love lost between you.'

'A strange expression, isn't it? On the contrary, all love was lost between us when she decided she would get her claws into Lee. She was bad for him. She was bad, simply. I know about bad girls, Mr Bright. I was one myself, believe it or not. They decide what they want and they go for it and nothing stands in their way. If they get what they want they can become good girls and do nothing but good in the world. But if they are thwarted – as Lee I believe thwarted Chloe – their wickedness gets out of hand. I'm afraid that is what has happened here. It would not surprise me if Chloe killed Lee. I told him she would. He insisted on marrying her because she was pregnant. I told him, pregnant? She may be pregnant now but I promise you she won't be after you marry her. And of course I was right. They go to London. He marries her. She has got what she wanted and suddenly she is not pregnant any more! He wouldn't listen to me. He left me. He left his father's business. He left his own country and his own kind. For that.'

'Yeah, well. Is there anything we can do – I mean – to make things easier?'

'I have made arrangements. The body is to be flown here when the coroner releases it. We will have a memorial service, though Lee has been gone so long he probably has more friends in London than he has here. But his father's family . . .'

'And your family?'

'I have no family. I was raised in an orphanage. What you call a foundling? A nice word. For a not so pleasant condition.'

'You come across as pure aristocrat,' he said. 'I wouldn't have suspected.' He wished he could get over the impulse to call her ma'am like his previous superintendent in Kentish Town.

'I never sold myself cheap. I met Clement Han. I got the highest price. He knew the value of the things he bought. And I gave him the best value always.'

'You're still doing that, I guess.' He had no idea where this conversation was going. He was surfing it.

'Yes. This business could have gone down the tube when Hong Kong became a container port. He was old then and had forgotten how to move with the times. I turned this business round. It makes more profit now than it ever did.'

'So I hear.'

'And all of it is above board.'

'A-ha?' He kept his voice dead flat, no innuendo.

'I pride myself on that.'

'So you should.'

Her bloomy eyes rested on him. He felt like she was caressing his face, dammit. He felt like he was being fondled. He had to swallow this sudden rise of saliva into his throat. He had to get his concentration back. But while she talked there was this other conversation going on underneath, like she was undressing him, like— He had an erection for Christsake, sitting here on a sofa four feet away from the woman. A woman he didn't like and didn't fancy either. He found her repellent. But he wanted to fuck her. He was bewildered. He was excited. And somewhere really deep down he was scared. She was a dangerous opponent – no holds barred, no time called. She'd use any weapon that came to hand – no double meanings intended. He wasn't out of his depth yet. But it wouldn't take many steps down the slope . . .

She said, 'You're an unusual policeman, Mr Bright.'

He gave her his squint and one raised eyebrow. It wasn't much.

She said, 'You have the gift of inscrutability. It's unusual in a Westerner.'

'A-ha.' All this flattery. Who was buying who?

'I wouldn't like you to be my enemy,' she said.

'Why should I be your enemy, Mrs Han?'

'My name is Eloise.'

'Why would I be your enemy?'

She turned her face to give him a look from the side of her eyes. She tucked in the corner of her mouth, the furthest she probably went in the way of a smile. 'Mr Bright—'

'My name is John.' He was starting to enjoy himself.

'I do not believe, John, that you have come here simply to bring condolences for the death of my son.' She waited to give him time to deny that. He didn't. She went on. 'I believe you have come here because you think Han Enterprises, and perhaps even I in particular, might be implicated in his murder.' Again she gave him the chance to demur. Again he did not. 'I can only assure you that this is not the case. No doubt you have been told that Han Enterprises has been investigated more than once by the Hong Kong Police Bureau and also by the Customs and Excise Bureau, and they have found nothing. They have found nothing not because we are clever but because we are clean. Clean.' She stood. Her fingers spread out. She stood in all this dazzling light and radiated light herself, it seemed to him, like in the comics when someone shimmers with rage, sending out jagged lines like electric current. She was truly outraged by the calling into question of her squeaky-clean business image. He wanted to laugh but didn't; he nodded, slow, watching her. She calmed down a bit. 'Anyone is welcome to study the books. My business *is* an open book.'

'That right?'

'Yes, that is right!'

'Only – I mean – all these deals going down all over the world – there must be deals that have to be kept pretty – well – discreet? Nothing illegal necessarily, but just a fair bit of discretion on behalf of your customers, right? I mean you couldn't be a completely open book. Could you? I know what it means to broker a deal. I've seen a fair bit of that in my time. And the principle is – well – your discretion. As a broker. What I'm saying is, your customers have got to know, given the choice between them and the investigating authorities, which side you'd be on. Or you'd lose your customers, right? Stands to reason.'

'I'd only lose customers who had something to hide.'

'A-ha. You got it. That's what I was trying to say.'

'So customers of that kind know that if they want to broker a deal they do not come to me.'

'A-ha.' His voice assumed its purring tone like a sleek black tomcat. He watched her from behind his mask of amusement. He let things simmer a little without talking, just looking at her. She was nice to look at. She went to the desk and took a cigarette from a black enamel box and lit it with a desk lighter, a big grey stone. Granite. A handy weapon. He watched her. She turned back to face him. He thought it was time to change the subject. He said, 'So you still hate your son, even now he's dead.'

She bore down on him like a cobra. He felt like ducking but he sat still just where he was. Not moving a muscle but ready.

She stopped just in front of him. 'How dare you? How dare you? What do you know about it? Are you married? Do you have any children? No, you don't, I can see you don't. You know nothing about that particular passion. The strongest and the least wanted. That kind of passion makes you weak and I cannot afford to be weak. The parent is like a rejected lover. The child is always moving away from you, always leaving you. I do not like to be in that position, it is not a position I accept, it is humiliating.

The ingratitude of children is beyond belief. I offered Lee everything. Everything I – everything his father – had built up. His inheritance. His empire. Lee was good. And he was clever. He could have used his power and his intelligence for good purposes, for anything he wanted. But no. He turned it down. Casually. As if I were offering him cheap trash from Stanley Market.' She sucked on the cigarette like its smoke was oxygen, filled her lungs with it and kept it there. Like a forties film star. Bette Davis or someone. One of those larger than life ballcrushers that can put the fear of God into you even though they're way over the top in the acting stakes. And she was only a little thing when you looked at her, no more than five foot three. She meant every word of it, that was the thing; that was the power of her – she burned with this intense heat like a blow torch, and a blow torch right in your face has quite an effect.

She let out all the smoke on a long breath. 'So don't speak about what you don't know.' She sat down again. A little bit closer than before. 'I did not and do not hate my son. I love my son.' Her voice gave out. She waited a second. 'More than life or death,' she said. The emotion might even have been real. She ground out the half-smoked cigarette in the big glass ashtray on the glass coffee table that reflected all the windows. 'But I do not forgive him.' She joined her hands in her lap and turned to face Bright. 'And now I never can,' she said. 'It is now too late.'

No question: this was the real thing. He did not believe even she could fake that particular despair. So he suddenly knew that she was not responsible for Lee's death except by the process of chronology and accident or – if you like to call it that – fate; that what had happened, though originally maybe caused by her, was not what she had wanted at all. Not at all. In the secret recesses of this woman's fantasy she played a reconciliation scene with her son. And someone had cheated her of that scene. He might have an ally here. If he played his cards right. She was a businesswoman. But her feeling for Lee might override that. If so, it was the only thing in the world that could.

Suddenly she put out a finger and touched the back of his hand. Lightly, like a breath, then removed it. But a shiver went through him like she had run her fingernails all over him. And his hackles rose again. This woman knew just what she was doing. She got you mesmerised, off your guard, then back went the cobra head, and she darted in for the kill. Christ, she took his breath away.

She said, 'So you see, John. We are on the same side.'

'That's what I wanted to know,' he said. He managed to stand up, in spite of that sofa sucking him into its depths. In spite of the fact that he felt he'd been three rounds with Prince Naseem. In spite of his desire to feel the touch of her fingers on him again. 'So I can rely on your help to nail his killers,' he said. 'Whoever they may be.'

'Whoever they may be.'

'So if Chloe contacts you—'

'Whoever they may be.'

'Okay. Okay.'

As he walked towards the lift he heard a child's voice. It was quickly quelled, but he had heard it. An unmistakable sound. It had come from the end of the room at right angles to the river and the street. The wall was blank, some shelves with nice Chinese jars and horses and clay figures like the stuff he'd seen yesterday down the Hollywood Road, but no door. No visible door.

He gave no sign that he had heard this sound. His step never faltered. But he knew that Chloe Han's baby, this woman's grandson, was in this apartment on the other side of that wall. And where the child was it was not unlikely Chloe was too. And he knew that Eloise Han would get Chloe and the kid out of there like a dose of salts, before he could get the Hong Kong police on to it. And he could do sod all about it, because if he did he would ruin his own case by becoming a witness on Hong Kong jurisdiction.

So he carried on to the lift like he'd heard nothing, and she pressed the button and he heard the lift clanking up from below and when the doors opened he stepped in and as the doors closed he said, 'Thanks.'

In the lift he sweated. He'd been on the point of saying, 'I saw Roger Gould at your house last night.' If he hadn't heard that cry he might have said it. He might have screwed up everything. He felt he'd escaped some catastrophe, a shipwreck or a plane crash. Even his legs felt weak. But of course he'd escaped nothing yet. He tried the mobile. Useless. No signal inside the lift. The lift doors opened, on the reception area he was glad to see – he'd half expected some dank basement. The pigeon-suited heavy on the desk was just putting down a phone. Bright stepped out and crossed the floor-space fast. The smart guy came out from behind the desk. Bright tried to open the heavy glass door. It didn't budge.

'Excuse me, sir.' Thick Chinese accent. High pitch with a reedy camp sibilance more frightening than a big butch rumble. Bright readied himself for the sudden accident that was about to befall him. His centre of gravity was lower than Smart Guy's, good for one unexpected throw, but after that he wouldn't have a chance. A hand shot out of the immaculate shirt cuff. Bright did not duck or flinch – just. The hand pressed numbers on a pad on the wall by the door. The door slid open.

'Goodbye, sir.'

Bright sauntered out then swung round to give Smart Guy a kind of salute. It was just an excuse to turn, make sure there was no weapon aiming at his back. But Smart Guy was already inside the door. Arms folded. Staring out.

The hurrying hordes of people swallowed him up. He was

grateful, for their speed, their proximity, their fixation on their own affairs. He got out the mobile. The only problem was the noise – traffic, shouting, klaxons, alarms. He backed into a doorway to dial. He heard Albert's voice, cracking up, coming and going, distant, as if heard over water or up a mountain. 'The kid's in the Han building,' he said. 'Top floor, right side looking from the front, no visible access. There might be another way out; if so it'll be back right, on to the harbour.'

Albert said, 'Vincent already has the Small Boats Division in the harbour behind the building.'

Then Bright felt a blow in his back, a jab in the kidneys that made him shout out in pain. He tried to turn round in the doorway but he doubled over and found himself on his knees. The blow had winded him. He couldn't get his breath. He needed to see who had thumped him but he could see only the legs of the thickening jostling moving crowd. He felt he might black out. He pulled himself up using the edges of the door panels. He had to get out of this doorway.

The pain had gone now, strangely. But his back felt numb, his head felt whuzzy, his eyes had a swarm of flies in them and his legs were made of rubber. Keeping close to the buildings he hauled himself along using window ledges, corners. He reached the edge of the building next to the Han building as Chloe came out.

She had long hair, right down her back, but there was no mistaking that eel-like walk, those crazy long, long legs. A taxi drew up. The passenger door of the taxi opened from the inside, but the passenger stayed inside.

Chloe made straight for the taxi. She moved fast, weaving through the crowd. She put her hand out to the open taxi door. But before she could get in, she was surrounded. Bright saw the taxi zoom away from the kerb with its door still open. A police car howled after it, waggling in and out of the traffic. Both screeched across a red light.

Then he saw Chloe again. A man either side of her held her arms. A third man showed her his ID. The third man was Albert. They pushed her inside an unmarked car. Albert looked around. He looked straight at John Bright, then got into the front seat of the car, and the car drove away.

Bright had been holding his phone close to his body. He looked at it. The phone and his hand were sticky. His shirt was crimson and wet and stuck to him. The blood had seeped round his body and through the front of his shirt. Oh, shit, he thought, with a sense of distant mild surprise, *it wasn't a punch.* The buzzing flies in his eyes and in his head swarmed louder and thicker. *I've been stabbed.*

42

The country was so dark. None of the amber half daylight that passed for night in London. Now and then a pair of headlights reared up, dazzled, then passed her, leaving her feeling alone on the face of the earth. She took the wrong turn time after time, pulled over, stopped, turned the map this way, that way, got her bearings, found her way back to the route. It was hard work driving with one arm more or less out of action. She had to lean on the steering wheel with her right arm to control the steering while she changed gear. She felt mad. But in the mad world she had come to live in the mad are sane.

All she had were Dan's descriptions, and Bright's. And now at last she thought she was getting there. Out night after night in the hunt for George she'd become conscious of the phasing of the moon as she had never been before. Tonight was the last little sliver, mostly clouded out, before tomorrow, when there would be no moonlight at all.

She found herself at the coast before she was ready. The big wide estuary, a shining satin ribbon folding and unfolding under and over the slice of moon, over there to her right. She stopped under a lone tree and rolled the window down. A plaintive bird-call made her shiver. She could go no further in the van. She had to get out.

She climbed down on to the road and stood next to the van. A river wind fingered her with its icy touch. She waited for her eyes to get used to the dark. Her hands were cold but that was nerves more than the wind. She took the torch from the pocket in the van door.

She heard a noise, just a rustle, and her eyes caught the tail of a fox as he crested the bank on the other side of the narrow road. She held the torch like a weapon, wishing now it was her left wrist that Brennan had nearly broken. It was stupid to be here like this, not even two good arms to defend herself. *Get back in the van and drive like hell away from here, woman. Go home!* Noise of water. And this eerie bird's lament that sounded the way she felt, herself – a persistent rhythm of grief.

But seeing the fox was something. It meant she could see well enough now to move. She walked away from the protection of the van, on down the grass verge. Rustlings in the grass – wild creatures or just the wind. An unmetalled road went to the right towards the river, alongside a high wall. Ten yards along, this road ended in a high grass bank. She clambered up the bank to the top.

A big old landing stage made of railway sleepers jutted out high over the water. She walked out on to it. Her footsteps sounded a muffled echo, loud in the dark. She crept to the edge. She could see the water, black, with jiggling silver coins of reflected moon spilled over it. She turned her back on the water.

Now she could make out, back beyond the wall, a massive square black lump. That must be the house. It must be. She could hear her heart. What was she doing here? They must have guards, dogs. Brennan was a thug. He was the master of thugs. They wouldn't hesitate to throw her in the river if she could be of no use to them. *Oh Christ.* She heard a dog bark. Then another. A light went on in the house. She lay flat on the slimy cold wet sleepers. She wriggled backwards towards the edge behind her. Her arm sent screaming messages of pain up into her shoulder. The toe of her right foot touched earth, the bank at the side of the jetty. The bank was steep down to the river. She slid, toes first, grabbing with her left hand at the soft wet brown paste that released a foul smell. Her feet touched flat earth, a clump of grass. She turned to the river, standing upright, squeezed against a cold iron stanchion studded with sharp little shellfish.

She heard footsteps, quiet voices, then a dog barking. She squeezed backwards further under the jetty, this ghostly rickety cathedral, up to her knees in viscous muddy water. She crouched. Water was supposed to nullify human scent. She had never believed this theory and wished she had chosen a less critical moment to test it out. Two lots of footsteps, over her head now. And the dog. Only one dog, she thought, its toenails scraping and clicking on the wood. She did not breathe. The sharp edge of a rusted metal stave cut into her hip.

She couldn't hear what the men were saying, just the flat drone of their voices as they wandered round the jetty above her head. The dog made whimpering sounds in its throat. Then she heard, 'Come on, then, boy.' And the steps went back the way they had come, away from her, off the wooden sleepers. The dog hung back, whimpering and panting. The man gave another low call, 'C'mon!' The sudden scrape of the dog's nails on the slimy wood and then its light footsteps as it went to obey its master. *Please, please, go back to the road and home to bed! Please not down here. Please!* No sound. Not a whisper or a thread of a voice or a footstep. Just the grieving night-bird over the water. Jude let her head fall forward. Oh the relief of letting the tension go. She crouched for minutes that stretched like hours, giving the men and their dog time to go thoroughly away, praying all the time to the fates, *Please just don't let them see the van.* Glad that the van was painted dark green to blend into the tree that sheltered it, and the fields, and the night.

She pulled herself upright. Her legs trembled in water thick as sewage. Her boots were embedded in sucking grey mud, they were full of the stuff, squidging between her toes. She tried to lift a foot. The mud sucked her boot away, gripped her leg in a soft enveloping vice. At last, clinging with her good hand to one of the rusted metal loops that rose up the stanchion like a ladder, the little crustaceans cutting into her palm, her fingers, she slurped her right foot out of the mud, and out of her boot. She placed her foot on the lowest metal loop and pulled with all her strength. The suction of the mud seemed to tighten as she pulled. Panic and fear rose like a tide in her body and urine spurted down her leg. She felt shame and this somehow curtailed her panic. She moaned with rage and gave a frantic heave and the sucking mouth of mud reluctantly relinquished its hold. She held precariously with her one good arm and, now, both feet to the metal ladder. She would have to jump from there back on to the tussocks of reeds on the bank. A darkness closed round and she let go and leapt.

She landed safe, on what she now thought of as her good side. Her legs on reeds, her head on grass. She lay there panting, looking up at the grey clouds. The little slice of moon slid out so bright it hurt her eyes, lighting the silken river and the sculptural jumble of rusting iron, broken bottles, cans. And the man lying half in and half out of the mud a few feet away from her.

43

'John? It's Albert. Where are you?'

'I'm in the Kowloon hotel. In the lucky room. This bloke is attacking me. With a needle and thread. He says he's got medical qualifications. He's got skills in physical torture, that's for sure. Ah, Christ.' He handed over the phone. 'You talk to him.'

A Chinese conversation followed. It sounded like a fight but Bright was used now to the high pitch of energy the Chinese put even into their casual chat. He took the phone back.

Albert said, 'You didn't see who stabbed you?'

'Not a clue, mate.'

'Seriously?'

'Seriously.'

'Where were you?'

'You don't want to know that, Albert.'

'No. Of course.'

'Doesn't matter. You got Chloe.'

'Yes, she is apprehended. We have questioned her along the lines you laid out. She is now in the police building awaiting a hearing with the magistrate.'

'Yes! Who was in the taxi that came to pick her up?'

'I'm afraid he got away.'

'He? You saw him?'

'Enough to see it was a man. That's all.'

'That's something.'

'We ran a check on the taxi. It's not registered. A fake.'

'The same fake we followed up into the hills maybe?'

'The same.'

Bright tried to say *Yes!* in a triumphant tone but managed only a feeble croak.

'The doctor told me you're lucky—'

'Getting stabbed is lucky in Chinese?'

'—the knife just missed your kidneys.'

'Okay, that's lucky.'

'But he says you mustn't move.'

'I get it. He's stitching me up in more ways than one. Whose side is he on?'

The doctor cut the thread and covered the wound with a dressing strip. He held out a small brown plastic bottle. 'Take one of these four times a day after meals. They are quite strong painkillers. Do not drive.'

'You hear that, Albert?'

Albert laughed and put down his phone.

Bright said, 'If Albert didn't know about this, how come you turned up?'

'Kim called me.'

'Albert's brother-in-law Kim?'

'That's right. My nephew Kim. You came back to the hotel in a taxi. You were losing a lot of blood.'

'I don't remember!'

'If Kim had not called me, you might have bled to death.'

'I see what you mean by lucky.'

A knock woke him from something like sleep. He watched the door open. The smart guy from the Han Building filled the doorway. *Ah shit. I'm gonna die like this, in lucky number eighty-eight, in a hotel in Kowloon?* Then this cool voice said, 'I'll call you if I need you,' and Smart Guy went outside and closed the door.

Bright said, 'Come to finish me off, have you?' He reached for the phone and felt the stab wound afresh.

She said, 'It was not I who had you stabbed.'

'No? Some passing commuter suddenly got an urge, that it?' He started to dial.

She said, 'If you tell them you have twice seen me alone, your case will be completely invalidated.'

'If I tell them Roger visited your house and stayed three and a half hours the case will be invalidated. I don't tell on Roger, Roger don't tell on me.'

She said, 'I have no desire to harm you.'

'Is that right?'

'On the contrary, I need you alive.' She stood there in her skin-tight frock and opened her lovely arms. 'I have no weapon.' She never took her unblinking eyes off him, circling his face like a caress, like a physical caress.

No weapon? In spite of the situation he was in, in spite of the fact that paradoxically she made his blood run cold, he was in danger of getting a hard-on again. He'd have laughed, only it hurt like hell. She said, 'If I wanted you killed, you would be dead. I would not waste my time talking with you first, believe me.'

'I believe you.'

'I have a proposition to put to you.'

Holding her gaze he slowly put the phone back on its rest. 'Okay,' he said. 'So shoot. And I don't mean that literally, okay?'

'Some time ago,' she said, 'a businessman in London made contact with me through a Chinese group operating there. This Chinese group had its origins here in Hong Kong. They had stolen a cargo, part of a cargo, from the container port here. It was a well-planned, well-executed robbery. It had a bad effect on my business, on my reputation for discretion, as well as being a great financial loss for all concerned. Something had to be done about this group. This London businessman is clever. He had been approached by this group to make a partnership to dispose of some of this – cargo – in the UK. He contacted me.'

'How did he contact you?'

'He sent Roger Gould.'

Bright breathed out so hard his wound hurt. He put the phone back on its rest. 'This businessman paid for Roger's trip?'

'He – made the arrangements.'

'You got proof of that?'

She gave him that look, head cocked on one side: *You think I'm stupid or what?*

'So what was his aim?'

'To buy into my business by performing a service for me.'

'The service was to teach this gang a lesson.'

'You might put it that way, yes.'

'Which he did.' Bright's surge of excitement was stronger than the weird turn-on he was getting off her. It went back to the Triad shooting in Essex. He knew it. His case was going to crack. He had to calm himself down. He could feel his breathing getting bothersome, each breath a sharp jab.

'Now this man is becoming a nuisance,' she said. 'He wants more of my business than I am prepared to let go. He is using every weapon he can against me to force me to give him what he wants.'

'What weapons?'

'You know.' She wouldn't say her son, she wouldn't say Lee's name.

'Apart from your son,' he said. 'What weapons?'

'My grandchild and the mother of my grandchild.' There was just the slightest hurry in the way she said this, out of kilter with her normal measured speech.

'Is this why you wouldn't come to London to see your dying son? Because of Brennan?'

'I know no one of that name.'

'Reynolds then.'

She repeated in the same flat tone, 'I know no one of that name.'

'A-ha. Right. Okay. No names no packdrill as my old ma always says. It's still why you didn't come to see Lee when you knew he was probably gonna die?'

'My son left many years ago. We had had no contact since he left.'

'Oh well then, no reason to make the trip just because he'd been burned to death by some low-life drug-dealing prick that you were doing business with.'

She didn't move. She sat more still if anything, like she was reorganising all the bits, putting them back together in the shape that would best serve. She was like a Buddha. A female Buddha. You didn't ask was she right or wrong or good or evil: *I am who I am.* He got new respect for Brennan, doing deals with this woman. But then, he recalled, Brennan hadn't met her.

She said in the same quiet voice, 'It is no use for you to abuse me. You don't understand the history. I am not here to explain it. My relationship with my son is my own affair. I have caused it. I have to live with it. I will live with it. I do live with it. That is not the issue here.'

Oh but it was. It was the issue. 'What is the issue then? What are you doing here? What have you come to trade?'

'Roger tells me you have come closest to putting an end to the activities of – this businessman. You had a case against him.'

'Which was screwed by your friend Roger.'

'You don't know that.'

'I did not know that. I do know it now.'

'You can't prove it.'

'Not yet.'

'Do you know how you can prove it?'

'I have a few ideas.'

'You came here to find Chloe Han. My ex-daughter-in-law.'

'That is quite true.'

'Roger also came to find her.' At this point she stopped caressing Bright's face with her eyes. She looked towards the window. Neon lights were flashing on and off, colouring her face, chrome – turquoise – crimson – gold. 'Roger came to find her on his own account,' she said. She turned to face him again. 'Chloe was – if you like – sold to Roger by our businessman friend. She was his – mistress seems an old-fashioned term, but that was her function. A gun . . .'

Ahhh . . . Bright hoped he had not made a sound but he couldn't be sure.

'I believe a gun was removed from the scene of a crime. The only witness against the businessman had been killed with this gun.'

'A-ha.'

'And Roger Gould was at the scene before you.'

'A-ha. Big Rog from AMIP was the man in charge.'

'AMIP?'

'Area Major Incident Pool. Co-ordination it's meant to be. Interfering bastards is how we generally think of them. It's a job for the high-flyers. Like dear old Rog.'

'You are bitter.'

'A-ha, that's right. In this case I am.'

'Very well. I know what happened to the gun.'

'Oh you do.'

'Roger kept it. He did not destroy it. He knew he could use it at some future date if he needed to. It kept the balance of power between him and the businessman. But he could not keep hold of it himself, of course. It would incriminate him.'

'He gave it to Chloe. To keep for him.'

Her eyes told him yes.

'The poor sap trusted Chloe?'

'Oh give him some credit. He is not stupid.'

'Excuse me. He is stupid. He thought because Chloe needed drugs and protection and he could supply them he had Chloe in hock to him. He's a stupid corrupted bastard, he's an asshole that shouldn't be allowed to— He's the worst. The lowest form of life. The Brennans of this world, they have one function: they're criminals, that's their life, that's their job, but the Brennans couldn't function in this world of ours if concupiscent shits like Roger Gould didn't pave the way for them— Never mind, never mind, carry on.'

'Concupiscent?' she half smiled.

'A-ha, yeah. Long word for a thicko copper, right? Let's get on with this. Chloe has the gun.'

'She does not have it. Airport security.'

'No, she could hardly bring it here, stuffed down her baby's nappy.'

'She knows where it is.'

'So what? The chain of evidence is broken. The gun is no use now to anyone.'

'I know the name of the policeman who saw the gun at the scene before it disappeared. He was paid to keep his mouth shut.'

'He was promoted to AMIP as well.'

'So you already know so much.'

'That's quite a high pay-off for a creep like him.'

'He can be made to testify, surely,' she said.

'He can be made to do anything. Obviously.'

'Yes. As can anybody.'

'You think so?'

'Even you.'

'Oh yeah. Everyone has their price. Money, power, sex. Just get the price right—'

'The currency,' she said, 'rather than the price. With you for instance money would not work. Nor would promotion to a position of power in your job – you wouldn't want that except on your own terms. Nor sex?' She came close to him and with her fingernails she lightly scratched the back of his hand from the wrist down to the knuckles and on down to the tips of his fingers. He felt all over him the fine sharp needles of a pleasure that verged on pain. He did not make a sound or a sign but she looked into his face with a frank knowledge that contained compassion. He knew, for the first time with a woman, the desire to kill. He felt breathless with it. But he kept his breathing quiet. He kept his eyes on hers. She smiled slightly and touched his hand with a cool fingertip. 'Perhaps not,' she said. 'With you now . . . Oh yes, I know. I know what currency will buy you.'

'Oh you do, ha?' Great repartee. He blamed the painkillers.

'Yes, I do. If the removal of the gun were to come to light, you would be under suspicion of removing it, or causing it to be removed, from the scene of the shooting. You could be disgraced in your profession. I believe this would hurt you, I believe this would horrify you. You pride yourself on being above the criminals, different from them. That is your particular vanity: that you could never be corrupted. So to be accused of this, of being in the pay of this man you call Brennan? Yes . . .' She stepped back a little and looked at him speculatively. 'Yes, I think you could be persuaded by the threat of this. No?'

'What – get corrupted by the fear of looking corrupt? A-ha, that makes a lot of sense.'

'Roger Gould's word against yours? Which would they believe?'

'Do you think I'd leave London and come here without covering my tracks? You think I'd come here without hard evidence against him?' At last he'd got over his appalling desire to call her ma'am. He had to be careful though: she'd calculate precisely how rattled he had to be to start insulting her. Careful,

careful. Go easy. Making her angry was not his aim. He needed to get Roger Gould. The way she was talking, it was going to be him or Roger. So she should think she'd got him. The trouble was, she was watching his thoughts as though they were printed on ticker tape, moving across his forehead.

She said amused, 'You can stop thinking so furiously, trying to outguess me. Us. You are in our control. The only really hard evidence is the gun. The gun can be found and the trail of evidence can lead back to you. You will be suspended pending an inquiry. Two witnesses, officers in this – AMIP – will give evidence against you. The businessman's lawyer will intimate to the investigating officer that you were in the businessman's pay. Even if it is kept quiet and, knowing your tabloid press in the UK, it will not be kept quiet, you will be disgraced. Your colleagues, the team you head, would be disillusioned. Your mother would never quite know whether to believe you or them. Your friends. The women who are important to you. They would never after this trust you again.'

His heart was actually pounding. Did she know she had just revealed to him the driving spark of his existence? He could have paid a psychiatrist for ten years and not got this close. As with a shrink, so with her, it was no use pretending. Except to be just a little bit more stupid than he was? If she had sussed his Achilles' heel, he had sussed hers. He said, 'I never realised that.'

'What?'

'That that's what matters most to me.'

'What?'

'To be trusted. For folks to think I'm trustworthy.'

'All your life and you didn't know?' She smiled, the thick smooth brown-pink lips slightly parted.

'No!' He laughed and thrust a hand through his hair, that gesture he had. Then ran the hand over his face. The small square capable hand. She watched him. 'It's a bit of a shaker,' he said.

He watched her with his squint full-on, so, though she watched him close, she could not tell how close he watched her. 'You're a clever woman,' he said. And he saw the frisson of pleasure it gave her to be told that. Your greatest weakness is your greatest strength. Hers was her cleverness. She held her quiver of pleasure in check but he saw it. 'I need to be trusted!' he said. 'Fuck . . .'

'If you go along with us, the gun will be returned. There will be an unbroken chain of evidence against the businessman. You will have your case.'

'I'll have Roger Gould.'

Again the little smug tuck at the corner of that beautiful mouth. 'Perhaps. Who knows? Who can predict the future?' She gave him the gaze again, concentrated on his mouth. He was right: to be the cleverest wasn't enough; she wanted to be the sexiest too. Mirror mirror on the wall. And she was that all right. No contest.

He gave her his cat smile, not a muscle moving. The urge to move in, to touch the skin of her bare arms, to press his mouth on the matt flesh of her mouth, to part those firm soft lips with his tongue, to feel that clever body fit itself to his, and that clever mind working on the things she could do to him – that excited him and she knew it – the idea of that clever mind always just a little bit detached no matter the pleasures of her body . . . And all the time he's thinking. He's weighing up her offer.

She came close. He could smell her perfume. He'd smelled it before. Where? He shut his eyes a moment. Jude Craig? Her red hair and her freckles and her childlike blue eyes and her simple blue cotton frock. She used the same perfume as Eloise Han? It wasn't possible. He said, 'What's that perfume?'

'I have it shipped to me personally from Paris. It is Vent Vert by Balmain.'

'It's incredible,' he said.

She said, a step closer, 'You are quite subtle, you know. You are more subtle than a man generally is.'

'More subtle than Big Rog? Surely not.'

'Ah, poor Roger. So simple. He likes them young.'

'But you're ageless.'

Flattery, most people, you could lay it on with a trowel, no problem. But her? He hadn't got the measure yet of how far he could go. The thing was, he was telling the truth. He meant every word. Ageless she specialised in. He said, 'I mean, you're Lee's mother so even if you had him when you were fifteen—'

'I was not so stupid, even at fifteen, to become an unmarried mother, believe me. He had to be my husband's child to inherit the business.' She moved closer to him. 'But yes, I am ageless if you like. Any woman can be ageless if she wants to be . . .' She came very close.

He said, 'What do you want, Eloise?'

'I want my grandson.'

'You won't get him if I tell them how you're implicated in this.'

'You won't tell them if you are dead.'

'So what's the trade-off ?'

'You finish the activities of the businessman but you keep my name and my business out of it.'

'And?'

'I give you Roger.'

44

She knew who he was. She recognised his feet. Or rather his shoes. She gingerly put out a hand and with two fingers searched for the pulse in his ankle. Yes, there was a pulse. His head was close to the water line. The tide was coming in. She could hear water lapping. She didn't know when high tide might be or how fast it might happen. She wondered why she cared whether he lived or died. There was no way she could pull him out of there. He weighed more than she did. And she was, due to his less than perfect manners, lacking the use of an arm. Some people now, she'd have tried anyway. But this bedbug in the mattress of humanity – no thanks; she was getting out of here. She struggled to her feet and the act of standing in itself steadied her. Her mind clicked in. He was obviously not conscious. He hadn't got down here by accident. And he was not likely to have been left for dead by one of his own employees. She started hauling herself up by her good arm.

Easy it was not. She was wet. Her mud-caked clothes clung to her flesh, thick and heavy and smelling foul. For every step she climbed, she slipped back three. But at last she sprawled on the bank by the landing stage. She heard voices over by the house and a vehicle driving off; not in her direction. Quiet fell all round. Even that heartbreaking bird had stopped calling. The chill in the air told her it was late, nearly dawn. She had become expert in the stages of the night. She crawled to the edge of the grass bank. Eyes well used to the dark, she could see no people, no movement, no dogs.

To her left was a vast expanse of marsh; to her right the house. She slid down the bank. She ran on the grass at the edge of the road. Her boot made no noise, but her bare foot was agony. When she got level with the house she cut away across the corner of the field. She longed for a bush, a hedge, a rock, anything to stand up and shelter her from view in this bald flat landscape under that shining slice of moon. She heard voices again and fell flat, lying there with her heart beating in her ears as though the ground itself was beating. A car door banged and, to stop herself uttering a sound, she pressed her face to the earth and got a mouthful of muddy wet soil. Then an engine started and headlights beamed her way. She felt their light all over her. The car didn't stop, no one called out. The engine died away down the road. She stayed, waited, her mouth in the mud and the mud in her mouth. No sound. No lights. She turned her head at last – a faint light thrown from the house. She got to her knees and wiped her mouth and spat and waited again. She crawled a short way, on stones, in water, on grass again. She got to her feet. She felt so exposed she just ran, ignoring the pain in her foot. She had no control left. She stumbled and fell several times before she reached the road. She could see the tree where she'd left the van.

No van.

She heard herself whimper like a little dog. They knew she would eventually come here to get the van. They only had to wait for her to come. She was too tired now to carry on with this mad scheme. She'd had it. She was done. When the headlights came round the bend she didn't even try to hide. She sat where she was on the wet ground and simply waited.

The car stopped. A man got out. He was coming straight towards her across the humpy field, stumbling like her. And she still didn't move. She couldn't. He said, 'Mrs Craig?'

She didn't answer so he had to come up close. He said, 'Niki Cato, Kentish Town CID.'

She laughed.

He said, 'Come on, we've got to be quick.' He grabbed her arm and hauled her to her feet. She was so tired her legs would barely move but she still laughed. They ran doubled up, every step searing to her bare foot, back to his car. He pushed her in. He turned the car to go back the way he'd come. She said, 'Where's Dan? Where's my husband?'

'That's what we'd all like to know. We thought you knew.'

'So did I.'

He rolled his window down. She was already aware of the smell coming off her. It was disgusting beyond belief. She remembered she'd wet her pants. But just this minute she didn't give a damn. She said, 'I need to go to the house back there.'

'You have got to be joking.'

She didn't answer. He only hesitated a moment then he turned the car round.

There were lights on downstairs. She pressed the intercom. An oily voice said, 'Yes?'

She mouthed at Cato, 'Who's this?'

'The lawyer.'

'This is Jude Craig,' she said to the intercom.

The shortest silence then, 'Yes?' He didn't waste words.

She said, 'I know where Michael Brennan is. I'll tell you where he is when you give me back my husband.'

'I do not have your husband.'

'Then you won't get Brennan.' Cato stood there with his mouth open staring at her. She lifted her shoulders, her eyebrows, she shook her open hand at him: *What do I say now, what do I do?*

Cato made a gesture: *Keep rolling.*

She said, 'You must have some idea where my husband is. When I saw Brennan he was close to death. Someone has badly injured him and it's not likely to be one of you, so we'll assume it was Dan. In which case Dan can't be that far away.' She stood silent now, waiting. The oily voice didn't speak and she started to wonder if he'd gone. She wanted to wait him out but she couldn't. She said, 'Where is my van?'

'Ah, the pretty green Rascal?'

'Where is it?'

'Taken care of.'

So Dan hadn't found it and driven it off. She said, 'Well . . . ? Are you going to tell me where Dan is?'

'Just a moment.'

Her lungs felt dry and airless. She tried to take a deep breath but the air wouldn't go deeper than her throat.

Then he said, 'I am told your husband was last seen near a farm on the road to Southminster. Layland Farm.'

'When I find him I will tell you where your boss is.'

'How do I know you will keep your end of the bargain, Mrs Craig?'

'You don't.' She pulled Cato away from the door. 'We've got to go where he said.'

'That's what they want you to do.'

'But they've pinched my van. They think I'm on foot, that I can't get there before them.'

Cato groaned. 'Christ, you're right.'

He did a three point turn and they were back on the road, so flat it was like driving along a causeway. No hedges, no hills, just horrible bumps like the car had a wheel loose. Cato punched numbers and held the phone under his ear. He gave their whereabouts and pumped questions. 'Okay.'

They reached a barrier: *Private Road. No access without permission*. 'We're here.' Cato threw the car to the left, a narrower lane but smoother. He slowed. They peered into the dark. 'You look out that side, I'll do this side.' Shadowy buildings loomed ahead. A distant dog barked.

Jude said, 'Stop.' She said it very quiet, very low.

Cato stopped the car.

Jude got out.

Cato shone the torch. She saw the feet. Cato moved the beam of light up the body to the head.

Cato said, 'That's a dog did that.'

So she knew then that he was dead.

Cato turned away and murmured into his mobile.

Jude knelt down. She bent her head and rested her forehead on Dan's back, then put her arm across him as though like that she could keep him warm.

The paramedics had to lift her off him to get him into the ambulance. There were three police cars. She said to Cato, 'Brennan is on the mud next to the landing stage.'

The grey-haired superintendent said, 'Next to the house?'

'Yes. To the right if you're looking at the river, down on the mud.'

'Alive or dead?'

'Unconscious when I saw him. But alive.'

Two police cars roared off.

Cato pushed her back into his car and followed the ambulance. He said, 'The place will be deserted when they get there.'

'Sinking ship,' Jude said.

Cato lit his pipe. 'You mind this?'

She didn't bother to reply.

'It's like you said.' He puffed hard to get it going. 'They thought you were on foot. They'd catch up with you before you found this place. Then what? I just don't want to think.'

As they approached the hospital entrance she said, 'How come you were there?'

'We've had you under surveillance since the attack. Orders of the DI.'

He parked. She did not want to get out of the car.

45

Roger stood up with a look of shock, which he tried to replace with an expression of concern. He did not quite convince. But then no one was looking at Roger.

Albert helped Bright to a chair and sat down next to him.

Lawrence gave him a cup of that reviving tea. 'Glad you could join us, John.'

'Me too,' Bright said.

They all laughed. Including Roger, who said, 'Where did it happen, John?'

'Shop doorway. Busy street downtown. Must have mistaken me for someone else, Rog, eh? No hard feelings. One of those things. Let's get on.'

'Ms Chloe Han was apprehended leaving the Han Corporation Building at eight-twenty this morning and brought here for questioning. She says she came to Hong Kong only to bring her son to visit his grandmother whom he had never met. She denies all involvement in the death of her ex-husband Lee Han. She denies being at the scene of the fire, and any part in cutting off Lee Han's life support.'

'Well, she would, wouldn't she.'

'And she denies that there was a passenger in the taxi that stopped outside the Han Building apparently to pick her up,' Albert said.

Roger ran the side of his forefinger over his upper lip and kept it there concealing, and controlling, his mouth.

'She has been taken to the reception centre for the Lai Chi

Kok Women's Remand Centre,' Lawrence said, 'to await the hearing in the extradition process.'

'We questioned Eloise Han who admitted that Chloe's child is in the Han Building in her private apartments. Her lawyer was present. We were shown a document signed by Chloe Han giving her child for adoption to Eloise Han in return for a substantial allowance for the rest of her life. It was also signed by Eloise Han and witnessed by her lawyer.'

'Did Chloe have Mun-yi Wong's passport on her?'

'I'm afraid not. But a false passport and papers and immigration documents for Australia were found in her possession, plus a large sum of money.'

'How much?' Bright said.

'Three million Australian dollars.'

'Just to be going on with.'

'Oh yes. She had details of a bank account in Sydney with a deposit of five million.'

'What's she got over on Eloise Han to get that sort of a deal?'

'That is what we would all like to know.'

'These documents are bagged up?'

'Yes. They are listed in evidence and will go to London in your safekeeping.'

'Better if they're listed in evidence and come back with Chloe,' Bright said.

'Do you agree, Roger?' Lawrence turned to Roger Gould. All eyes were upon him. He hesitated, visibly.

Bright nudged him along. 'Going by what's happened to me, Rog, we'll be lucky if we get back in one piece.'

'Quite right. Quite right.' Roger had no choice.

'Don't worry. She will be flown back under armed guard.'

'Good, good.' Roger gave a chirpy smile.

'Eloise Han of course denies all knowledge of Chloe's possible involvement in her son's murder. Chloe arrived on her doorstep as it were, with the child, and Eloise took her in, out of the goodness of her heart: when she saw her grandson, all was forgiven. She offered to adopt the child and Chloe asked for an allowance which Eloise, generous woman that she is, was glad to provide.'

'And the false papers for Australia?'

'Ah, well. Eloise denies all knowledge of those. And so does her lawyer of course.'

'Any chance of tracing them back?'

Lawrence gave an elegant shrug. 'We continue to question Chloe. But Chloe will soon be back in London. You will be in a better position there to negotiate with her some – arrangement in return for information. Isn't that so, Roger?'

'Oh yes, Lawrence. Absolutely, yes.'

Bright had a shower, another high-powered pounding with hot then cold. Wrapped himself in the robe. Lay on the bed propped on pillows. Drank half a bottle of the same pure spring water he drank in London. It had come a long way. Like him.

The painkillers loosened his grip a bit – held life at a distance. But he did know Albert was coming for him at ten to take him to the airport. Plenty of time but he'd better get dressed. He put on his new gear. It didn't hurt too much if he was careful. That cool fresh feel of new cotton against the skin, made him think of Jude Craig. He checked his watch. Seven and a half hours difference. The early shift should just be coming in. He phoned home.

Helen told him the news.

He didn't say a word.

'How are you, John?'

'I'm fine, Helen, I'm fine.'

He phoned Superintendent Derek Cooper in Essex.

'Don't get your knickers in a twist, John. Everything's in order. Under twenty-four-hour guard in the hospital.'

'And Jude Craig?'

'Doc's seen her. She'll survive. Cato's got her under his wing.'

'I arrive at the crack of dawn. I'll come straight to you.'

Coming back was easy. The flight was eleven-thirty at night – bedtime. He thought about a scotch or two, but decided the whisky/painkiller cocktail was probably not a good idea. After dinner he settled on his little pillow, pulled up his scrappy blanket, covered his eyes with the daft little mask and made a decision to sleep. No movies. No distractions. It was like sleeping on sharp rocks in a high wind. His wound throbbed. It was fitful. But it was sleep.

Roger came through customs looking like death. Maybe business class wasn't all it was cracked up to be. Or maybe Roger had other troubles.

'Hospital smells really get up my nose,' Bright said.

'Very funny, guv.'

'How long was he in intensive care?'

'Just under twenty-four hours.'

The consultant met them outside Dan's room and refused them entry. 'Little bit groggy, I'm afraid, folks. Later this afternoon perhaps he'll be more compos mentis.'

Even Bright didn't contradict consultants. He said to Cato, 'Where's his wife?'

'I left her at the local nick with your mate, Derek Cooper. She offered to make a statement.'

'You stay here, Cat. Anyone asks, you don't know where I am.'

'Anyone?'

'You know what I mean. Use your famous discretion, Sherlock.'

The car-park was at the back. A grey Merc was parked there. Bright recognised the registration number. He barged straight in the back way, banging doors. 'Where's Jude Craig?'

'Who's asking?'

He flashed his ID. 'It's my case.'

'Oh, sorry, sir. The bloke from AMIP's with her.'

'And where's your superintendent?'

'He's with her too.'

'Where?'

Bright's concentrated mix of alarm and rage constituted an unmistakable threat. The guy just said, 'Okay, okay, this way,' and led him through to the interview rooms. Bright didn't knock.

He was shocked. Cato had said she was in a bad way but he was looking at a grotesque travesty of the gorgeous girl he'd held in his head all this time. One eye was shut by swellings all colours of the rainbow from yellow to indigo. Her amazing hair was tied back and she had dressings on her neck. Her arm was in a sling. Her foot was bandaged. She was wearing a jumble of clothes that had obviously been lent to her.

'Hi, Rog,' Bright said. 'Who told you she was here?'

'Well, Superintendent Cooper of course. Dreadful goings-on round here last night.'

'Shouldn't she be at the hospital with her husband?'

'Well, I asked for a little debriefing first.'

'Ith okay. I offered.' Her speech was full of swelling, thick, fat, difficult.

'Mind if I sit in?' Bright pulled out a chair and sat. He had that cheerful breezy energy that was the sign of a pure clean anger that was going to do somebody a lot of damage. Maybe not now. Maybe not tomorrow. But sometime soon.

'Of course, John, of course!'

'Have you made a statement, Jude? To Chief Inspector Gould here?'

'I juth tol' him wha' happen' lath night.'

'A-ha.' Bright looked at Gould. 'How's Brennan? You seen him?'

Gould put out a hand and rocked it from side to side. It shook slightly. *'Comme si comme ça,'* he said.

'He in custody?'

'He's in intensive care, John. Under police guard. We can't read him his rights till he's conscious.'

'Same hospital as Dan Craig?'

'Yes.'

'His lawyer says he was attacked by Craig. That true?'

'It appears to be true, to be true, yes. Yes.'

'Where's Mrs Craig's statement? Being transcribed? Recorder's not on.'

'Oh well, you know, just an informal debriefing, as I said. Mrs Craig will be in a better condition to make a formal statement tomorrow perhaps. She's sedated just now.'

'I'm doped to the eyeballth,' Jude said. 'Ith true.'

She smiled, which made Bright madder than before.

'So what have you told my esteemed colleague here?' he said.

Jude saw he'd got these metallic hard little jags of light in his eyes. His eyes flicked from her to Gould like switchblades. She felt scared and safe in equal proportions. She knew there was something wrong. She knew she must not say more than she had to. He did not need to tell her this in words; she felt his anger – directed at this pompous man, she thought – like the sharp end of a rope. Even though she was thickly Valiumed she knew she had to be careful.

Roger Gould drawled, 'She had just got to where she found Michael Brennan under the landing stage. She recognised him by his shoes.' Gould gave her a sophisticated smile. 'Isn't that so, Mrs Craig?'

'I'd been thtaring at them long enough the other night.'

'So somehow you got up out of the mud?'

'With one mighty bound.' Trying to grin was painful.

'Where was your van?'

'By the only three.'

'Eh? Oh! Tree.'

'But it had gone. I thought Dan had taken it.'

'Has it been recovered?' Bright asked Gould.

'In a garage behind the property.' Gould wasn't saying things twice any more. In fact he was hardly saying things at all.

'Can I have it back?' Jude said.

'We'll be going over it for prints and stuff, but then?' Bright looked at Gould who nodded. Twice.

'Thankth. Can't manage withouth ith. Oh shith. Thorry. Ith tho hard to thpeak.' She hoped she wasn't laying it on too thick.

'I think we should leave this whole thing till tomorrow. Don't you, Rog? Her place is with her husband at this time, right? And it looks as though she could do with a rest. We don't want to be accused of exacting statements under duress, do we? Especially from a witness who can hardly speak.'

'Anyway thath when Theargent Cato found me, tho . . .'

'Yeah, we got Sergeant Cato's version. You were with Cato from then on?'

'He never lef' my thide.'

'Well there you are. Come on. Let's go. I'll give you a lift to the hospital.'

Roger stood, blocking their way. 'I asked them to call me when Mr Craig regains consciousness.'

'This is her husband we're talking about, Rog.'

'Yes, of course. I'm so sorry, Mrs Craig. We policemen get carried away when it comes to intelligence gathering.' He opened the door with great dignity. 'We'll all reconvene tomorrow.'

'Sure, Rog.' *Not if I can help it*, Bright did not say.

46

At first she thought it wasn't Dan. They'd shaved his head. And a line of stitching ran like a ladder down the left side of his face missing the eye by a millimetre. The vermilion bruising gave him a piratical appearance. He looked leaner, stronger. Clearer, with harder outlines. The soft look had gone with the boyish curly hair. His eyes were hard too. He stared at her with no expression, not defiance, not shame, not gladness or hope. And emphatically not with love. She came close to the bed.

He said, 'I was expecting the police.'

'John Bright said I could see you first.'

'Ah, how kind.'

'Well, it is, actually.'

'We're a matching pair. The walking wounded.'

'Your friend Michael Brennan did this.'

'He hinted as much. I tried to kill him.'

'I know,' she said. 'I found him. I was looking for you.'

'You should have been glad to be rid of me.'

'He's alive, did they tell you?'

He closed his eyes. 'Shit,' he said through his teeth. 'Nothing I do ever goes right.' But she could tell it was relief he was feeling. He opened his eyes and a wisp of his boyish expression was back there.

'He's here in the hospital,' she said.

'Under police guard too?'

'Yes. Like you.'

'They surely can't have found anything to arrest him for.'

'Assault.'

'I assaulted *him*!'

'Assault on me.'

'He'll find a way out of that.'

'It enables them to hold him for questioning while they accumulate their evidence.'

'How is he?'

'Recovering from concussion. And his leg was fractured in the fall from the landing stage.'

'Is that all? Life's a big disappointment, isn't it?'

'Dan – I have to ask you . . .'

'What?'

'George has disappeared.'

'Oh Christ. Shit.'

'You didn't . . . ?'

'Didn't what? Try to harm your familiar spirit? Me? You think I was hanging round the neighbourhood to kidnap George? Come off it, Jude.'

'Michael Brennan seemed to know something about it.'

'Oh, bollocks. George'll be back.'

'You don't know that.'

'No.'

'And you don't care.'

'At this present moment? Not a lot, no.'

'I don't think I've ever known you very well.'

'Well, there you are.'

'Yes. There I am.'

'Who've you been more worried about, him or me?'

'What's going to happen to us, Dan?'

'You've got to let me go, Jude.' He looked at her, determinedly expressionless except for the hard coldness of his eyes. 'Let me go,' he said.

'You've already gone, haven't you?'

'This time you came after me. Next time – don't.'

'Where are you going next time?'

'Not home to you.'

She sat there looking at this new Dan. The shaved, stitched head gave him a thuggish appearance. She didn't want to hate him. 'Okay,' she said.

'Well, where is this policeman? I haven't been to confession since I was seventeen. They say it's good for the spirit. I never found it so. But maybe it works better with a copper than a priest.'

She went to the door. Bright was outside. He gave her one quick look and came to the door. 'Dan wants to talk to you now,' she said. She was going but Dan said, 'Stay.'

She looked at Bright. 'Can I?'

'Sure. And I'm afraid my sergeant has to be present too.'

'What the hell. The more the merrier.'

'Only he's been delayed for a few minutes, finding a tape recorder. We have to record you here, as you're not able to come to the station just yet.'

Dan didn't answer. Jude felt scared. Bright was going to interview Dan with only her for witness?

Bright said, 'There's something you need to tell me, Mr Craig. And I want you to tell me now and tell me fast. What has Michael Brennan got over on you? Shoot.'

'Bless me Father for I have sinned,' Dan said, 'it's twenty-five years since my last confession.'

Bright sat still, never moved a muscle, like a bird was hopping near to him and he must not frighten it away.

'I killed my mother,' Dan said.

Nobody spoke. Jude's head came up. She understood everything. Everything.

'Why?' Bright said, very quiet.

'She was ill. She was dying. She was in pain. She was begging me. She was begging me for over a year.'

'Why wait a year? Why leave her suffering that long?'

'I couldn't do it. I couldn't. I thought I should but I was more afraid of my conscience than I was of her right to choose her way out. In the end there's this night. I'm there, drinking myself into oblivion, and Michael comes to visit. He visited her every month. She was a second mother to him, to a lot of the kids in those flats. He said, she's begging you, what's the matter with you, went on about all this Catholic guilt rubbish. I'd asked the nurse who came to give her the injections why they couldn't control her pain better. She said, because we could be accused of bad practice. I realised no one could put an end to her suffering but me. I said this to Michael. The next day he brought me a syringe. Showed me what to do. I couldn't do it, my hand was shaking. But I had to be the one. In the end he held on to my wrist while I – I had my eyes shut. When I opened them she was gone. I missed it.'

'What?'

He put it in quotes. '"The moment of her passing." Michael paid for the funeral. Grand Catholic celebration, wasn't it, Jude? Oh, everything done very well. Great send-off, everybody said.'

'Nobody questioned the cause of death?'

'Doctor said a woman of a lesser constitution would have been dead two years ago.'

'So that's what Brennan had over on you.'

'I couldn't bear to go near the flat after. He offered to take it off my hands, always there to solve your little problems, that's Michael.'

'He rented it off you?'

'He said he'd buy it the minute it was legal for me to sell.'

'Then he paid you fifty thousand.'

'It was in a separate account. I transferred it so that Jude . . .

In case of anything untoward happening to me, Jude would have access to it.'

'And what did you have over on Brennan?'

Dan was about to answer but Bright held up a hand. 'Hang on. I think we'll get my sergeant in on this.' He stood up and went out, closing the door behind him.

Dan said quickly, 'Do they know about you and Lee Han?'

Jude nodded.

Bright came in again. 'This is DS Cato.'

'We've met.'

'Hello, Mr Craig.' Cato pulled a small Walkman out of his pocket. 'This is all I could find.' He switched the thing on and announced the date, time, and people present.

Dan was about to begin.

Bright said, 'Mr Craig has just told us that Michael Brennan killed his mother two years ago. Mr Craig has felt guilty over this ever since. Mainly because he then let Mr Brennan take over his mother's flat and eventually buy it. Mr Craig has a very sensitive conscience and he felt that he'd thereby profited from his mother's death. Mr and Mrs Craig will both confirm that this is what Mr Craig has just told me. Right, Mr Craig?'

Dan stared at Bright, dumbstruck.

Bright said, 'Please say yes for the recording, Mr Craig.'

'Yes?'

'Right, now let's get on to the arson attack on Lee Han.' Bright gave Dan his most impenetrable gaze, and waited. Dan said nothing. Bright spoke encouragingly. 'Well, for instance, did you know about this attack before it happened?'

'No.'

'But you were seen hanging about outside the premises when it did happen.'

'I was worried.'

'You didn't know it was going to happen but you were worried?'

'My wife was— Jude was— I'm sorry . . .' Dan covered his eyes.

'You suspected that your wife and Lee Han were having an affair, right?'

'Yes. I was upset about that. And I made the mistake of telling Michael.'

'Michael Brennan?'

'Yes.'

'You seem to make that mistake about a lot of things.'

'I was down here discussing the house with him. We were drinking. And Michael says, Don't you worry my old son, I'll take care of it. I said no, that's the last thing I want, don't you get involved, but it was too late. Don't give it a thought, he says, I like to kill two birds with one stone. It's economical. Your troubles are over. I said no, don't, it's all a mistake. He said, don't worry, I'm just going to give him a bit of a frightener. That's why I was hanging round outside Lee's place. I was worried. What if anything happened to Jude?' He put his head in his hands. 'If anything was going to happen I wanted to be there. I wanted to stop it. When I saw Jude come out safe I was relieved. Then I couldn't leave because Chloe, the girl who used to be married to Lee Han, she was there and then other people hanging round. And then . . .'

And then. And then. And then . . .

Bright drove her home. They didn't talk much. She kept wiping her eyes. She looked bereft when they got to her house. She stared up at the blank windows.

'I'll come in with you if you like.'

'Oh, would you?'

She felt pitiably grateful. She couldn't have faced going in alone. She didn't call George. She'd given up on that. Bright asked if he could use the ground-floor cloakroom so she went downstairs alone to put the kettle on. George was sitting outside the french window waiting to be let in, just like he'd never been away. When he saw her he opened his mouth, showing all his teeth, indignant with her for not being home.

She thought this hallucination was caused by the medication the police doctor had given her. But she opened the door anyway. George yowled in complaint and trotted in. He jumped on to the worktop to look for his food. She fed him. While he ate she felt him all over for injuries. He was thin – she could feel all his bones – and his fur was dusty and dry. But as far as she could tell, he was fine. In the middle of eating he broke off to rub his face against her face, this side then that side, purring and spraying food pellets.

She turned and saw John Bright standing on the stairs watching her and George. She couldn't fathom his expression. 'He's always been a messy eater,' she said.

47

Chloe came back in Albert's safekeeping. Bright went to question her in the remand section of Holloway. He didn't like prisons. He especially didn't like women's prisons. He didn't like the noise or the smell. Walking down a corridor he heard babies crying. He knew Chloe's Chico wasn't one of them. He was being raised in luxury by one of the wickedest women in the world.

What would a couple of months banged up in Hong Kong have done to Chloe? He knew she'd been prescribed methadone. So he'd still be talking to a junkie. And as methadone was more addictive than heroin he'd be talking to a double junkie.

He wasn't prepared for how bad she looked. The up-to-the-minute black clothes like she'd just been shopping at Muji, now looked skimpy, creased, spotted with little knots of lint. Her hair wasn't black satin any more, it was just black and it came nearly to her shoulders and had ragged ends. Her lips looked chewed. Her lidless eyes looked dead.

'Hi, Chloe.'

The eyes swung slowly in his direction and away again to this really interesting spot on the wall.

'How they been treating you?'

She crossed her thin arms across her body, gripping above the elbow.

He pulled out a chair opposite her and sat down. 'Look, Chloe, I'm not gonna mess with you. You can help me and I can help you. You're looking at a murder charge here. You're going down for life.'

'You can't prove anything.' She said that like she'd said it a lot before and the needle had stuck.

'You were seen, Chloe. And not just by Daniel Craig. You came out of Lee's place. A few minutes after Jude Craig left, four minutes before the fire. That's enough for conspiracy to murder at the least.'

'I was just visiting my ex.'

'You went in. You came out. Three minutes you were in there at the most. That's not visiting.'

'Lee was asleep. No point staying. You can't prove anything.'

'Chloe, you have associated with a lot of dodgy people. We know that. We know now who these associates are. You can tell us a lot of stuff that will help us to put these dodgy people away. For ever, Chloe. You'll do time, but they'll do for ever. They'll be banged up where they can't harm you ever again.'

'Oh yes? And where is that by the way?'

'We will protect you.'

She laughed, a cracked little hoarse little scrape in her throat. 'Oh really?'

'You got the choice. You were seen at Lee's place just before he got burned. You were seen at the hospital on the morning he was murdered. You were seen using the staircase down from the burns unit. Next thing you're on a plane to Hong Kong, a trip carefully arranged by your dodgy friends. We have evidence. We have witnesses. The girl whose passport you travelled on – Mun-yi Wong? Her family are helping us. You know why? Because she died, Chloe. And so did her baby. They were found in a building site off the M4, heads bashed in with lumps of concrete, next to a wrecked car, meant to look like an accident only we found no trace of the driver and the accident was never reported.'

She didn't shift her gaze and she didn't change her posture but something stiffened like she'd forgotten to breathe for a minute.

'Didn't know that, did you? Why do you think he let you go, Chloe? You know a lot about him. You're dangerous to him. Why wasn't it you over that motorway embankment? Eh? Why, Chloe? Because that wasn't his doing, was it? That was the doing of another powerful friend of yours.'

'My powerful friends are really powerful. More powerful than you.'

'Oh yeah? How come you're in here awaiting trial for conspiracy to murder with your little baby thousands of miles away that you're never gonna see again? Has your powerful friend got you out of here?'

She moved one shoulder. She tried to make it a dismissive shrug. It didn't quite come off.

'You think about that at night, don't you? Why you're still here? Where's his end of the bargain? When's that bit gonna happen like he said?'

'He'll keep his end because I've got too much on him.'

'Who we talking about, Chloe?'

Her dull black eyes rested on his with lifeless contempt. Her mouth moved. She intended a little sneer, an attempt at mockery. Again, it didn't quite work.

'And now we've got too much on him, Chloe. We're going to have him. And we're going to make it public. And then he won't be powerful any more. He's done nothing to help you because he knows he's within that—' Bright held up his thumb and forefinger pressed together right in front of her face and she flinched – 'he's within *that* – of being exposed.'

The reedy thread of her smug little voice. 'So why don't you go ahead and expose him then?'

He pushed his fists hard into his pockets. 'We're about to do that, Chloe. Now you can go down with him – and it's gonna be a long one for you, you've been involved in a lot of bad stuff including selling your baby – juries always love women who abandon their kids – or you can help us and – okay, I'm not saying you won't go down, but we can lighten it up for you. We can lighten it a lot. You can help us and you won't go down for life.'

'If you could get him without me you would. So you need me. If I go with him he'll look after me.'

'You think so? I'll be straight with you. I have a newspaper article written by Lee. It wasn't published because at the time it was libellous, they wouldn't risk it. But now there's evidence to back it up. It's gonna be published. Now questions are gonna be asked. Your friend can issue denials. But mud sticks. Your friend will be forced to resign, take early retirement, and within his profession he'll be disgraced. The friend who's protected him is gonna be banged up, for life this time. So he's not gonna be rich or powerful any more. The funny handshakes don't have quite the same clout when you're banged up for life. So think: what's gonna happen to him? Think he's gonna worry about you? The most he'll do for you is have you silenced, love. That is a fact. And you've been here long enough to know that it wouldn't be that hard. Junkie killer found hanged in her cell while the balance of her mind was disturbed? Who'd care?' He got up and walked about. He leaned on the wall and watched her. A little black and white doll someone had left there, abandoned, forgotten. Only they wouldn't forget Chloe. He sat down again opposite her. He said, 'They can't just forget you and leave you to rot. You know too much. They got to deal with you. And you're expendable. With your help I can do it properly. I can go in through the front door instead of the back. I don't like bent coppers. I want to root out scum like your friend. It's only with the connivance of scum like him that villains like your Mr Brennan can carry on. I want him. If you help me I will be grateful, believe me. Trust him or trust me, Chloe. Take your pick. But I am being straight with you – your choices are a bit limited, love.'

She didn't move. She might have been behind plate glass for all she reacted to his words. If he didn't go now he'd start shaking her and he might not stop. If her scum friends didn't kill her maybe he would. He got up suddenly, swept his scruffy leather jacket off the back of the chair. The movement roused her. She looked up at last. He said, 'I'm off. Things to do. This was a social visit, Chlo. No recording, you notice? Just came to see you out the goodness of my heart. You think it over. I'll be back tomorrow. And tomorrow we'll have the recorder on. You give me an answer then. So long, Chlo.'

At the door he looked back. She was still slumped in the chair, long long legs stretched out straight, arms across her body, hands clenched in her armpits, head turned away. He pressed the buzzer by the door. This huge warder came to the peephole, then opened up to let him out. Built like a brick shithouse, face like Mount Rushmore, hands like hams, she stood there with her arms folded, and gestured with her square chin at Chloe. 'Up, you,' she said. Chloe stood. Bright would have obeyed her too.

Next day he went back. Official this time. With Cato: *The time is . . . Present are . . .* She had a lawyer. Legal aid. A greyish dandruff-spattered man with clammy hands. You could tell she could hardly bear to sit next to him. The lawyer said, 'My client has written out a statement. Here it is.' He leaned across the table and the smell that came off him – stale cigarettes and a bad digestion – Bright shifted his chair an inch or two back and flicked through the three sheets of A4 covered with neat lines of handwriting. 'Is this statement written by you?' he said to Chloe.

'Yes.'

'Is this your signature?'

'Yes.'

'Have you been coerced in any way to produce this statement?'

She stared at him. Her eyes mocked him bitterly. But her voice said flatly, 'No.'

'We'll stop the recording while we read this statement.'

Cato told the recorder the time and offered Chloe and the living-dead lawyer a cup of tea.

Chloe said, 'No milk.'

Bright moved his chair to a corner under a glaring sixties spotlight, freckled with paintspots from each time the room had been decorated, different shades of green or cream. *I came to London with Lee Han in February 1994. We got married. A month later when I found out I wasn't pregnant after all he started to treat me badly. He accused me of cheating him, which I hadn't. I liked going out. He didn't. We had different friends. We were not getting on. In 1996 I met Michael Brennan. He fell in love with me. He wanted me to leave Lee. But Lee wouldn't let me have a divorce. Michael set me up in a flat. He used to have parties there with other girls and men he knew. That was where I started using drugs. At first it was cocaine, then when Michael asked me to do favours for his friends I starting using other things. He wouldn't let me have my drug if I didn't do favours. I would do favours for my drug. His friends were wealthy.* Here the writing faded off in a squiggle as though she'd gone into a dream, fallen asleep, who knows, maybe the pen had run out. Then it took up again, stronger. *In 1998 I went back to Lee because I didn't want to stay around Michael B. any more. I wanted to get clean. Lee took me back. He sent me to detox. I came out clean. But then I got pregnant. It was Lee's baby. I went back on the stuff. After the baby was born Lee was angry all the time. I was scared he would hurt me so I left and went to stay with this friend of mine. She lent me her flat when I left Lee in November 1999.*

I needed a supplier again so I got in touch with Michael Brennan again and he brought this man to see me. He was a police officer. I did not know that at first. Michael asked me to do him a few favours. This man fell for me. He wanted to have me to himself. I know

Michael made a deal with him over me. He said this police officer would protect us all. He was going places and soon would be in a very powerful position. But because my baby was born addicted Lee started writing articles about Michael Brennan, accusing him of criminal activities and revealing stuff about him. That was why I had to go with Roger, this police officer, because he could protect Michael in return for favours and stuff.

Bright read that bit over again. And again. And again. *Roger. This police officer.* A languorous looseness seeped through his body, all his limbs relaxed. He read on, skimming the surface: . . . *Brennan said he wanted to give Lee a fright. I had to keep watch at the front of the house till the gardener went. Then I went through to the back and gave the signal to someone on the shed roof. That person must have started the fire. I don't know who it was. I did not know there was going to be a fire. I didn't know that fire was so quick and that it would do so much damage. He said I couldn't be blamed. Roger would make sure of that. And then when Lee was in hospital it was the same. I just had to lead this man to where Lee was, that's all. I didn't have to do anything and anyway I didn't know they were going to pull the plug on him. And he wasn't going to live anyway. A taxi was waiting outside the hospital to take me to the airport. And the taxi driver gave me an envelope with this passport and tickets in it for Hong Kong. I just wanted to introduce my baby to his grandmother that he had never met. That's all.* Signed *Chloe Han* and the date and the address of the prison.

Bright passed the last page to Cato. Then he reached into his folder and brought out a photo in a plastic envelope. He held it up facing Chloe. 'Can you identify this man?'

Cato said, 'Chloe Han is being shown a photograph—'

Chloe said, 'It's Michael Brennan.'

Bright said, 'Do you know this man, Michael Brennan, under any other name?'

'Mick Reynolds, Mike Ryan. And other names I forget.'

'And this man?'

'Chloe Han is being shown a photograph of—'

'That's Roger.'

'—of Detective Chief Inspector Roger Gould,' Cato said.